BURIED ANGELS

PATRICIA GIBNEY

SPHERE

SPHERE

First published in 2020 by Bookouture, an imprint of Storyfire Ltd.
This paperback edition published in 2022 by Sphere

1 3 5 7 9 10 8 6 4 2

A CIP catalogue record for this book
is available from the British Library.

ISBN 978-0-7515-8266-6

Printed and bound in Great Britain by
Clays Ltd, Elcograf S.p.A.

Papers used by Sphere are from well-managed forests
and other responsible sources.

MIX
Paper from
responsible sources
FSC® C104740

Sphere
An imprint of
Little, Brown Book Group
Carmelite House
50 Victoria Embankment
London EC4Y 0DZ

An Hachette UK Company

www.hachette.co.uk
www.littlebrown.co.uk

To Lily Gibney
Aidan's mother and my wonderful mother-in-law

PROLOGUE

Afterwards, the detective would say he had never seen anything like it in all his years on the force.

'Stand back.' He held out his hand, preventing the young garda from entering. 'I'll take a look first. You wait outside.'

'But—'

'But nothing. If you don't want your breakfast mingling with the blood on the floor, you'll do as you're told. You hear me?'

'Yes, sir.'

Once he was free of his charge, the detective closed the door behind him. The coppery tang held the air hostage. He wiped his mouth with the back of his hand, inhaled a deep breath, pinched his nose between thumb and forefinger and walked through the kitchen, paying no heed to the orange Formica cupboards or the broken dishes on the floor. Pieces of crockery crunched beneath his boots. Out of the kitchen to the hallway. Small and compact. Coats draped on the banister; the cupboard door under the stairs hanging off its hinges; footprints in blood on the tiles. With one gloved finger, he pushed at the door to his left and stepped inside.

The couch on its side. A bare foot sticking out from behind it, shielded by a flat brown cushion. Gulping down a large swallow of acrid mucus, he moved cautiously around the furniture without touching anything. Involuntarily he slapped his hand against his mouth as he looked down at the woman on the floor. Blood had dried on her face and throat and pooled to a brown stain on the carpet. He reckoned she was at least twenty-four hours past the time when anything bordering on an attempt at resuscitation could be made. The fetid air clogged his nostrils and narrowed his throat, but still he tasted the decay on his tongue.

Retreating from the room, he stood in the hall, the sound of his breathing breaking the silence. Staring upwards, he listened to the drip of a tap somewhere above his head.

The bottom stair creaked under his weight. When he reached the last step, it too creaked. He stood onto the small square landing. Four doors. All closed. His heart thumped so hard against his ribs he was sure it was trying to escape its bony enclosure. His mouth dried up and his nose became blocked, and he found it hard to breathe despite the thunder in his chest.

The door was old. Brass knobs. Steel hinges. Loose nails. He twisted the nearest handle to him and pushed the door inwards.

The bathroom.

Green tiles. Yellowed bath. White ceramic toilet bowl and sink. A mishmash of colour. A whiff of bleach, no blood. He exhaled slowly and backed out of the room. He sniffed at the stale air of the landing before twisting the handle of the next door. It rattled. Then opened.

The change in odour was seismic. Brutal copper assaulted his struggling airways. He closed his eyes, blinding himself to the scene before him. But it was useless. Forever more, when he laid his head on a pillow, the enduring image would be an abattoir of human blood. His dreams would become nightmares and he would never again sleep peacefully.

Children.

Pre-teenage babies, he thought. How could someone do this?

Two girls clothed in unmatched pink and yellow pyjamas. One of them had one bare foot, the other sheathed in a fleece sock, half on, half off; her leg outstretched as if she had been trying to flee. The second girl was over by the window, her hand similarly outstretched seeking escape, her mouth frozen in a silent scream. The curtains shielded the tightly shut sash window.

He remained frozen in his footsteps. There was nothing to be gained by walking further inside. He did not want to disturb the crime scene. The killer had long since carried out this vicious attack and fled. Or else …

The detective froze. Was the killer behind one of the other doors?

He backed out of the room, turned to the third door and eased his hand towards his shoulder holster. The thought of shooting dead the author of this devastation fuelled him with adrenaline.

'I'm coming in,' he warned, though he wasn't sure he said it loudly enough to alert anyone who might be inside.

The room was another bedroom. Indiscriminately coloured bedding and two pillows lay on the floor. The sheet on the bed had a pool of damp in the centre. He was certain it wasn't blood. More than likely whoever had been sleeping here had wet the bed. One of the girls? Had they been awakened by the noise of the intruder? Was this the master bedroom? he wondered, as his white-faced reflection stared at him from the mirror on the wardrobe door.

The window hung open and a curtain fluttered back into the room from the breeze. He knew he shouldn't venture in further, but he had to be sure. Kneeling, he glanced under the bed. A dusty suitcase and a pair of suede slippers. He stood again and noticed a door to his right. An en suite? He crept over, unsure why he was fearful of making noise. He had declared his presence. He had a gun in his hand. What had he to fear?

The door hung on two hinges; the third was busted. Behind it, a shower with an old-fashioned plastic curtain, and a small toilet. The room was empty.

Three bodies. Mother and two daughters? Was there a father, husband or partner? If so, where was he? Had he carried out this brutal attack on his family before escaping?

He backed out of the room and glanced into the last room. A single bed. A free-standing wardrobe against one wall, a small cabinet with an unlit lamp beside the bed. A narrow window with lightweight flowered cotton curtains. Light streamed through the slit, casting a cone of dust motes through the centre of the tiny room.

He hurried down the stairs and rushed outside. Bending over, hands on knees, he gulped in fresh air and attempted to keep his breakfast in his stomach.

'What did you find?' his uniformed colleague asked.

'A mother and two kids. Girls. Dead, all dead.' He gasped for air, trying desperately to rid himself of the stench of death; of the images indelibly etched behind his eyes.

'Two kids?'

'Yeah. I didn't come across their father. Not yet. The bastard.'

'Did you say two kids?'

'For feck's sake, are you bloody deaf? Why do you keep repeating it?'

'I'm not sure … I thought the report said …' The garda fumbled in his jacket pocket for his notebook. Flipped over the pages. 'There should be three kids.'

The detective stood up straight and wiped his brow with trembling fingers. As he searched his pocket for cigarettes, he said, 'So where the hell is the third one?'

Twenty years later

Removing the frozen goods required brute force and, of course, gloves.

I found a pair in a box, beneath a conglomeration of garden equipment, refuse bags, slug repellent and weedkiller. I held a debate with myself over the possible use for the weedkiller, but eventually I threw it back in the box. In a toolbox I located a roll of duct tape. I left the shed and made my way to where my work would take place.

The lock on the first of the three chest freezers snipped open with pliers. I felt the air heaving with anticipation. I raised the lid and got to work taking out the frozen meat. Two legs of lamb and a side of beef. This was the decoy if anyone came nosing around. Once the false bottom was removed, the offending article lay there, frozen to the sides.

Lifting it out took some effort. The plastic wrapping tore in places. When it was eventually fully excavated, some of the plastic remained in the freezer. Nothing could be done about that now. Without paying too much attention to the slab of meat (for want of a better description), I dumped it on the floor. I didn't really want to look at it. I knew what it was. I'd seen it before it was frozen.

The refuse bags came in useful. I slit them and laid them out, and then rolled the slab onto them. The frozen flesh was visible through the torn wrapping, yellow and creased.

When it was fully encased in the sacks, with duct tape wound around, I replaced the false bottom in the freezer, followed by the decoy meat. The job was almost complete. Now the cargo just had to be transported under cover of darkness and disposed of. It had been moved once before. This would be the last time.

I had two more freezers to unload. I worked methodically. I had a lot to do before the sun rose.

CHAPTER ONE

Sunday

Slowly they lowered the coffin into the soft earth.

A cry, more like a melancholic sigh, rose into the air. Lottie Parker glanced to her right. Grace Boyd, glassy-eyed, was facing straight ahead, her face smeared with tears. One hand was at her mouth as she chewed at her fingernails. A dribble from her nose rested on her upper lip, and Lottie longed to take a tissue and wipe it clean. But she remained stock still, rigid.

Though it was the last week of May, the Atlantic Ocean blew a tornado of cold air in over the west coast, ripping through Lottie's light summer jacket. The hilltop graveyard was open to the elements; its tall Celtic crosses stippled in green moss; one even had seashells embedded in its uppermost point. The sparse trees were bending in supplication to the wind. The bushes of purple heather ruffled sharp fronds against the noses of the mountain goats nuzzling the bog cotton. It could be an idyllic scene if not for the sadness.

The priest sprinkled holy water into the six-foot hole where the coffin now lay. He directed the chief mourners to do the same. For a moment Lottie was all alone as the others moved forward. With a small shovel they dug into the mound of earth and let the clay fall on the wooden box with its brass cross. Grace lingered, then picked a lily from the floral wreath and let it drop down, down into the depths of the gaping earth, its white petals bringing light to the darkness below.

Another sharp breeze rolled up from the sea. Lottie shivered, memories of her husband Adam's funeral laid bare and raw. The smell of lilies, so potent, clogged her nostrils and her hand flew to her mouth, covering her nose. But she did not shed a tear. Enough tears had gushed from the depths of her being over the years, and she had no more left to share.

'In the name of the Father, Son and Holy Spirit ...' The priest concluded the prayers and Lottie stepped back to allow the steady stream of locals to offer their condolences to the family.

Standing at the thorny hedge of blackberries that marked the boundary on the cliff side, she let the ocean breeze whip her face, welcoming the touch of nature. She had no idea how long she stood there before she sensed approaching footsteps in the soft grass behind her. She didn't turn around, her eyes fixed on the vastness of the water, with its hazy horizon in the distance. She wished for a moment that she could be carried silently on the crest of a whitecap wave to somewhere far away from where she now stood.

When she felt the hand slip into hers and squeeze her fingers, she turned. With the other arm tightly around the shoulders of his sister, Boyd rested his head on her shoulder.

'A fine send-off for Mam,' he said. 'It's over now, Lottie.'

She feathered his forehead with a tender kiss.

'No, Boyd, it's only just begun.'

Grace Boyd sat huddled in the corner of the snug, a forlorn figure, unnaturally quiet, still biting her nails.

'I don't know what to do about Grace,' Boyd whispered to Lottie when she appeared carrying two glasses of sparkling water. He took one from her before her elbow could be jostled by the swelling crowd in the pub.

'Come outside,' she said.

Out in the sunshine, she inhaled the fresh sea air. 'Leenane is beautiful. This is where they filmed *The Field*, isn't it?'

'Yes. Mam has … had Richard Harris's photograph hanging on the living room wall.'

'I don't know what to say, Boyd.' Despite having suffered so much grief in her own life, Lottie found she had no idea how to react to someone else's.

'Tell me what to do about Grace.'

She pulled out a chair from a wooden table splattered with bird dirt and pointed for Boyd to sit. She leaned against the table as he brushed at the chair with his hand.

'It's a difficult one,' she said. 'Grace has lived all her life with your mother. Living alone will be a major change for her.'

'That's the point.' He sipped his pint. 'I don't think she *can* live alone.'

Lottie eyed his drink. 'Where did you get that?'

'It is a bar, Lottie.'

'You shouldn't be drinking while on treatment.'

Boyd had been diagnosed with a mild form of leukaemia over six months previously, and though he was doing well and his treatment had been reduced, his health was a constant worry. His immune system was weak and he was susceptible to infection. She was worried that the stress of his mother's death would harm his recovery.

'My doctor said I can have the odd drink,' he said petulantly. 'Stop nagging.' He lowered his head. 'Grace tries to be independent, but we know she can't be left to her own devices. She needs someone to watch out for her.'

Lottie put out a hand and lifted his chin, looking into his sad hazel eyes. 'Your mam was great, and she'll be missed. It's a shock for you all. Especially for Grace.' Then she said the words she knew he wanted to hear. 'Maybe you should bring her with you back to Ragmullin.'

'I'll have to evict Kirby.' Boyd smiled wryly.

'It's high time he found his own place anyway, and if my half-brother Leo comes through with the money on Farranstown House, we can buy somewhere together and Grace can live with us.'

She thought of the wrangling back and forth with solicitors over legal documents, none of which she understood. She just wanted to sign and get the money, but things were never that simple. Leo Belfield had appeared in her life following a difficult case in which her true family heritage had been revealed. She was still trying to come to terms with it.

Boyd eyed her over the rim of his pint glass. 'You'd do that for me?'

'You know I'd do anything for you.'

'You sound like something out of a romance novel.'

'You read them, do you?'

'Smart arse,' he said with a smile, the first time she'd seen that glint of devilment in his eye in a long time.

He put down the glass and wrapped his hand around hers. She felt the warmth of his touch seep through her skin and into her bloodstream. She gazed out across the sparkling water in the bay to the lush green vegetation on the sides of the mountains that guarded the inlet.

'I know you're ill, Boyd, but you make me so very happy.'

A crash and the tinkle of breaking glass reached them from inside the pub. A second of stunned silence paused the mumble of chatter before a scream pierced the air.

'That's Grace,' said Boyd as he got up from the chair, but Lottie was already through the door, where she was greeted by pandemonium.

A semicircle of sweaty bodies had formed in one corner of the sweltering pub. She elbowed her way through the three-deep ensemble. Curled up on the bench, knees clutched to her chest, Grace Boyd cried and sobbed, her hair wild and her arms scratched.

'All of you, stay away from me,' she snarled through gritted teeth.

'Hey, Grace, why don't you come outside with me?' Lottie said as she reached the distraught and dishevelled young woman.

'I only asked her where she'd live,' one man said. 'She lost the plot when I—'

'Give her a break,' another interrupted.

Lottie had heard enough. She needed to calmly extricate Grace from the melee.

'Stand back. Give her some air. Fetch a glass of water.' She stared at the crowd. 'Now.'

At last the gathering dispersed and someone thrust a pint glass of water into her hand. She slid onto the bench next to Grace.

'Sip this. It will help cool you down.'

She was surprised when the other woman took the glass and gulped a mouthful, without raising her eyes.

'Don't mind what any of them are saying. What do men know about grief, eh?'

Grace began to hiccup.

'Slowly. Just sips. Come on.'

'I'm not a child.' Anger flashed in her eyes.

'Do you want to come outside? Mark's out there. Maybe you can tell him what's wrong.'

'He doesn't get me, Lottie. No one does. Not even you.' Grace wiped her nose with the back of her hand, childlike.

'I have a fair bit of experience with my own gang; why don't you try me?'

Grace shook her head and handed back the glass. 'I want to go home. Can you bring me?'

'Sure I can.' Lottie handed her a napkin from the table. 'Dry your eyes and let's get out of here.'

Grace stood and wiped her face. She scrunched the napkin and stuffed it into her handbag. 'I like you, Lottie, and I'm glad you're sticking with my brother.'

'That's sweet of you, but listen to me. I'm here for you too.'

'But my mam ... I'm going to miss her so much. Can you understand that?'

'I lost my husband, so yes, I understand it better than you can ever know. Now let's get the hell out of here.'

'I'd love a plate of bacon and cabbage. Do you think you could cook that?'

Lottie groaned inwardly. Culinary expertise was not on her talent list. Grace was craving something her mother had cooked. Something to keep her alive in her mind.

'Where was your mother's favourite place to visit?'

'The Twelve Pins.'

'Well then, that's where we're going.'

'You're so good, Lottie.' Grace sniffed. 'Thank you.'

The lump in Lottie's throat bulged. She found it difficult to be this sympathetic with her own kids, so how was it she could mother this thirty-something-year-old woman? Unable to find the answer, she walked over to Boyd, who was standing by the door.

'You know the way?'

'Yes, boss.' He winked at Grace, whose face broke into a sad smile.

'And then I have to head back to Ragmullin,' Lottie said. Lowering her voice, she whispered in Boyd's ear, 'With or without you.'

CHAPTER TWO

Monday

The three-bedroom 1950s detached house with a square patch of overgrown grass and a cracked path up to the front door was the second in a line of ten houses. Someone had constructed a ramp and a rail to the side of the two front steps. Jeff's aunt, Patsy Cole, had only been sixty when she'd died in bed here two years ago, but that didn't worry Faye. She didn't believe in spirits or ghosts. She was happy. At last they had a place to call their own. Once they had it renovated and decorated, she would be able to escape from their tiny apartment. She rubbed her hand over her white cotton shirt and with a thrill of excitement felt the as yet invisible bump beneath it.

The key turned easily in the lock. She shoved open the door and stepped onto the grey linoleum with its discoloured lines down either side from Patsy's wheelchair. That would have to go, she thought as she moved into the living room.

The fireplace was on the wall across from her. Tiger-striped tiles around the broken grate and smoke residue on the flowery wallpaper. Jeff had already taken a lot of the furniture to the recycling centre, and most of the rubbish had gone to the dump. There wasn't even anything worthy of bringing to a charity shop. All that remained of the furniture in this room was an old armchair and the threadbare orange carpet.

Faye paused at the window. She touched her stomach again and smiled. Their very own place. She looked around and decided that the first thing to go would be the wallpaper. It was garish and faded, blackened and torn, and it made the room look smaller than it actually was. They planned to knock down the wall dividing the living room from the kitchen. She tried to envisage an open-plan area, but standing here with the three-bulb light fitting whispering over her hair, she wondered if that would even work. It really was very small.

From a miniature toolkit she extracted a paint scraper, then filled a plastic basin with yellow water from the kitchen tap and began to dampen the wallpaper in the corner by the window. At first she moved slowly, fearful of nicking the plaster beneath, but then she felt an adrenaline rush forcing her to rid every wall of the hideous paper, and within an hour she was over by the fireplace. Her feet were surrounded by scraps of damp, mouldy wallpaper, which stuck to her jeans and white Converse shoes. She didn't care.

The paper to the left of the fireplace came away more easily than any other area. She used her fingers to pull and tug, and it ripped off in one long strip. With the paint scraper, she tapped the plaster. It sounded hollow. She knocked on the wall to the right of it. Solid.

She stepped back and regarded the wall. The plaster on the two sections appeared different. One was fresher than the other. She wondered why this was so. Then she remembered Jeff saying that there used to be a stove-like range in this room, but that his uncle had taken it out and installed a fireplace before he'd built on the back kitchen. She knew then that the extension had to go. The roof was flat and leaking.

She sighed at the amount of work they had to do. They'd agreed to carry out the upgrade themselves. It'll be cheaper, Jeff had said, and we're in no hurry. But she was. She wanted to move in before the baby arrived. That gave them less than six months. Maybe if they knocked out this piece here, she thought, they'd have a nice alcove. She could get IKEA shelving. It would go well with the woodchip burner she'd already picked out. A trickle of excitement built up in her chest.

In the kitchen, she found Jeff's larger toolbox. She picked up the lump hammer and went back to the living room. Now or never, she thought, and swung the hammer at the centre of the plaster. Soon she was covered in grime. A weave of dust motes swam in front of her eyes. She should have put on the goggles. Taking a step back to admire her handiwork, she sighed. She'd only made a small hole, even though she felt like she'd been hammering for hours.

With her fingers, she tugged at the plasterboard, trying to draw it away from the wall. At last it came away in her hand. A bigger hole opened up beside the old tiled fireplace. Maybe Jeff's uncle and aunt had left a time capsule inside, she thought. That would be exciting.

Suddenly the tiny hairs stood up on the back of her neck beneath her scrunched-up ponytail. Maybe this wall was never meant to come down.

Trying to shrug off the weird feeling gripping her, she picked up the hammer again and thumped the wall with all her strength. The plaster cracked and tore and fell apart. Coughing and spluttering, she swatted her hands around, attempting to clear the air, praying the dust wouldn't damage the baby growing in her womb.

When the last motes had shimmered away, she stepped forward and squinted into the dark space. A tsunami of dread shook her whole body, her teeth chattered, and bubbles of cold sweat trickled down her spine.

The hole wasn't empty.

She gasped and leapt backwards as the thing in the wall came crashing out, landing at her feet. Two sightless eyes stared up at her.

Only then did she scream.

CHAPTER THREE

Lottie awoke with her grandson fast asleep beside her. When she'd returned from Galway last night, he'd been crying in Katie's arms.

'He has me wrecked, Mam,' Katie had said, her voice as frazzled as the little boy's whimpers. 'I don't know what's wrong with him.'

'He could be cutting his back teeth.' Lottie dropped her overnight bag behind the couch and took Louis from her daughter. 'What's the matter, little man? Did you miss your nana?'

She was rewarded with another loud cry.

'I gave him a spoon of Calpol half an hour ago,' Katie said, 'but it made no difference.'

'You need to have patience with him.' Lottie cradled the boy on her lap and soothed him with kisses in his soft hair. 'Go on to bed. I'll mind him.'

'You've work in the morning. I don't want you blaming me if he keeps you up half the night.'

'I won't blame you,' Lottie said.

Now she was awake with a headache and she was going to be late for work. She eased out from under the warm duvet and took a quick shower. She pulled on her black jeans and a white long-sleeved T-shirt. It would save her having to apply sun lotion if her work took her outdoors today.

Louis stirred, turned over, and, with his thumb in his mouth, slept on soundly. She would have to wake Katie. Tiptoeing across the landing, she tapped on the door and looked in. Her daughter's long black hair fanned out over the pillow, which moved with each breath she took.

'Katie? Hun, you need to wake up.' She brushed her fingers over the girl's bare shoulder and shook her gently.

'Ugh? What? What time is it?'

'Early, but I'm late for work.'

'Knew you'd blame me.'

'I never said a word about you. Louis is asleep in my bed. Go and lie with him. He seems rested. I think he's just teething.'

'Yeah, yeah.' Katie threw back the duvet and stumped across to Lottie's room.

At Sean's door, she rapped more loudly. 'Sean. School time.'

'Yeah, yeah,' her sixteen-year-old son said, an imitation of Katie's words a moment ago. 'I'm awake.'

She hesitated at the third door. Eighteen-year-old Chloe had dropped out of school. No amount of cajoling, bribery or rows had worked, and what with having to deal with Boyd's illness and Sean's bad moods, Lottie had given in. Chloe worked full-time in Fallon's pub and it seemed to suit her. But come September, Lottie was adamant her daughter was going to finish her education.

She moved away without knocking and went down the stairs to snatch a slice of toast to chew in the car.

She hoped it would be a quiet week.

CHAPTER FOUR

The drone was great fun. It whizzed along at such speed, the boys found it hard to keep up. Jack Sheridan was delighted with the images displayed on his phone attached to the controller. They were clearer than the Mediterranean Sea in high summer. He knew all about that because he'd been to Majorca last year on his holidays. His friend Gavin Robinson, on the other hand, had only gone to Connemara.

'Does your mam really believe we're using the drone for a school project?' Gavin said.

'Course she does. My mam believes everything I say. Doesn't yours?'

'Are you joking? I get grilled more than the rashers every single morning.'

Jack laughed. 'As long as you don't tell her where we go before school, we should be okay.'

'Well, I'm twelve next month,' Gavin said, 'and I'm going to ask her for a drone for my present.'

From the bridge over the railway track, Jack glanced back at the town lying low in a dip behind him, the cathedral spires standing guard like they were protecting Ragmullin from evil monsters. Jack had heard his father talk about evil monsters and he'd had plenty of warnings about not talking to strangers. Did they think he was five years old or something? Monsters were only a figment of the imagination.

The sun was rising quickly in the sky and Jack knew today would be as warm as yesterday. He slipped off his jacket and balled it into his school bag before hefting the rucksack onto his back. Then he turned his attention to the tracks below.

'Will we do the canal or the railway?' he said.

Gavin was already climbing down the shallow steps at the side of the bridge. 'We did the canal the other day. I thought we agreed we'd do the tracks today?'

'Yeah, but I don't want the poxy commuter train slamming into Jedi.' He'd had a competition among their friends to name the drone. Now that he thought about it, he realised it wasn't really a competition because there was no prize, and anyhow, he'd chosen the name himself.

'The early train's long gone,' Gavin said, 'and the next one's not for an hour. Come on.'

Jack made his way down the steps after his friend. He had to admit that for eleven years old, Gavin talked like a grown-up at times. It got on Jack's nerves and he often thought of finding a new best friend, but Gavin knew about things he didn't, like the train timetable, so it was good to have him around.

He made sure the camera was working on the drone, checked the SD card was in place to record, steadied the controller, and set Jedi off down the tracks.

'Don't let it fly around that bend,' Gavin roared. 'Stop it now, dickhead. It's going to disappear. We'll never find it.'

'I'm looking at it on the phone screen, dope.' Jack ran ahead of his friend, keeping one eye on the screen and the other on Jedi as it skirted a blackberry bush and disappeared out of view.

When Gavin reached him, Jack slowed down and walked a few steps forward, making sure to leave a foot of space between himself and the tracks, just in case Gavin had got the timetable wrong. That wasn't likely, but you'd never know what could happen. He didn't want the Ragmullin to Dublin train ploughing into them, mashing them into mincemeat. Yuck.

'What's that?' Gavin said, pointing at the screen.

'What's what?'

'Back Jedi up. Make it go over that piece of track again.'

Jack eyed Gavin and noticed his friend's eyes dancing frantically in his head.

'I thought I saw something between two sleepers,' Gavin squealed. 'Are you recording?'

'Of course I am.' Jack reversed the drone back over the route and studied the screen.

'Hover it. Keep recording.'

'I'm not stupid,' he said. He stopped walking and stared.

'Jack?' Gavin's voice trembled. 'What is that on the tracks?'

Jack hadn't a clue, but it reminded him of one of those monsters that was supposed to be a figment of your imagination.

'It looks like a zombie. Like something Spiderman would tackle.'

Gavin said, 'It looks like a headless body.'

Jack zoomed the drone in closer, hovering it over the thing on the railway track, and then watched in horror as Gavin vomited all down his school uniform.

CHAPTER FIVE

Eventually Faye calmed down enough to find her phone and call Jeff. Within fifteen minutes, he was by her side.

'I thought you'd been murdered or something,' he said as he sat her into his aunt's smelly armchair.

'Don't make light of it, Jeff. I was terrified of that … that thing.' She wiped her forehead with the tissue he'd thrust into her hand. 'What is it? Tell me it's not real.'

'It's probably fake. Some sort of prank.'

'But it's been plastered up behind that wall for God knows how long. Surely someone wouldn't put a fake skull in there, would they?'

'It looks to me like someone did.' He sat on the floor next to her. 'Why were you knocking down the wall anyway?'

'I was pulling off the wallpaper and I noticed the difference in the plaster.'

'What difference?' His voice was measured, but Faye thought there was an unusual edge to it. She tried to keep calm by admiring the straight line of his jaw and the smoothness of his chin on his long face. His blue eyes dazzled her in the half-light. She wanted him to hold her tight so that she could nuzzle into the soft cotton of his shirt, but he sat monk-like on the floor, his long legs crossed at the ankles. He was twenty-nine to her twenty-five and she was hopelessly in love with him.

'That section was fresher.' She pointed to the hole in the wall. 'And when I hit it with the paint scraper, it sounded hollow.'

'And you had to hammer the shit out of it. Why?'

Faye shrugged her shoulders wearily. 'I'm sorry. I thought that if there was a space there, we could insert a shelf unit.' Her voice had returned to normal, though her throat felt raw from screaming. 'A cheap one. I know you don't want me wasting money we don't have.'

'You shouldn't have set about demolishing a wall. Did any of the neighbours come in to investigate what the noise was about?'

She shook her head. 'No. I suppose most of them are at work.'

'Probably.' He got up and moved over to investigate her demolition job. Then he scrutinised the skull lying in the middle of the floor. He nudged it with his shoe. 'It looks fake to me.'

'It looked quite real at the time. It's tiny. Scared the living daylights out of me.'

He stretched to his six-foot height and started to pace the floor in circles. 'Do you need to visit your doctor?'

'Why would I?'

'The baby. You got a shock and—'

'Jeff, the baby is fine. I'm fine.' She wondered how she would ever rid herself of the image of the skull landing at her feet. 'I think we should call the gardaí.'

Jeff stopped his anxious pacing. 'Good God, no. We'd make a holy show of ourselves.' He laughed before gripping her hand and staring earnestly into her eyes. 'It's fake. Probably left over from Halloween years ago. No need to waste the guards' precious time with it.'

'But who put it there, and why?' She felt his fingers kneading her dust-covered flesh. 'Did you know there was a secret cubbyhole in there?'

He dropped her hand and stood back, hands on hips. 'No. It could have been there years before my aunt and uncle bought the house, but I know they took out a range at some point.'

'Can you find out?'

'Find out what?'

Faye sighed. Jeff was being impossible. 'Find out when the wall was plastered over and when the skull might have been placed there.'

'There's no one to ask. Mam and Dad and Uncle Noel all died years ago, and Aunt Patsy's gone too.'

'There has to be someone else.'

'I'm the only one left, and you need to stop thinking about this skull. I'm putting it in the bin. Forget all about it. I'm taking you into town for a cappuccino and a warm croissant.'

Jumping up, she said, 'How can you think of food when that thing could be someone's head lying on our living room floor!'

She hadn't meant to shout, but every pore on her skin was screaming at her that this was something bad and they had to take it seriously. She started coughing, dust caught in her throat. Tears sprouted from her eyes and she swayed on the spot. Jeff caught her arm tightly, and she staggered against him.

'You're so melodramatic, Faye. Look at me. I'm saying we forget about it. I mean it.'

Frozen in place, leaning against the wall for support, she watched Jeff as he picked up the small skull.

'Have we refuse sacks here somewhere?' He turned the skull around in his hand, poking his fingers through the eye sockets.

'I don't think—'

'Ah, Jesus, Faye, stop.' He took a breath and looked at her. 'I'm sorry. Sorry for swearing at you. It's just awful … it has me rattled too. Stay there. I'll find the sacks myself.'

He marched out of the room still holding the skull, and Faye heard him pulling out drawers in the small kitchen. She looked out of the window at the world rushing by. Cars on the road. Two teenagers laughing loudly on the footpath as they chased each other. Probably skipping school, she thought. A bird landed on the cherry blossom tree in the small front garden. She watched it, concentrating as it twitched its head. Anything to keep her mind off the eyeless skull that had rolled out at her feet.

At that precise moment, she felt it for the first time. A fluttering, just like a trapped butterfly lurching around in her tummy. A tiny being created by her and Jeff.

But for some reason it did not make her feel happy.

CHAPTER SIX

Detective Larry Kirby parked the unmarked garda car on the verge beside the bridge. He always thought it was such a misnomer, because every child and crook in the town could recognise an unmarked car a mile off.

Uniformed officers had set up a one-way system and were directing irate drivers back down the narrow hill. All the trains had been halted, causing pandemonium in the station, with buses having to be hired to ferry commuters. Planting an unlit cigar in the side of his mouth, he extracted himself from the car and waited for Detective Maria Lynch to join him. He had to admit she was looking healthy and fit after her maternity leave.

'And the little bugger sleeps all night?' he said, chewing the end of his cigar.

'He's much better than the other two were. Needless to say, Ben is delighted, because we won't have to share the night-time in and out of bed with a bottle lark.'

'Good, good,' Kirby said, searching his pocket for a lighter. He knew nothing about babies or bottles or any of that. Unless the bottle contained alcohol, of course. He had no children and it was looking like he might never have any, being divorced and his girlfriend having been killed in the line of duty. Lynch's husband, Ben, was welcome to his kids.

Eventually he succeeded in lighting the cigar, while Lynch spoke briefly with the uniformed officer.

'Put that out, Kirby,' she said. 'We have a bit of a walk after we get down on the bank. Should have worn my trousers.' She set off down the steps located to the side of the bridge.

Standing in a huddle of uniforms at the bottom were the two youngsters who'd made the grim discovery.

'We should have a chat with them first,' Kirby said.

'They're being looked after. I have all the details. Come on, lazy bones.'

He would have taken the words as an insult from anyone else, but he'd worked a long time with Lynch, so he just chuckled to himself and set off after her. Maybe things might get back to normal now that she had returned to work. And hopefully Sam McKeown would shift his arse back to Athlone. McKeown had been a good addition to the team when he'd filled in for Lynch, but he tended to rile Kirby for no good reason.

'Is it far?' he shouted at Lynch as she headed along the grassy verge by the railway tracks.

'Only about half a mile.' Her voice carried back to him on the warm morning air.

'Only?' he muttered. He found a grubby handkerchief in his pocket and dabbed away the perspiration dripping down the folds of skin on his neck.

As they rounded the next corner, the white-suited scene-of-crime officers came into view. Kirby trotted after Lynch. She was almost suited up by the time he reached the huddled group. He grabbed a suit for himself, but before he could attempt to pull it on, he found himself forced to bend over, hands on knees.

'You okay?' Lynch said.

'Catching my breath.'

'Maybe you need to join a gym.'

'I have no energy for it.' He raised his head and studied her. Lynch had retained very little of her baby weight, and her face was slimmer than he remembered. He put a finger up to his own flabby jowls and thought maybe she had a point.

'Get that suit on and hurry up, for God's sake,' she said.

He muscled his way into the tight forensic suit, hat, booties and gloves. He could smell what awaited them even before he entered the warm tent. He pulled his mouth mask up over his nose, but was still inclined to gag.

'Not a pretty sight,' said Jim McGlynn, head of the SOCO team. Kirby knew that the man enjoyed his banter with his boss, Detective Inspector Lottie Parker, though neither she nor McGlynn would ever admit it.

'Oh my God,' Lynch said, her forehead paling beneath the short whisper of fair hair that had escaped from her hood.

'Jesus, Jim, what is it?' Kirby stalled at the entrance to the tent. He felt his head wobble. The heat or the cigar? Maybe the gym wasn't a bad idea. Scrap that. He couldn't afford it.

'Will you give me a chance?' McGlynn sounded irritated.

Once he'd regained his equilibrium, Kirby peered over Lynch's shoulder for a better look. Tight between two sleepers was a body, or more correctly, part of a body. Torso, no head. Legs cut off at the hips, arms at the shoulders. It was hard to tell if it was male or female. And it was small, very small. The skin was putrid and oozing in places, and in other places, it looked like …

He scratched his head. 'Was it frozen?'

'Yep. She's been thawing out for quite a few hours by the looks of it. Hopefully frozen shortly after death, so we may get lucky.'

'Lucky?' Kirby itched to get the hell out of the tent.

'Yes, Detective Kirby. Freezing a body close to time of death preserves DNA and fibres. We might get samples to analyse forensically and possibly inform us of the cause of death.'

'Good, good,' Kirby said. 'And time of death?'

'Won't know anything until the state pathologist does her work. Where is she?' McGlynn stared at him accusingly.

'I'll check if she's on her way. You think the torso is female?'

'At the moment, yes.'

'When do you think she was killed?'

'My middle name is not God, so I have no idea. Are you going to let me get on with my job?'

Kirby took his chance to escape out into the fresh air, quickly followed by Lynch. She looked green in the face when she whipped off her mask. She spoke to a uniformed officer at the entrance to the tent as she stripped off the protective clothing and stuffed it into a brown evidence bag. Kirby moved to her shoulder.

'You okay?' he said.

'Fine,' she snapped. 'Jane Dore will be here within the hour.' She shook her hair loose, as if freeing each strand of the stench that clung there. 'What the hell is that in there, Kirby?'

'I'm not sure, but if I was pushed, I'd say it's the body of a child.'

CHAPTER SEVEN

Lottie wasn't one bit happy as she stood in front of her new superintendent. She herself had been in line for the promotion after Superintendent Corrigan had formally retired on grounds of ill health. She had been overlooked for the temporary position in favour of David McMahon last time around, but this time she had not even bothered to put in an application. McMahon had spewed on his bib and was spending his suspension kicking pebbles on Dollymount Strand while Internal Affairs raked up the dirt on him. From what Lottie had heard, there was enough to fill two wheelbarrows. Karma, she thought. And yet he was on paid leave pending a full hearing.

To date, she had had little interaction with Deborah Farrell, who'd been promoted quickly up through the ranks. Lottie was glad to see a woman getting the job, but not so sure she wanted to be working under this particular one. There was little grapevine chatter to draw on, so she had to depend on official sources, which were tight-lipped.

Deborah Farrell had arrived in Ragmullin two months previously with a steady record. At forty-five she matched Lottie in age, but Lottie had a good three inches on her. That was something, at least, she told herself. Not much good sitting down in an interview, though. Farrell's eyes were a dark shade of grey, and her hair, an insipid brown, was tied in a tight bun at the back of her head. Not one strand was loose. Even her hair didn't suffer insubordination.

But her white uniform shirt was in need of an iron, an epaulette had come undone on her shoulder and her tie lay in a knot on the desk.

She ran a ringless finger around the open collar. 'Detective Inspector Parker.' A statement, not an enquiry.

'That's me, Superintendent Farrell.' Lottie sat up straight.

'We can drop the formalities. Okay if I call you Lottie?'

'Sure.'

'Outside that door I'm Superintendent Farrell, but between ourselves I'm Deborah.'

'Fine by me.' Lottie had no idea where this was headed, and wrong-footed by the superintendent's cosy tone, she couldn't decide whether she should be relieved or wary.

'Detective Sergeant Boyd is off on sick leave, but I have an application here requesting his return to work on a part-time basis.'

'Really?' Lottie leaned forward. News to her.

'I'd like to have your opinion on the matter. I believe you and Boyd are … intimate?'

Heat flared on Lottie's skin before she could prevent the blush. How to handle this? With the truth, she supposed.

'We're engaged to be married, Superin— Deborah.' Gosh, it felt awkward addressing her boss informally. 'I don't wear an engagement ring. It doesn't seem appropriate, you know, being a widow and all.' Why was she making excuses? 'Boyd was diagnosed with leukaemia last December. His treatment has taken a lot out of him, but the latest results are showing improvement.'

'What do you mean by that?' Farrell ran a hand along her chin, almost manly.

'He has responded well to treatment. According to his oncologist, that's as good as they'd hoped for at this stage.'

'I heard his mother died recently.' Farrell leaned her head towards Lottie, dropped her hand from her chin, both elbows on the desk,

'Yes,' Lottie said. 'She was buried yesterday.'

'How has that affected him?'

Fiddling with the cuffs of her scruffy T-shirt, Lottie wondered about all the questions. Farrell's voice was soft and soothing. A great tone for extracting information from witnesses and suspects alike. Which category did Lottie fall into? Why was she even here, answering questions about Boyd? Farrell could bring him in and grill him if she felt the need.

'Honestly, he's fine.' She shifted uneasily.

'Do you think he's up to a return to work?' Farrell persisted.

Damn, Lottie thought. Now she was being put in an awkward position. Boyd had mentioned in passing that he'd asked his consultant about returning to work part-time, but she hadn't really been listening. She thought it'd be good for his emotional and mental state do be doing something meaningful again, but was he physically up to it? How would it affect her team? Maria Lynch was back from maternity leave and Sam McKeown had not been reassigned to Athlone yet. She didn't want to upset the equilibrium. But also, she couldn't watch Boyd struggle. The chemotherapy had caused some side effects. How to be diplomatic? she wondered.

'I think it's a matter for his doctors,' she said eventually, worrying a hole in her thin cotton sleeve. Farrell's eyes were like a pair of bullets bearing down on her.

'Mmm. I wanted an insider's knowledge, but I see you don't want to betray an emotional interest. I get that, and—'

'No, it's not that at all,' Lottie blurted. 'I actually want to leave personal issues aside and look at this professionally.'

'I'm beginning to doubt that.' Farrell's friendly demeanour fell away and her mouth flatlined.

'I beg your pardon?' Lottie said.

'I don't think it's going to work.'

'What's not going to work?' She was floundering now, hands on the desk, almost pleading, because she knew exactly what was going to come out of Farrell's mouth next.

'You working with Detective Sergeant Boyd. I'm trying to give you an out here, but you're not grasping it at all.'

Lottie shook her head. Had she missed something in the conversation?

'I'm not sure I follow you, Superintendent,' she said, dropping the Deborah shite.

'I thought you were cleverer than that. You disappoint me.'

'You'd better explain what you mean,' Lottie said defiantly.

Farrell picked up the tie from the desk and slid it under her shirt collar. With deft fingers she had it knotted and in place in four seconds flat, effectively shrinking her neck. 'You can tell me Boyd isn't ready to return to work, even part-time; if not, either you or he will have to be transferred to another district. Emotions can't come into this job. What's it to be?'

Resisting the temptation to tell Farrell that her epaulette was undone, Lottie stood and slid the chair under the desk. She wasn't about to fall into the baited trap. 'I believe it's a matter for you to decide.' With her hands resting on the padded back, trying to still her jittery fingers, she added, 'Is that all?'

'That's all.'

Escaping out the door, she leaned against the wall. She closed her eyes and waited until her breathing returned to normal.

'You okay, boss?' Kirby waddled towards her.

'What are you doing up here?' she said.

'The super asked to see the report on the drone body.'

'What's a drone body?'

'Shit, sorry. Forgot you didn't know about it. Will I fill you in before I talk to …?' He nodded towards the door.

Lottie gripped his elbow and steered him back down the corridor.

'Yes, you damn well better fill me in.'

CHAPTER EIGHT

Kevin O'Keeffe's first self-imposed duty of the day was to remove the recyclable materials and trash from the utility room and bring it to the wheelie bins outside. He attacked this daily chore with gusto.

With his hands sheathed in disposable gloves, he lifted the lid off the first bin and pulled out the clear plastic bag. He punched the side of it lightly, twisting it around in his hand as he peered through the clear plastic. It looked okay. Food remnants wrapped haphazardly in newspaper. The waste management company had yet to provide brown bins for food waste, and much as it pained him to have to do it, he went out the back door and deposited the bag in the black rubbish bin. The smell of bleach erupted when he lifted the lid. He kept his bins clean, hosing them inside and out after each collection.

Next he opened the small indoor recycling bin. It was empty. That was odd. Surely there should be cardboard, food cartons and plastic wrapping from vegetable trays? What was Marianne up to now?

Back out in the morning sunshine, he opened the blue bin lid, smelling the bleach again. There on the bottom was the bag he had expected to find inside. As he brought it back in with him, he noticed something leaking, trailing brown liquid behind his footsteps. Upending the bag, he spilled the contents on the kitchen floor. Among the shredded papers and flattened boxes, he found the offending article. A Coke can, not properly drained, though in fairness it had been scrunched up.

'Marianne!' he bellowed.

'In here.' Her voice drifted from the living room, where she had set up a little office for herself.

'What's the meaning of this?' He held up the can.

Sitting at her desk, she glanced over her shoulder. The sun streaming through the window highlighted her brown hair. It looked shinier than normal. He wondered if she'd had it dyed without asking him first.

'I haven't a clue what you're talking about.' She gave him that half-smile, the one where he never knew whether she was mocking him or admiring him.

Slamming the can on top of the paper she'd been working on, he swivelled her chair around so he stood behind her and laid his gloved hand on the nape of her neck. Just the barest of touches, but he felt her shy away, bending her head, moving out of his reach. He pinched her skin tighter, snagging the short hairs at the base of her neck.

'I do the recycling, not you, and this is why.' He nudged the dripping can.

'Kevin, don't be ridiculous. The bag was full, so I put it out.'

He felt the heat flush up his neck and flare on his ears like sunburn. He balled his hands into fists, his skin sweating beneath the synthetic gloves. Her voice grated on his nerves. It sounded like an out-of-tune piano. High-pitched. Unnatural. Whiny.

'Is there something in there you wanted to hide from me?' he said. 'Something you're writing that you don't want me to see? Is that why you shred everything?'

'Of course not. You're being irrational.'

He knew the signs so well. She was trying to be bossy, but she was cowering. He smirked and gripped her neck tighter, sliding his fingers up under her hair and twisting her head so she had to look at him.

'You know I am *never* irrational, sweetheart.'

'Please, Kevin. You're hurting me.'

He smiled. He knew he wasn't hurting her, but he could if he wanted to.

He leaned over, pointed to the page she'd been working on. 'What's this about?'

'It's a work in progress, you know that. That's why I need to shred the pages. I don't want anyone to read it in its unfinished state.'

'Are you writing about me?' He wouldn't put it past her to invent obnoxious untruths.

'I write fiction, as well you know.'

'It wouldn't stop you making me into some kind of monster, would it?' He laughed nervously. She shouldn't worry him like this with her rambling writing.

'You know I couldn't do that. Stop, Kevin. You're hurting me now.'

He withdrew his hand. Her head flopped and she reached to her neck. Long fingers with red polished nails.

He took a step forward, grabbed her hand. 'Who is this for?'

'What in heaven's name are you talking about— Ouch!'

He'd slapped her without realising he'd done it. It was her own fault.

'Take that off your nails.' He moved away from her without apology. When he succeeded in breathing normally and reducing the screech in his voice, he said, 'In future, drain the cans and cartons and wash them out before you crush them. I'm in charge of taking out the rubbish and recycling.'

'I didn't think—'

'You never do, do you? Not unless it's about making up some poxy plot for a book that will never be published. Give it up.' He walked to the door, then turned back and stared until she looked up at him. 'I'm serious, Marianne. It's time you put that laptop on eBay and forgot your silly notions. You'll never be a writer.'

He returned to the utility room to complete his morning duty. He couldn't help feeling pleased with himself. One leaky drink can and he'd put her firmly in her place. Hopefully it was a good omen for the rest of the day.

CHAPTER NINE

Once Jim McGlynn had finished his examination around the dismembered body, and Jane Dore, the state pathologist, had cast an eye over it on site, the torso was removed to Tullamore Hospital mortuary. The pathologist had said she'd have to wait for it to fully defrost under sterile conditions at the morgue. Kirby filled Lottie in on the early-morning activity and left her to read over the two boys' statements.

In the general office, he flipped the tab on an energy drink and said, 'We'll get a call when the pathologist is ready to start the post-mortem.'

'Where are the two witnesses?' Lynch said, plonking herself on her chair and kicking her shoes under the desk.

'They gave their statements and their mothers brought them home. The drone footage is now in evidence.'

'Poor kids.'

'Not that poor. They owned a drone. Expensive toys.'

'You know what I mean.' Lynch folded her arms.

'This might soften your bite.' Kirby pounded the keyboard with stubby fingers. 'I got the tech guys to put the SD card from the drone into a USB. It's ready to watch.'

'Could you not do that yourself?'

'You know me and technology. Do you want to look at it or not?'

'Sure.' She wheeled her chair over and tucked her legs under his desk.

Kirby was suddenly conscious of his body odour and wished he'd nipped to the locker room for a spray of deodorant. No point in fretting now, he thought, and opened up the link on his computer.

'You have to hit play,' Lynch said.

'Give me a chance.'

'You sound like McGlynn.'

'Normal service is resumed, so,' Kirby laughed.

The images were surprisingly clear. Following the line of the tracks from up above, Kirby imagined the boys running behind the drone watching it on the phone screen, unaware of the horror they were about to uncover.

'Pause it there.' Lynch pointed at the screen and Kirby was sorry he hadn't let her take over. He found the correct key and hit pause.

'That's about a hundred metres from where the body was found,' he said.

'I know, and I'm trying to get a feel for the terrain. How could someone get a body, a frozen body, down that far? There's no road. It's virtually a train track through fields.'

'The canal is to the left as we look at it, with a towpath for walkers. Maybe the body was transported along the path, or by boat?'

'A boat is a possibility all right,' Lynch said. 'No trace would be left behind that way. What about it being dumped from a moving train?'

'Is that baby brain you've got?'

'I take offence at that comment.'

'Oh, sorry.' Shit, had he said something politically incorrect?

Maria Lynch laughed and tied her hair back with a bobbin. 'I'm joking. But you're right, there's no way someone could conceal a frozen body on a train before hefting it out a window.'

'It's small. Jesus, Lynch, I'm sure it's a child.'

'I'm curious as to how long it's lain there,' she said as a uniformed officer distributed files on detectives' desks. 'There were two trains this morning before the boys made their discovery. I've organised for the drivers to be interviewed to see if they noticed anything on the tracks. We'll have to speak to the passengers too.'

Kirby flicked through the file that had just been dropped on his desk. It looked like it had been quickly typed up by one of the new clerical assistants. Things were changing as fast as their new superintendent could sign them off.

'The two boys reported that today was the first day they'd flown the drone over the railway rather than the canal. Could the body have been there a while?'

'I doubt it.' Lynch shook her head. 'I'm sure a train driver would have noticed a torso in a great big block of ice.'

'That's the point, isn't it? If it had been there much longer, more ice would've melted. The state pathologist should be able to give us a good idea of when it was dumped, based on the time taken to melt a frozen body in this weather. Let's continue with the video and see if we notice anything.'

Pressing a key, he watched the footage intently as the drone flew over the single-line track.

'Pity it's not flying closer to the ground,' he said. 'We might discover some clues.'

Lynch said nothing. That unsettled him. He tried to concentrate on the screen, but his belly was rumbling and a headache began to thrum behind his eyes.

'Don't know how youngsters watch screens all day. I'm not five minutes here and already—'

'Stop it,' Lynch said.

'I'm only—'

'The film. Video or whatever. Pause it. Back it up. There. Do you see it?'

Kirby leaned closer to the fuzzy image. 'What?'

'All the stones between the sleepers are uniform-looking, wouldn't you say?'

Kirby shrugged. He had no idea what the hell Lynch was talking about.

'You must see it! Zoom in closer.'

'How do I do that?'

'Are you having me on?' She stared at him.

He clicked the mouse a couple of times. The image grew grainier and fuzzier, but at last he noticed what his colleague had seen.

'That's not a stone,' he said. 'What is it?'

'I'm not sure, but it could be ...' Lynch sat back in the chair, frowning.

'Lynch?'

'We need to get back to the railway now.'

'What is it?' he repeated.

She leaned in again, squinting. 'Bloody hell, Kirby, it's a fucking hand.'

CHAPTER TEN

The insurance business was not what Kevin O'Keeffe would have picked for himself, but life didn't always turn out the way you planned. A2Z Insurance was located on a retail street, with a breaker's yard to the rear. It was noisy both inside the building, with its open-plan desk formation, and outside with the crunch of machinery from the yard.

'You're late!'

'Sorry.' Kevin threw his laptop bag under his desk and picked up his headset. 'I had a bit of a problem with Marianne again.' He mimed raising his hand to his mouth as if he was drinking. His go-to excuse. Everyone in the office believed his wife was a roaring alcoholic, and this garnered sympathy for him from his colleagues, though he wondered if his boss, Shane Courtney, could see through the lies. Courtney was younger than him. Thirty-something, with an attitude tattooed into his prim mouth and steely eyes. Kevin felt irritation scratch his skin as his boss wended through the maze of desks towards him.

'She needs to see someone. It's impacting on your performance, Kevin. Do you think she might need to go into rehab?'

Biting the inside of his cheek so as not to lash out, Kevin nodded. 'You're probably right, but have you seen the cost of those places? Even on your salary I wouldn't be able to afford it.'

'You have no idea what my salary is, and anyway, it's not me that needs drying out. You've had five lates this month. Unacceptable. Get your family life sorted or you'll have no salary at all.'

'Okay, okay … sorry.'

Moving back towards his office, Courtney said over his shoulder, 'And you're nowhere near reaching your targets this month. Crack on.'

As he drew an intake of breath in relief, Kevin noticed the hush around him. He felt his cheeks burn. Fuck Courtney. Why did he have to reprimand him in full view of the rest of the staff? He shook his head and entered his computer password.

'Are you okay, Kevin?'

He looked up over the partition at Karen Tierney. She was in her twenties and pretty in a forgettable way, her fair hair bunched untidily on top of her head. The combination of blue jeans, red blouse and pale make-up made her look like the American flag. And sometimes, like today, she could be a nosy cow.

'I'm fine,' he muttered. 'I need to get busy.' He tapped the keyboard, hoping she got the message.

'I saw Marianne in the supermarket at the weekend. She doesn't look at all well. You really should do what Mr Courtney suggests.'

'Karen?'

'What?'

'You should mind your own business.'

Her head disappeared behind the partition and Kevin got to work, wishing he was anywhere but stuck in this gossip-mongering hellhole. Once he had his computer up and running, he latched on the headset then checked the national news app. It usually gave him something for small talk when he had a difficult client on the end of the phone. The breaking news ticker tape drew his attention and he tapped it.

'Holy shit,' he said.

'What's wrong?' Karen popped her head back over the partition, gripping the blue edge, nails studded with diamonds as fake as her eyelashes.

Waving her away, he continued to read about the torso found on the railway. His headset beeped with an incoming call. He transferred it to Karen. Best to keep her busy while he read the news.

*

The Bank, one of Ragmullin's newer coffee shops, was quiet enough. Faye sat in a nook while Jeff ordered their drinks. He returned with two coffees and toasted croissants filled with cheese and ham. Her stomach lurched.

'I couldn't manage a thing.'

'You need to eat something to get over the shock.' Jeff tore open sugar sachets and emptied them into her steaming mug. 'Drink up.'

'Honestly, I can't.' Faye leaned back in the chair, which was too soft and too low. Her knees were higher than her belly button; she wanted to throw up. 'What did you do with it?'

'With what?'

She watched as he stuffed croissant into his mouth, melted cheese sticking to his bottom lip.

'The skull,' she whispered.

He blew on his coffee before gulping down a mouthful.

'It could belong to a body. Where's the rest of it?'

'Please, Faye, forget about it.'

She leaned forward and lifted her own mug. Her stomach flipped again as the aroma of crushed coffee beans reached her nose. She stood. 'I'm going to the loo.'

Black spots traced her line of vision and she felt Jeff's hand reach out to steady her. She swatted him away and went to the dimly lit ladies' room.

Leaning over the ceramic basin, she drew in deep breaths of air. When she looked at herself in the mirror, she recoiled in shock at her appearance. Beads of perspiration had burst out on her too-white skin. Her fair hair was matted and dusty; even her hands were still covered with a sheen of fine plaster particles. A ghost, she thought, I look like a bloody ghost.

With water pouring from the tap, she hastily squeezed soap from a reluctant dispenser and washed her hands, then shook the dust out of her hair. Holding a paper towel under the gurgling stream, she dabbed the soaked tissue across her forehead and cheeks.

After she'd peed and washed her hands again, she felt no better. The butterfly fluttering continued in her stomach and she wondered how she was going to cope with a little human being in her life when she couldn't even deal with the fact that she'd probably found a dead one in the house she was trying to make into a home.

A dead one.

'Really?' she asked her reflection. *Forget about it*, Jeff had said, but Faye was not one to forget about things just because someone told her to. No way. She turned off the dripping tap and straightened her shoulders. She would find out if the skull was real or not. First, she had to discover where Jeff had put it.

As she opened the ladies' room door, a shadow fell over her. She looked up.

'Jeff?'

'You were ages. I was worried. Are you okay? The baby?'

'Will you stop fretting over me like I'm a sick puppy. I've had a shock; I'm fine now. You need to get back to work. Drop me to the house first. That wallpaper isn't going to scrape itself off.'

CHAPTER ELEVEN

Lottie reached the place Lynch had spotted on the drone video. Suited up, she crouched next to the railway sleepers.

Kirby puffed and huffed beside her. 'It's about a hundred metres from where the body was found.'

She viewed the activity in the distance. A small army of SOCOs like white ants were scouring the area from where the body had been removed. She glanced around her. A thick blackberry bush stood out from the nearby hedge. On the opposite side of the tracks there was a wooden stile leading up and over to the wide bank of the canal. Most likely a fishing location, she thought.

'Maybe the body was transported via the canal,' Kirby said, 'and whoever was carrying it exited onto the railway from here. They might have dropped the hand on the way to the main dumping site.'

Lottie scrutinised the location. Kirby was probably right. But where were the rest of the body parts?

'It's definitely a hand,' she said inspecting the frozen flesh without touching it. 'The entire railway line will have to be fingertip-searched.'

'The *entire* line?' Kirby said. 'From Sligo to Dublin?'

'No, I mean from town out to where the torso was found, and then a little way beyond.'

'Still a lot of manpower.' He scratched his head. 'We could just fly a drone over the track.'

Lottie smiled behind her mouth mask. 'Kirby, that's the most sensible thing I've heard from you in a long time.'

'Is that a compliment, boss?'

'You can take it as one. However, it might be better to call in the air support unit, and we still need feet on the ground. Organise it.'

She stood up and glanced at the hedges, bits of paper and plastic caught in the branches. The bank along the tracks was studded with litter too. Probably the same on the canal towpath.

'I want the surrounding area searched as well. Seems to me that whoever dumped this body was careless; that's if it wasn't intentional.' She pondered her own musings. 'Perhaps they threw away something that might help us incriminate them. Where's Lynch?'

'I'm here.'

Lottie watched as Maria Lynch struggled with the zipper on her protective suit.

'It's stuck. And don't mention baby weight, because I haven't got any.'

'You're looking great, Maria, and don't let anyone tell you otherwise. Can't say the same for Kirby. What's up with him?' She watched as the burly detective mooched off to one side, fiddling with his phone.

'What's *not* up with him?' Eventually Lynch's zipper shot into place.

'Good work discovering the hand. If you hadn't, the wildlife would have had a feast.' Lottie noticed two members of the SOCO team making their way towards them.

Lynch was bending over the hand, staring at it. 'It looks like it was wrapped in plastic. Do you think it is part of the torso?'

'I hope so, otherwise we'll be dealing with two bodies.' Lottie crouched down beside Lynch. 'We have the torso and one hand. I'd like to know where the rest of the body is.'

'If we have one hand, the other should be around. Who in their right mind would drop one hand?' Lynch said earnestly.

'It may have been dropped by accident. We're not dealing with someone in their right mind,' Lottie pointed out.

McGlynn arrived beside them. 'You're interfering with my crime scene as usual, Detective Inspector Parker.'

'Looking, not touching. I'm learning,' Lottie said.

'Good,' he said grudgingly. 'How is young Boyd?'

'Boyd is doing fine, thanks.' Lottie grinned at the older man with his inquisitive green eyes. He was like a thorny bush; in among the thorns there had to be some roses, though so far she had been unable to find them.

'Dear Lord, I'll soon have the two of you stamping all over my crime scenes again. God give me patience. Now out of my way until I see what we have here.'

'Will I be able to get fingerprints from the hand?' Lottie asked.

'You won't but I might. I'll let you know when I know.'

'Jim, is the body really that of a child?'

'I think so.'

She left the SOCOs to their forensic work, and she and Lynch walked over to Kirby.

'We need to scrutinise all our missing persons files,' she said. 'Even though we only have parts of a body, this was a human being, a child, and someone out there is missing a loved one.'

CHAPTER TWELVE

Faye watched Jeff drive off. She dropped the rancid curtain and looked around. He still refused to tell her where he'd put the skull, saying she needn't worry her head over it. He's missing the pun, she thought wryly.

It had to be somewhere in the house.

In the kitchen, she went through the trash can. She searched every cupboard, swatting away flies and spiders, unafraid but careful all the same. If she saw one pebble of mouse dirt, she was out of there.

They'd have to dump the crockery at some stage, she mused as she moved cups and plates around, and the stained cutlery would have to go too. All the mouldy foodstuff had been chucked out ages ago, for fear of inviting in rodents. Faye shivered. She wasn't afraid of much, but they were one thing she would run a mile from.

The chest-high refrigerator hummed as she opened the door. The light spilled into the kitchen, illuminating the laminate cupboard doors. Frost and ice clung to the bottom of the ice box and its drawer looked frozen solid. She tugged at it but it wouldn't budge, so it was logical to assume Jeff hadn't put the skull in there. She glanced around the kitchen. She couldn't wait to demolish it. Garish colours and dirt and grime. They would need another skip once they got started. Excitement built in her chest as she envisaged what the house would look like once it was renovated.

Jeff hadn't brought the skull with him when they'd left for coffee, so where could he have put it? She recalled he'd used the toilet. She climbed the stairs slowly. This was the part of the house she hated the most. It gave her a ghoulish feeling right between her shoulder blades. On the landing, she paused and listened. Her heart was drumming in her chest and the baby was fluttering away innocently. All four doors were slightly ajar. Three bedrooms and a bathroom. She reached out a finger and pushed at the bathroom door.

A tap dripped in the bath, leaving a brown copper trail to the plughole. The ironwork was corroded, and a cracked rubber hose was still stuck to one tap. The shower curtain hung limply, fungus growing up the length of it. The toilet smelled as if it hadn't been flushed in years, but Jeff had used it, hadn't he?

With one eye closed, Faye squinted into the toilet bowl. The water was clear. She flushed it anyway. Mistake. The pipes in the attic groaned and rattled as the water filtered noisily from the tank to the cistern. She felt as if the entire room was shaking as much as she was. Edging out backwards, she pulled the door shut.

They'd agreed that the box room would be for the baby and they would use the biggest room because it looked out over the road at the front of the house. The third bedroom, at the back, had a view of the overgrown garden for which they had zero budget.

As she moved to enter the front bedroom, she thought she heard a noise from the box room. She paused, breath held, heart thumping. No, it was just the pipes in the attic. She took another step and heard it again. One hand flew to her mouth and the other to her stomach. Acid rose into her throat and the black spots returned to her vision.

'Is there anyone there?' she said, once she had found her voice.

Silence.

What had she heard? Was it the thud of a footstep? *Don't be silly.*

'Hello?' she said tentatively.

Should she run or stay? Reaching out a hand, she pushed open the box room door. There couldn't be anyone here. Only she and Jeff had keys, and they'd been in and out most days over the last few months.

She took a step inside and screamed.

The animal lunged at her, scratching her face with one vicious swipe. Its claws caught in her hair, and she flailed at it, trying to dislodge them. Then, as suddenly as it had appeared, it fled, and she slid down the wall, her body convulsing in tremors. How had a cat got stuck up here? The room was empty, except for an old chipboard wardrobe standing in one corner. She'd joked with Jeff that if they turned it on its side, they wouldn't get another thing into the room. Now it seemed to glare at her as if it was threatening her, with one of its double doors slightly ajar. Had the cat been in there? Maybe it had kittens and was only trying to protect them. Could that be why it had attacked her?

She really didn't want to remain alone in the house any longer. But something continued to niggle on the inside of her skin, pushing up the hairs on her arms. And she wanted to find the skull.

Still crouched against the wall, she waited and listened.

There was only the rattle of the pipes overhead and the dripping of the tap in the bathroom. Nothing else apart from her own breathing.

Getting to her feet, she moved towards the wardrobe, its partially open door challenging her to peek inside. She pulled it outwards quickly; too quickly. The handle came away and the nail that had held it in place impaled itself in her hand.

'Shit!' She looked at the blood oozing from her hand. She'd need a tetanus injection for sure now. She was about to turn away, to go down the stairs and out into the fresh air, when her eyes were drawn to the shelf at eye level inside the old wardrobe.

The tiny skull.

Eyeless sockets staring at her.

She turned and fled.

CHAPTER THIRTEEN

'I really hate school, don't you?' Sean Parker leaned against the canal bank wall and kicked out at his rucksack. The canal skirted around Ragmullin, and he liked this section because it offered seclusion from the school down the road.

From under his too-long fringe he eyed his friend Ruby O'Keeffe. She had a cigarette in her mouth and a lighter in her hand and was trying to look cool, which was difficult dressed in her school uniform. Her hair was styled in a short dark bob and her cheeks had a few acne craters, but Sean supposed she was pretty. He liked her, but not *that* way. They shared an interest in gaming and had become good friends when his school turned co-ed last year.

'Want one?' she said, offering him the packet.

He shook his head as he looked down at her. Ruby was tall but nowhere near Sean's height. He was almost six foot. He'd turned sixteen in April, though his mother still treated him like a child.

'You know I hate them. My dad died from cancer and now my mam's friend, her boyfriend, has leukaemia.' Sean dropped his eyes to the grass at his feet to avoid Ruby's watchful stare.

'Did your dad smoke?' She pulled her light jacket around her waist. Sean knew she was self-conscious about her weight, but she looked fine to him.

'No.'

'If it wasn't the fags that killed him, you need to chill out.' She lit the cigarette.

Sean watched her blowing smoke out the other side of her mouth, away from him. 'Boyd, that's my mam's boyfriend, he smokes.'

'Does he still smoke even though he has cancer?'

'He has an e-cig, but I've seen him sneak a cigarette a couple of times.'

'Do you like him?'

'Yeah.'

'You don't think he's trying to … you know … take your dad's place?'

Sean couldn't put his finger on the reason why, but this remark annoyed him more than Ruby's smoking.

'No one could ever take my dad's place. Boyd knows that. He's a nice guy. He's good to my mam and to me. He notices me. Do you get that?'

'Yeah, I do. That's good, you know; it can't be easy living in a houseful of girls.' She grinned.

'Tell me about it.' Sean gulped down a breath of fresh air, catching the entrails of Ruby's cigarette smoke. His two older sisters were crowding him out of the house. Even his little nephew Louis was a pain in the arse at times, now that he was walking and pulling everything from the cupboards.

'He'll eventually come to live with us,' he said.

'Who?'

'Boyd.'

'Have you got a room for him?'

Sean had given this a lot of thought and wasn't sure he liked it very much. 'He'll probably share my mam's room.'

'That's gross. It's like … disrespecting your dad or something.'

Now Ruby had truly pissed him off, because this thought had plagued him over the last few months. Despite that, he felt he had to stand up for Boyd.

'It's five years since my dad died. I think Mam's entitled to some happiness,' he said defensively. 'Anyway, the house we shared with Dad burned down and we're living in a rental now. All our stuff went up in flames, Dad's stuff and—'

'Hey! I was only saying.'

'Yeah, and everyone else will be saying it too, but I don't care. I like Boyd.'

'But … will he die on you too?' Ruby threw down the butt and scrunched it out with her shoe.

'Shut up. Come on, we'll be late back to school.'

'We're already late,' she said. 'We should have stayed in Pizzaland.'

'The pizza was gross. Anyway, I've computer science now and I don't want to miss it.' Sean picked up his school bag and hoisted it onto his shoulder. Ruby's words bounced around in his brain, knocking at the inside of his skull. She had asked the one question he was terrified to answer.

Death.

When would it come knocking on his door again?

*

Marianne O'Keeffe closed her laptop. Two thousand words wasn't bad, even if it was all rubbish. First drafts were universally terrible, she'd heard. Hers were anyway. Perhaps that was why she had yet to have a book published.

He would be here any minute. The appointment had been agreed weeks ago, but she had to be sure Kevin would be at work, so she'd rung the office half an hour ago to confirm the visit could go ahead.

She sprayed a dash of her best perfume behind her ears. Millions. *Not like you'll ever make millions*, Kevin had said the Christmas before, when he'd presented her with the expensive perfume in a gift set. 'I will if I have my way,' she muttered as she spritzed her hair and down her legs for good measure. She grimaced in the mirror, thinking how Kevin hadn't even paid full whack for the perfume. The skinflint. She'd found the Boots half-price sticker on the back of the box. She was sure he'd left it there on purpose.

The doorbell chimed and she checked her appearance once more. White cotton blouse with a red silk camisole underneath, skinny black leather jeans, and her two-inch-heel black ankle boots. Rarely in their seventeen-year marriage had Kevin complimented her on her looks or style. But she knew she looked good, so fuck him.

She rushed to open the front door.

'Hello,' the young man said. 'Mrs O'Keeffe?'

Navy suit with brown shoes. Her pet hate, but she supposed it was the fashion.

'Call me Marianne. Come in.'

His name tag swung from a lanyard around his neck. Aaron Frost. She had to admit he looked anything but frosty. Steaming hot, if she was honest.

'The kitchen is the most comfortable place to have a chat,' she said, leading him down the narrow hallway into the vast bright room with integrated appliances. In truth, she suspected Kevin had bugged the room where she worked. Paranoid? Maybe. 'Tea? Coffee?'

'A glass of cold water would be good. Caffeine makes me hyper.' Aaron laughed. Marianne thought he sounded a bit nervous.

'Tap water okay?'

'Sure.'

She filled a glass. Kevin didn't allow bottled water. *Too much plastic ruins the environment*, he'd said over and over again. As if he knew all about it. Kevin knew fuck all about anything but liked to give the impression he was an expert on everything.

'Here, have a seat.' She guided Aaron over to the centre island, and he pulled out a stool for her. So sweet.

'Your house is beautiful. The extra-large bay windows at the front are very classy,' he said. 'New-build?'

'It's about eighteen or nineteen years old. I designed most of it with my father's help.' She didn't need to tell him it was her father's money too. 'I had it painted and redecorated last year.'

He looked up at the wall. 'Wow. Is that a sixty-two-inch?'

Marianne glanced at the flat-screen television. 'I've no idea,' she laughed.

He ran his hand over the counter top. 'Granite?'

'Quartz,' she said, knowing he was impressed.

'I can start straight away,' he said, loosening his tie and undoing the top button of his white shirt. Was she making him uncomfortable? She hoped not.

'Have you worked with the company long?' Small talk.

'Er … I joined after I left college, years ago, when I was twenty-four.'

He didn't look old enough to have finished school, let alone college, but she supposed he must be in his thirties.

'Do you like your job?'

'It's okay.' He gulped at his water. 'Decent wage. But my degree is history and English. I want to teach at some stage.'

'Why don't you?'

He shifted uncomfortably on the stool. 'Applied to a few schools, but when I didn't even get called for interview, I knew I had to earn a living somehow. So here I am, doing house valuations for my father's estate agency.'

'Why could you not get an interview for teaching?'

'You can't get a teaching position without experience and you can't get experience without a job.'

'Catch twenty-two.'

'I suppose.'

Gosh, but he was too sweet for words. Marianne leaned over and gave his hand a squeeze. His eyes flashed with something akin to horror. Was she really that old and horrible-looking? She was only thirty-eight, for feck's sake. She pulled back and pointed to the folder on the table.

Aaron stood and slid a business card across the quartz counter. 'I'll leave this for you. Now, where do you want to start?'

Where indeed? Marianne smiled to herself. This was going to be fun.

She watched Aaron work for twenty minutes, measuring from wall to wall in every room, with an app on his phone and a beeping gadget in his hand. She saved her own room for last.

Leading the way across the plush carpet, she said, 'And this is the master bedroom. Don't mind the mess.'

There was no mess. There never was any mess in her luxurious home. And yes, it was *her* home, though Kevin liked to give the impression to anyone who cared to listen that he owned it. The title deeds were in her name. It was her one victory over him. He might think he controlled everything in her life, and she had to admit that he scared the shit out of her at times, but it came in handy to let him think she was a doormat.

'Nice room. It's so big,' Aaron said, and his little machine beeped again. 'Your house is amazing. It's worth quite a lot of money. You'll see once I have the valuation calculated. But there'll be no problem selling it if that's what you want.'

He'd taken off his suit jacket downstairs and rolled up his shirtsleeves. They'd settled into a friendly routine as they'd gone from room to room. She had offered to help, and he'd said he could manage. She could see his hands shaking as he held the two devices and spoke into the recorder on his phone. He checked and double-checked that he had everything correct. His steel-rimmed designer spectacles had slid down a little on his nose and patches of sweat had spread under his arms, but all she could smell was a woody cologne.

'I like to think of the house as a work of art,' she said. 'As I said, I designed it myself, though my husband likes to think he had some input. See that hideous mahogany wardrobe?' Aaron nodded. 'He insisted it had to be in our room. It was his mother's. Can you imagine waking up every morning to see your mother-in-law's old wardrobe?'

'I suppose it is a bit weird,' he said.

She eyed him and noticed a smile at the corner of his lips.

'More than a bit,' she laughed.

'Why keep it if you hate it?'

'Don't know.' But she did. She kept it to let Kevin think he'd won a victory over her.

'It's very big.'

'It's handy for spare sheets and pillows.' She was sorry now that she'd mentioned it. 'There's an en suite, with gold-plated taps. Do you need to measure in there?'

'Er, I'll have a look.'

When he went inside, Marianne smoothed out the creases in her blouse. A glance in the mirror told her the outline of her red lacy camisole was visible. Good.

She sat on the bed, crossed her legs and waited.

When he came out of the bathroom, she patted the bed. 'Sit for a moment, Aaron. I'm tired from all this traipsing around the house.'

'I'd better get going, Mrs O'Keeffe. I have to go back to the office. It's—'

'Shh. Sit.'

She was surprised when he did as she asked. The cologne was more pungent now that he was closer. She reached out and took his hand in hers. He jumped up.

'I really have to go. I'm sorry if I gave the wrong impression. This is my job and—'

She rose and pulled him by the hand towards her, then kissed him on the lips, blocking his words.

He tugged his hand free. 'Are you out of your mind?'

She stifled his words with another kiss, crushing his mouth with her own and pushing him back on the bed. Heat convulsed her body and she cast off all her inhibitions. This was what she wanted. A hot man writhing beneath her.

Suddenly he wasn't moving. Lifting her mouth from his, she stared into his open eyes. Was he dead?

She fell backwards as he shoved her away and leapt from the bed, rushing from the room. She heard his feet on the stairs, the snap of the lock and the soft thump of the door as he pulled it shut behind him.

'Fuck.'

*

Aaron Frost walked in circles for miles around the town, going as far as the Dublin bridge and back round towards the Railway Bridge. He was rattled, though not because of the O'Keeffe woman. Creepy bitch. Who did she think he was? No, he had a lot of other more important things on his mind and he didn't want to go back to the office.

Like a child, he kicked stones into the murky green water of the canal and watched the ripples spread through the slime. The reeds rustled and he thought he saw a rat scamper up on the opposite bank. He shivered and continued walking.

He should go home, change his clothes, then he'd go and meet them and tell them to forget about everything. His phone pinged and he checked the message.

DID YOU SEE THE NEWS TODAY?

No, he hadn't. He tapped into the news app, went into the regional category and scrolled down. A torso had been found on the Ragmullin railway tracks. The Dublin side of town. The opposite end to where he was walking. Still, he looked around frantically.

Slipping the phone into his pocket, he continued walking. Faster now. Kicking up pebbles as he went. Something in the news report raised goose bumps on his skin. No, it had nothing to do with what he'd found out.

His phone pinged again.

DID YOU READ IT?

All capitals. Why? He typed back.

Yes. Nothing to do with me.

ARE YOU SURE?

Yes. Fuck off.

THE DEAD HAVE BEEN WOKEN.

What type of shit was that? He loosened his tie as if that could keep the feeling of dread from choking him to death. Frantically he looked all around, twisting his head like an idiot. No one, only himself on the path, and ducks and rats and fish in the water. Why then did he feel like someone was watching him?

Fuck this, he thought, and broke into a run.

CHAPTER FOURTEEN

Lottie missed having Boyd in the office; his presence had a calming effect on everyone. They could do with his organisational skills too, she thought as she eyed the mess on Kirby's desk.

'Right so, until we get word from the state pathologist, we don't know what we're dealing with. Because the body had been dismembered and frozen, it's a suspicious death.'

McKeown wandered in with an ice pop in his hand.

'You could have got one for everyone,' Kirby moaned.

'Piss off.' McKeown plonked himself at Boyd's desk now that Lynch had reclaimed her own.

'Can we take our meeting into the incident room, where we can be serious?' Lynch said.

'We will,' Lottie said, 'when we have more details. What's the latest?'

'Irish Rail have been on to us,' Lynch said. 'They want to know when they can get trains moving again.'

'Not until we're sure there are no more body parts along the tracks. Have the train drivers been interviewed?'

'There were two trains this morning. The 6.05 and the 7.55. Neither driver noticed anything on the tracks, but the cab's high up and the torso was lying between two sleepers, so that's not telling us anything.' Lynch checked her notes. 'I also contacted yesterday's train drivers. No one saw anything.'

'When was the last train yesterday evening?'

'Arrived into Ragmullin on its way to Sligo at 8.20 p.m. Driver has been interviewed. He reports seeing nothing either.'

'I called in the air support unit,' Kirby said. 'No drones, but the helicopter should be in the air already.'

'Good. We also need to establish how the body came to be placed or dropped on the tracks, and when. Tell the pilot to scan the canal too.' Lottie scratched her forehead, trying to think on her feet. Literally. She could still feel the emotion of the weekend funeral weighing her down. 'Who interviewed the two boys? What are their names?'

Kirby flicked through the pages of his notebook but McKeown had the answer after one tap on his device.

'Jack Sheridan and Gavin Robinson. They've given statements. All the details are here.'

Lottie groaned. She sensed the animosity in the air as if it was a tangible object. There was going to be trouble between those two detectives.

'Print them out for me.' She preferred working with paper. 'I'll give the boys a shout later.' Leaning against the timber-framed wall, she heard a creak and hoped it wasn't her knees. 'And I want regular updates from the air crew.'

McKeown's iPad pinged. 'That was quick,' he said.

'What was?'

'The helicopter crew spotted something in the water. Two hundred metres down the canal from where the torso was found.'

'Who's going to call Irish Rail?' Lynch said.

'You do it. There's to be no resumption of trains for now. Let's go.'

Lottie picked up her bag, slid her phone into her jeans pocket. She knew it was a universal cliché, but all she could think was that the case had taken another grisly turn.

*

Walking along the bank as quickly as the undergrowth allowed, Lottie glanced over her shoulder to make sure Kirby was keeping up with her.

'What do you think is going on?' she said.

'I can't understand why the torso was dumped on the tracks where it could be easily found.'

'If they were disposing of it at night-time, they might have thought they were further away from town.'

'They didn't bank on two kids with a drone, did they?'

Lottie reached the location and looked up at the helicopter hovering overhead, its rotors swishing the reeds back and forth. McKeown was already there and radioed the air crew to continue searching. With a last twirl in the sky it headed back along the canal.

She peered into the tangled mess in the centre of the water. 'Is that a leg?'

'Looks like it.' McKeown said. 'Whatever it was wrapped in has disintegrated. The skin is bleached from the water. It's hard to know how long it's been there.'

'Where's McGlynn?'

'Still at the site of the torso.'

'I thought it had been moved to the mortuary.'

'Yes, but he's scanning the area for evidence.'

'We'll need divers to retrieve this body part,' Lottie said.

'I can go in.' McKeown sounded like an over-eager schoolboy wanting to please the teacher. 'But we still need divers to search further, in case there are more remains in there. It's very black and mucky.'

'Don't go in,' Lynch said. 'Wait for the divers with the proper equipment. You'll catch Weil's disease.'

Lottie eyed Lynch and McKeown and wondered how a rapport had sprung up between them so quickly.

'Get a cordon erected immediately, otherwise we'll have Cynthia fecking Rhodes sniffing around.' She glanced over her shoulder as if the mention of the reporter might cause her to appear. But she knew there was no chance of that. Following a recent scoop, Cynthia had secured a slot on primetime television, a step up from her two-minute reports on the news. No doubt a new Rottweiler would be sent to Ragmullin shortly.

'Right so,' McKeown said. He began unwinding a roll of garda tape. As Lynch assisted him, Lottie stood with Kirby and stared at the portion of leg protruding from the stagnant water.

'It looks like a child's,' she said softly and blew out a troubled breath.

'Yes, it does.' Kirby sat on the bank and took off his shoes and socks.

'You can't go in there. Like Lynch said, it's—'

'We can't leave it any longer. Someone has to take it out.' He shrugged his arms out of his jacket and rolled his trousers up to the knees.

'It's deeper than that. Wait for the divers,' Lottie said, though she knew where Kirby was coming from. It wasn't right to leave part of a child in such a mire.

'I'm going in.'

She watched as Kirby waded into the foul water. The reeds rustled as he moved, and a dark shape swam away from the body part and crossed to the other bank. Something licked her ankles. She squirmed. It was just the wiry reeds rustling about her feet in the soft breeze.

She moved back a step. 'McKeown, tell SOCOs to hurry up with the tarpaulin.'

'Should I have put gloves on?' Kirby shouted.

'Doesn't matter now. Just get it out of there. Hurry up. You'll catch a cold ... or something.'

She held her breath as the water reached Kirby's chest. He paused, then carefully lifted the body part and waded back towards the bank. Springing into action, she instructed the arriving SOCOs where to lay the plastic sheeting and watched helplessly as one of the forensic officers took charge of the leg, laying it reverently on the plastic. A lump formed in her throat. Goddammit, she thought. Ever since Boyd's diagnosis, she'd found it hard to control her emotions. She shook herself back into professional mode.

'Someone, fetch a towel for Kirby.'

'I'm fucking freezing,' he said.

McKeown shrugged. 'You should have thought of that before you decided on a Superman impression.'

Lynch sniggered.

'Thank you, Kirby,' Lottie said.

The SOCO opened a large steel case and handed Kirby a black towel and a forensic boiler suit to change into.

'I've a set of clothes in the car, thanks.'

Lottie stared at the leg. It had been cut off at the knee, the toenails on the little foot blackened and bruised. The threads of a sock remained around the ankle, with frayed pink nylon ribbon that might once have been tied in a neat bow.

She felt her heart contract and her throat tighten. The sight of the remnants of the child's sock caused her more heartache and nausea than the smell of decay and the imprint of rodent teeth on the hardened flesh.

'It belongs to a little girl,' she said.

Rushing towards the bushes, she did her best not to throw up. She breathed in through her nose and out again, blinking furiously. Through the bushes she could see the railway tracks running parallel to the canal. The waterway led to Dublin in one direction and Sligo in the other. She knew little about it but was aware that there were different depths along the route.

'Do you think there are lock gates close by?' she said as she returned to the small, silent crowd.

'Five miles that way,' the SOCO said, pointing east.

'What are you thinking?' Kirby said as he unfurled one sopping trouser leg.

'That maybe the body parts were dumped in a lock chamber and were released when the lock was opened.'

'Still doesn't account for how the torso and hand came to be on the railway,' McKeown said.

'I know. I haven't thought that far.' Typical of McKeown, she thought, skewering her attempt to put logic into an illogical scenario. 'Radio the air support crew. Tell them to fly over the locks to check them out.'

As McKeown did as he was asked, Lottie noticed Lynch bending over at the edge of the plastic sheeting, staring at the little leg and foot.

'You okay, Lynch?'

The detective shook her head. 'Not really. Who would do this to a poor little child?'

At last Lottie could breathe normally. 'Whoever it is, I intend to find them before they can do it to someone else's child.'

CHAPTER FIFTEEN

Jack Sheridan filled a glass of water from the tap and sipped, but still his chest shuddered. What he and Gavin had found had resulted in a day off school, but it wasn't worth the trauma gurgling in his stomach. He sipped some more, trying to slow down the awful churning.

'Jack? What in God's name were you doing mitching from school?'

The sound of his dad's voice caught him by surprise. He dropped the glass into the sink and water splashed everywhere. His dad was off work on sick leave, though Jack wasn't sure what was wrong with him. It was usually his mother who doled out the punishments, especially when she was stressed after a long shift at the hospital.

His little sister Maggie crawled between his legs and took up residence under the table, scooping crumbs into her mouth. His nine-year-old brother Tyrone sat on a chair, his head bowed. After Jack had made his statement at the garda station, his mother had decided to pick Tyrone up from school and bring them both home.

'I wasn't mitching,' Jack said. 'Me and Gavin were flying the drone before school.'

'But you're not in school now, are you?'

'I had to go to the garda station. The police wanted to ask me questions.'

'Right,' his dad said, his voice softening. 'Are you okay?'

'Not really.'

'You'll be fine in time, but I knew that drone was going to cause trouble. You're too young for it. Where did you put it?' His father began going through his school bag, throwing books and pens on the floor. 'I don't care how much it cost; it's going in the bin.'

'It's not there, Dad. The detectives kept it. They said it's evidence or something.' Jack wanted to cry, to run, to puke, but he also didn't want his dad to see him as a weakling.

'Leave him alone, Charlie. He's had an awful shock. Go up to your room, Jack. I'll bring you a cup of hot tea in a minute.' Jack's mother came in from the clothes line and threw the laundry basket under the table. Maggie shrieked. 'Oh, I'm sorry, Mags. Did I scare you? What are you doing down there?' She picked up the two-year-old and plucked sticky crumbs from her hair.

'I don't want tea,' Jack said.

'Of course you do. With sugar for the shock.'

Jack knew that was a load of shite. Sugary tea was just to give him something else to think about. He stuffed his books back into his bag and made to leave the kitchen. No one listened to him any more. Only Gavin. He was sure Gavin's mother wasn't making him drink sugary tea that he didn't want.

'Stop dragging your bag,' his father said. 'You're scratching the wooden floor. It took me two weeks to get that shine on it.'

Sometimes Jack thought his dad cared more about the floor than he did about him.

*

As they made their way towards the cordoned-off area near the bridge where the car was parked, Lottie pointed to a house across the fields. 'Have all the homeowners in the locality been interviewed?'

Kirby followed the line of her hand, his feet squelching in his shoes. 'It's ongoing. That's where Jack Sheridan lives. One of the boys who found the torso. I interviewed him at the station this morning with his mother.'

'Has a family liaison officer been assigned?'

'The mother said they were fine, didn't need anyone. We're stretched, so I didn't argue.'

'Hope it doesn't come back to bite us. Superintendent Farrell will have a field day.' Lottie wondered how Farrell would cope with all the media attention. Better than she herself would, probably. 'Let's visit them.'

'You're hardly going to wade across the canal, are you?'

'I'll admit I'm a bit of a maverick, Kirby, but I'm not that bad yet. We'll get the car and then drive up to the house. Okay with you?'

'I need to change out of this suit first.'

By the time they got to the car, Kirby was puffing and panting. He sat into the back and tore off his rancid clothes, changing into baggy jeans and a white shirt. He found a pair of runners and some rolled-up socks in the boot and pulled them on, then bundled himself into the driver's seat and took a cigar from the dashboard.

'Don't even think about it,' Lottie said.

He drove the car away from the cordoned off area and eventually he turned onto a narrow road running alongside the canal, with grass growing up the centre.

'Do you know where you're going?'

'I have the address.' He pointed to Google Maps on his phone.

'We should have taken one of the squad cars with a built-in sat nav,' Lottie said, eyeing the phone's cracked screen. She was hot and sweaty and it was making her ratty. If Boyd had been driving, he'd have said something smart and she'd have tried not to smile, or she'd have smiled against the window where he couldn't see her. Yeah, she missed his smart-arse comments. She shivered despite the heat, the worry for his health creeping silently like a ghost into her bones.

Kirby veered away from the canal and drove along an even narrower lane. 'Should be up here.'

There were no gates, just overgrown hedges and wild bushes scraping off the sides of the car. Maybe it was just as well they were in this battered vehicle and not one of the newer ones.

The house was an old two-storey grey farmhouse with white PVC window frames now yellowed from the weather, and a door that had seen too many bad winters. There were net curtains at the windows, drawn to the side.

Lottie got out of the car, her soft-soled shoes crunching on the sharp gravel, and pressed her finger to the old bell. She glanced around as she waited for the door to be opened. It was a long time since any farming had been carried out around here. The ditch surrounding the house was untended, and briars grew wild everywhere. A series of dilapidated barns and sheds stood to the side, their galvanised roofs broken and falling inwards.

'They can afford a drone and not a lawnmower,' Kirby said, a little too loudly, just as the door opened.

The man who stood there was tall and wiry, with a grey hue to his face. His dark hair fell to his shoulders and he hadn't shaved. Lottie guessed he was in his late thirties. His clothes were casual. Jeans, and a T-shirt sporting an iconic image of the Irish singer Hozier.

'I suppose you're the detectives who interrogated my son,' he said as he led them through the house.

'Detective Kirby here interviewed him. I'm Detective Inspector Lottie Parker. And you are …?'

'Charlie Sheridan. This is my wife, Lisa.'

He pointed to the woman sitting at the table nursing a mug. A little girl perched on her knee. The kitchen was modern but unfinished, as if they'd run out of money. Shabby chic, Lottie supposed you'd call the furnishings, though they were definitely more shabby than chic.

'Hi, Lisa,' she said. 'How's Jack doing?'

The woman looked up at her with brown eyes, flecks of hazel glinting in the sunshine pouring through the window. Her fair hair hung limp on her shoulders as if she hadn't had time to wash it. She wore a white tunic and navy slacks.

'He's fine. More than a little shocked. He didn't go to school after … afterwards.'

Charlie pulled out a chair. 'Excuse my manners. Have a seat.'

'Thank you.' Lottie sat at the table. 'Where is Jack?'

'He's in his room,' Charlie said, moving to the kitchen counter. 'Tea, anyone? The kettle's boiled.'

'No thanks.' Lottie wondered why Charlie wasn't at work. 'Did you both take time off work to look after Jack today?'

'I've been off a couple of weeks,' Charlie said. 'Haven't been well. Lisa is a nurse. Works in the hospital.'

Lisa rolled her daughter's curls around her finger absent-mindedly. 'Of course, once I got the call from the gardaí, I changed my shift.'

'How can we help you?' Charlie said, leaning his back against the patio door, which was stained with tiny handprints.

The kitchen was untidy. Clothes on most available surfaces. Some folded, others strewn on the backs of chairs. The hallway they'd just walked through had boots and shoes lining one wall, with coats and jackets hanging on hooks on the other side.

'We're just following up for our investigation. I'd like a word with Jack, but I also want to ask you both a few questions, if that's all right?'

'Sure,' Lisa said. She continued to hold the little girl, who had a beaker of juice clamped to her mouth. 'Why don't you sit?' she said to Kirby.

Lottie lifted a bundle of clothes and placed them on the table, and Kirby sat beside her. She noticed that Charlie had remained standing, his hands shoved into his trouser pockets. He looked drained.

She said, 'As you know, Jack and his friend found body parts on the railway tracks this morning while they were using his drone.'

'He didn't do anything wrong,' Charlie said, and crossed his arms.

'Of course not. Your house faces the canal and railway. I'm wondering if either of you have noticed anything unusual recently. Lights at night? Boats on the water?' She looked at their blank faces, trying to read them.

'There'd be no boats yet. Bit early for them,' Lisa said. 'To be honest, we might only see five or six the whole summer.'

'What she said,' Charlie offered. 'Only a couple through the summer and you'd only notice them during the day. I haven't seen one boat in all the time I've been off work.'

Lottie looked at him thoughtfully. 'Can you see lights from boats at night-time?'

'You can, but I haven't seen any yet this year.'

She turned to his wife. 'Lisa, have you noticed anything unusual?'

'I work every hour God sends. I'm due back in tonight after swapping my shift this morning. Charlie was minding Maggie.'

'So, you haven't seen anything?'

'No, nothing.' Lisa stared at her tea, a film of grease forming on top.

The kitchen door opened and a young boy burst in, tears streaming down his face. 'Jack hit me. I only wanted a lend of his spare controller and he wouldn't give it to me. Mam! Make him give it to me.'

'Tyrone! We have visitors,' Charlie said. 'Go back to your room.'

The boy ran out, and when the kitchen had returned to silence, Lisa said, 'I drove over to the school to drop Jack off, but he was green around the gills so I just picked Tyrone up and brought them both home. Saved me having to go back again for him.'

There was something off with this little family. Lottie could sense vibes permeating around the kitchen like microwaves. The shock of their son finding a torso on the railway? Or something else?

'Is everything okay?' she asked.

Charlie moved from the patio door and came to stand behind his wife. He laid a hand on her shoulder. 'We're all in shock. Poor Jack is in a terrible state. He's told you all he knows in his statement. What else do you want from us?'

'I'm grateful to him for that. It's just that we've made additional discoveries since this morning, and I'm following up on anything that might help us discover who dumped body parts in the canal.'

'Body parts?' Lisa said. Her face paled significantly, and her eyes flew to Charlie before settling back on Lottie. 'God, this is awful. And we have to live here! What else did you find?'

'I'm not at liberty to say, but I have to call at all the houses on this route.'

'There's not another house for miles out this way,' Charlie said. 'The next one is down at the locks. No one has lived in it for donkey's years.'

Lottie nodded. 'Okay, thanks. Can I have a quick word with Jack now?'

'It might traumatise him even more,' Lisa said.

'It really would help,' Kirby said.

'Maybe it would be good for him to talk, Lisa,' Charlie said, bending his wiry frame towards his wife, squeezing her shoulder gently.

Lisa squirmed, and as if sensing her mother's discomfort, the little girl dropped her beaker and started to wail. Orange juice splashed all over Charlie. Lottie watched carefully to see his reaction, but he just smiled, took the child from Lisa's arms and cradled her to his chest. Fatherly, she thought.

There was a crash and bang out in the hallway and the door smashed open against the wall. A boy she assumed was Jack tumbled in, clutching his brother's hair. Both were screeching. He seemed quite tall for eleven, his hair as fair as his mother's. His school shirt was unbuttoned, and his brother was tugging the hem.

'It's mine. Give it back, you wanker,' Jack yelled.

'You're a meanie,' Tyrone cried, and tried to pull away.

'Boys! Stop!' Charlie handed Maggie back to Lisa and went to separate his warring sons. 'That's enough. These are detectives and they'll lock you up if you don't behave.'

That stopped them. Jack released his brother and stared at Kirby with terrified eyes.

'I didn't do anything wrong. It was just the drone. It's not my fault. Gavin wanted to do it, not me. I swear, Dad. I did nothing wrong.'

'No one's saying that, Jack,' Lisa said. 'Please stop fighting with your brother. God knows what the summer holiday's going to be like with you both at home in a few weeks.' Tears sneaked out of the corners of her eyes and she clutched the mug tightly.

'Look, you have a lot to deal with today,' Lottie said, hoping she wasn't giving up too easily. 'This is my card. Please give me a ring if any of you remember anything that might help us. No matter how inconsequential you think it might be.'

'Sure.' Charlie grabbed Tyrone by the arm and pushed him towards the door. 'Both of you, upstairs, and I'll talk to you about controllers in a minute.' He turned to Lottie and Kirby. 'I'll show you out.'

Lottie put her card on the table and slid it towards Lisa. 'I mean it, Lisa. If there's anything bothering you, ring me.'

The woman continued to stare into her mug of cold greasy tea.

CHAPTER SIXTEEN

Kirby drove slowly down the lane. Lottie turned the rear-view mirror towards her so that she could see the house fade behind them.

Charlie stood at the open door holding his daughter, watching them leave.

'What do you make of all that?' Kirby said. He picked up his cigar, then thought better of it and stuffed it into the door pocket, which was already full to bursting.

Lottie was silent until the car reached the wider road and the house disappeared.

'I don't know what to make of it yet. I'm going over it all in my mind.'

'Oddballs, if you ask me.'

'I didn't ask you. I said I was thinking.'

They approached the activity at the bridge.

'They looked guilty of something,' Kirby said, and idled the engine.

'I don't think it was guilt, that look.'

'They were scared, then.'

Lottie thought for a moment. 'Their son found a torso on the railway this morning; that's a pretty terrifying experience for any family.'

'Maybe they don't like detectives knocking on their door,' Kirby offered.

'It's the shock. Let's call to the other boy's house.'

'Gavin Robinson lives over the bridge,' Kirby said, and sniffed. 'I really need to take a shower soon. I stink.'

'That's nothing new.' Lottie was only half joking. She needed one as well.

Gavin Robinson lived in Canal Lane, a new development about a hundred metres beyond the bridge. Kirby drove into the horseshoe estate, passing an area surrounded by hoarding, and some unfinished houses that the builder had abandoned at the time of the economic crash. Gavin lived in a block of three-storey apartments. Single flats on the ground floor and duplexes on the first and second floors.

'Which one?' Lottie said.

Kirby consulted his notebook and pointed.

She climbed the steps to the first floor and rapped loudly on the door. It was opened after a second round of knocking.

'Is your mammy or daddy here?' she asked the boy who stood there.

'My dad's dead, but yeah, Mam's in her … er … office. Upstairs.'

'Hiya, Gavin,' Kirby said. 'Can you get her to come down?'

Lottie peered inside. The hall was narrow and cramped, with a door to the right and an open one in front of her. Gavin moved back to allow them to enter. He stood on the bottom step of the stairs. Though he was the same age as Jack Sheridan, he was small and thin.

'She's doing a story, a video, and said she didn't want me to disturb her. She told me I've disturbed her enough today.' He curled his lip grumpily.

'This is important. I need to talk to you, and you have to have a responsible adult with you. Can you ask her to come down?'

As Gavin tramped up the uncarpeted wooden stairs, Lottie depressed the handle on the door beside her and stepped in. It was a sitting room, but everything to sit on was piled high with boxes and bags. 'What is this stuff?'

A young woman flew down the stairs. 'Hey! Who said you could go in there?' she said sharply, then immediately composed herself. 'I'm sorry, it's messy in there. Why don't I bring you into the kitchen? I'm Tamara Robinson, by the way. Gavin's mum.'

Lottie cast her eye over the room again. It was crammed with boxes of cosmetics and hair products. Tamara waited until they were all out in the hall before directing them to the other door.

As she passed the young woman, Lottie noted Tamara was tall, blonde and dressed like she was auditioning for a part in *Next Top Model*. A light blue chiffon blouse tied at the waist and skinny white jeans. She was a stark contrast to Lisa Sheridan, pale and tired in her nurse's uniform.

The kitchen was bright and modern, like one you'd see in a show house. It reminded Lottie that she and Boyd had a viewing on Saturday, and she quickly crossed her fingers that her half-brother Leo would come through with the money for Farranstown House, sooner rather than later.

'Nice place you've got,' she said.

'I earned it.' Tamara shooed Gavin into the kitchen behind Lottie and Kirby, and the space suddenly felt too small for all of them. She'd have to remember that, when she went viewing houses. Her family was large – all adults except for Sean and Louis, and Sean was taller than all of them. Then there was Boyd's sister Grace to think of. Jesus, they'd be like the Waltons.

'What do you work at, Tamara?' she said.

'I'm an influencer.'

'What's that?' Kirby asked.

'Instagram.' Tamara rolled her eyes. 'You wouldn't understand, and it would take too long to explain.'

'You were making a video, were you?' Kirby said.

'For my stories, and now I have to do it all over again. You' – she pointed at Gavin – 'were told not to interrupt me. I told you to lie on your bed and rest.'

'We need to talk to you and Gavin, Mrs Robinson.'

'You can call me Tamara. Everyone does,' she said, like it was a badge of pride. Lottie wondered if it was her real name. Looking at the luscious blonde hair, perfectly made-up face and too-long eyelashes, she suspected she'd been christened with it and had spent her life making sure everyone knew it.

'I know Gavin made a statement,' Lottie said, 'but I wanted to ask him a few questions.'

'I'm not sure he should be talking any more about it. He won't sleep tonight.'

'Well, in a way I'm glad you don't want him to talk about it. It's a live investigation. We need to control the information until we have a suspect in custody.'

'So it was a murder!' Tamara clapped her hands to her mouth.

'We don't know what we're dealing with yet.' Of course it's a bloody murder, Lottie thought, and turned away from the doll face, directing her attention at Gavin. 'Do you and Jack fly the drone every morning?'

'Some mornings. Not all the time.' Gavin looked embarrassed by his mother and kept his eyes trained on a spot outside the kitchen window. His hair was shaved on one side and long on the other. He was dressed in a football jersey and tracksuit bottoms.

'What team do you support?' Kirby said.

Lottie smiled as the boy rolled his eyes like his mother had done and pointed to the crest on his jersey. 'Man U.'

'I think they're good.'

Lottie butted in before Kirby made a total ass of himself. 'This morning, were you not scared that a train might be along any minute?'

'I know the timetables. I have an app on my phone. Tells me when the next train is due. I'm curious about things like that.'

'You should have gone straight to school. Perhaps stay away from Jack for a while.' Tamara turned to Lottie. 'Those two are thick as thieves. God knows what they get up to.'

'But he's my friend,' Gavin whined. 'My only friend.'

'You have me, don't you?'

'Mam! You're gross.'

'Maybe I should have brought you to school after you gave your statement. But you told me you were too shocked and couldn't go in.'

The lack of empathy was almost physical. Tamara was entirely self-absorbed. Lottie wanted to tell the boy that it was okay not to feel okay. Instead she said, 'Tell me, Gavin, when you got down on the tracks, what did you do?'

He tugged at the crest on his jersey. 'It was all Jack's idea. I didn't want to go on the tracks, but it's his drone, so I followed him.' He wasn't able to hold Lottie's gaze, and she thought he might be lying.

'How many times have I told you to stay away from the tracks?' Tamara said. 'And stop fiddling with your jersey; you'll rip it, and it cost me nearly a hundred euros.'

'No it didn't,' Gavin sulked. 'You got it free when you put me in one of your Instagram stories.'

'Look, Tamara,' Lottie interjected, 'I just want to know what the boys did this morning. You can reprimand him later, okay?'

'Right, but I'm busy.'

She choked down a retort. 'Gavin, did you know you would find something on the tracks this morning?'

'What kind of question is that?' Tamara's eyes flared fuller than her Botox-filled lips. She was quick, Lottie had to give her that.

'I'm establishing facts.'

'You're trying to incriminate my son.'

'It's okay, Mam.' Gavin turned to Lottie, his cheeks puce. 'I saw it first. On the phone screen attached to Jedi. That's what we call the drone. I saw this lump on the tracks. You know, like a bag of coal but not a bag of coal. It was scary, so it was. Jack puked all over his clothes.'

'What did you do then?' Lottie had read the report and knew it was Gavin who'd puked.

'It looked like a headless zombie. We ran back to the bridge and I called 999. That's it. We waited for the guards and then we were brought to the station until our mothers came for us and we gave our statements.'

Lottie could see that Tamara had paled beneath her bronzer.

'Why are you making him relive it like this?' Tamara said.

'I'm okay.' Gavin shrugged off her hand.

'Do you and Jack fly the drone every morning?' Lottie repeated her earlier question.

'Most.'

'And evenings?'

'Not really. Sometimes we do.'

'Did you notice anyone else around this morning, or yesterday maybe?' Lottie said. 'Do you think you might have disturbed anyone?'

The boy blanched. 'You mean we might have seen the killer? Or ended up dead?'

'Not at all. I'm trying to establish a timeline of the events of this morning and the days leading up to it.'

'I saw no one. Unless there's anything else on Jedi's camera. You have it. Check it out.'

'We will,' Kirby said.

'This is a quiet area,' Tamara said. 'You wouldn't think it, but most people here work in Dublin. Gone early in the morning, home late, and in all night. Very quiet.'

'This is my number,' Lottie said, passing the woman her card. 'If Gavin remembers anything at all, please call me.'

'Sure thing.' Tamara clutched the card with her long red talons.

Gavin said, 'Is Jack okay?'

'Like you, he's still in shock,' Lottie said.

Tamara followed them to the door. 'I'm sorry. For earlier. Being a bitch and all. I am very protective of Gavin. His father died when he was a baby. Heart attack. I am all he's got.'

'I'm sorry for your loss,' Lottie said, knowing just how hard it was to bring up children single-handedly.

'Keep an eye on him,' Kirby said.

'Do you think he's in danger? Because of what he found?'

'I don't think so,' Lottie said, 'but there's no harm in being more vigilant than normal. And ring me if you notice anything unusual, or if he remembers anything else.'

'I will. And that stuff in there …' Tamara nodded to the sitting room, 'it's all gifted. Just in case you think I stole it.'

'Of course,' Kirby said, and Lottie shoved him ahead of her out of the door.

CHAPTER SEVENTEEN

Back at the station, Lottie had no time to get stuck into her paperwork. Jane Dore rang to say she'd completed her preliminary examination of the torso. Lottie fetched her car and flew along the motorway to Tullamore Hospital, where the mortuary was located.

She parked up in the last empty space she could find and immediately thought of Boyd. This hospital was where he spent several hours a week for his treatment. She locked the car, her heart aching. She wasn't sure if she believed in a God any more, but she silently prayed that he would let Boyd get better. Her prayers had gone unanswered with Adam.

'You owe me one,' she whispered to the sky.

The morgue was at the end of a winding corridor, the odour stronger the further she walked. She thought she'd be used to the smell by now, but it clawed at the back of her throat, and she fetched a mouth mask from the supply cabinet. The Dead House mortuary was aptly named, even though it had been modernised ten years ago.

Lottie stood with Jane in her office as the state pathologist perused her notes.

'The torso on the tracks is definitely female.'

'I gathered that,' Lottie said impatiently.

'I'm doing you a favour here,' Jane said. 'No need to be cranky.'

'Sorry.' There was no point in having the pathologist on the wrong side of the fence. 'It's just that it's getting late and I've to keep on top of Sean's homework. He has exams and I'm certain he's way behind on his schoolwork.' She was rambling on because she didn't want to think about the butchered girl lying on a table in the cutting room.

'How is Sean?' Jane said.

'He has his dark moods, but he's doing well considering all that's happened over the last few years.'

'And Detective Sergeant Boyd? Is his treatment working?'

'I hope so. He wants an overnight cure, but you and I know that won't happen. He's so impatient, it's annoying.'

Jane smiled.

'What?' Lottie raised an eyebrow quizzically.

'You and Boyd,' Jane said. 'You're so alike. When are you giving me an excuse to buy a hat?'

'I can't imagine you in a hat other than the hood of a forensic suit.'

'Then you don't know me at all,' Jane said, studying her notes.

'We really need to make time for that coffee, don't we?'

'Yes, but another few years waiting for coffee is okay by me.'

Sighing, Lottie thought how she had no real friends any more. Between trying to keep tabs on her children and staying up to date with her work schedule, she never seemed to have time for anyone else. Other than Boyd, that was. Or did she delegate Boyd further down her list of priorities too? Now was not the time to consider the implications of that scenario.

'How about Saturday?' she said, hoping Jane would say no.

'I can't do Saturday. I have a date.'

'The same guy?'

'Have you ever known me to date the same guy twice?'

Lottie wasn't sure how to answer. Truthfully, she knew little about the pathologist's private life.

'Let's get on with the report, shall we?' Jane said.

'Of course.'

'As I was saying, the victim is a girl. I'd estimate she was aged between seven and twelve.'

Lottie felt her stomach somersault. She couldn't bear to think of a child being mutilated in such a barbaric way. 'Oh, the poor little angel. This is terrible.'

'The torso was almost defrosted by the time it arrived here, thanks to the unusually hot weather. I've sent samples to the lab.'

'How did she die?' Lottie wasn't sure she wanted to hear the answer. She could feel the blood draining from her face.

'It's tough. Kids always are,' Jane said. 'Try to detach yourself.'

'Not possible.' Lottie gulped, her voice unsteady. 'Someone killed this little girl, cut her up and dumped her body. Part of her body.'

'The other body parts are being sent to me, so I'll know more when I get them. You still don't have her head, but the damage to the bones in the neck leads me to believe she was strangled and then decapitated.'

'You can tell that, even though the head was sawn off?'

'It wasn't sawn off, but yes, I can. There's enough of the hyoid bone present to prove she was strangled.'

'If it wasn't sawn off, then how?'

'A single chop with an axe or a similar type of blade.'

Lottie felt her stomach churn. 'Tell me she was dead at the time, right?'

Jane nodded without answering.

'How long has she been dead?'

'The short answer is, I don't know.' Jane consulted her notes. 'It's only preliminary at the moment. I have a multitude of tests to run yet, so don't push too hard or I might give you a wrong diagnosis.'

'You can't diagnose a dead person.'

Jane laughed. 'You *are* awake.'

'Sorry.' Lottie knew the pathologist had caught her yawning. 'Long, hard weekend.'

'Boyd must be better.' Jane winked.

'His mother died. I was over in the west for the funeral. Got back late last night.' She'd talk about anything to keep from thinking of the dead child.

'Give my condolences to Boyd. I didn't know.'

'It's okay. She died suddenly. Heart attack. It leaves Boyd in a predicament over his sister, though.'

'Why so? She's in her early thirties, isn't she?'

'She is, but it's a long story. I'll tell you over that coffee,' Lottie said, wondering if they would ever get to make the time. 'Can you tell me anything else about the body?'

'I've sent the stomach contents for analysis. There wasn't much. The body was dismembered soon after she was murdered and frozen straight away. There's a skein of skin missing from her lower back. It's more than likely still in the freezer where she was kept.'

'Why? I don't follow.'

'You own a freezer, yes?'

Lottie nodded.

'If you put raw meat in to freeze and leave it there for months, or even years, it will adhere to the surface of the freezer. When you try to extract it, part of the outer layer may be left behind.'

'Do you think she was frozen for years?'

'Yes.' Jane picked up a small plastic bag from a tray and handed it over.

'What's this?' Lottie turned the bag over in her hand. Inside was a strip of paper with illegible ink marks.

'The sort of dated tag that's stuck on a plastic freezer box or bag. I figure the body was in the bottom of the freezer and containers were placed on top of it. They were probably never moved until the body was extracted. It may give you an idea of how long she's been in a particular freezer, but she could also have been moved to a different one. It's a long shot.'

Lottie agreed with Jane's logic. 'I can't decipher it.'

'I put it under the microscope. It's written in black ink, probably a ballpoint pen. I'll have it analysed, though I can't guarantee anything.'

'Will that tell us a date?'

'No, but I could read the date under the microscope.'

'Go on.'

'The twelfth of June 1997.'

'Jesus, she's been dead for twenty years if that's the case.'

Jane shook her head. 'All it tells you is that something was placed in a freezer with that date attached. And the body was put in the freezer either before or after it.'

'Where did you find the label?'

'Just above her buttocks.'

Lottie stared hard at the piece of paper. 'It's possible it has nothing to do with the time of the child's death.'

'It is, but so far it's all you've got. I did get some fibres that I've sent to the lab. Could be clothing she was wearing at the time of her murder.'

'Or they could be from her killer.'

'Or they could be carpet fibres. Let's not speculate at the moment. I've taken a swab for DNA comparisons also. And an interesting thing …'

'Yes?'

'There were some flecks of paint on the torso and some on the railway sleepers. McGlynn did a good job.'

'Really?' Lottie was curious. 'Why are flecks of paint relevant to a body that might have been frozen twenty years ago? They must have come from something on the tracks.'

'I don't think so,' Jane said. 'They're tiny blue flecks. Three in total. One on the body, two on the sleeper.'

Lottie bit the inside of her mouth, thinking. 'Any idea what it could be?'

'No. All sent for analysis in any case. Okay?'

'Sure. Let me know as soon as you have results.'

Watching the pathologist scroll through her report, Lottie was thankful for McGlynn's meticulousness and Jane's professionalism. She didn't know how she would cope if she had to dissect a child's body. That made her think of what type of person could kill and dismember a child. Too awful to dwell on. She handed back the evidence and turned to leave.

'If we had the head, it would help identification,' Jane said. 'And there's one other thing ...'

Pausing at the door, Lottie hoped the pathologist had good news.

'You're not going to like this.'

'Go on.'

'The hand you brought in ... it doesn't belong to the torso. It's that of an adult male.'

CHAPTER EIGHTEEN

Following the altercation with the cat and a visit to the A&E, Faye had to go home and lie down. Her hand and face were throbbing, and the pain was even worse after she'd showered and carefully bathed her wounds. Jeff was standing in the bedroom doorway watching her.

'I don't understand why you left it there like that,' she said as she plumped up the pillows on the bed in their one-room flat.

'You were freaking out. I had to leave it somewhere while I decided what to do with it. It just feels weird, finding it in my aunt's house.' He sat on the bed.

'You told me you'd dumped it. I thought you meant in a bin.'

'What else was I supposed to say? Jesus, Faye. I wish you'd never found it.'

'Me too. But if it's real, who is it? And why was it there?'

'I don't know. Maybe it's fake, maybe it's not, but it's too scary to think about.' He paused. 'How are you feeling?' He raised her hand to his lips, but she snatched it away quickly.

'I'm fine. The injection was the worst thing.'

When he eventually stopped fussing, Faye said, 'Honestly, tell me why you think a skull was left behind the wall in your aunt's house.'

'Please, Faye. Stop talking about it.' He got up from the bed. 'I've had a rough day and you've had a horrific one. Just drink your tea and have a nap.'

'I think we should tell the guards.'

'No. We can't be wasting their time.' He turned towards the door.

'Where are you going?'

'I have to do a run for my boss. Up to Dublin and back. To make up the time I lost this morning. I should be home by midnight.'

'I don't want to stay here alone. That cat scared the shit out of me.'

'Thought the skull scared you more?'

'Yeah, but you told me not to talk about that.'

'Look, hun, I have to work. Try to have a good long nap. Okay?' He smiled, leaned over and kissed her tenderly on the forehead. She made to draw him down to her, but he was out the door before she could wrap her arms around him.

The tea was insipid. She wouldn't mind a proper drink, but he hadn't offered her one, and anyway, she was pregnant. At the thought of her baby, she cradled her tummy with her uninjured hand and tried to think happy thoughts. Like painting the nursery yellow because they didn't know if they were having a boy or a girl.

Now, though, the thought of that room being decorated for their new baby was tainted by the image imprinted in her mind of the mad cat jumping out and attacking her. She didn't think she could ever erase that. As if in protest, her cheek stung and her hand throbbed. She had to do something. And this was one time where she was going to defy Jeff.

Picking up her phone, she googled the number for Ragmullin garda station. Before she made the call, she scrolled through Twitter for the latest news. What she saw caused her to bolt out of the bed. She pulled on a light cotton dress, the nearest thing to hand, dragged a long cardigan over it and shoved her feet into a pair of trainers. She checked the phone again. The news of the discovery of a torso was everywhere. How had she missed it? Her stomach churned and her baby fluttered against the wall of her womb.

A headless torso had been found on the railway tracks.

She'd found a skull.

The threads began to stitch together.

She picked up her bag, dropped her phone inside and left without ringing or texting Jeff. He was not going to like it, but she had to tell the police.

CHAPTER NINETEEN

On the way back from the morgue, Lottie called Boyd.

'I'm heading to Ragmullin later on,' he said flatly.

She thought of how the trauma of his mother's death on top of his treatment must be affecting him.

'I just wanted to hear your voice,' she said.

'You sound upset. What's happened? Are the kids okay? Little Louis flying around dragging everything out of cupboards?'

She could hear the whine of an engine in the background and wasn't sure if it was her own car or if Boyd was driving too. She could hardly see out through the windscreen, her tears blinding her.

'Mine are fine. It's a little girl, Boyd.'

'Who?'

'The new investigation.'

'Oh shit.' His voice stalled before he said, 'Are you talking about a murder or an assault?'

'A frozen body. Dismembered. Found in the canal this morning. No, that's not right. The torso was found on the railway tracks, and a leg in the canal. We have divers looking for the rest of the body. She was so small. What type of monster does that to a defenceless little girl?'

'Monster is the right word. Have you checked the missing persons database?'

She sniffed and wiped her nose with her sleeve while indicating for the slip road to take her off the motorway. 'Jane thinks the body had been frozen for some time.'

'I thought Jane dealt in facts, not hypotheses.'

Lottie smiled. Trust Boyd to bring her back to reality. There was no point in getting upset. Emotion could only hinder her investigation. 'She found a tag, a label, attached to the skin. It was dated June 1997.'

'Oh,' Boyd said. Lottie knew he understood the enormity of her task. He continued, 'Sounds like a historical case. You'll have some job going back over old files.'

'It might be on PULSE. The historic files were transferred to the database, I think.'

'You should also check local and national newspaper reports for that year; you might strike lucky, and it could be quicker. Yeah, try the local papers if PULSE turns up nothing.'

'Thanks, Boyd. I knew you could help.'

'I'll get back to Ragmullin tonight. Mind yourself. See you shortly,' he said.

Lottie was composed by the time she reached the station, though her heart was still thumping loudly, and she knew that if anyone looked crooked at her she'd either chew their ear off or burst into tears.

The heat of the station was oppressive as she entered the main door, and by the time she reached her office, she felt she needed to change her T-shirt. Damn building. So much for the fortune spent on refurbishment. It was a furnace in summer and an icebox in winter. That thought brought her back to the body. Gathering the team together, she led them into the incident room and relayed the information she'd gleaned at the mortuary.

'The state pathologist tells me this is all preliminary at the moment. Lots of tests and analysis have yet to be undertaken.' She looked at the notes she had scrawled on the white board.

Victim - Torso
Female
Aged 7-12
Strangled
Possibly an axe used to dismember
Fibres - analysis
DNA - comparisons
Label - 12/6/1997
Flecks of blue paint - one on body, two on railway sleeper

Leg - not yet examined.
Threads of a pink ribbon, possible part of a sock

Victim - Hand
Adult Male
Right hand
Ringless

Kirby said, 'So we have two victims. Could the leg belong to a third?'

'I hope not.' Lottie had not considered this. 'It still has to be examined but it must belong to the same child.' She sat. 'Are the divers still on site?'

'Yes. Found nothing else yet. They'll break for the night and return at first light,' Lynch said.

'And Irish Canals? Have they been contacted?'

'I phoned them.' Lynch consulted her notebook. 'They've instructed all registered boat owners to check in with them and issued instructions to terminate the use of the canal for the foreseeable future. But they have no real control. Truth is, anyone can take a boat out at any time.'

'Okay. Check the homeowners along the route. See if there's any CCTV,' Lottie said.

'Will do.'

'Put out an appeal for anyone who walked or cycled along the canal path in the last few days. Someone might have noticed something. Have you checked the locks?'

'A team of divers carried out an inspection earlier. Nothing to report.' Lynch shut her notebook. 'The railway's been closed all day. When do you think it can be reopened?'

'I don't know. Update the appeal. See if anyone who travelled by train over the last few days witnessed anything unusual along the line. People acting suspiciously, that kind of thing. It can be opened again once it's been comprehensively searched. But run it by Superintendent Farrell first. She'll have to deal with the fallout.'

'Right.'

Lynch didn't seem particularly pleased, but that wasn't Lottie's concern. She rubbed her eyes and stifled a yawn. She knew her tiredness was a reaction to the shock of the discovery of the child's body. She wondered how young Jack and Gavin were coping.

'We need to go through every missing person file from around June 1997. Check for children in the relevant age range. I doubt we'll have DNA on file, but if you find anything close to a likely candidate, let me know. McKeown and Kirby, take that on between you.'

Her two detectives nodded in unison. About the only thing they agreed on.

'Lynch, I want you to oversee officers checking through the litter collected from the banks of the canal and the rail tracks. Something might have been discarded that's pertinent to the investigation, something that might identify whoever dumped the bodies.'

'That's a shit job,' Lynch said, her eyes shooting sparks of anger. 'Can't someone else do it?'

'I'm only asking you to oversee it; you don't have to get your hands dirty. You have a good eye for what's relevant and what's not.' Lottie hated stoking egos, but Lynch had been a thorn in her side for years and she knew how to work her. 'But leave it until the morning. I don't know about you lot, but I'm knackered.'

When the team had dispersed, Lottie pinned up the gruesome photos. First the torso, *in situ* on the tracks. Then the hand, and finally the leg, with its pink ribbon attached to the string of fabric around the tiny ankle. She prayed it was part of the torso, because she couldn't bear to contemplate the horror that she might be dealing with two murdered little girls.

CHAPTER TWENTY

Kevin O'Keeffe knew the second he put his foot over the threshold that a stranger had been in the house. He smelled cologne. And it wasn't his.

'Who was here?' he called out. 'Marianne? Where are you?'

Goddam that woman! She liked to play deaf when it suited her. He felt the anger twist like a roll of barbed wire inside him. It wasn't good enough. He'd had a bitch of a day and needed his dinner and a whiskey. A double. No, make that a triple, he thought as he tramped into the living room and opened up his mahogany bar. He sniffed. The odour of the pungent cologne hung in the air here too.

He poured a decent measure into the Waterford crystal glass and cast his eye over and under her antique desk. The bin was empty. Opening a drawer, he shoved around the pens and paper. There was nothing there to interest him. Marianne was an open book as far as he was concerned. A boring book at that. A book that would never be finished, always a work in progress. She tired him out. She was tedious and life-draining, but he was too proud to cast her aside. And too broke. He needed somehow to register the house in his name. The only thing he owned was his mother's wardrobe. A damn ugly monstrosity, but he'd won that battle. Dragged it across town on the roof of his car just to teach Marianne who was the boss of the house, even if she still owned it. Fuck her.

'Marianne?' he yelled, louder now, fuelled with alcohol. He refilled his glass and made his way into the kitchen. 'I want to know who was here while I was out.'

'Dad, what are you on about?'

His daughter, Ruby, was seated at the table in the dining area with a friend. That detective's son. What was his name? Parker? The boy kept his eyes down, staring at the PlayStation controller in his hand. Ruby held one also, and they had linked the PlayStation to the television screen. A multitude of coloured cables lined the table.

'You should be doing your homework,' Kevin said.

'Sean is heading home soon,' Ruby said. 'I'll start then.'

'I'm looking for your mother.'

'Haven't seen her.'

'It's not a mansion.' But he knew it was the next best thing.

'Maybe she's in the bedroom,' Ruby said. 'I haven't been upstairs yet. Well, only to bring the PlayStation down.'

'Finish up that game and get your books out.' Kevin turned on his heel to the sound of the teenagers moaning.

Upstairs, he entered the bathroom, put the glass on the sink, turned to the toilet bowl and peed. When he'd finished, he washed and dried his hands, drained the glass of the remaining whiskey and left it there. *She* could bring it downstairs.

In the bedroom, he paused inside the door. Something was different. He scanned the room, and then it hit him. The sheets. Why had she changed them? Once a week was enough, he'd told her. Saturday mornings. He didn't see the need for wasting water or electricity by having the washing machine working every second day. So why had she defied him by doing the washing today? He peered through the window. On the clothes line at the end of the expansive garden, sheets and pillowcases billowed in the evening air. Why? And where was his wife?

He glanced into the en suite. A trace of steam lingered on the mirror. An afternoon shower? And then he remembered the sensation he'd got when he'd entered the house. Someone other than his daughter and the Parker boy had been here today.

'Marianne!' he yelled, racing back down the stairs.

Fuck the bitch.

He was going out.

CHAPTER TWENTY-ONE

Before she left for the evening, Lottie took a call from reception.

She hung up and turned to Kirby. 'There's a young lady in the interview room. The desk sergeant tells me she arrived just as I started the team meeting and was asked to wait.'

'What's it about?'

'She claims to have found a skull in her boyfriend's house. At first she thought it was fake, but then she saw the news about the torso and now thinks the two might be connected.'

'Can't be a coincidence,' Kirby said.

'It's all a little macabre.'

She was almost out the door when she thought of protocol. 'You come too. Bring a notebook and pen. I've no idea where to find mine.'

As usual, Interview Room 1 was stuffy, and the odour of its last visitor hung in the air, like a rack of damp clothes left beside a radiator for too long.

'You must be Faye.' Lottie held out her hand to the thin young woman seated at the table.

Faye half stood. Her hand had a plaster on it, and there was an ugly scrape on her tired face, her hair swept to one side in a ponytail.

'I'm Detective Inspector Lottie Parker, and this is Detective Larry Kirby. How can we help you?'

They sat down, Kirby making a play of opening his notebook and uncapping his biro.

'Please, I don't want this recorded. I just want to pass on the information.'

'Okay,' Lottie said. She was too tired to argue. 'Go ahead.'

'I'm probably being foolish. Jeff would kill me if he knew I was here.' Faye's hand shook as she wound a stray strand of hair around her finger. Lottie noticed a blush flare high on the woman's cheekbones. 'I mean, he'd be angry; he wouldn't really kill me. Wrong choice of words to use in here. Sorry.'

'Don't fret. Just tell me what you found. Where and when.'

'It was this morning. Jeff dropped me off at the house before he headed to work.'

'What's Jeff's surname?'

'Cole.'

'Where did he drop you off?'

'At his aunt's house. Well, it's his house now. His aunt died you see. I'm sorry. I'm nervous. I've never been in a garda station before. Well, I was. To get my passport form signed, but not like this … Sorry.'

The young woman was clearly petrified, twisting her hands into knots. The three steri-strips on her face had burst slightly, oozing a soft trickle of blood. Lottie wanted to ask how she'd been injured, but first she had to know about the skull.

'You've nothing to be nervous about. Where is this house?'

'It's the second one.' She'd stopped twisting her hands and had tangled her fingers in her hair again.

Lottie wanted to tell her to stop fidgeting, but instead she said, 'What's the address?'

Faye lowered her hands and clasped them tightly in her lap. 'Number 2 Church View. Do you know it?'

'The old estate behind Tesco?'

'That's the one.'

'So Jeff dropped you off. What were you doing there?'

'It needs a lot of work before we can move in. She was an old woman, Jeff's aunt. The house is in a state. I wanted to sell it, but Jeff said no. He was firm about it. We can't afford to pay anyone to decorate it, so now we're doing it ourselves.'

'So this morning, what had you to do?'

'I wanted to scrape off the wallpaper. You should see it. Rotten. That's what I was doing when I found it.'

'The skull?' Lottie was exhausted, but she needed Faye to tell her everything in her own words.

'Yes.' Faye shivered and her lips trembled. 'It was hideous. I screamed and phoned Jeff to come, and—'

'Faye, where exactly did you find it?' Lottie wanted to lean across the table and shake the answers out of the woman, but she knew that wouldn't do her reputation any good.

'Like I said, I was scraping the paper off the wall. I noticed the plaster to the side of the fireplace was different to the rest of it. I remembered Jeff saying there used to be a range there … you know, a stove?'

'I know what a range is.'

'Well, it got me thinking there might be a nice nook behind the plaster where we could put in a shelving unit. I got a hammer and smashed the plaster. It was hollow, so it was easy enough, and then it rolled out on the floor. Oh my God, it was awful.'

'Let me get this straight. You broke down the wall and there was a skull behind it. Is that correct?'

Faye nodded frantically.

'You called Jeff. Then what?'

'His boss, Derry Walsh, is good to him and let him off for a bit. Jeff arrived within ten minutes of me calling him.'

'What did he say when he saw the skull?'

'He told me it had to be fake, and he'd get rid of it.'

'Was it fake?'

'Looked real to me.'

'What did you do then?'

'Jeff brought me into town for coffee because I'd had a shock, but I went back to the house later. Even though I hated the sight of the skull, I had to see it again. I thought he'd put it in the bin, but it wasn't there.'

'Did you find it?'

'Yes. That's when the cat did this to me.' Faye pointed to the angry scratches on her face.

'The cat?'

'It jumped out at me when I went into the baby's room.'

This was like unravelling clues in a logic puzzle, though Lottie couldn't see the logic anywhere. 'What baby?'

'I'm pregnant.'

'Congratulations.' She wasn't too far along, Lottie thought. She hadn't noticed a bump before Faye had sat.

'Thanks.' Faye paused. 'I'm talking about the room we were going to turn into a nursery. Now, I'm not sure I want my baby in there.'

'I'm certain once it's decorated it will be fine. Did you find the skull in the … er … baby's room?'

'Yes. It was in the wardrobe.'

'Had Jeff put it there?'

'Yes.'

'Why did he do that?'

Faye shrugged. 'I asked him, and he said he didn't want to dump it yet. He said he had a weird feeling about it, being his aunt's house and all, but he didn't want to freak me out. Hello? Like I wasn't already crawling up the walls. He'd put it there until he decided what to do with it.' The young woman's brown eyes bored through Lottie. 'He kept saying it was fake, but I'm sure it's not. Then I read about the body found on the railway. I don't know what to think now. It all sounds so far-fetched and impossible.'

'You think the two incidents could be linked?' Lottie asked.

'Likely, isn't it?'

'Is the skull still at the house?'

'It must be. I didn't bring it home with me and I doubt Jeff moved it.'

'And why did it take you so long to contact us?'

Faye shrugged. 'I wanted to this morning, but Jeff thought I was being ridiculous. I'm here now, though. You see, Jeff had to go to Dublin for work and I was all alone and everything was spinning around in my head. I had to tell someone who would listen.'

'You were right to come in. Do you have a key to the house?' Lottie found Faye's sincerity authentic and her anxiety contagious. She had a feeling it was going to be a while before either of them got home this evening.

Opening her bag, the young woman took out a single key and placed it on the table.

'Will you accompany us to the house?' Lottie said, picking it up.

'I'm really tired. And I've work in the morning. I do alterations and I wasn't in today and … Sorry. I'm talking shite.'

'I'll have you back home in no time,' Lottie said. 'I drive fast.'

Faye's scratched face lit up with the first smile since Lottie had entered the room.

'Let's go then,' she said.

*

The noise from the kitchen downstairs was like someone driving a drill through Aaron Frost's skull. The pain was real, he knew that.

An overload of tension, strumming away like an out-of-tune guitar. High-pitched. Off the wall. Bloody hell.

Marianne O'Keeffe was totally loola, he concluded. He should report her for sexual assault. But that would only attract attention to himself at a time when he wanted to be invisible. Who knew being an estate agent could be such a tricky job?

He paced in circles around his bedroom. It felt miniature compared to the opulence of the O'Keeffe house.

He opened his laptop. It was all over the news.

His phone beeped with a text.

No, he wasn't going to read it. He wasn't involved any more. No way was he doing anything else.

But the text was adamant. Another threat.

GET THE KEYS.

What keys? he replied.

When a message arrived with the address, he couldn't understand what it was all about. With conflicting emotions, he sent back another text.

This is the last time.

There was no response.

He pocketed his phone and walked slowly down the stairs.

It was definitely the last time.

CHAPTER TWENTY-TWO

Number 2 Church View was a forgettable house in a line of other similar 1950s detached dwellings. The small iron gate creaked between two pebble-dashed pillars. The grass had grown into a wilderness from inattention over the years, though Lottie noticed a flattened section behind the front wall with a wooden post lying among the weeds.

Kirby took the keys from Faye. He opened the door and stepped to one side to allow the two women to enter before him. They hadn't called in SOCOs. Lottie had to know what they were dealing with first. And anyway, the skull had been dislodged, handled and moved.

She noticed the smell the second she put one foot into the hallway. Cat's piss, as her mother would have said. More than one cat.

'Did Jeff's aunt own cats?'

'I don't know, but it's likely.' Faye led the way to the living room.

Following the young woman, Lottie could see a dusty haze hanging in an inverted V from the light streaming through the grubby window. She stared at the work Faye had done. Wallpaper hung in shreds from two of the walls, and the others were clear of the yellowing paper, leaving behind remnants of decades-old decor. She moved closer to the nook. The plaster was cracked and broken, the debris in a haphazard heap on the floor, the opening only half exposed.

'It fell out of here?' Lottie said, pressing her nose into the dark gap.

'I was hammering like a woman possessed. Once I set my mind to something, I keep at it until I succeed. It fell onto the floor. Don't know how it didn't smash.'

'How do you think that happened?' Lottie pulled back from the empty space.

'Maybe from the vibrations of the hammer?' Faye shrugged like a little girl. 'All I know is that it frightened the life out of me. Those hollow eyes … it was awful. I'm sorry.'

'No need to apologise,' Lottie said, though she wasn't sure what Faye was sorry for. 'Where did Jeff go with it after he picked it up?'

'Out to the kitchen.'

Lottie moved into the small kitchen. She could smell the mildew. Fungus curdled in the corners of the room. The walls were stained sepia, probably from cigarette smoke. She opened cupboard doors, finding nothing of interest inside.

'I'll have a look upstairs, if that's okay.' She was treating Faye gently because of the fear emanating from the young woman in waves so strong she felt she could touch them.

'Will you go up there alone?' Faye said, her voice low and trembling, her hand lifting to her sore face like a child who'd been told not to touch it in case she made it worse. 'I don't want to meet that cat again. I don't want to go into that room ever again and I can't imagine bringing my baby into this awful house.' She looked earnestly into Lottie's eyes. 'Can you feel it, Inspector?'

Pausing on the bottom stair, Lottie felt confused. 'Feel what?'

'I'm not superstitious or anything, but it feels to me like there's … I don't know … menace seeping out through the walls.' As if to give effect to her words, Faye shuddered violently.

'Kirby, take her back into the living room and sit her down. I won't be long.'

Lottie made her way up the stairs, the cat odour more pungent on the landing. She glanced into the bathroom, but there was nothing to see there. She entered the smallest bedroom. The carpet was a dirty brown, stained in big blobs, and the tiny window was shut tightly. When she looked at the wardrobe, she felt a wave of uneasiness swamp her body.

The doors were open; the handle from one of them lay at her feet. And when she moved closer, she knew without a doubt that the skull was real.

She made sure her forensic gloves were on properly. She should wait for SOCOs, but it had already been moved by Jeff and disturbed by the cat. Gripping it with both hands, she took it from the shelf.

It was small. A child's or a young adult's, she figured. She thought of the dismembered leg with the pink ribbon around the ankle and shivered. Turning the skull carefully around in her hands, she examined it by sight. There was a crack running down the cranium. Her experienced eye told her that was post-mortem damage. But the centre of the forehead told a different story.

A hole.

Too large to be a bullet hole, she surmised, but she was sure the wound had been made with a pointed implement. Someone had struck the victim in the centre of the forehead. Death might have been instant, or not. It might have been painful, or not. Pathology and forensics would interrogate the bone structure and tell her the unequivocal truth of what had happened. Then she would set out to find who had inflicted such a horrible death.

'Kirby,' she shouted back down the stairs. 'Call SOCOs and get this house sealed off.'

The little skull looked so sad and lonely in her hands.

'Don't worry,' Lottie whispered to it, 'I'll find you the justice that's been denied to you all these years.'

Once the house was sealed off, they brought Faye back to the station. SOCOs wouldn't be commencing the on-site examination until morning. McGlynn had arrived in a huff, inspected the skull and given permission for it to be sent to the state pathologist once it had been photographed.

Lottie oversaw the taking of Faye's official statement. The young woman gave her consent to a DNA swab, and her fingerprints were taken for comparison purposes. They would catch up with Jeff Cole first thing in the morning. Faye didn't want anyone to accompany her home, so Lottie watched as she left the station, her head bent so low between her shoulders that she looked more like a little old woman than a young woman with her life before her. Her dress was grubby and her cardigan appeared to be a few sizes too big. She looked so lonely and pathetic, Lottie almost called her back. Instead she told Kirby he could finish up for the evening.

Sticking a photo of the skull on the incident board, she studied it with her hand on her chin, feeling the weariness seeping into her bones. She was too tired to make sense of all that had happened. She had to go home. To eat. To hug her children and cuddle her grandson. She hoped it would make her feel more human in an inhumane world.

As she switched off the light, she yearned to feel an arm around her shoulders, a squeeze of her hand; to be asked if she was doing okay by someone who knew she wasn't. She needed to see Boyd.

*

Walking away from Ragmullin garda station, Faye thought of calling Jeff. She had to tell him everything before the detective talked to him. He wouldn't be pleased to see the house wrapped in crime-scene tape, but she had done what she felt was right.

A bell clanged loudly in the evening air. She jumped, dropped her phone into her shoulder bag without making the call and looked across the road at the imposing cathedral. It was in shadow, the setting sun behind it. The sky was filled with grey clouds, a thrust of pink cutting a line along the tree-topped horizon. The soothing scene contrasted with the turmoil turning like a roller coaster in her chest. She felt dirty and smelly and needed a long hot bath. Then she remembered they had no bath in the flat, just a slow shower that dripped constantly. She supposed it was better than nothing, and her baby fluttered in agreement. She smiled to herself and let her hand rest on the small swell of her abdomen.

Turning right, she passed the coffee shops that lined the narrow road and moved onto Main Street. It was quiet. Ragmullin was falling asleep. A car with heavily tinted windows and a scrape along the door pulled up alongside the taxi rank, and she smiled in recognition. It was their car. Hers and Jeff's. He must have finished the job early. She waved, then opened the passenger door and slipped inside, pulling it shut behind her.

'I'm wrecked. Such a day,' she said, snapping on the seat belt. The doors locked with a click. As she moved her bag, her phone fell out and she bent over to pick it up. 'I've just been thinking of jumping into the shower, then bed.'

The car pulled away and swerved down Gaol Street, jumping the light that had gone from orange to red in a flash. And then she realised something.

'How did you know where I was?'

Turning to look at the driver, she felt a chill creep like a finger along her shoulders and settle in the nape of her neck. She reached for the door handle, but the slap caught the side of her face and her hand fell away.

She slid down in the seat, clutching her handbag to her chest, the seat belt restraining her movement, and prayed to the God she thought might be housed in one of the cathedral's twin spires to help her and her unborn baby.

CHAPTER TWENTY-THREE

As usual, the house was a mess, but Lottie liked to think of it as organised chaos. Her half-brother, Leo, hadn't been in contact for some time, but in his most recent email, six weeks ago, he'd said the documents were close to being finalised in relation to the old family home, Farranstown House. Lottie had signed her share of the inheritance over to Leo after he'd agreed to pay her upfront before he put the property on the market. It was a generous offer, and even though she didn't entirely trust him, she felt she had nothing to lose. But he was taking his time paying over the money.

The house she lived in with her family was a rental. After her home had burned down, it was only because of the generosity of housing developer Tom Rickard, baby Louis' grandad, that she could afford this one. The sooner she had Leo's money, the sooner she and Boyd could seriously start house-hunting. The viewing next Saturday was to get a feel for houses. For a moment, that filled her with excitement, and then she rolled up her sleeves and began to stack the dishwasher with the lunchtime dishes.

The doorbell buzzed. She heard Katie talking in the hall before Rose Fitzpatrick marched into the kitchen with a large dish in her hand.

'Hello, Mother,' Lottie said.

'I won't make a habit of this, but I had a full chicken in the fridge near its best-before date, so I made a casserole.'

'You have to eat too,' Lottie said, inhaling the delicious aroma.

'I took a bowl for myself. The rest is for you and your starving kids.'

Lottie didn't rise to the bait. 'Thanks.'

'Where's your handsome young man this evening? Did he not come back with you from the west?'

'He had to sort out things with Grace but he is coming back.'

'Poor pet. She'll be lost without her mother.'

'He is bringing her to Ragmullin. In the short term.'

'He's a good lad, that Boyd. I always told you so.'

Lottie turned and stared at her mother. 'You *are* happy that we plan to get married, aren't you?' She'd not discussed her decision in great detail with Rose, and for once her mother had been unusually quiet on the subject.

Pulling out a chair, Rose sat at the table and began folding laundry from the basket on the floor. Maybe she shouldn't have started a conversation, Lottie thought wearily, as her mother cleared her throat.

'I think he's great for you, Lottie, but you have to let him be who he wants to be. Don't suffocate him. He has enough to contend with, what with all that horrible cancer treatment.'

'I know all about that. It's been a tough few months, but I honestly think he's on the road to recovery.'

'You're wearing blinkers, Lottie.'

'What do you mean?'

'The treatment is managing the disease, not curing it. He might still need a bone marrow transplant.'

Thanks a lot, Lottie thought, but she kept her lips pressed together in a thin line. It was not okay to be told things she knew but kept at bay. She did not need her mother or anyone else to tell her how to live at this stage of her life.

'You went through so much with Adam's illness, and then after his death ... well, you know all that, and—'

'What's your point?' Trying desperately to keep from snapping, Lottie lifted the lid from the dish and began filling a bowl with food.

'My point is,' Rose said sharply, 'don't let yourself get into that situation again.'

Lottie slammed down the bowl and turned on her.

'What do you want me to do? Drop Boyd because he has cancer?'

'I did not say that.' Rose put down the clothes and folded her arms.

'You implied it. I love Boyd and he loves me. I think I'm entitled to a little bit of happiness, don't you?'

'I do, and that's not what I'm saying at all. Why do you insist on twisting my words?'

'I don't.' Lottie sighed, knowing she sometimes did. 'Tell me exactly what you're trying to say.'

'As a mother, it was so hard witnessing what you went through with Adam. It almost broke you, and I don't want to see you back in the depths of grief again. You were so bad: the drinking and the pills, and you damaged your children and—'

'Damaged my children! How dare you! Everything I do is for them.' She paused to take a breath, averting her eyes from the hurt in Rose's. 'I admit we went through bad times. I admit I went off the rails for a while. And yes, I admit I put my children in danger through my job. But no! I will not admit to having damaged them. They're doing just fine, thank you very much.'

'What are you hiding, Lottie?'

'What?'

'What are you hiding in that heart of yours? What is making you so angry?'

Lottie slumped onto a chair, the food forgotten, her hunger evaporated, anger seething beneath her skin. She held her words on the tip of her tongue. She could say that she was angry at Adam for dying and leaving her to cope with three teenagers who were going through the most formative and difficult years of their lives. She could say she was angry at Boyd for getting sick just when they were on the brink of a new life together. Or she could say she was red-hot angry at Rose herself for all the lies and secrets on which she'd built Lottie's life.

There was so much to be angry about, but she could not let loose at Rose. She loved her mother despite all that had gone before. And she loved Boyd even though she knew he could never replace Adam in her heart. But Boyd was part of her present. She did not want to dwell on how long or how short that time might be. And she definitely did not want Rose dictating how she should feel.

'Answer me.' Rose put a hand on her clenched fist. Lottie forced herself not to pull away. Rose was ageing fast and it was unfair to be angry with her.

'I'm not hiding anything. Yes, I am angry. Angry at everything that fate has dealt me. But I'm strong too. I can get over anything. I've proved that.'

'But can your children get over it?'

'What do you mean?'

'They lost their father so quickly. They've only recently been able to cope with it. How will they feel if ... you know ... if Boyd doesn't survive his illness?'

That did it. Lottie stood, flew across the floor and opened the kitchen door. 'Thanks for the dinner, but I'd like you to leave. I can't deal with you now. Please go.'

'I've hit a nerve, haven't I?'

She wanted to call Rose an interfering busybody, but in her head she had to agree. The foremost thought in her relationship with Boyd was how it affected her children. Was she a bad mother to put her own feelings ahead of theirs just this one time? She'd thought she was right in what she was doing, but now, with Rose questioning her, she wasn't at all sure.

Watching her mother walk slowly to her car, she felt tears gather in her eyes, blinding her. She would not cry. She would not let Rose make her cry.

'Nana. Nana.'

She closed the door and scooped her grandson into her arms. Feathering his hair with kisses, she said, 'I love you so much, Louis.'

'Love you, Nana.'

'You hungry?'

'Cheese?'

'You can have a cheese string, but don't tell your mammy.' Lottie smiled, her tears forgotten, and went to fetch her grandson his snack. But her heart was as heavy as the little boy in her arms.

CHAPTER TWENTY-FOUR

The apartment was too small for all of them. On the drive home from the west, Boyd had phoned Kirby to tell him. When Boyd and Grace arrived back, after eleven, Kirby's belongings were packed up in one corner and he was not in the apartment.

Boyd left his sister sitting on the couch while he went to fetch clean sheets. He would've loved to fall fully clothed onto the bed and sleep for eight hours straight. He wasn't sure if it was the drugs in his system or the stress and grief from the last week, but he had no energy.

Hearing the bell ring and Grace open the door, he peered out to the living room. His flat was contained and small. Living room and kitchenette, bedroom and bathroom. All in dark colours. He rarely pulled up the wooden blinds on the windows. His world, his home. A home he'd shared with Kirby for the last five months, though most of the time he'd either been in Galway, over at Lottie's or in hospital. Now Kirby had to find another abode.

'Hello, soldier,' Kirby said. 'Sorry for your loss. Did you give your mother a good send-off? Sorry I couldn't get down to it. Work. That new super never stops cracking the whip.'

Boyd looked into Kirby's weary eyes. 'Long day?'

'I don't want to bore you with it. You've enough on your plate.'

'Please, Kirby. I can do without you treating me like a condemned man. Enough that all the women in my life are at it.'

Kirby smiled weakly. 'Sorry, bud. Too tired to talk tonight.'

'About all this …' Boyd said, nodding towards Grace, who'd curled up on the couch and closed her eyes.

'No worries. I'm just going to put my stuff in the back of my car and I'll be out of your hair.'

'Have you somewhere to stay?'

'Yes, yes. Of course I have.' He was lying.

'Tell me where, in case I need you,' Boyd pressed.

'The Joyce Hotel. Got a room for tonight.' Kirby looked shifty. 'I'll figure everything out tomorrow.'

'Leave your stuff for now.' Boyd sat on the arm of the couch, his legs unable to hold him up any longer.

'All joking aside, you don't look great,' Kirby said.

'Treatment's going well. Almost finished. It's the funeral … I'm just tired. Grace too.'

'I'm sorry for disturbing you this late. Appreciate all you've done, putting me up the last few months. I know I should have had myself sorted out before now, but it was easier not to think about it.'

'Glad of the company, to be honest. It made a huge difference having you around.' And it had, Boyd thought. Kirby had been something of a life-saver, albeit an untidy one who'd done his head in more than once. But having someone to fill the void in his home had been welcome. Kept him from dwelling on his ill health.

'Thanks anyway.' Kirby picked up a Tesco bag for life.

'I can loan you a suitcase if you—'

'No, not at all. Got a spare shirt, underwear and washing gear here. More stuff in the car and I'll pick the rest up another time, okay?'

'Sure.'

'Get some sleep. You look like shit,' Kirby said, blunt as ever.

Boyd smiled. 'Call around tomorrow and we can talk about your plans.'

'What plans?'

'Where you're going to live.'

'Oh, that. Right.' Kirby curled his lip and dropped his eyes.

Boyd forced himself up from the couch, conscious that Grace had not stirred throughout the conversation with Kirby. At the door, he said, 'I'm trying to get back to work, you know.'

'My advice is to take your time. Look after yourself first.' Kirby put a hand on his arm and Boyd felt the pressure on his bones.

'Desk duty, that's all I want. Otherwise I'll go mad. I need to have something to focus on other than myself.' He desperately wanted to ask Kirby about the case Lottie had mentioned on the phone, but he didn't want to put his friend in an awkward situation.

'You have Grace to worry about now.' Kirby hoisted the sagging bag onto the crook of his arm, sounding a little too like Lottie.

'I don't need anyone to worry about me,' Grace said from the couch.

'See?' Boyd said.

Once Kirby had gone, Boyd finished making the bed, this time with Grace helping.

'I don't want to take your bed,' she said.

'You're having it,' Boyd said. 'No arguments.'

'But you're s—'

'Do not say I'm sick, Grace. Please. Okay?'

'That's fine. I'll go to bed now. You can have the couch. Good-night.'

Later, lying on the uncomfortable couch, still in his clothes, Boyd smiled. Grace was direct. No filter, his mother had always said. With so many people pussyfooting around him lately, he looked forward to some straight talking. His mother had been a straight talker too. Though he'd not seen her much in recent years, he missed her. And then for some unknown reason, he thought of his ex-wife, Jackie.

Now why the hell had she popped into his mind? He hoped it wasn't a forewarning of dire things to come. Bad news always preceded Jackie. Damn her.

He would close his eyes just for a moment, to blot out her cheating image. Then he would fetch a blanket.

Before he finished the thought, he was snoring.

The ringing of his phone woke him ten minutes later.

*

'I hope I didn't wake you,' Lottie said when she heard Boyd's voice yawn a hello.

'No, I'm just getting ready for bed.'

'Liar. You know you shouldn't have driven back from Galway.'

'Too late now.' She heard the grin in his voice.

'Your insurance won't cover you if you crash.'

'I'm a good driver.'

'You're having chemo treatment. Check your policy.'

'I'm sure you've already done so, Mrs Fussy Boots.'

'I have. Don't drive again, Boyd. Your brain is unbalanced from all the toxins you're being fed. Chemo brain, it's called. If you need to go anywhere, ask me.'

'Yes, boss.'

'No need to be smart.'

He laughed then. 'Stop worrying, Lottie. I'm fine. I'm sure this week's treatment will be the last. All my vitals were good last time. My consultant says the chemo is working. Don't be worrying about me. I'm not going to die on you any time soon.'

'I hope not.' She stifled a sob.

'Oh shit,' Boyd said. 'I'm so sorry, Lottie, that was thoughtless. You know me, I'd never—'

'No, it's okay. It's not that.' She found a tissue up her sleeve and blew her nose. 'It's the little girl. It's breaking my heart. I need a drink.' She hadn't touched alcohol in months, and in truth, she knew she couldn't stop if she started.

'I'm coming over to you.'

'If I need you, I'll call round to yours. Okay?' She was too jaded to think, let alone talk any more. 'I don't think I've even got a bottle of Coke in the house, let alone a bottle of wine.'

'Are you sure you don't want me to come over?' Boyd's voice was laced with anxiety.

'I'm certain. We'll chat tomorrow.'

'Lottie, I need to ask you something.'

'What?'

'I want to go back to work. Let me help with the investigation.'

'No way. Don't even think about it.'

'Send me the file, then. I'll have a read of it here. Please let me do something.'

'I'll think about it,' she said wearily.

Her bones creaked as she moved off her couch. She switched off the sitting room light and shut the door before turning out the hall light. She checked the lock was secure on the front door and pulled the security chain across. Was Chloe home? Shit, she couldn't remember if her daughter was working in the pub tonight. She'd have to go upstairs and check. She heard Louis cry out in his sleep.

'Are you gone?' Boyd said.

Lottie realised she was still on the call. 'I'll talk to you tomorrow.'

'I really want to help.'

'I know you do.'

'I love you,' Boyd said.

'I know you do.' She hung up and crept up the stairs.

CHAPTER TWENTY-FIVE

She shouldn't have got into the car without double-checking who was driving. But it was their car, she was sure of it. The little china Liverpool FC ball that Jeff had bought at a match last year hung from the rear-view mirror. But how …? She was certain of one thing. She'd made a huge mistake.

A violent pain surged in her stomach, and she turned over and vomited yellow bile onto the sticky floor. The liquid seeped beneath her prone body, and she felt it bleed through her clothes. She gagged from the smell, but nothing else came forth from the depths of her being. She hoped that whatever she had sipped from the water bottle beside her had not harmed her baby. Please flutter again, little butterfly, she urged the child in her womb. But there was nothing, save for the nausea burning away at her intestines.

She hadn't the energy to lift her head to orientate herself, but she figured she was in a small enclosed space. Her feet touched a wall. Slowly she reached forward, and her fingers brushed another wall. She raised them upwards, but they flashed through the air. At least the ceiling wasn't pressing down on her. She tried to see through the darkness, to lift herself on her elbow, but she couldn't move. She thought she could see a star in a black sky above her. Was she hallucinating?

Fear gripped her insides like a hand squeezing a stress ball, and she dry-retched. She tried to shout out, but she heard only the echo of a strangled cry, like the cat she had disturbed in Jeff's aunt's house. Where was she?

Slowly she turned sideways, the pool of bile spreading beneath her as she moved. Here, the darkness was complete. It was so intense she could feel it as if it were a solid mass. Who had taken her? She had originally thought it was their car and the driver was Jeff, so she had not hesitated in sliding in when the door opened. But once the central locking clicked into place, she was totally aware that it was not Jeff.

Stupid.

The driver had been vaguely familiar. But who was he and why did he have their car? And where was Jeff? She hoped he was okay. A mad thought streaked through her brain. Had Jeff arranged this? Because she went to the guards about the skull? That fucking skull. She wished she'd never picked up the hammer and smashed it into the wall. Now she and her unborn baby were trapped in this coffin-like dark hole with an imaginary star above her.

Her breathing came in short, sharp bursts as panic set in. She had to calm down. She had to get out. But she didn't know where she was. Her breathing increased at an alarming rate, and her heart beat so quickly she was sure it would burst out of her ribcage.

And then the space filled with light.

'Now, missy.'

She could not be sure it was the same person who'd taken her in the car.

'What do you want?'

'I want to know everything you know.'

'I don't know what you mean.' Her throat felt raw, as if it belonged to someone else.

'Tell me how you knew the skull was in that particular place.'

'Didn't know. Accidental. No idea.' She caught her breath. 'How could I?'

'You think I believe that bullshit? Don't fucking mess with me. How did you know it was there, and what else did you find? What do you know about me?'

'I … I don't know what you mean. Found nothing. Only a … skull.' She was finding it harder to breathe, to concentrate on the words. Her mind was mush, words floating …

She followed the trajectory of the voice. She couldn't make out the face and fear travelled so quickly through her body that bile had spewed out of her mouth before she even retched.

'I … need a towel. Something. Please.' Another wave engulfed her, and she cried out. Pain split her abdomen in two and she thought she had been stabbed. But it was coming from inside. Deep in her womb. Her baby objecting to the frantic emotions racking its once placid watery environment.

A hand came down. She sensed it like a cold breeze before it struck. The contact sliced open the wound on her face.

She cried out again. Tasted the blood as it curled into her mouth. 'My baby. I'm pregnant. Please don't hurt my baby …'

'You'd better tell me what you know.'

Emotionless. That was how she would describe the voice if that tall, exhausted-looking detective asked her. A deadpan voice devoid of anything. And that made her blood freeze. No matter what she said, she was not getting out of this alive. She thought of all she had planned for her and Jeff. The love and happiness in her future, her baby, her life. All for nothing. All about to end in the darkness of the unknown, the unseen.

She had no answers to the shouted questions. And then he was silent.

Despair made her eyelids close. The cold steel cut into her back, and she heard it snap one of her ribs. The pain might be worse than childbirth, but she'd never know the intensity of that miracle. Never know the joy of holding a new life in her arms.

The knife was extracted and her body spasmed, but her cries were not for herself. She was crying for the little life that would never see daylight. She was dying. She knew that. As the knife entered her body again, she ignored the torture within which she became engulfed and concentrated on the final soft fluttering in her womb before it ceased all movement.

Then, at last, Faye gave way to her pain, to the horror and terror, slipping silently into an eternal world with her final thought.

She would see her baby at last.

CHAPTER TWENTY-SIX

The moon held the sky captive in a surreal light, shining down on the canal and making the water look like something out of a Disney movie. Jack Sheridan had watched from his window as the garda forensic team and divers worked in and around the canal. Now they were tidying up for the night, and a few officers stood around guarding the site.

There was nothing else out there tonight. Not that there was on any other night. Except for … No, he didn't want to think about that. He couldn't upset his parents any more.

He jumped off his bed and rooted in the bottom of the dresser drawer for his binoculars. Mam had bought them for his ninth birthday, when he'd told her he was interested in birds. *I hope it's the feathered kind*, his daddy had laughed. He used to laugh more back then, Jack thought. Not like now. Now his daddy was … Jack tried to think of the word. Maybe … uneasy? Sick? He shook his head.

With the binoculars clutched in his hands, he raised them to his eyes and focused them. They weren't much good really. Maybe he could ask for night-vision goggles for his next birthday. But he was told when he got the drone last year that he wasn't getting any more expensive presents. They couldn't afford them. Couldn't even afford to finish Mam's dream kitchen.

He watched intently. The divers divested themselves of their suits, working swiftly under lights that had been erected earlier in the evening. He'd love to know what was going on in the tent with the blue roof and white sides. What had they found in the water? Was it more parts of the body? He shivered and dropped the binoculars, which thudded against his chest.

He didn't want to think about what he and Gavin had found on the tracks. But he couldn't stop thinking about it, and it made him feel sick. He hoped it wasn't someone he knew. And he hoped whoever had put it there didn't know he was the one who had found it.

He folded up the strap of his binoculars and slid them back into their case. Then he pulled down the blind on the window and fell onto his bed. He put his hand under the pillow and felt for the tiny USB stick. He had downloaded last night's images onto it. He wasn't sure what they were, but somehow he knew they might be important. He had no idea what to do with the USB. He just knew he had to keep it safe until he figured everything out.

He wrapped his fingers around the tiny stick and stayed that way for a long time, wondering how Gavin was doing.

*

The duvet cover was sopping wet from her tears. Ruby O'Keeffe did not care. Her PlayStation flickered and her phone vibrated with notifications, but she ignored them all.

She stared. Stared hard. The photograph in the silver frame on her bedside cabinet mocked her. She must have been aged about six or seven, always a tomboy. Dad standing beside her. Fishing rods in hand. And a sick-looking fish dangling from the hook he was holding. Happy times. Or were they? Had it all been an illusion? A smokescreen to hide what was really going on in his life. Ruby wanted to lash out and knock the photo to the floor. To get up out of bed and smash it into tiny pieces.

But she did none of those things. She just lay there staring at the smile on her dad's face.

The longer she stared at the photo, the more she thought the smile was not a very nice one.

The longer the night wore on, the harder her heart grew.

By morning light, Ruby O'Keeffe was convinced she hated her father.

Twenty years earlier

They were all dead. My mother and sisters. I'd seen the blood. I had to escape.

I climbed out of the window and ran as fast as I could. I ran as if I was on the heels of the wind itself. I ran as if the devil was in pursuit. I heard his footsteps, trundling through the grassy field behind me.

My feet were bare and torn. Blood stained my hands and probably my face, but I didn't care about that. I had to keep running.

I veered away from the canal and into the field on the right, following its natural trajectory. Though it was dark, I could see the rusted steel wheels and pits. I skirted around them without dropping my pace. I knew I was in the middle of the old filter beds. We had played here, my sisters and I. An out-of-bounds warren of adventure. Now it was a snare, a treacherous hazard, and my feet would betray me at any second. But I could not slow down. I did not want to think what might happen if he caught me.

Before me, the road intersected the land like a long grey snake. Beyond it was the graveyard. I thought it might give me protection. A place for the dead to hide; a place where no one would look for a living being. But how to get across the road unseen?

He was somewhere behind me. I struggled to listen, to hear anything above the crashing thumps of my heart. The birds were silent in the trees, but I heard the rustling leaves and the scurrying of small creatures in the grass about my feet.

I had no plan. No reason. No skill.

I was fourteen years old.

I had to escape.

With a hurried glance up and down the road, I flew across the tarmac as though I had wings on my bleeding heels.

No! Too late I realised that there was a thick chain with a rusted padlock on the tall graveyard gate.

I ran along the wall, hoping for a way through. Monster trees loomed out over the dark road, their shadows like angry claws, urgent in their quest to snap me into their midst.

I felt a hand on my shoulder. A human hand. And I knew then that there was only one way I could ever escape.

CHAPTER TWENTY-SEVEN

Tuesday

Lottie knocked on Chloe's door and entered her daughter's bedroom.

Chloe sat up with a start. 'What's wrong? House on fire?'

'Not this time.' Lottie sat on the side of the bed. 'I want to talk to you about Instagram.'

'Mam! It can't even be five o'clock in the morning.' Chloe pulled the pillow over her head.

'It's six thirty.'

'It's like, still night-time. I was working till twelve. Let me sleep.'

'I will. But first you have to explain Instagram.'

'Are you mad?'

'Nope.'

'You're not going away, are you?'

'Nope.'

Chloe sat up and dragged her phone out from under the other pillow, charging cable attached.

'Don't even start,' she said, catching Lottie's look of horror. She tapped the screen. 'It's just people's stories.'

'How can someone get stuff gifted?' Lottie said.

'If you advertise for free, a company will send you products. I don't really know how, but it's way cooler than Facebook.'

'Can you check if Tamara Robinson is on it?'

'Tamara? She's like … huge.'

'Really? I never heard of her before yesterday.'

'She's a massive cosmetics influencer. I've spent a week's wages based on her recommendations.'

'You did not.'

'I did so.' Chloe tapped the phone and turned it towards Lottie again. 'See those there? They're people's stories.' She tapped one of the circles. 'That's Tamara.'

Lottie took the phone and watched as Tamara Robinson demonstrated how to apply eyeshadow, all the time showing the brand of the palette she was using. The young woman looked beautiful. 'Is she paid for doing this?'

'I don't know if she gets like a salary, but she gets products for free.'

'Maybe you could try doing this, Chloe. Then you wouldn't have to spend all your wages on make-up.'

'And how would I get fifty thousand followers?'

'Good God. Is that how many Tamara has? Is that even possible?'

'Yeah.'

'Jesus.'

'You are so out of touch, Mother.'

'Can you set me up on Instagram?' Lottie asked. 'Obviously you need to use a fake name on the account. I don't want people knowing it's me. Okay?'

'Now? It's five o'clock in the morning.'

'It's six forty now.'

Chloe groaned. 'You're not going to let me go back to sleep, are you? Give me your phone.'

*

A shrill cry woke Boyd at 6.45 a.m.

He sat up quickly, his bones screaming in protest. He had no idea where he was. When he realised he was lying on his own couch, he stretched out his legs, trying to get some life into them. Pins and needles paralysed his knees as he walked towards the bedroom.

Grace was lying in a tangle of sheets, the duvet on the floor. She was still asleep, from what he could see, but she was crying softly, clutching a picture frame in her arms. He picked up the duvet and spread it softly over her quivering body. His sister was so sensitive to everything, he was afraid he might wake her. She stirred, turned over and continued her uneven sleep.

He wanted to reach down and wipe away her tears, but there was no point in disturbing her. The trauma of their mother's death was an unknown vista for them both, and together they would have to survive it. Grace operated in a black and white life. Right and wrong. Good and bad. Boyd had never known her to waver anywhere in the middle, and he had no idea how she would cope without their mother's logic and advice to guide her. He would have to take Mam's place and he couldn't imagine how that was going to work out.

In the kitchenette, he switched on the kettle and spooned coffee into a mug. He needed a long hot shower, but the bathroom was situated off the bedroom and he was afraid he might wake up his sleeping sister. With his coffee made, he returned to the couch and sat in his sweaty clothes wondering what he was going to do about Grace.

His phone beeped with a text. Lottie.

Instead of taking the time to text back, he rang her.

'Good morning, gorgeous,' he said.

'Did you get some sleep?'

'A little.'

'I just texted to see how you were doing. Is Grace okay?'

'She's asleep. I have to decide what to do.'

'What do you mean?'

'I have to do what's best for her, and I don't think sleeping in my bed with me on the couch is it.'

'Call over to mine this evening if you want to talk it out. Bring Grace.'

'I'll see how she is. What are you at?'

'Getting ready for work.'

'Wish I was too.'

'Don't start, Boyd. Take your time. You don't want to meet the new super before you absolutely have to.'

'Is she that bad?'

'I don't know enough about her yet. I think I'll be skirting around the edges of her trouser leg for a while.'

'Don't get into trouble.'

'Oh, you know me. Trouble is—'

'Your middle name,' he said.

She hung up with a laugh and the sound warmed him. He put down his mug and counted out his ration of tablets for the day. He was thinking they looked like a line of balls on an abacus when he heard a voice behind him.

'Each day is a bonus.'

He turned quickly, knocking some of the pills to the floor. 'Jesus, Grace!'

'My name is not Jesus. Just Grace.'

She was standing in the doorway, her hair mussed, her nightgown buttoned to her neck. For a moment he thought how much she looked like their mother.

'The kettle is boiled if you want to make a coffee.' A tremor took hold of his hand.

'Have you any fresh orange juice? Caffeine gives me the shakes. I can see your hands shaking already.' Grace was as straight-talking as they came.

'It's the pills, not the coffee.'

'I'm sure you're telling me a fib, Mark. I don't like fibs. Now what about that orange juice?'

'I'll go to the shop to buy some.' He didn't want to go to the shop. He wanted to go to work.

'Thank you.' She returned to the bedroom. 'Make sure you tell Lottie you need a lift to your appointment today.'

Boyd wondered if inviting his sister to stay with him was the worst idea he'd ever had. But what else could he do? He didn't think Grace was capable of living alone.

'By the way,' her voice echoed from the bedroom, 'I'm not going to be here permanently. I'm perfectly capable of living on my own, in Galway.'

Oh God, had she read this mind? What was he going to do?

CHAPTER TWENTY-EIGHT

The mood at breakfast was strained. Jack liked that word. He'd read it somewhere. Probably to do with peas or pasta. This morning it felt like his mother and father were pushing each other through tiny holes in a sieve. He tried to ignore the silence being broken by grunts and single-syllable replies to whispered questions. He attempted to spoon his cornflakes into this mouth without gagging. He was trying so hard to act normal when all he wanted to do was run away and hide. It was all his fault, this tension. He'd brought it on his family when he found the body.

His brother sniggered at him from across the table and Jack glanced down to see the cause of his mirth. Milk had dripped down his uniform shirt, a long streak looking like he'd been sick. It didn't bother him as much as the memory of what he'd found yesterday and what he thought he'd seen the night before that. He hadn't thought much about it at the time. But maybe it was the reason he'd gone down the tracks with Gavin yesterday morning and flown his drone along there.

He let his spoon fall into the bowl and milk splashed up. He had to talk to Gavin.

'I'm off to school,' he said, jumping up from the table.

'Jack, please be careful. I'll take you,' his mam said.

'I'll be fine. I *am* fine, honestly.'

'Then wait for your brother,' his mam said as she watched Maggie spoon Cheerios into her mouth.

Jack groaned. He didn't want to babysit Tyrone on the walk to school. 'He isn't even ready yet.'

'Bring him with you, and that's final.'

'Why? You usually drop him off.'

His dad stood up suddenly. He towered so tall his head almost scraped off the light bulb. 'Jack, we all know you had a shock yesterday, but there is no need for cheek. Do what your mother tells you.'

His mam tried to calm the situation as Maggie started to whinge. 'Jack, honey, there could be a killer out there. You boys have to mind each other.'

Yeah, Jack thought. He noticed his mother was still in her PJs. 'Are you going to work today, Mam?'

'No.' She lowered her head to her daughter's head of bouncy curls before letting the toddler down to the floor. 'I think I might have caught your father's bug. Maggie! Don't put that in your mouth.'

Jack watched as his mother scooped up his little sister.

He faced Tyrone. 'I'm going now, ready or not.'

'I have to finish my breakfast.'

'Tough luck. I'm leaving.'

'Wait for your brother,' his mam said.

He felt a hand nudge his back and looked up into his dad's eyes. 'Do what you're told.'

With a long, exaggerated sigh, Jack sat down and scowled at Tyrone. The little prick smiled back at him, his mouth milky white, cornflakes stuck to his teeth. God, but in that moment he wanted to thump his brother.

They walked along the canal and over the bridge bridge past the guards who had the traffic flow almost back to normal. It wasn't a busy area anyhow. When they reached Gavin's apartment, they trudged up the steps.

'You better not open your mouth,' Jack said to Tyrone.

Tyrone made a zipping motion across his lips with his finger.

Jack rang the doorbell and shouted, 'Gavin? We're going to be late. Hurry up.'

Eventually he heard the chain being pulled back and the door opened. Tamara stood there in pink fluffy slippers and a white silk robe. Her hair was hidden in a towel twisted into a turban, like she'd just stepped out of the shower. As if she'd had a shower with her make-up on. Then again, knowing Gavin's mother, she probably had to do her face before she showered, and she most likely brought her iPhone in with her to make a story for her Insta page.

'Hello, Jack. How are you?'

'Er, hi, Tamara. I'm fine. Is Gavin ready?'

'He's not going to school today.'

'Oh. He didn't text to tell me.' Jack thought it strange. Gavin told him everything. Or so he'd thought.

'Well,' Tamara said, 'he's traumatised after yesterday, so I'm keeping him home for a day or two. How are you doing, Jack?'

'I'm okay, I suppose.' Jack bit his lip, thinking how he really wasn't okay and maybe his mother should have kept him home too.

'Keep safe, Jack. Bye, Tyrone.' She shut the door and Jack heard the lock engaging and the chain snapping into place.

'Is Gavin sick?' Tyrone said as they plodded down the concrete steps.

'Shut up.'

Walking in silence, Jack dawdled outside the crime-scene tape at the bridge. He stared at the activity, which had wound down considerably since yesterday. It still looked like something out of a movie, and then he wondered if the killer had returned to watch. They did that in the movies. In real life too, according to the true-crime documentaries he watched with his dad. A sliver of fear coursed down his neck and spine, and his uniform shirt, still with the milk stain, clung to his skin. There had to be a killer. There was no way that body had cut itself up.

Uncharacteristically, he grabbed Tyrone's hand. 'We'll be late for school.'

Tyrone tried to disentangle himself. 'Why are you holding my hand, pervert?'

'Shut up and hurry up.'

Jack didn't want to admit it, but he was clutching his brother's hand for comfort.

*

From her office window on the top floor, Tamara watched the Sheridan brothers walk out of the estate. They would be okay; they were tough kids. She wasn't sure about Gavin. He'd had terrible nightmares all night long. She scanned the expanse of unfinished houses and settled her gaze on the bridge.

She swallowed hard and pointed her phone at the scene. Zooming in, she tried to make out what exactly was going on. There were still plenty of guards and vans around. The helicopter had resumed circling in the sky. Had they found more body parts? She'd scrolled Twitter for ages trying to garner as much information as possible, but when the chat became too gruesome to be believable, she'd returned to Instagram. Maybe she could put out Gavin's story. Make him a mini celebrity. But wouldn't that take the limelight away from her? She could weave in a little fake news and make herself the hero. Mother of brave son. She would make the headlines sing.

She felt the familiar swell of excitement. Yes, she could turn this horror show to her advantage. Maybe get a slot on *Prime Time* or *True Life Crime*.

What to wear? She looked around her office. Racks of clothes hung with labels intact. One wall she kept free to use as a backdrop. It made the room look like a bedroom, with a bed and large wardrobe in the distance. Perception was everything in her business. She knew that better than anyone. But what Gavin had seen, that was reality.

She heard him mooching around in the kitchen. She needed to speak to him. But Tamara Robinson, who was at such ease communicating with her family of followers in internet land, had no concept of how to talk to her son. She scrolled through her phone contacts. There was one person who might be able to help her. She tapped the phone and listened to the dial tone.

CHAPTER TWENTY-NINE

Without Boyd at work, untidiness had crept into the office, evidenced by the stack of empty photocopier paper boxes tottering in a corner, and the trail of paper clips leading across the floor from the filing cabinets to Kirby's desk. Boyd would have had it all tidied away, boxes flattened for recycling and the paper clips swept up and deposited on a desk to be reused. She wondered where her detectives were this morning.

'Kirby? Where's McKeown?'

'No idea.'

'He's always disappearing.'

'Probably in the canteen. He can't live without a hundred cups of coffee a day.'

'He should be at his desk,' she said, knowing she sounded petulant. 'Any word on the skull?'

'Nope.'

'Are SOCOs at the house in Church View?'

'Yep.'

'You're full of chat this morning.'

'Didn't sleep great.'

'Where did you stay?'

'The Joyce.'

'Uncomfortable?'

'I got so used to being squashed up on Boyd's couch, I couldn't settle in a proper bed.'

'Right.' Lottie was in no mood for dishing out sympathy. 'I read Faye Baker's statement from last night. We need to interview her again, but first I need to speak with the boyfriend. Jeff Cole.'

'Will I ring him?'

'I've tried already. No answer from his phone. I sent uniforms round to their apartment first thing this morning to bring him in for a statement, but there was no answer there either. Faye must be at work and he probably is too. She mentioned that his boss is called Derry Walsh. Ring any bells?'

Kirby stared at her.

'What?' she said.

'Derry Walsh is a butcher.'

*

Upstairs in the canteen, Maria Lynch paid for her breakfast. Getting out to work was harder by the day since she'd had the baby. She sighed and looked around for somewhere to sit.

'Anyone here?' she said, placing her tray on the table and pulling out a chair opposite Sam McKeown. He was nursing a cup of milky coffee.

'You're welcome to join me,' he said, half standing in a good-mannered sort of way.

She sat and tore the cellophane from her sandwich before glancing up at him. He looked tired. Trawling through missing persons files, not knowing who you were looking for, had to be almost as bad as searching bags of rubbish. She bristled at the thought of what faced her for the day.

'Are you settling back okay?' McKeown said, making small talk.

'Please, don't you start. It's like I was never away, if you really want to know.' Biting into her sandwich, she chewed loudly before adding, 'What do you make of the new super?'

'Deborah? I knew her in Athlone many moons ago. Haven't seen her in a few years.'

'Knew her or *knew* her?' Lynch smirked.

'Ah, yeah, that's funny.' He flashed a crooked grin, but his body stiffened.

Lynch thought she'd lost her chance to snatch some insider information. 'I'm only asking.'

McKeown ran his hand over his shaved head. 'I know Deborah Farrell, okay? She's a good guard. A great administrator. That's her strength, which is ace for the superintendent job. What more is there to know?'

'Does she like our inspector?'

'You're talking double Dutch, Lynch.'

'I'll rephrase it. What do *you* think of our inspector?'

'I'm not sure I know what you're getting at.'

'Ah, come on, McKeown, don't act innocent. You're a detective. You know where I'm going with this. She's giving us all the shit jobs. It's not fair. I think the super needs to know.'

He straightened his back. 'Lottie Parker is a great detective. Might not always do things the way I would do them, but she gets the job done. If there's something you're not happy about, don't involve me.'

He picked up the wrappers from the table and stomped over to the bins, leaving Lynch wondering if she had targeted the wrong person.

CHAPTER THIRTY

Walsh's butcher's shop was located in a small shopping centre on the edge of Mooreclon, a large housing estate on the north side of Ragmullin. The Spar shop beside it doubled as a garage, with fuel pumps on the forecourt. At the sliding doors of the shop, a trolley stood with briquettes and bags of short sticks. Not much call for those in the current weather, Lottie thought as she parked on double yellow lines. There was one parking spot available beyond the forecourt, but that was reserved for disabled drivers, and her disregard for parking laws did not extend that far. Not yet.

She rolled up her sleeves against the morning sun and entered the cool interior of the butcher's shop. It sold vegetables and sauces as well as meat; everything required to make a full meal. If only they'd cook it too, she mused as she stood at the counter.

'How can I help you this morning? Chicken fillets are on special offer. Four for a fiver. Won't get cheaper anywhere.' The squat man smiled pleasantly. His name badge informed her that this was Derry Walsh. He was in his fifties, maybe even sixties, she estimated.

'I'm wondering if I can have a word with Jeff Cole.'

'Oh, sorry, can't help you there.'

'Why not?'

'He didn't show up for work this morning.'

'Really? Did he ring in with an explanation?'

Walsh stepped back a pace, wiping his hands on his white apron. 'And who wants to know, if you don't mind telling me?'

She introduced herself and added, 'I need to speak with Jeff. Do you have any idea where I might find him?'

'I'm not his father, only his employer, and he's turning out to be an excellent butcher. I taught him everything he knows. He learned from the best, I can tell you.' He puffed out his chest, causing Lottie to smile.

'Jeff isn't at home and now I find he hasn't come to work. Would you have any idea where he might be?'

'Haven't a clue.'

'But he works with you every day. Has there been anything on his mind recently?'

Walsh leaned on the clear glass counter and stroked his stubbled jaw with his hand. 'He has been a bit distracted the last few months. I put it down to the house. You know he inherited a house from his aunt, Patsy Cole. Annoying she was too. Had me deliver meat every week, and nine times out of ten she'd tell me it wasn't what she'd ordered. Always looking for a bargain, that woman. Broke my heart, so she did.'

'Why would the house cause him to be distracted?' Though with her own preoccupation over Farranstown House during the last year, she understood how Jeff might have become sidetracked.

'First off, Faye wanted him to sell it. She got him to believe it was his decision. That's women for you. No offence. She even went and got it valued. And you'd think in today's market they'd make a fortune out of it, but no. Too much work needed to be done to bring it up to scratch, according to anyone who viewed it. Jeff decided to take it off the market and renovate it. I told him it would take a long time to do that. But he said it wasn't like they were out on the street waiting for it. Wasting money on rent, though. You know they're renting that apartment and—'

'Mr Walsh, Faye said Jeff was working late yesterday. Was he driving somewhere for you?' Lottie had the impression that Derry would prattle on all day long if she let him.

'Yes. He had to go to Dublin to pick up an order. Drove my van. Dropped it with the meat back here, must have been around nine but I wouldn't swear to it on a stack of bibles, if that's what you're asking. No idea what he did after that.'

'Do you know anything more about Jeff's family or the house?'

'I'm not one to gossip.' He picked up a knife and ran it along a steel sharpener that hung from his hip on a leather scabbard. 'Ask Jeff.'

'I will when I find him. You sure you have no idea where he might be this morning?'

'Isn't that what I told you?'

'I think so,' Lottie said with half a smile. It disappeared as an image of the frozen torso crept into her mind. 'Do you have freezers on site here?'

'I do. In this weather, sure the meat would be cooked before I got it out on display.'

'Can I see them?'

'Sorry. Health and safety. I can't let you go beyond the counter.'

'What if I had a warrant?'

'Ah, now that would be different,' Walsh said, dropping his eyes, his face suddenly shaded. 'But I don't know why you need to see my freezers.' With the hem of his apron, he wiped an imaginary spot from the glass counter.

She couldn't read his expression, but what he was doing must surely be breaking one of his regs. 'Just a mad notion. I'm prone to them from time to time.'

'Not so mad at all from what I've heard about you,' he said. 'You have a strong reputation for solving crimes in and around Ragmullin. You must be dealing with the frozen dismembered body investigation.' He winked. 'Detective Inspector Parker, I can guarantee you, my freezers only hold animal meat. Nothing human.'

'I'll come back with a warrant.'

'Do that. Are you going to get one for every butcher in town? The judge will love you,' he chuckled.

She needed to think it through. Why was she harassing this happy-looking butcher? But she knew why. Jeff Cole worked here, and a skull with a hole in its forehead had been found in his house. A house that had belonged to his aunt. A house that, if you believed what Derry Walsh had not said, harboured a secret. She had to get back to the station to arrange a warrant and investigate the house further. She needed to locate Jeff and she'd have to talk to Faye again.

At the door, she turned. 'Thanks for your help.'

'Are you sure you don't want a half-pound of rashers and sausages? On the house, if you like.'

'Not now, but I'll be back.'

'I'm sure you will, and when you locate Jeff, tell him he's just about on his last chance.'

CHAPTER THIRTY-ONE

Karen Tierney had been glad to have the day off and to be out of the office. Working at A2Z Insurance was a pain at the best of times, but recently Kevin O'Keeffe was being a total ass. There was only so much moaning a girl could take. She'd planned to catch the one o'clock train to meet her friend Maxine in Dublin for the afternoon, but when she arrived at the station she discovered the frigging trains were not running because of the body found on the tracks. Such bad luck, and the bus would take forever to get there. If she'd known about the trains, she could have got an earlier bus.

As she stood in the angry bus queue, she chewed her Nicorette gum and plucked a loose stud out of her gel nail. Damn. Now she'd have to get them redone. She turned her phone over in her hand and tapped up Instagram to see what was trending. At that moment the bus appeared at the top of the hill and the queue compacted as everyone surged forward. Someone nudged her shoulder and she dropped the phone on the tarmac.

'Fuck's sake!' she yelled. 'Take it easy.'

She dropped to her knees, scrabbling about for the battery, which had flown out. The screen was smashed too. Damn, she'd have to buy a new phone. As she knelt there, surveying the damage, she saw something odd. Straight across the tarmac, in the first line of parked vehicles. Something, drip, drip, dripping from the boot of a car. Had a bottle smashed in a bag of shopping? She hoped there was nothing valuable in there, because it was surely destroyed. Her mind flashed to her job, and she tried to think if car insurance covered damaged goods left by the owner in the car.

As the bus stopped, the crowd surged once more. She shoved the remnants of her phone into her fake Michael Kors bag and found her ticket. The driver stamped it and she made her way to the seat behind him. She tried to see out through the dirty window. The car was bugging her. Maybe if she did something now, she could help avert an insurance claim.

The bus filled up, and the air brakes gushed as the driver put the vehicle in gear and swung it out on the road.

Karen jumped up. 'Sorry! Hey! Can you stop? I forgot something.'

'If you get off, I'm not waiting for you.'

'That's fine.' What was she thinking? This was madness.

The door screeched open and she stepped outside. She waited as the bus headed up the hill towards the bridge before making her way over to the car. As she approached the rear of the dark green Honda Civic, she did indeed feel a little mad. Glancing around to see if anyone was watching her, she stuck her bag under her arm, crouched down and stared at the small pool of liquid on the ground. She dipped her finger into it, hoping to God it wasn't oil, or she would definitely need her nails redone.

She raised her finger to her face to see the substance more clearly.

It wasn't oil.

It was blood.

CHAPTER THIRTY-TWO

Lottie rang Kirby to get the name of the place where Faye worked. It was on Main Street, but before she could head there, McGlynn was on the phone demanding her presence at Church View.

She parked down the road from the house and approached the front gate. Her eye was drawn to the post in the grass, but before she could investigate, McGlynn bustled to the front door.

'You took your time. Come on. Get suited up.'

'Not sure there's a need. I walked through the whole house yesterday without one. My DNA and fingerprints are on file for comparisons.'

'Put it on anyway. We can eliminate you later.' McGlynn turned away from the door and disappeared into the narrow dark hallway.

To placate him, she quickly suited up, then signed in and went in search of him.

'In here,' he called, his voice muffled behind his mask.

The stench of cats seemed more pronounced today, but she was sure nothing feline had remained in the house when it was locked and sealed last night.

'What are you doing?' she said.

McGlynn was on his knees, enlarging the hole from where the skull had allegedly fallen.

'Oh, there you are.' He got up and set off past her towards the stairs. 'Follow me.'

Lottie shook her head and fell in behind him. 'What's going on?'

'Give me a chance and I'll show you.'

He stopped at the bathroom door. A technician was on his knees inside, sweeping softly at a skirting board with a short-handled brush.

'Give us a minute,' McGlynn told him.

The technician dipped his head towards Lottie as he passed her on the way out.

'I'm turning off the lights. Just to let you know. Come in, woman. Shut the door.'

Lottie sighed, her breath coming back at her from the mask. She closed the door behind her. A sheet of forensic tarp hung from the window, blocking out the daylight.

'Is that luminol?' she asked, knowing exactly what McGlynn was using.

He nodded. 'Now, look at this.'

She felt her mouth hang open.

'Aye,' McGlynn said, acknowledging her astonishment. 'It's had a good scrubbing with bleach, but there's still some left behind. Not visible to the naked eye, of course.'

'Sweet Jesus. What happened in here?'

'A bloodbath?' McGlynn suggested. 'Someone was hacked to death right here.'

'Not a dismemberment after death, then?'

'From what's left, I'd say there was way too much blood spatter. I found my forensic heaven down behind the skirting boards.'

'Shit.'

'There are traces in the living room and kitchen also. Just so you know. Haven't got to the rest yet.'

'Recent murder?'

'Offering you an educated guess, I doubt it. It's probably linked to the skull, possibly the torso.'

Lottie felt her face turn pale and was glad of her mask. 'Someone went on living in this house after a butchery occurred. That's too barbaric to contemplate.' As she said the words, her thoughts returned to Jeff's job and Derry Walsh's reluctance to let her look in his freezers.

'The guy who inherited this house, he's a butcher.'

'Might be clever to have a word with him.'

'I need to locate him first.' Lottie opened the door and stepped out onto the landing, thinking that Jeff was too young to be involved if this was connected to the torso. He would only have been around nine years old in 1997. 'Thanks, Jim. Keep me informed of anything else you find.'

'Sure will.'

She tried to recall everything from the PM on the torso. Blue paint. Fibres. 'Jim, take samples of all the carpets in the house, and any other fabrics. We need to test them against fibres found on the torso. And see if there's anything with blue paint.'

'Will do.'

'Has anyone found freezers anywhere?'

'Not so far, but we haven't got to the garden or the shed yet.'

'Can I have a look?'

'Only if you bring one of my team with you and touch nothing.'

The back garden was more overgrown than the front. Lottie stepped tentatively along green-mossed slabs to the shed. It was unlocked.

She pulled the door open and depressed the grimy switch on the wall. A light bulb flickered to life, casting a yellow hue inside. There wasn't much to see, which disappointed her. A free-standing wooden unit that served as a cupboard and workbench. A few long-handled tools – a rake, shovel and the like. An old lawnmower, not used in years by the looks of the garden.

Nothing hung on the walls. Three paint cans, magnolia shade, stood just inside the door. She opened the cupboard. More paint cans, and brushes that had been put away with paint stuck to the bristles. She moved the cans around with the tip of her finger. Empty. Nothing behind them.

'No hacksaws or axes?' McGlynn loomed in the doorway behind her.

'No.'

'Don't worry. We'll go through the place,' he said.

As she stood to leave, her head touched the light bulb, causing it to sway. The beam of light caught a corner of the ceiling.

She stopped. 'Have you got a torch?'

McGlynn passed her one. 'What do you see?'

'Give me a chance,' she said, echoing his mantra. 'Thought I spotted something lodged up here.'

She scanned the area, spiders fleeing in the light. She brushed away cobwebs and stepped in closer.

'I can see a blade,' she said, her heart racing. 'Holy shit. It's an axe.'

'Not unusual to find one in a shed,' McGlynn said.

'But why is it hidden away up here?' Lottie stood to one side while a technician took photographs.

The camera flashed. She knew why the axe had been hidden. 'I can see bloodstains on the blade.'

CHAPTER THIRTY-THREE

Lottie left McGlynn and his team fussing over the best way to remove the axe from its hiding place without disturbing evidence. She didn't know if they'd find anything else that could have been used as a weapon, but the hairs on her arms were standing erect, giving her goose bumps, and she had to leave them to it.

As she drove into town, she mulled over the weird smelly house. It had to be linked to the body parts they'd found. The place was a crime scene, but which crime? Hopefully Jane could match the skull to the torso, narrowing their investigation somewhat.

With no one able to locate Jeff Cole, she rang Sewn, where Faye worked. The supervisor told her that Faye wasn't in. She tried the young woman's mobile again. Nothing. It was dead. Then she tried Jeff's. It rang out. A trickle of foreboding wetted the back of her neck. She did not welcome the feeling at all.

She headed along Main Street before turning left, the cathedral imposing its shadow over the bonnet of the car. Before she reached the station, the radio burst into life and a squad car roared past her.

'Shit.'

She swerved the car around the excuse for a roundabout at the cathedral and sped back the way she had come, following the squad car.

It was heading for the railway station.

*

Sam McKeown lifted his tired eyes from the missing persons list he was studying. He was seeing double. He'd found nothing of interest. No one he could link to the body parts on the railway line and in the canal.

'A mother or father has to have reported a missing child,' he said.

Lynch raised her head then lowered it again without commenting.

'What do you think?' He probed for a reaction.

'Maybe the child wasn't missing. Maybe the mother or father killed her. Then they wouldn't report her missing, would they?'

'Maybe you're right,' McKeown said. He began sifting through the mounds of files on his desk.

'Did I say something intelligent?'

'I think you just might have.' He picked up a photocopied page and strolled over to Lynch's desk. 'Here, I found this earlier.'

'What is it?' Lynch folded her arms.

'Look, I'm sorry about this morning, but I'm not that long at the station so I don't want to rock the boat.'

'Have it your own way.'

'Right. See this?'

'I'm not blind.'

'Jesus.' He snapped the page from the desk.

'Wait. What is it?

'A copy of a page from the local newspaper. The inspector said to check local papers around the date found attached to the torso. I printed off a few articles and then forgot about them. Until now.'

'Okay. Why the mad flurry now?'

'This is dated April 1997 and it's about a mother and her two daughters who were brutally murdered in their Ragmullin home. Says here it was classed as familicide.'

'Before my time in the guards,' Lynch said. 'You could look at the murder file, but if the family are dead, what's that to do with the body?'

'The father and a third child were never found. The thinking at the time, per this article, was that the father murdered his family and then disappeared, kidnapping his own son. What if he then went on to kill and dismember the son?'

Lynch unfolded her arms and yawned. 'Our torso is female. You'd better keep trawling the missing persons files, McKeown.'

He folded up the page and went back to his desk. 'For a minute there I thought I'd found the answer to everything.'

CHAPTER THIRTY-FOUR

A group of young women were huddled by the bus stop.

'Which of you is Karen Tierney?' Lottie said as she approached.

Diamond-studded nails twinkled in the sunlight as a hand was raised tentatively. 'Me.'

'Can I have a word?'

She led the young woman away from those who appeared to be comforting her and made her stand with her back to the guards who were hurriedly unrolling tape around the green Honda.

'Tell me everything. From the start.'

'I can't remember it all.'

'Try.'

'Er ... I wanted to get the train, but they're not running today. You know, after the body was found yesterday. Of course you know that. Sorry.' She swiped at her eyes and stopped with her hand mid-air as if she'd only just remembered the blood dried on her fingers. 'So I had to get the bus ...' She faltered.

'Go on, Karen.'

'It's awful. I can't stop shaking.'

'It's the shock. We don't yet know what you've found. It might be nothing.' But Lottie knew it wasn't nothing. Uniforms had run the registration number. She knew who owned the car.

Karen was talking again. 'You see, I broke my phone. Waiting for the bus. Someone nudged me and it flew straight—'

'Okay, Karen, just give me the details, as quickly as you can.'

Karen bit her lip and Lottie thought she was about to clam up, but the young woman lowered her voice and said, 'I saw liquid dripping from the boot. Thought it might be a bottle of Coke or something spilling. I was thinking of an insurance claim. I work in insurance, you know. A2Z. I notice things. Bit of a hazard, if I'm to be honest. Can't even go to a nightclub without warning people not to slip on spilled drink.'

'That's a good skill to have.' Lottie was thankful the girl was so observant. She knew of A2Z Insurance. Her son was friends with Ruby, whose father worked there.

'I got on the bus, but it was bugging me, whatever was dripping out of the car boot, so I asked the driver to stop and got off, even though I knew I couldn't use my ticket again. I went over to the car, got down on my knees and dipped my finger into the … I knew it was blood.'

'Did you call 999 straight away?'

'I couldn't. Not immediately. I'd just broken my phone, so I ran up to the station office. Grumpy Boots behind the desk wouldn't let me use the phone there. I didn't know what to do, so I came back out and that woman over there had arrived for the next bus and let me use hers. I don't even know her name.'

'Thanks, Karen. You've been very helpful. If you don't mind, I want you to go with Garda Brennan there and she'll bring you to the station and take your statement.'

'I want to go home.' Tears clogged in the glue of Karen's false eyelashes and Lottie felt a wave of sympathy for the young woman.

'You can go home, just as soon as we get your statement.'

Lottie watched Karen dipping her head as she sat into the squad car. She waited until it had reached the bridge before she turned towards the cordoned-off vehicle.

'Anyone able to open the boot?'

'The keys were on the front seat,' said one of the two guards standing by the car.

'Has the interior been photographed?'

'Did it with my phone.'

Lottie pulled on gloves. Without removing the keys, she pressed the boot icon on the fob and heard the boot click. She half expected it to spring open, but it remained firmly shut. The sound of car horns from the bridge, the squeal of brakes as the traffic lights changed too quickly for an inattentive driver, the chatter of kids in a garden over in the apartments and the clash of metal at the car dismantler's yard behind her filled the air, and then it all faded as she put her hand on the lock.

She pressed and lifted.

The smell of decay exploded from the confined space.

She hung back, her eyes averted, but the smell told her what she already knew.

At last she looked.

A body lay curled on its side, sheathed in clear plastic. She could see where the blood had pooled and leaked through a gaping hole in the wrapping. Swallowing and breathing in the clear air, she said, 'Radio for SOCOs and call the state pathologist.'

She didn't know who was standing beside her to take the order, but she heard the air whoosh as they moved away, leaving behind a vacuum. She steadied herself, straightening her shoulders, swallowing her horror.

The coppery blood mocked her. She put out a hand but stayed it above the body, unable to touch it. She could not turn it over. She knew who it was.

The car was registered to Jeff Cole.

She'd been looking for Jeff Cole.

Instead, she had found Faye Baker.

*

It was another hour before Jane Dore arrived from Tullamore. In that time, Lottie set uniforms the task of interviewing the group of women who had waited with Karen. She ensured the scene and the station were sealed off. Irish Rail were throwing more hissy fits. She sent other uniforms to Faye's apartment to seal it until she could get there.

Grumpy Boots, as Karen had called him, was Pete Reilly. He sat in an office behind the screened-off counter with a heater under his desk at his feet. He was holding a tissue to his nose, sneezing and coughing, eyes and nose red from a cold. The air was stifling.

'It's like she said.'

'Tell me yourself.' Lottie rolled up her sleeves and swatted a fly from her neck. A half-eaten breakfast roll was poking out of the bin, and the room stank.

'She came knocking on the screen. Wanted to use the phone. Told her she couldn't.'

'Is there a public phone?'

'It got vandalised so many times it was removed by the powers above.'

'Were you so busy that you couldn't let her make a call?' Lottie couldn't hide her dislike of the man.

He snorted and coughed loudly. 'I know there are no trains, but the buses are still running. It's busy and I have to work my shift one way or the other. You let one person use the phone, then everyone will want to use it.'

'This was an emergency,' she snapped.

'She didn't say that.'

'Was she distressed?'

'Sure she was. But *everyone* is distressed these days.' He smirked.

Lottie bristled. 'I need all your CCTV footage. Including the car park. From yesterday afternoon. Say four p.m. until now.'

'You'll have to ask the manager.'

'Where is the manager?' Her patience was stretched so thin, she wanted to smack him.

'At home with the flu. She can stay at home, but I have to come in. Says a lot about who's important round here.'

Lottie couldn't follow his logic and didn't care. 'Don't make me get a warrant. The paperwork alone will mean you sitting in here on your arse for a week ticking boxes.'

'Huh! The car park is run by a different company. Not sure I can give you anything.'

'For fuck's sake, Mr Reilly. Just download the damn footage onto a USB or DVD and let me out of this fever-infested cubbyhole.'

'All right. No need to blow a gasket.'

He shuffled his chair across the floor and opened a door that Lottie had thought was a cupboard but was in fact another small office.

'Hey, Mickey, the guards are out here. They want our CCTV footage.' He shouted out the relevant times.

Mickey replied, 'It'll be a few minutes.'

'Do you want to wait?' Pete said over his shoulder.

'I'll get someone else to take it into evidence,' Lottie said. 'And Mr Reilly, next time someone looks distressed and wants to use the phone, let them.'

He bent double in a coughing fit and she left him to his germs.

Jane was at the car, leaning over the body, scrutinising it.

'What do you think?' Lottie said.

'She's been stabbed. Two wounds that I can see without moving her. Looks like she was in or on the plastic at the time. The blood pooled. It was then wrapped around her and she was moved. All conjecture at this stage, but I'll know more later.'

'Time of death?'

Jane shook her head. 'In this heat and without knowing where she was killed or how long she's been enclosed in the boot of the car, I wouldn't want to speculate.'

'Try. For me?' Lottie said, gulping fresh air.

Jane pulled off her forensic gloves and dumped them in a brown paper bag. 'I'd estimate sometime in the last twelve hours. I'll let you know when I get to the post-mortem.'

'This is the woman who found the skull,' Lottie said, unable to keep her eyes off Faye's body in her blood-drenched dress.

Jane looked around at the busy scene while SOCOs took control. She clutched Lottie by the elbow, like Boyd would, and moved her to one side. 'I had a quick look at it early this morning. It's the skull of a child, Lottie.'

'Oh shit. Shit.'

'I'll run tests. You'll want to know if it's linked to the other body parts as soon as possible.'

'Yeah, thanks.'

'About the leg … from the way the bone was severed, I can say it was cut with the same tool used on the torso. I still have analysis to do. Don't quote me yet. I'm only telling you because you look like you need something to keep you sane.'

'Thanks, Jane. And the hand. You're sure it's an adult male?'

'Quite sure.'

'So, including the skull, we could still be looking at three bodies?'

'It's possible, but I've yet to do a full examination of the skull.'

Lottie watched Jane get into her car, her garda driver shutting the door and walking around to the other side. As bad as her own job was at times, looking at the aftermath of violence from the outside, she would hate to be Jane, cutting up little children to see what had happened to them from the inside out.

CHAPTER THIRTY-FIVE

Walsh's butcher's shop was quiet when Jeff rushed through the doorway.

'Where the hell have you been?' Derry said, puffing and panting as he slung a side of beef over his shoulder before slapping it down on the stainless-steel table.

'Something came up. I'm here now.'

'Have you done something you shouldn't have?'

'What do you mean?'

'There was a detective here earlier, looking for you.'

'For me? A detective?'

'That's what I said. You look guilty as hell.'

'I've done nothing.' Jeff could feel the nervous tic in his jaw and was powerless to hide it.

'Where's Faye?' Derry said.

'Faye? Why are you asking about her?'

'I put two and two together. Beat her up, did you?'

'No, I did not fucking beat her up. What's going on?'

'That's what I asked you.'

'She wasn't home last night when I got back from Dublin. I don't know where she is. We had a … misunderstanding about something to do with the house. That's all.' Jeff pushed past his boss and fetched his white apron. Derry followed him to the back room.

'What's up then?'

'I don't know, to be honest.'

'Best get to work. Go out front and restock the counter. I've been flat out all morning. And Mrs Stokes is like a bull. You left the bones for her dog out of the order. Again. Don't keep making mistakes or you're out on your ear. Do you hear me?'

'Yeah, yeah.'

Once he was behind the shop counter, Jeff sighed. Mrs Stokes and her dog bones were the least of his troubles. He tidied up the rashers to make it look like he'd restocked the tray, then moved over to do the same with the mince tray. It was only half full. He pushed the mince around with a ladle. No way he could make it look full. He'd have to put the mincer on. He didn't feel like working, but he'd had to put in an appearance. He'd try to calm his shattered nerves before he headed home.

'And another thing …' Derry said, standing at the doorway, a meat cleaver dangling from his hand. The sight of the four-inch-wide blade caused Jeff to back up against the wall just as the shop door swung inwards.

'Josepha. Good morning,' Jeff said, diverting his attention from the cleaver. 'How can I help you?'

'You look like you've seen a ghost,' laughed the woman, dragging a buggy in behind her.

'Sorry,' Jeff said. 'What can I get you?'

'A babysitter would be a good start.' Josepha unwrapped a lollipop from the jar on the counter and handed it to the child in the buggy.

'Can't help you there, unfortunately. Anything take your fancy in the meat line?' He knew he was delaying the inevitable row with his boss.

'Four rashers and a pound of mince.'

Now he really did have to put on the mince machine. He counted out the rashers and weighed the meat. 'It will take me a minute or two to get more. Unless you want something else instead?'

'I need it to make bolognese.'

'You don't mind waiting, do you?'

'As long as Joey has his lollipop, I can enjoy a moment of peace.'

In the back of the shop, Derry had resumed his chopping. Jeff fed the mincer.

'What's going on at that house of yours?' Derry said.

'What do you mean?'

'Just heard it on the radio. The guards have it all sealed off. Rumours that dead bodies were found under the floorboards.' He slammed the cleaver into the side of beef. The sound of the blade striking through onto the steel table rang in Jeff's ears like an alarm bell.

'Dead bodies?'

'Yeah. Don't keep Josepha waiting. That little fucker in the buggy will eat all the lollipops.'

The lollipop jar was already half empty. Jeff tipped the mince into its steel tray, weighed out a pound, bagged it and was shutting the till drawer before he realised he'd finished serving the customer.

He closed his eyes and heard the door open and shut. When he opened them, he saw a tall woman with angry green eyes standing there, and he knew he was in trouble.

*

Lottie waited while Jeff took off his apron and pulled on his jacket, even though it was too warm for it. She was still feeling the effects of Pete Reilly's stuffy office. Jeff's face was ashen, and his eyes darted everywhere except to hers.

He said nothing on the drive to the station, and she remained silent too.

In the interview room, his anxiety manifested itself in a sour sweat that peeled from his smooth skin, the beads like welts. She left him alone with his thoughts and went to find someone to sit in on the interview.

As she reached the office, Superintendent Deborah Farrell stepped into her path.

'What's this about a body in the boot of a car?' Farrell was spitting fire. 'Why don't I hear these things first-hand? You know, Parker, I'm not liking you very much.'

Not my problem, Lottie thought. 'I heard about it in the car when I was returning to the station, so I flew down to catch the scene. I didn't have time to park and come in to tell you.'

'Insubordination colours your file, and I can see why.'

'If you say so.' Lottie edged to move past her superior officer. She didn't want to leave Jeff Cole too long or he'd start screaming for a solicitor.

'Who is the victim?'

'Faye Baker. Aged twenty-five. Pregnant.' She felt a lump gather in her throat as emotion threatened to overwhelm her. Why had Faye been killed? It made no sense. Murder never did.

'Domestic dispute that spilled over?' Farrell probed.

Lottie shook the emotion from her shoulders. 'We don't know yet. Two stab wounds. Wrapped up in plastic, shoved in the boot of her partner's car and abandoned at the railway station.'

'Did the partner do it and then do a runner on the train?' Farrell folded her arms and leaned against the door, satisfied-looking. This maddened Lottie even more.

'The trains are cancelled because SOCOs are still working the torso investigation on the tracks, so no, he didn't make a getaway on a train.'

Farrell flexed her fingers before balling them into fists. Lottie guessed she didn't like smart-arses.

'What about the bus? Another car? He has to have fled some-where.'

'Doubt it,' Lottie said.

'Why are you so sure?' Farrell stepped into her personal space. Lottie didn't flinch.

'Because I know where Jeff Cole is.'

'And where might that be?'

'He is sitting in Interview Room 1. I've just picked him up at his place of work.' She didn't want to tell her boss that Jeff was a butcher, and that a bloody axe had been found at his house, along with specks of degraded blood behind the bathroom skirting boards. Not yet.

Farrell's cheeks flushed. 'What are you doing up here? You should be down there, interviewing him.'

'I will be. As soon as you let me pass. I have to get Kirby or McKeown or Lynch or someone, anyone at all, to conduct the interview along with me. Excuse me.' She dipped around her superior and headed into her office. She counted to five while Farrell disappeared down the corridor.

Kirby poked his head around the door, flustered and red-faced.

'That poor young one,' he said. 'She was so timid and frightened last night. Why was she murdered?'

Lottie let a long, sad groan escape her lips. 'Maybe it was the boyfriend. Lost his rag over her telling us about the skull. Or maybe it wasn't. We need a warrant for Walsh's butcher shop. All I know is that an innocent young woman and her unborn baby died violently. It sucks, Kirby. Fucking sucks.' She took a few deep breaths and blew them out. She felt an aching sorrow for a young woman she'd only met for the first time yesterday. 'Sometimes I hate this job.'

'It's a bit of a mess all right.' Kirby turned to leave.

'Don't disappear. I need you in the interview room.'

CHAPTER THIRTY-SIX

Jeff had taken off his jacket, and Lottie could see dark patches under both armpits when he stretched out his arms. Pleading for answers? Yeah, well, she wanted answers too.

'What's this about? Why am I here?' He twisted his hands feverishly while Kirby finished up the mantra for the recording.

'When did you last see Faye Baker?' Lottie tapped the table idly.

'Faye?'

'Your pregnant partner.'

'She's my girlfriend. Partner makes her sound ancient. She's only—'

'I know what age she is. This time when I ask a question, I expect an answer. Okay?'

'Okay.'

Lottie felt a sudden sadness for the young man. Where did that emotion spring from? For all she knew, he had butchered his own baby and its mother.

'When did you last see Faye?' She repeated the question into the malodorous air.

'Yesterday. Late afternoon. She was in a state. You see, she found … she found a fake skull in the wall of my aunt's house. Well, it's my house now, but I still call it my aunt's house. That's what I always knew it as—'

'Go on.'

'She wanted to tell you lot about it, but I told her not to. Didn't want to be wasting your precious time.'

'You argued with her?'

'Not really. We discussed it and then I had to leave for Dublin to pick up stock from a supplier for my boss.'

'Where did you talk with Faye?'

'At our apartment.'

'What time did you arrive home from Dublin?'

'Not sure. I think it was before midnight. Dropped the van at the shop and walked home. There were no lights on. I thought she was fast asleep. But she wasn't there.'

'Where did you think she was?'

'I thought maybe she'd gone to visit her mother. The car wasn't there. I was knackered, so I went to bed without ringing her.'

'Did she often disappear back to her mother's?'

He shook his head vigorously. 'No. Not at all. But she was upset. Over the skull. I wouldn't listen to her. I didn't want any hassle. Work is hard at the moment. Derry's good, but I'm wearing him thin. He'd already given me time off yesterday when I had to go to calm Faye down.'

'And then this morning when she still hadn't returned home, did you try to look for her?'

'I woke around six. I rang her. No answer. The phone was dead, actually, now that I think of it. Hey, why are you asking all these questions? She reported it, didn't she?'

'Reported what?'

'The skull. Derry said it was on the radio. He said the house on Church View is taped off and all.' He paled, the colour fading from his face in one flash of awakening. 'Oh no.'

'What?'

'She's dead, isn't she? In the house. That's why you have crime-scene tape there. Oh God, Faye. Nooooo.'

His voice echoed off the walls, deafening Lottie. She knew raw emotion when she saw it. And Jeff was in genuine mental pain, even though she had yet to confirm Faye's death for him. Or was he putting on an act?

When his voice eased to a puppy-like whimper, she said, 'You slept alone all night, got up, tried calling her and then went to work. That right?'

'Yes,' he whispered.

'Did you call her workplace? Her boss? Did you not think she might be there?'

'I wasn't thinking straight. I'm exhausted. I had to go to work. I can't afford to lose this job. Not with the baby and the cost of refurbishing the house. Everything is money, money, money, and we have to work for it.'

'Why didn't you want Faye telling us about the skull in the wall?'

'I told you why.'

'Not really.'

'I thought it was fake.'

She was determined to get as much information as possible before she confirmed to him that Faye had been murdered. She was almost certain he had nothing to do with his girlfriend's death, but she still wasn't a hundred per cent sure. For all she knew he could be a very good actor. She kept the interview going because if she stopped, she would see the image of the young woman bundled up as unceremoniously as a side of beef in the boot of the car. It made her angry. So angry. She bit her lip, dug her nails into the palms of her hands and tried to funnel that anger into finding out what had happened to Faye, and why.

Jeff scraped at an imaginary crack in the table, as if he was filing his nail, which was already bitten, she noticed.

Kirby said, 'Do you know where your car is?'

'It's not at the flat, so Faye must have it.'

Lottie said, 'Do you know what happened to Faye?'

'I'm waiting for you to tell me.' His head hung low, his chin resting on his chest, saliva dribbling from his mouth and tears wetting his T-shirt.

'This morning Faye's body was found in the boot of your car parked outside Ragmullin train station. I'm sorry to tell you that both she and her baby are dead.'

Jeff shook his head from side to side, mouthing words that refused to be spoken. He tightened his lips and tears spilled from his eyes like a waterfall. And still he shook his head.

Lottie let the silence go on so long that when Kirby nudged her elbow, she felt like she was awakening from a restless sleep.

At last Jeff spoke. 'I know what you're thinking, but I didn't lay a finger on her. I couldn't. I love her.'

'Can you account for your whereabouts yesterday evening?' Lottie still had to get confirmation of time of death, but that might take a while. The body had yet to be removed to the mortuary. McGlynn was throwing a tantrum about having to be moved onto a new site yet again. She toyed with the idea of calling in support from another division, but Jim was the best and she wanted him.

'I told you. I drove to Dublin. Collected the stock and came back. Dropped the van at Derry's shop, then walked home. I'm sure you can track me on the motorway CCTV, and the warehouse has cameras too. Here, take my mobile. It has GPS.' He tugged the phone from his jeans pocket and flung it on the table.

'The thing is, Jeff, we don't know what time she was killed. It could have been after you returned home. Derry told us you were back by nine. You say it was midnight. Faye wasn't found until this morning, and I know she was still alive at eight thirty last night. That's the time she left the station.'

'I ... I went to the pub. I had a lot to think about.'

'I'm finding it hard to believe you. Twice now you've said you went straight home after dropping off the stock. Why didn't you tell me about the pub first off?'

'Didn't think it was important.'

'Every second of your day is important in a murder investigation, Jeff.'

'Okay. But Faye ... I don't understand.'

Lottie ignored his tearful pleas. 'Which pub?'

'Cafferty's.'

'I'll check it out.'

'There was a crowd there. I didn't talk to anyone.'

'If you were there, I will find out. What time did you leave?'

'Didn't check. I had a few pints and went home.'

'Are you telling us the truth this time?' Kirby sounded dubious.

'Yeah.'

Lottie wondered where to go next with her questions. Something awful had happened in that house in Church View, and she needed more evidence before plunging in. She thought of the blood specks McGlynn had found. They had the skull too.

'Jeff, are you aware of what might have happened in your aunt's house?'

He looked at her quizzically. 'I thought you said Faye was in the boot of the car.'

'I'm talking about the skull.'

'It's fake.'

'It's not.'

'Really? Shit. I know nothing about it. You have to believe me.'

'We found specks of dried blood in the bathroom. I know we will find more.' Lottie stared at the young man. His face scrunched up in confusion.

'What are you saying?'

'I'm asking if you know of anything that might have happened at number 2 Church View that resulted in murder.' She was going out on a limb here, but what the hell.

'I … I …' His features slackened, his mouth drooping. 'I haven't a clue. You have to believe me. Can I see Faye?'

'We need to take your fingerprints and a sample of DNA,' Lottie said. He had not asked for a solicitor. That in itself did not signify innocence, even though he looked shocked; trembling uncontrollably.

'Why?'

'We're carrying out a forensic examination of your aunt's house. You will have left traces there, so we need your sample for comparison and elimination purposes.'

'You can have what you want. I didn't hurt a hair on Faye's head.'

'You may not have done that, but did you stab her?'

'Oh God, no, no, no …' He slumped down in the chair, cradling his head in his hands, sobbing.

Lottie knew a defeated man when she saw one, but was he being truthful? She'd have to determine that in time.

They brought Jeff to a holding cell after they took his DNA sample for analysis. She asked again if he wanted a solicitor.

He didn't want a solicitor. He wanted everyone to leave him the fuck alone.

So they did.

CHAPTER THIRTY-SEVEN

Lottie paced in front of the incident boards, scanning the crime-scene photos.

'What's the connection?'

Before anyone could reply, her phone vibrated in her pocket. She glanced at it.

'Sorry, guys. I have to take a couple of hours' personal time. I'll be back in the afternoon.' She gathered up her files and bag and made for the door. 'McKeown, check out the CCTV at Faye and Jeff's apartment. We need to track that car.'

'Anything wrong, boss?' Kirby said.

'Can we help you with anything?' Lynch added, curiously.

'It's personal. Kirby, you take over from me. I'll be back later. Make sure someone checks the train station CCTV and documents all activity around that car. If you see anyone, track them through traffic cams. You know how to do your jobs.'

Lottie fumed for the entire drive to the oncology unit in Tullamore. It wasn't Boyd's fault. It was her own fault that she'd forgotten today was his treatment day.

Grace said, 'Please don't drive so fast. We're not late.'

'I know, but if your brother had reminded me, I would have been more organised and maybe a little bit calmer.' Boyd was in the back seat, the belt keeping him upright, his head drooping to one side as he dozed. She added, 'I'm afraid he might not get his treatment today.'

'Why not?' Grace said.

'His platelets could be too low from all the stress. A family death takes a lot out of a person. He wouldn't slow down. Wouldn't listen to anyone. He's worse than a teenager.' Lottie knew she shouldn't be talking about this with Grace, but she had to get it out of her system.

'I don't think Mark was ever a teenager. He had to grow up quickly in our house. I'm sorry.'

'Sorry for what, Grace?'

'For being a nuisance to my family.'

'Don't say that. You were loved and cherished by your mother. Now Boyd and I will continue to care for you and love you.'

'Ha!'

'What?' Had she said something to offend the young woman?

Grace folded her arms over her seat belt, pushing her bottom lip out in defiance. 'I don't need to be cared for. I am able to look after myself.'

'I know you are. But you're mourning your mother's loss, so you need all the support you can get.'

'Support? When my brother won't do what's best for his own health? I'd be better off at home, even if it is on the side of a mountain with only goats and sheep for company. Lottie, I want to go back to Galway.'

'I'm not sure that's wise at the moment.' Lottie wondered if Boyd had discussed the situation with his sister. 'Has he spoken with you about his plans?'

'What plans?' Grace said.

'Yeah, what plans?' Boyd mumbled.

Lottie glanced in the rear-view mirror to see him sitting up straight. 'You weren't asleep, then?'

'Dozing.'

'Feel any better?'

'I felt all right until you started driving like a maniac.'

'Mark,' Grace said, 'what plans have you for me?'

'I don't know what you mean.'

'Don't pretend to be stupid. Are you going to sell Mam's house out from under me? Lottie said you have plans.'

'I never said that.' Lottie wondered what she might have implied.

'Yes you did. You asked if Mark had spoken to me about his plans.' Grace unfolded her arms and slapped the dashboard triumphantly.

Lottie groaned.

Boyd said, 'I will talk to you, Grace. After I've had my treatment. And Lottie, honestly, there was no need for you to drive me.'

'Oh yeah? Getting fined for driving without insurance wouldn't do your application to return to work much good.'

Grace's jaw dropped. 'You never said you were going back to work.'

'I just put in an application. Look, Grace, we have a lot to discuss and now is not the time.'

'When is the time?'

'Later.'

'Always later, and then it's never until I find out myself. Have it your own way.'

Boyd rolled his eyes and Lottie winked at him in the mirror.

'And for your information, I'm asking my consultant today to certify that I'm fit to drive, so that will put an end to that argument.'

It was an understatement to say that the oncology unit was busy. Boyd waited in line and eventually signed in. They hung around in the long, narrow corridor until seats became available in the waiting room. Boyd had to have his bloods taken first; the results would determine whether he had his chemo. Lottie had intended heading back to work once the drip was up and running, and then returning to collect him when it was finished. She glanced at her watch as they got three seats together.

'You can go,' Boyd said.

'You know the drill,' she told him.

'What drill?' Grace asked.

'I wait until the IV is set up.'

'Okay,' Grace said. 'But I'm here today, so you can go now, Lottie.'

'Mark Boyd?' a nurse called, and he followed her to a cubicle.

Grace stood, but Lottie stayed her with a hand on her arm. 'He'll be back in a few minutes.'

'Does it take long for his blood results?'

'Maybe fifteen minutes, but it's very busy today so I don't know.'

'Can I ask you something?'

'Fire ahead.' Lottie leaned back on the hard chair, her head resting against the wall.

'Do you think Mark is going to die like our mother?'

'Good God, Grace. Of course not. He's getting the best treatment and the consultant said his prognosis is excellent.'

'But I looked it up. There are so many forms of leukaemia. He might need a bone marrow transplant.'

'I think he's responded well to treatment, so that won't be necessary. But if it is, the doctors will tell us.'

'I'm his only living relative. I don't know if I could do it.'

'Do what?'

'Give my bone marrow.'

'Don't worry your head about it. There's loads of tests needed first, and anyway, it's not going to come to that.'

'How do you know? You're not a doctor.'

'And neither are you. And neither is Google. Stop worrying.'

Boyd rejoined them, his face yellower than earlier.

Sitting in the waiting room with sick people was Lottie's worst nightmare. It brought back the times she had waited by Adam's side while his bloods were being checked. The day they told him they could do no more chemo. The day they were told to get their affairs in order. The day they found out he was going to die.

She felt her eyes fill with tears and hoped she wasn't going to cry. Not in front of Boyd. She couldn't handle the way he might look at her.

The door opened and a man walked in, tall and wiry. His shoulders slouched as he automatically ducked his head beneath the lintel. He found an empty chair and sat himself down heavily, stretching his long legs in front of him in the crowded space. It was Charlie Sheridan, the father of the boy who'd found the torso.

'Mark Boyd?' Another nurse stood at the door, a clipboard in her hand, a thick file under her arm.

'That's me.'

'Can I have a word?'

Boyd followed her, leaving Lottie and Grace to wonder what news he was about to receive.

'Should I go with him?' Grace said.

'No. He'll come back if he wants us,' Lottie said.

Charlie Sheridan raised his head at the sound of her voice. The two of them locked eyes across the stifling waiting room. Neither moved a muscle. Then he nodded, stood and walked out the door.

Lottie stood too, but Grace held out a hand and stopped her.

'Whatever it is, Lottie, you're here for Mark.'

Lottie sat back down, feeling torn. Grace was right, she told herself. Boyd was her priority while she was here.

*

She drove slower on the way home from the hospital. Boyd was in the front seat and Grace in the back.

'Are you okay?' Lottie looked sideways at him.

'It must be all the activity last week,' he said. 'Just a glitch, according to the nurse.'

'I tried to tell you. You wouldn't listen.'

'I'll take it easy for now.'

'Do. Please. It's the only way to get your platelets back up to an acceptable range for your treatment to take place.'

'I don't think it's a good sign.'

'Stop. You have to be positive.'

'I suppose so. Thanks.'

'For what?'

'Being with me. I wanted to do this on my own, but I realise I need you by my side to get through it.'

'Is that why you proposed?'

'Feck off, Lottie. I'd proposed long before I knew I had cancer.'

'That word evokes such horrible memories. Change the subject.'

'Okay. Who was the man that ran out of the waiting room?'

'The case I'm working on. His eleven-year-old son found the torso on the tracks.'

'Weird to meet him there.'

'Small towns, small country.'

'Do you suspect him of anything?'

'Not at all. But he and his wife looked terrified yesterday when Kirby and I were at the house.'

'Maybe he had this appointment hanging over him, or perhaps it was just because of what his son had found. Don't be quick to jump to conclusions.'

'But why did he rush off the minute he saw me at the hospital?'

'That, I don't know,' Boyd said.

'Neither do I.'

She indicated off the motorway and Grace gazed out of the back window. They remained in their own thoughts until they reached Ragmullin, when an Instagram notification pinged on her phone. She read it and called Kirby.

CHAPTER THIRTY-EIGHT

Kirby came with Lottie to the apartment. Tamara opened the door quickly.

'Oh. It's you again,' she said. Her make-up was heavier than yesterday, appearing more like cement in the blazing sunshine.

'Can we come in?' Lottie said.

'Why?'

'We need to talk to you.' Lottie pushed past and Kirby slouched in behind her.

'Oh, come in, why don't you?' Tamara shut the door.

'Why did you put Gavin up on the internet?' Lottie said, leaning against the counter, folding her arms in case she lost her temper.

'The internet? What are you talking about?'

'Instagram,' Lottie said.

'That? It's just a story. I put it on YouTube too. A thousand views already. Amazing. And I've had national television news on to me. They want to interview Gavin. And two national newspapers. Imagine!'

'I advise you not to do that,' Lottie said.

'I'm not asking your permission.' Tamara mirrored Lottie's folded arms.

'You're putting your son in danger.'

'He only said he and his friend found the body. They're heroes, Inspector.'

'It mentions flying the drone over that area for a week. What's that about?'

'I don't know. Gavin doesn't even own the drone. It's Jack's.'

'And did you get permission from Jack's parents to drag his son into this before you posted it?'

'We didn't mention Jack by name.'

'No, but anyone can find out who Gavin's friend is.'

Tamara sulked. 'Well it's done now.'

'Remove it.'

'I can't do that.'

'You can't or you won't?'

'I don't want to, and you can't make me.'

Jesus, Lottie thought, Tamara looked like a teenager being told to go to her room. She supposed the damage was already done, but it galled her to think of a mother exploiting her son in this way.

'How much did they offer you? The newspapers?'

'None of your business.'

Unfolding her arms, Lottie moved towards the woman. 'If any harm comes to Jack or Gavin, I am holding you personally responsible. Remember that when you're banking your cash.'

'I'd like you both to leave.' Tamara pointed to the door.

'Keep a close eye on your son. I'll have to tell the Sheridans what you've done and how you've put their son in the sight of a killer.'

Lottie was glad when she got the required reaction.

'No, don't say anything to Lisa.'

'Lisa? What about Charlie? Does he not care for his son's safety?'

'He does. Please, don't tell them. I'll take it down.'

*

'You're back early.' Lisa was hanging clothes on the line.

'Where are the kids?' Charlie said.

'Maggie's having a nap. The boys are still in school. What did the consultant have to tell you?'

'I didn't see him. There was a full waiting room and I was too anxious. I had to get out of there.'

'Ah no, Charlie. You can't let your anxiety get the better of you. I should have gone with you.'

'You had to mind Maggie. Hospital is no place for a two-year-old.'

'You'll have to wait weeks for a new appointment.'

'I won't. I'll tell them I'm dying or something. I'll get an appointment quick enough.'

He watched as Lisa pegged Maggie's little white dress on the line. She picked up the basket, and as she walked towards him, he felt himself shrink away. He went into the kitchen and took a can of lager out of the refrigerator.

'Jesus, Charlie, you can't drink at this hour of the day.'

'I need it.'

'But it isn't good for you. Anyway, make a new appointment immediately. You need to know what's wrong. This uncertainty is driving me insane.'

'You and me both,' he said, placing the drink on the counter.

She moved towards the open patio door.

'Lisa, please don't turn your back on me.'

'You're not yourself.' She was at the line again, moving pegs around. 'All this anxiety about the consultation, then everything with poor Jack and what he found, it's not good for you.'

'And do I not know what's good for myself?' He could feel the anger taking the place of his anxiety. Curling around his veins like a hungry snake.

'Sometimes you need others to remind you.' She moved Maggie's dress along the line and stuck another peg on the hem. The sun glinted through the thin white cotton. Charlie felt blinded for a moment.

'That may be true. But I don't need you to tell me anything. Do you hear? I've had enough of your lies.'

She paused then, and he wondered if at last he had penetrated the shield she so artfully erected when she needed to.

She said, 'I never lie to you.'

'You lied to me for years. How could you, Lisa?'

'I told you a thousand times, I'm sorry.'

'How do you expect me to believe you?' He fetched his beer, gulped it down and returned to his vigil by the door. 'Sorry doesn't make it better. It's just a word.'

He watched as she pegged up Jack's football jersey, her back still to him.

'I don't know how to make things right,' she said.

He knew then that she was crying.

'You can't make them right.' He finished his beer, crushed the can and flung it as far down the garden as he could. Then he fetched another one. 'Aren't the boys due home soon?'

'I can go pick them up if you watch Maggie for me.'

'You watch her. I'll pick them up.'

'You've had a drink, you shouldn't be driv—'

'Lisa! For once, can you please just shut up.'

He grabbed his keys and closed the door softly because he knew she'd be expecting him to bang it and he wanted to piss her off. Really piss her off. His day had been shit.

'Feck off, Lisa,' he shouted as he drove down the narrow lane.

*

The knock on the door was insistent. Karen Tierney unwrapped the throw from around her legs, pulled herself off the couch and opened the door.

'Kevin! What are you doing here?' She was surprised to see her colleague. 'Do you want to come in?'

'Sure. Thanks.'

She led him into her cramped bedsit and indicated the couch. He sat, and she pulled a stool across for herself.

'Are you all right?' he said. 'It's the talk of the office. I read about it online. You must have got a terrible shock.'

'It was awful. I'm not the better of it yet.'

'Do you need anything?' He was wringing his hands like he was washing them.

'I need to rest. That's what the guards said.' She'd never seen Kevin so agitated, not even when he was getting a bollocking from the boss.

'Did they say anything else? The guards.'

'Like what?'

'About what happened to … to the woman in the boot.'

'No, they just took my statement. Twice. I had to go to the station. They were very nice. Got me tea and a Kit Kat.'

'Have they any suspects?'

'Kevin, what is wrong?'

'Nothing.'

'Why are you here?'

'Er … the boss, Shane, he sent me to see if you were holding up okay.'

Karen got off the stool and sat beside him. 'You and I both know Shane doesn't give a shit about me. But I'm glad you do.'

She flinched when he edged away from her. 'It's not like that, Karen. I swear.'

'Oh, so now you don't give a shit about me either?'

'You're twisting my words.'

She stared at him, seeing stark terror written like a quotation in his eyes. 'I'm not going to jump you like you jumped on me at that conference last year. Did you ever tell Marianne about that?'

'I'm sorry, Karen.' He struggled to stand up from the low couch. When he did, he towered over her. 'Tell me what the guards are thinking about that body.'

'What are you really after?'

'Information. There might be an insurance claim. She was found in a car insured by us. I checked it, and Shane is worried.'

'Like fuck he is.' She followed Kevin to the door, noticing the sweat colouring his white shirt orange.

'If you think of anything that struck you as suspicious or if you remember any information the guards let slip, tell me first. I need to be ready for any claim that lands on my desk.'

Before she could reply, he was out the door and driving off with a screech of tyres and a spurt of smoke from the exhaust. She wondered if he'd forgotten to take off the handbrake.

She went over the frantic conversation in her head. Something Kevin had said struck her as odd.

The guards had instructed her not to talk to anyone about what she had found. Everyone at the scene had been told it was important to remain silent for operational reasons. And nowhere online or on the news did it say the body was that of a woman. How then did Kevin know?

In her handbag, she found the inspector's card. She felt a loyalty to Kevin because she liked him and they'd slept together, albeit just the once, but then when had he ever shown her any loyalty in return? She should really call the detective to tell her about Kevin's visit, shouldn't she? Then she remembered her phone was in bits. She'd have to get it repaired or buy a new one. Later.

Lying down on the couch, she pulled the soft throw up to her chin. The room suddenly felt ice cold.

CHAPTER THIRTY-NINE

The traffic in the town was bedlam. The buses couldn't get into the station car park, so with nowhere else to go, they lined up along the green area at the shopping centre, causing a jam. Lottie's mood hadn't improved by the time she arrived at the office. She was angry with Kirby because he'd scuttled off to the smoking pagoda to catch a few puffs of his cigar. She was angry with Boyd for not resting more. She was angry with Tamara for putting her own interests before the safety of her son and his friend. She was angry, full stop.

She called Lynch and McKeown to follow her and to bring the relevant uniformed officers with them. In the incident room, she tried to pull her thoughts back to before she'd left to go with Boyd.

'Has the train station CCTV been checked yet?'

'Yes,' McKeown said. 'I took over when Kirby left with you. We can see the car being driven in around eleven p.m. It's bad quality and we're trying to get the images enhanced.' He passed her a print. 'A man getting out of the car. Throwing the keys on the seat and closing the door. He walks away. CCTV doesn't pick him up at the railway bridge, so we think he walked the other way, down towards the industrial estate. The Hill Point apartments are over there. There could have been someone waiting for him. God knows where he went.'

'I don't care if God knows or not; *I* want to know.' Lottie stared at the blurry image. Useless. 'It could be a man. It could be a woman. It could be a fecking alien.'

'Don't think it's an alien,' Lynch said drily.

McKeown cut in again. 'We're running through our own camera footage and I've canvassed the businesses in that area. We're gathering their videos. There's no CCTV at Faye's apartment so we can't see when the car was moved. A lot of the CCTV around town either doesn't work or it's just dummy cameras.'

'Tell me something I don't know,' Lottie said.

Lynch said, 'We're knocking on doors in her apartment block to check if anyone saw anything around that time last night.'

'Any idea where she was taken from and to? We know she wasn't killed in the car.'

'Her flat has been searched. It's clean. No sign of her phone or handbag. No signs of a struggle.'

'Jeff Cole says he went to Cafferty's. Has anyone checked if that's true?'

'I'll get on it,' Lynch said, and stood.

'Sit down until we've finished,' Lottie snapped, and then took a deep breath. 'Sorry. Bad day.'

'No problem.'

'We know she left here at eight thirty last night. Where did she go if she didn't go back to the flat? She was walking. What route did she take?'

'I'll check that,' McKeown said.

'Let me know as soon as.' She paused to order her thoughts. 'Anything from forensics on the car?'

Kirby bustled in, preceded by the odour of cigar smoke. 'Her bag and phone were under the body.'

'See if there's anything on the phone. Calls or texts that might tell us how she ended up dead. She must have been picked up off the street. Has she any friends we can check with?'

'I'll ask Jeff,' Kirby said. 'We're still holding him.'

'We really don't have anything on him, do we?' Lottie said.

'He hasn't asked to leave.'

'If he knows something, maybe he feels safer here.' She frowned, wondering about the young man and the house he had inherited. She'd have to have another run at him soon.

'Don't think I'd feel safe here with the mood today,' Lynch said under her breath.

'What's your problem, Detective Lynch?' Lottie said.

'Nothing.' Lynch flipped through a file, clearly not one bit sorry.

'Anything else to report from Church View?' Lottie said.

'The skull has to be connected to the body parts found in the canal and on the railway,' McKeown said. 'Could it be some kind of satanic ritual?'

'We know nothing until we get results from the lab, so don't speculate and definitely not outside these four walls. There's a media scrum at the front door already.

'"Satanic ritual in Ragmullin". Can you imagine?' Lynch said.

Lottie ignored her. 'I'll check with the state pathologist to see if she's linked the skull to the torso. Anything else?'

'The axe has been sent for analysis,' McKeown said. 'Luminol showed up blood residue. Could be animal, but more than likely human. I'll let you know when results are in.'

Lynch looked over his shoulder at his iPad. 'Any freezers at Church View?'

'No,' he said.

'Any progress on the warrant for Walsh's shop?' Lottie said.

'I'm working on it,' Kirby said.

Lottie turned to the photos on the board. 'There's a wooden post lying flat on the grass in the garden. Has anyone had a look at it?'

'It's a For Sale sign. Ferris and Frost estate agents,' McKeown said.

Lottie thought about it. 'Faye and Jeff were going to sell the house and then Jeff changed his mind. What else have we?'

Lynch flicked through the file again and took out a small evidence bag. 'You asked me to oversee the collection of rubbish and litter from the area where the torso was found. Well, we found something.'

'Go on.' Lottie hoped it was a clue, because so far they had fuck all.

'It's all recorded, where everything was picked up and that. I'm glad to say there wasn't a whole lot. The anti-litter message must be getting through at last.'

'What did you find?'

'It might be nothing,' Lynch said with a glint in her eye.

'For Christ's sake, spit it out,' Kirby said.

'It's a doctor's card. You know, the one where they write in the date of your next consultation.'

'And?' Lottie ground her nails into her palms.

'It's a consultant called Mr Saka. Tullamore Hospital.' Lynch handed her the card in its evidence bag.

'The name of the patient isn't on it, and neither is the date or time of an appointment.'

'I know. But if the killer dropped it, or the person who transported the body, it might be something.'

Lottie thought of Charlie Sheridan and his quick exit from the hospital earlier. She squinted at the card. 'Or it could belong to someone who lives locally. Check Mr Saka's speciality. If he's in gynaecology, it might be linked to Faye, but she would have no reason to be at that area of the canal. I'll ask Jeff. Then again, I saw Charlie Sheridan in Tullamore Hospital today. I'll talk to him too. He lives near the canal.'

'Jack's dad?' Kirby said.

'Yes. And Lynch, run a check on Tamara Robinson while you're at it.' Grasping at straws came to mind as she added, 'The missing persons files; have you found anything yet, McKeown?'

'I'm cross-eyed looking at PULSE, and I've checked likely cases against the physical files. I discovered that not everything was transferred onto the database when it was set up. I'm still searching. I'll let you know if I find something.'

They would have to send Jeff Cole home. The barman in Cafferty's recalled him. Said he left sometime after closing time. They had evidence he'd slept in his own apartment. Nothing to show he'd picked up Faye and murdered her somewhere. They still had more CCTV to peruse and people to interview. But for now, Lottie had no reason to detain him.

She opened the cell door. He was sitting on the bench, cross-legged, facing the wall.

'You can go home, Jeff. We've searched your apartment and it's clear. But you can't go near your aunt's house.'

'It's mine.'

'It's a crime scene.'

She watched as he slowly turned, uncrossed his legs and stretched them out. He clutched the edge of the bench, his head drooping forward.

'Was that where Faye was killed?'

'No.'

'How can you be so sure?'

'Because it was already sealed off. Faye was last seen leaving here after giving her DNA sample and fingerprints.'

Jeff said nothing.

Lottie leaned against the wall. She should really bring him to the interview room again and talk to him there. But if she did that, the formality might cause him to remain mute.

'I want to help you, Jeff.'

'Unless you can resurrect Faye from the dead, you can't help me.'

'Did Faye have a consultant at Tullamore Hospital? A Mr Saka?'

'No, she was attending her own GP and Ragmullin Hospital.'

'Right. Where do you think she might have gone last night, if not back to your apartment? Had she any friends or acquaintances you're aware of?'

'Only the girls she works with. She never socialised with them.'

'If she was angry with you, who would she talk to?'

'She wasn't angry with me,' he snapped.

'But you had argued with her when she suggested reporting the skull.'

'It was just a disagreement. That's all.'

'Why did you not want her to report it?'

Jeff sniffed and swallowed. He raised his head and glared at Lottie. 'Why is the house sealed off?'

'The skull was found there, and I told you, we also found some blood spatter.'

'You found something else, didn't you?' His eyes were dead in his head. Lottie thought it was now or never, but she really should have this on tape.

'Will you come with me to make this conversation formal?'

'No. And I know you can't make me. I can get a solicitor to inform me of my rights.'

This was all wrong, but after making sure the door remained open, she moved over and sat beside him.

'Something bad happened in that house, Jeff. I need to know what it was.'

'I honestly don't know anything.'

'Come on. You suspected something.'

He sighed and leaned his head back against the wall, staring at the ceiling. 'I always got a bad vibe there. It's hard to explain. You can't even begin to understand what I mean.'

She did. She'd often experienced the sensation of evil in the course of her work, and she'd definitely sensed something malevolent in the Cole house. She thought this was what Jeff meant. 'Try me.'

'I can't explain it. When I was very young, I was always over there, playing with my cousin Polly. She was an only child. She was sick a lot and home-schooled. Then one day when I was about eight or nine, I was told I couldn't go there any more.'

'Where is your cousin now?'

'I've no idea. I wasn't in that house for years. Even after my mother and father died, I never visited. Then out of the blue I got a call from Aunt Patsy to say she hadn't long to live and would I visit to give her a hand. So I did. I asked about Polly, and my aunt said she had moved to England with Uncle Noel. I assumed Patsy had been unable to care of her, you know, with the drugs and drink back in the nineties. Anyway, it was obvious to me that any mention of her name was too painful.'

'Do you have any photos of Polly?'

'No. Nothing.'

'What age was she when you last saw her?'

'She was around my age. Nine, I think. At the time, my mother told me that Patsy had friends staying and that's why I wasn't allowed over. I'm not sure if that's true or not.'

'What happened to your mother?' Lottie felt a tingle at the bottom of her spine. Had Polly really moved abroad? Could the dismembered remains they'd found be hers?

'Mam died of a heart attack five years ago. Dad was long dead at that stage.'

She felt her skin bristle. On the one hand she was excited that they might have a name for the child's torso, and on the other disappointed because anyone who could tell her what had happened was dead. She should be recording this, but she couldn't stop him now.

'Did you ever hear of any incidents happening in the house?' she said.

'No. Only like I said, that one day I was no longer welcome there.'

'You sure?'

'I'm sure that Faye and our baby are dead. That's all I'm sure of.'

'I'm sorry, Jeff.'

'Why was she killed?'

Lottie stood and walked to the door. 'I don't know.'

'There's an awful lot you don't know.'

'Yes, but I intend to find out. You're free to leave for now. Come with me and I'll arrange it for you.'

The young man hesitated.

'Do you not want to leave?' she said.

'I've nowhere to go.'

'You can go back to your flat.'

'But is it safe?'

'You're worried about your safety because of what happened to Faye. That's understandable. Do you know of anyone who would want to hurt her?'

He shook his head vigorously. 'Faye was the kindest soul. She hurt no one and I can't see why someone would hurt her. Life will be so empty now.'

She let him walk out past her.

'Where are the keys to your car usually kept?'

'In the flat; that's if either me or Faye hasn't got them.'

'Has anyone spare keys or access to your flat?'

'No ... Wait a minute. The estate agent we rent it from, he might have a spare set.'

Lottie wondered if it meant anything. At this stage she had to consider everyone and anything. 'Who is that?'

'They have an office in town. Ferris and Frost. We dealt with Aaron Frost.'

*

Lynch found McKeown in the yard at the rear of the station.

'Didn't think you smoked,' she said.

'I don't. There's so few people smoking nowadays that I find it's the only place I can think undisturbed.'

'It stinks here.'

McKeown took a step away before turning back to her. 'Did you want me for something?'

'I think the boss is off her game.'

'She's doing fine.'

'Stop standing up for her. You can see as well as I can that she's distracted by Boyd's illness. I mean, she ran off to bring him to a hospital appointment straight after we found that young woman's body. That's unprofessional behaviour.'

'I see your point.' McKeown rubbed his shaved head.

'She does things her own way,' Lynch said. 'Not always by the book.'

'What evidence do you have for that?'

'She's just interviewed Jeff Cole down in the cells, alone and without any record being taken.'

McKeown drew in a long breath. 'That's iffy all right. What are you going to do about it?'

'You knew the super from her time in Athlone. Can you have a word with her? Tell her what's going on.'

'I think Superintendent Farrell is perfectly capable of seeing what's going on under her own nose. Why would I put myself in her line of fire?'

'If Lottie gets suspended, then we all can move up a notch. Boyd's sergeant position is up for grabs too, if he doesn't come back.'

'Are you the Grim Reaper as well as a snitch?'

'No, not at all. I like Boyd.'

'But you don't like the inspector. Why?'

Lynch sighed. She didn't like the way McKeown was drilling down to find her motives. They were best kept buried. 'It's nothing personal,' she lied. 'I just don't think she's doing a good job.'

'Pull the other one.' McKeown stood up straight and stretched. 'I'll tell you what. I'll keep my eyes and ears open, and if I witness something inappropriate or unprofessional, I'll determine the best course of action.'

'I suppose that's all I can ask.'

She watched him saunter in through the back door and wondered if in trying to create an ally, she had inadvertently made another enemy for herself.

CHAPTER FORTY

Lottie found she couldn't get Jeff's words about his cousin out of her head. She told McKeown to check if a passport had ever been issued for a Polly or Pauline Cole, and then she called the pathologist.

'Jane, I hate bothering you, but is there any chance you have news for me?'

'I had a look at the skull. The hole is not from a bullet. There's a slight indent beside it, so it was caused by something with two prongs, one shorter than the other. Possibly a poker.'

'That's what I thought. Is it definitely a child?'

'Yes.'

'A match for the torso?'

'I have no evidence one way or the other.'

'But it's likely, don't you think?'

'Lottie, I deal in facts and scientific analysis. Off the record, it's possible. Tests are being run as we speak.'

'If it's the same body, I can't understand why the head would not have been frozen like the rest of the remains.'

'Too easy to identify if everything was found together, maybe. It's a mystery you'll have to solve.'

Why dump the body parts now, years after the murder? Lottie wondered. None of it made sense. 'We've taken a DNA sample from Jeff Cole, the boyfriend of Faye Baker. I want you to run it against—'

'Lottie, I know how to do my job. I will test everything on Faye's body.'

'I know that, but I also want you to check it against the torso and the skull if you can.'

'Why? Do you think he's the murderer?'

'I want to eliminate him, but I also want to know if he could be related to the dead child.'

'Oh, right. I can try that. But results won't be quick.'

'Do your best. Thanks, Jane. It's all so disturbing and I'm tearing my hair out. I just need some clues, because so far I have nothing.'

'I sent you the blue paint analysis. Did you get it?'

'Haven't checked my emails. What's the result?'

'It's actually minute pieces of plastic. One of the products it's used in is recycling bins.'

'Oh, that's interesting. A possible mode of transport to get the bodies to the railway and canal.'

Lottie mused over this information. Was it even relevant? Maybe the blue flecks had been on the tracks all along and just adhered to the torso.

'Have you looked at Faye Baker's body yet?' she asked.

'She's next on my list.'

'Will you check for signs of sexual assault?'

'As I said, I know my job.'

'Sorry. Let me know as soon as you're ready to start the post-mortem and I'll try to get over for it.'

She was about to hang up when Jane said, 'The male hand. You didn't ask about that. It's also in the email I sent.'

'I've been run off my feet. Tell me.'

'I found a slight hint of what might be a tattoo on the wrist. Possibly the end of inking from an arm tattoo. It's indecipherable, but it might help in your missing persons search. I've sent you a photo now that it's all defrosted.'

Lottie hung up and browsed her emails. She read through Jane's report and studied the image of the ink on the hand. The pathologist was right. It was indecipherable. And the blue recycling bin angle was virtually useless. There were thousands of those bins throughout the county. She was getting no breaks at all. What to do next? Jeff had mentioned that the estate agent might have keys to his apartment. She decided to follow that up.

Ferris and Frost estate agents occupied a small unit on Friar's Street. Lottie walked quickly through the town and noticed the quietness of the street. She realised it was almost 5.30. The day had got away from her.

The office was small and modern. She was sure it had once been a chipper, and subliminally she smelled vinegar. She saw a young man behind a low desk under the window, which was gritty from exhaust fumes. Inside, she showed her ID.

'I'm looking to speak with Aaron Frost.'

'Sorry, he's not here at the moment. Can I help you?'

'Was he at work today?'

'He's been in and out. Busy. No point in him coming back now. I'm about to lock up, so I reckon he's clocked off.'

'Is Mr Frost the boss?'

'No, that would be Mr Ferris.' The young man indicated a photograph on the wall of two older gentlemen.

'Who's the other man?'

'That's Aaron's father, Richard Frost. He's no longer in the business.'

Lottie assumed that the younger man in the next photo must be Aaron Frost. He wore spectacles that enhanced a handsome face.

'Can I have a word with Mr Ferris?'

'He's been away on holidays for the last week. Not due back for another two.'

'Oh. So who is in charge at the moment?'

'Aaron is, but as I said—'

'And you are?'

'Dave. Dave Murphy. I've only been here six months.'

'I see,' Lottie said. 'Was Mr Frost working yesterday?'

'He was, but he was out of the office all day.'

'Can I see his diary?'

'Not really. It's on the computer. Linked to his phone calendar.'

'Can you print it off for me?'

For the first time the young man looked uncomfortable as he slid his finger over the shiny screen of his iPhone. His white shirt seemed too tight and his shoulder-length hair too slick. As if sensing Lottie's scrutiny, he rolled a bobbin from his wrist and tied his hair back.

'I'm not sure I can do that. I'd need permission or a warrant or something. Has Aaron done anything wrong?'

'I'm pursuing an active investigation. I'm not at liberty to divulge sensitive information.' Shithead, Lottie thought, quelling an overriding urge to tug his ponytail. 'Can you give me his phone number and address?'

'Don't think I can give out his address, but this is one of his business cards. His mobile number is on it.'

Lottie took the card. She could find his address easily enough, but Murphy was getting on her nerves.

'Do you keep spare keys here for properties you rent out?'

'Yes.'

'Can I check to see if there is a set for the property that's the subject of my investigation?'

'No can do. I'd imagine you'd need a warrant for that.'

'You'd imagine, would you?' Gosh, he was such a little prick. 'If I give you an address, can you check if the keys are here or not?'

'No. Sorry.'

Her patience was a thread that had started to unravel way too fast. 'Can you tell me what you were doing last night, say from eight p.m.?'

'I was in the Chinese having a meal with my girlfriend. It was her birthday treat. I went to hers afterwards. You can check.'

'I will. Does Mr Frost work outside of office hours?'

'What do you mean?'

Was he really this stupid, or was he playing silly buggers with her? Whichever it was, it riled Lottie up another notch. 'Does he carry out valuations and viewings after hours?'

'Oh, yes. For people who work during the day.'

'But you just said he's clocked off.'

'I meant he's not in the office for the rest of the evening. But he could still have appointments.'

'Did he have appointments last night?'

'I'm sorry, but—'

'You can't tell me.'

'No can do.' He shook his head, a slight smirk curling up the corners of his lips. She wanted to smack it off him but remained outwardly calm.

'Can you tell me anything about Aaron? What is he like to work for?'

'Oh, he's okay. Mr Ferris is the bully.' Murphy's hand flew to his mouth. 'I shouldn't have said that. Bad-mouthing my employer is not on. I take it back.'

Lottie had the impression that she was watching a performance. A bad one at that. There was a distinct odour of insolence in the air and she knew she was getting nowhere. She wanted to speak to Aaron Frost, not this whippersnapper.

'Right so,' she sighed. 'Here's my card. In case you get your brain cells working and think of anything important. I'll be back for that diary. I'd appreciate you having it printed off or ready to email when I request it with a warrant.'

'I believe it won't be a problem then.'

'You're sure making it seem like a problem.'

She turned and left without waiting for his smug reply.

CHAPTER FORTY-ONE

Lottie spent five minutes wandering around the car park behind the Ferris and Frost offices looking for her car before she remembered she had walked there. Definitely time to go home. She needed food. She needed to talk to normal people; that was if she could call her kids normal. She smiled then, thinking of the chaos that greeted her every evening, and she knew she wouldn't change it. Well, maybe a little bit once she and Boyd got sorted. Once he got well.

She suddenly felt cold, though the evening was warm. As she set off down Friar's Street, her phone vibrated. Pulling it out of her jeans pocket, she saw an unknown number. She answered the call. It was Karen Tierney. She listened, and when she hung up, she crossed the road and headed back the way she'd come.

A2Z Insurance had a *Closed* sign on the door, but she rang the bell anyway. A man opened the door on his way out. Lottie stepped inside.

'Hey, we're closed,' he said, pointing to the empty public area.

'I'll be just a minute. Where would I find Kevin O'Keeffe?'

He seemed anxious to head home rather than debate it. 'Up the stairs. Door on the right. Open-plan office. I'm sure he's still there.'

She followed his simple instructions, which wasn't hard because there was only one narrow staircase, with two doors at the top. The one on the left said *Toilets*. She pushed open the door on her right.

She counted sixteen desks set up in cubicles of four, separated by blue and grey dividers. Only five were occupied. There was a door at the end that she presumed belonged to the manager.

Holding up her ID, she said, 'I'm looking for Mr O'Keeffe. Is he here?' When he raised his head, she smiled. 'Hi, Kevin.'

'Lottie, what are you doing here? Is Ruby okay?'

'I'm sure she's fine. I'm afraid this is business. Can we talk in private?' She gestured to the remaining staff, who were ducking their heads, unsuccessfully trying to let on they weren't listening.

'My manager has left. We can use his office.' He led the way through the door at the end of the room.

'How long have you worked here?'

'A long time. Business is changing all the time. All about commission now. Not like the old days.' He was in his mid forties, around her own age. 'What's this about?' He seated himself in his manager's chair.

Lottie shut the door and leaned against it. It was late, and after a long day, she decided to be direct.

'How did you know we'd found the body of a female this morning?'

'What? I don't follow.' He began fiddling with the stack of forms neatly piled on the desk.

'It's a simple enough question.' She folded her arms and put one foot up against the door for support.

'Honestly, I've no idea what you mean.'

'Honestly?'

'Yeah. Well, I mean, I saw stuff online, you know, about the body at the railway. Found in the boot of a car.'

'Oh, and how did you know it was a woman?'

'I didn't.'

'You told Karen it was a woman.'

'Karen? What has she got to do with this?'

'You went to visit her. Before we officially released news that the body was female.'

'So what? It was probably on Twitter. Everyone knew it. There was even a video of you and the guards at the railway station rolling out crime-scene tape.'

Shit! There was no way to control social media accounts. Now that she thought about it, it was possible the information had been out there before it was officially released. All the same, she wanted to grill him a bit further. He was sweating, but so was she in the small windowless office.

'Why did you visit Karen?'

'She's my work colleague. I called round to see how she was.'

'To get information from her after you saw the videos online, is that it?'

'Maybe.'

'Why were you interested in it?'

'Just curiosity.' He blinked rapidly, loosened his tie and undid his top button. 'I wanted to make sure Karen was okay.'

'How did you know she was involved?'

'Er ... I'm not sure. She had the day off so I might have seen it online. Or maybe the boss mentioned it. I can't remember.'

'Try.'

'I've done nothing wrong. Why are you interrogating me?'

She laughed. 'Jesus, Kevin, you don't want to see me really interrogating you. This is like stroking a puppy compared to what I'm like in an interview room.'

He seemed to believe her, because the sweat was visibly blistering on his forehead. Kevin O'Keeffe had to be hiding something. He seemed very uneasy.

'Is something scaring you, Kevin?'

'Why would you think that?'

'Our children are friends. We've known each other for the last year through them.' Lottie considered this. She didn't really know much about the O'Keeffes, just that Ruby popped into her house from time to time and Sean went to Ruby's. Gaming. 'Tell me, why did you really visit Karen?'

'I was concerned about her. My manager, Shane Courtney, he was worried about a claim. We insured the car.'

'I don't believe you.'

'It's the truth.'

'How did you know it was a woman's body?'

'I … I can't recall.'

Lottie dropped her arms and launched herself across the room. She moved so quickly and slapped the table so hard that Kevin propelled himself against the wall behind him, the wheels of the chair snagging in the carpet tiles.

'Look, Lottie,' he said. 'I saw a tweet. It showed Karen in a group of people. The guards were just arriving to put up the tape. I think a comment under the tweet said it was a woman's body. That's the truth.'

'I don't believe you.' How many times had she said it now? He was lying through his teeth. 'I can check Twitter.'

'You can but it might have been removed.'

'Convenient.'

'Not really, because if it's no longer there, I can't back up my story.'

'Some story.'

'I've no reason to lie.'

'You must have a reason, because that's what you're doing. Lying.' She stepped back and opened the door. 'Our children may be friends, Kevin, but that doesn't mean we have to be. I'll be back.'

*

Saturated with fear, Aaron Frost could not get his heart to calm down. He'd gone back to the office, but had seen a woman talking to Dave inside. He just couldn't face speaking to a client. Not now. Not today. He'd gone home to his mother, and the smell of bacon and cabbage cooking on the stove had made him nauseous. He had to leave, despite her protests. Go for a walk or a run, anything rather than sit the fuck at home listening to his mother complaining about how it was high time he had a woman in his life.

He leaned his elbows on the canal bridge, the opposite end of town to where the body parts had been found, and stared at the unmoving water below. He thought he felt a hand on his shoulder. His imagination was in overdrive, but still he swivelled around on the heel of his shoe to check.

There *was* a hand on his shoulder.

And someone was standing so close he was unable to move.

He heard the traffic hum louder as it sped up when the lights on the bridge turned green.

'We need to talk.'

He knew he had no choice in the matter. The tremble in his voice betrayed his fear. 'Okay. Talk.'

'Not here, you dumb fuck. Follow me. My car is down there. Outside the Indian restaurant.'

'We can talk here or nowhere,' Aaron said, trying hard to be brave.

'You are in no position to argue. Now come on.'

He followed. What else could he do? He'd done all he'd been asked. Had he made a mistake and now he was being made to pay for it? He only hoped he didn't end up dismembered and thrown like carrion on the railway tracks or weighted down in a sack of stones in the canal. Or even stabbed and then abandoned in the boot of a car. He shivered uncontrollably as he got into the vehicle.

When the engine was running and the indicator on, Aaron put his hand on the door handle. 'You don't have to drive anywhere.

I don't think you're on double yellows and its past the time for a parking ticket. We can talk here. I've no idea what—'

'We need a little peace and quiet. I know the perfect place. Shut up and let me concentrate.' The car swung out, headed for the bridge. 'You can take your hand off the door. It's locked.'

Aaron silently fastened his seat belt. He stared straight ahead, watching the dipping sun. He hoped the driver would be silent, but that hope was cut short.

'You have to tell me who else knows.'

'I told no one. I swear to God.'

'That's a lie.'

He could see the hardening of the jaw. The narrowing of the eyes. The driver was angry. The lights turned from green to red, but the car sped through.

'It's not a lie. I never told another living soul.' He twisted his hands, interlocking his fingers. They were so sweaty he found he couldn't disentangle them.

'We'll see how long you hold onto that lie once I get going.'

Though he was thirty-five years old, Aaron Frost began to cry.

CHAPTER FORTY-TWO

Instead of going home, Lottie returned to the office and planted her feet on a box file that had sat for months under her desk. She could not prove that Kevin O'Keeffe was lying. She couldn't find the tweet he'd referred to and she'd been unable to contact his boss, Shane Courtney. Did everyone other than her switch off their phone the minute they walked out of their office? She'd have to follow it up tomorrow. And there had been no answer from Aaron Frost's phone either. He wasn't at home when uniforms had called to the house where he lived with his mother. She'd have to catch up with him later, or in the morning.

She glanced up to see Kirby standing at her door.

'You need to go home,' he said.

'We need to find him.'

'Who?'

'Aaron Frost.' She explained the situation, then said, 'Dave Murphy is only a minion in the office, but check him out just in case. Mr Ferris is on holidays, so Aaron is the only one we know of so far who could have got the keys to Faye and Jeff's apartment. At the very least I want to eliminate him and move on.'

'Okay. Want me to put an alert out on him?'

'Yeah, do that. Thanks, Kirby.'

McKeown stuck his head around the door. 'No record of a passport having been issued for Polly or Pauline Cole in the right age group. Maybe she changed her name or left without a passport.'

'Thanks, McKeown. I don't think she ever got a chance to leave. Something happened to her in that house. We need confirmation from Jane, but I think the body is more than likely that of little Polly. In the meantime, do what you can to find out if the girl is still alive or if anyone knows what happened to her. For now, Polly Cole is missing.'

Her mobile rang and skittered across the desk with the vibration. It was her half-brother ringing from New York. She waved McKeown and Kirby out of the office and answered the call.

'Hello, Leo.'

'Lottie, good to hear your voice. How are the girls and Sean?'

'Doing good.'

'And the little man?'

She knew he was building up to something and her gut wrung in a knot, warning her it was not going to be good news. 'Louis is fine. All okay with you?'

'Yeah, good, good. I met with Tom Rickard when your girls were over here at Christmas.'

Lottie closed her eyes and scrunched up her mouth. She knew what was coming. Tom Rickard, with his developer hat on, had talked Leo out of the deal with her over their inheritance, Farranstown House.

'What's up, Leo?'

'We've met up a couple of times since and he tells me there's no way I'll get planning permission to develop the land around the house. It backs onto the town's drinking water source, Lough Cullion. I didn't know it was a town supply and it makes the land virtually worthless.'

'I see.'

'Do you? I thought it could be worth up to ten million dollars as development land. That's why I made you such a generous offer.'

She wanted to strangle Tom Rickard. And she would have, if he wasn't Louis' grandfather. 'It's okay if you want to pull out. I really don't have the energy to argue with you. Not right now, anyhow.'

'I'm not saying I'm going to do the dirty on you. I'm not like my mother. Alexis was ruthless, but you're the closest living relative I've got. I want to help you.'

She wanted to tell him to fuck off. But she stayed silent.

'I can't pay you what I promised, but I am willing to sign the house and land over to you. I've more than enough from my mother's estate and my NYPD salary. You can have Farranstown. Who knows, in time it might be worth a hell of a lot more than it is now.'

'Have you fallen and bumped your head, Leo?'

'Do you want me to sign it over to you or not?'

Lottie thought it was a generous offer, but one with plenty of drawbacks. She'd have preferred the money up front, like he'd promised. 'Property taxes alone will be more than my salary.'

'Why don't you speak to Tom?'

'Tom is an arsehole.'

'No need to be so pig-headed. See, I've picked up your colloquialisms. Honestly, Tom would like to talk to you.'

'Well I don't want to talk to him.'

'I think he has a soft spot for you,' Leo laughed.

'I have to go.' She hung up.

CHAPTER FORTY-THREE

Before the front door even opened, Marianne knew Kevin was in a roaring bad mood. The jangle of keys in his hand. The rattle of the wrong one in the door. The thud of the bunch hitting the step. The invective that followed was loud enough to pierce through the glass and timber.

She closed her laptop quickly, secreted it in the desk drawer but didn't lock it. There was nothing like a locked drawer to infuriate her husband. She'd put it in the box under her bed later.

She rushed to the kitchen, folded her arms and stood upright against the cold counter. She was not going to allow him to intimidate her. Not again.

'What are you looking at?' he said when he eventually got the door open and almost fell through it, such was his temper.

'Dinner's ready.' Ages ago, she added silently, and turned to tap the microwave's digital display.

Having divested himself of his suit jacket, he rolled up his shirtsleeves and took a bottle of wine from the refrigerator. When he slammed the door shut, Marianne heard something inside clatter and fall.

She couldn't help her eyes travelling to the monster-sized clock hanging over the dining table. But she stemmed the words that were in danger of flying from her mouth. If he'd come home on time, his dinner would not need reheating. She waited patiently for the ping, then put the plate in front of him. She knew he was about to launch into a tirade, but she was saved by Ruby bursting through the back door, followed by Sean.

'Where have you been?' Kevin said, stabbing a slice of bacon with a fork.

'Out with Sean.'

The fork dropped and Kevin reached out, grabbing his daughter by the arm before she could escape. 'You've been smoking!'

Not a question. An accusation.

Marianne groaned silently and noticed Sean slide into the background. 'You know the rules, Ruby,' she said, trying to defuse the row that would surely follow. 'Sean, I think you should go home.'

'Ruby?' Sean said.

The girl twisted out of her father's grip, took the pods from her ears and rolled them round in her hand. 'I think it's best. I'll chat you later.'

Sean left. Marianne thought that would be that, but Ruby wasn't finished. She rounded on her father.

'I wasn't smoking. Some of the others were. The smell just sticks to your clothes, you know.'

'I don't know. Enlighten me,' Kevin said.

'Your dinner's getting cold,' Marianne intervened.

'It's cold anyway,' Kevin said. 'Disgusting food.'

'I'm going to my room. I ate with my friends.' Ruby fled towards the door, but Kevin put out a foot and his daughter stumbled.

'Not so fast. What friends? I don't want you hanging around with gobshites that smoke. Nor that Parker boy. He's trouble. His mother is trouble. You hear me?'

'I hear you. Can I go now?'

'No, you bloody cannot. Sit down. I want to talk to you.'

'I've homework to do. A project. It will take me ages.'

'Thought you were on your holidays at the end of the week.'

Kevin was bubbling up to something and Marianne warned Ruby with her eyes, but the girl was past caring. She could see it in the shape of her shoulders.

'So what? I still have to go to school. Still have to do my poxy homework.'

Kevin's hand caught Ruby's arm again and he twisted it up behind her. 'Don't answer me back!'

'Kevin!' Marianne screamed, catching his hand. She shoved her daughter out to the hall and heard her footsteps thump up the stairs. Kevin could do what he liked to her between their four walls, but she would not allow him to hurt Ruby. She turned to face him. His smirk was grotesque. He was holding the plate in his hand.

'I have to go back to work later on. This food is freezing. Heat it up for me again.'

The words she wanted to shout died on her tongue and she took the plate and put it back in the microwave.

Well, she was going out too.

Like a good little lady, she thought.

If he only knew.

Her knuckles turned white.

If he only knew.

*

Lisa watched Charlie pace an angry circle around Jack. He looked like her late father, who had been a sergeant major in the army.

'Leave him alone, Charlie.'

'I asked him a question. I want an answer. That's all. Come on, Jack. Please. Tell me.'

'I don't know what you mean.' Jack's eyes flitted to Lisa, his hands sucking the life out of each other as he wrapped them in knots.

'Did you see Tamara Robinson's Instagram post?' Charlie said.

'No.'

'Well, your mother and I saw it. Tamara says you and Gavin have been filming the canal and tracks for over a week. Is that right?'

'That's enough,' Lisa said.

Charlie swung around and glared, then resumed his pacing. 'Tell me, Jack.'

'I ... I don't know where Gavin got that idea. He doesn't even own a drone.'

'Yeah, but you do.'

'What is it you want to know, Charlie?' Lisa said.

'I want to know what Jack has been up to,' he replied quietly. 'What if whoever dumped that body saw him? What if they come after him? After Tyrone or Maggie? I'm trying to protect this family as best I can. I need to know what he was doing.'

'Leave him be. Maybe I can find out,' Lisa said as she placed Maggie at the table beside Tyrone, with a bowl of Coco Pops to keep her quiet.

'I'll handle it,' Charlie said with an edge to his voice.

She recoiled. The void between them was growing deeper by the day.

Charlie pressed his hand into Jack's shoulder. 'Look at me, Jack, and tell me what you've been up to with the drone.'

'Dad!' Jack squealed. 'You're hurting me.'

'For feck's sake, Charlie, stop it this instant!'

Maggie dropped the bowl of Coco Pops on the floor and shrieked loudly.

'This is a madhouse,' Charlie said, giving Jack a sharp push before storming out of the kitchen.

Lisa rushed to her son and hugged him, oblivious to Maggie howling to get down from the chair.

'What's Dad on about?' Jack said, his bottom lip quivering.

'I don't know.'

'He's so angry all the time. Why?'

'His health isn't great. He can't work at the moment, so he's going a little crazy in the house all day. Give him space.'

'Why can't you tell me what's really wrong with him?'

She wanted to, she really did, but Charlie had insisted the boys were not to know until it was absolutely necessary. 'All I can tell you is that he's having a lot of blood tests done at the hospital. We can't say anything more until we know for sure. We don't want you to worry unnecessarily.'

Jack whimpered, and Lisa bit back a cry when she saw the tears in her son's eyes before he wiped them away.

Maggie was eating Coco Pops from the floor. Tyrone was grinning at the table.

Lisa felt her life was going to shit.

CHAPTER FORTY-FOUR

Tamara had sent Gavin to the butcher's shop to get mince for dinner half an hour ago. It was only ten minutes there and back. What was keeping him?

She flicked her eyelashes, noticed the glue was visible and sat down at her mirror to sort them out. When they were fixed, she pulled off her bathrobe and had a look in the mirror to see how her tan was coming along. She didn't want to be orange, but she knew what television lights were like, so she had been a little heavy-handed.

She checked the time on her phone. Where the hell had he got to? She thought of all she still had to do. Early tomorrow morning she was going to the television studios in Dublin for an in-depth interview about Gavin's find on the railway tracks. This could attract a lot more followers to her Insta stories. More freebies. She paused, picking up the mitt to touch up her tan. She was going to kill him.

She tried his number again. No answer. She texted him, because she knew what he was like. He never answered his damn phone. Maybe he had called round to Jack's. She should phone there to check, but she didn't want the Sheridans cashing in on her limelight.

She went downstairs. In her stash room, she looked out of the window at the beautiful calm evening. The sun slanting down behind the apartments across the way, a pink hue lighting up the roofs. The calm before the storm? She hoped not. She hated driving on the motorway in wind and rain. Tapping her phone, she brought up the weather app. Clouds tomorrow. No rain. Good. If she did her hair tonight, it should be fine for tomorrow.

A loud rap on the door made her jump and clutch her chest. She hadn't seen anyone come up the steps; then again, she'd been looking out across the roofs at the sun. Gavin must have forgotten his key.

Opening the door, she found herself flung against the wall as the door was pushed inwards.

It wasn't Gavin.

'Tamara, I need to talk to you.'

She wasn't sure if it was anger or fear causing her to tremble as she followed her visitor into the apartment.

*

Gavin slapped the small plastic bag against his thigh as he walked. He hated mince. When his mother took it out of the bag, the kitchen always smelled like the butcher's shop. No amount of her floral diffusers or sweet candles could take away the lingering smell.

He nodded at the guard standing on the railway bridge. He wanted to go over and have a look, but he'd been close to it all the day before. That was enough for him.

He turned left into the winding avenue that led to the apartment. As he passed the boarded-up derelict house, he noticed the lock on the hoarding hanging open. He'd once heard adults saying that the developer should have demolished it when he was building the apartments, but someone else said it was tied up in pro … probate or something. Gavin couldn't remember and didn't really care.

He walked past the house regularly and no longer noticed it. No one noticed it. But now the lock was hanging open. Why?

Standing at the broken-down barrier encircling the house, he could see how easy it was to get inside. Just then he thought he heard a cry. Like a bird screeching high in the trees. He looked up but could see nothing. Had the sound come from inside the house? Maybe he should have a look. Maybe he should run, as fast as he could. But still he stood there. Listening. Staring.

He heard it again. It was definitely coming from the house. He pushed aside the two pieces of timber that acted as a gate and eased inside. Standing on the dried-up brown grass, he gaped up at the house with half its roof caved in. Now that he thought of it, it might be a good idea if Jack could fly his drone in through one of the smashed windows and then they could see for themselves what was inside. Yeah, that would be cool.

But it looked a whole lot scarier once he was on this side of the hoarding. The front door was damaged, like it had been kicked in, but someone had put a makeshift lock on it, which appeared to be open. He walked up what had once been a path, now cracked and stubbled with moss, still slapping the bag of meat against his leg.

At the door, he paused and glanced up at the sky. It was getting darker and he really should wait until Jack was with him. He could text him, but Jack's dad was being a grade A prick, keeping tabs on him like the devil himself was out to kill him. Another sound from inside made him shudder, and he let the bag fall from his hand. A root sticking up from the cracked concrete path punctured the plastic.

'Shit,' Gavin said, his voice echoing off the walls. He bent to pick up the bag and the smell of the meat made him gag. He peered through a crack in the door where the timber had split. He could see where the evening light shone down from the caved-in roof, lighting up a section in the centre of the hallway. Was someone really in there? It looked empty. He listened for the sound again. Must be birds, he thought.

Something skittered around his ankles and the bag of mince lurched as a black rat with a long tail dragged at the meat. Gavin jumped backwards. 'Fucking hell!'

He heard the sound from inside the house again. It stopped the beat of his rapidly thumping heart and he held his breath. Dragging his eyes away from the scratching at his feet, he looked through the crack in the door again. He really should turn and run.

A shadow skirted past an open doorway behind the light.

He blinked and looked again. Someone was in there.

From deep inside the house came a low, guttural scream. It kick-started Gavin's heart again and he heard the noise in his ears like a train gaining speed as it left the station.

Fuck this, he thought. He was getting out of here. He turned, and felt a hand grab the back of his neck. As he opened his mouth to scream, another hand clamped around his mouth.

Powerless, he felt himself being dragged against the rough clothes of an adult – someone bigger than him anyway. Shit, shit, shit. He was lifted bodily from the ground, his feet dangling, as the door was elbowed inwards.

He tried to cry out, but the sound was blocked by the hand across his mouth. He started to cry, and snot ran out of his nose over the hand.

He had to do something.

That thought spurred him to action. He struggled, twisting and turning furiously, but it was fruitless. He was held fast. He kicked back again and again and felt his foot strike bone. A yelp escaped his captor, but the grip did not loosen.

As he was carried into the body of the house, he cried silently. He wanted to shout for his mother, but he couldn't utter a word.

Inside, it was dark despite the gaping hole where the roof had once been. Rafters hung precariously and strings of electrical cable dangled dangerously close to his head. His captor seemed to have no fear of this. They reached what Gavin thought had once been a kitchen. Three chest freezers lined one wall. His breath stuck in his throat and he thought he might choke. He kicked out again, more from terror than a need to damage his captor, then felt the warmth along his leg as he peed uncontrollably into his pants.

A chair was kicked across the floor and he was dumped onto it. He tried to calm his breathing in readiness to make a run for it, but he was crying too hard and his nose was so blocked he could hardly breathe.

When his captor released him, he felt too terrified to move, so he just sat there, slumped like a wet jacket flung on the back of a couch. Stars jumped haphazardly in front of his eyes and he thought he was going to faint. The slap across his jaw startled him, and he stopped crying.

His captor stood in front of him now, a knife dangling loosely from one hand as if they were deciding how to use it.

Gavin eyed the freezers along the wall. Small green lights flickered on them and he saw that the electricity was wired up.

He thought of the body on the tracks and in the canal.

Terror ripped through his bones and he trembled all over, deep, dark shudders. He squeezed his eyes shut and prayed for someone to come quick.

A cloud passed over the open roof, and in the rafters a bird fluttered its wings. Sitting on the chair, Gavin Robinson cried and cried until he was engulfed in midnight black.

CHAPTER FORTY-FIVE

Sean threw down the controller. The game was shite. He had lost and now he had no interest in getting back in. He lay on his bed and stared at the ceiling. The flicker of light from his PlayStation bothered him, but he was too lazy to get up and switch it off. His phone beeped.

He yawned and checked it. Ruby was online.

What's up? he typed.

I'm going to kill my dad, Ruby replied.

My mam might have to arrest you. He added smiley faces. Ruby's mam, Marianne, was a bit wacky, and he hadn't much time for Kevin. He typed, *At least you have a dad.*

I'm serious, Sean. He nearly broke my arm. Then he stormed out of the house. I wanted to pick up a knife and stick him.

You need to talk to your mother about this.

I can't. She's a wreck. He's a prick. Thinks he owns the insurance business. Like fuck. He only answers the calls.

Have a smoke. It might calm you down.

I'm in my room, smoking out the window. ☺.

Sean paused before he typed. He'd known Ruby a long time. She was quiet. She was a nerd. She never got angry. Not like this.

Do you want me to call over?

No. If he comes back, he'll probably kill you too.

Drama queen.

I'm serious. He's never laid a hand on me before. It was scary.

Sean sat up on the bed. *I'll be over there in five.*

No. I'm just venting. He's a prick.

If you want me, just ask.

Ruby sent sad emojis and went offline.

Sean's door opened. His mother stood there. She looked tired and sad.

'What's up, Mam?'

'Everything. All okay with you?'

'Yeah, I'm fine, but …'

'But what?'

'It's just Ruby. She says her dad is a prick.'

He moved across the bed as Lottie sat beside him. She looked like she wanted to lie down and sleep for a very long time.

'I was talking to Kevin this evening,' she said.

'Really? Can you arrest him?'

'Can't arrest a man for being a prick, though I've often wanted to.' She laughed, but it sounded drained and forced.

'Are you okay, Mam?'

'Just tired. I'm heading over to Boyd's for an hour.'

'Okay.'

She stood and stretched. 'What has Kevin done to upset Ruby?'

'He hurt her arm. I've never known her to be so upset.'

'Want me to have a word?'

'No, no way. You'll only make it worse.'

'Ah Sean, I'm not that bad.'

'You're a tyrant.' If he was typing this conversation, he knew he'd add laughing emojis.

'It might be better if you stay away from the O'Keeffes for a while. No point in getting caught in family rows, plus Kevin is involved in my investigation, though I'm not yet sure how.'

'I'll be fine.'

'Make sure you are. I'll see you later. Don't be on that PlayStation half the night.'

'I won't.'

She closed the door softly, and suddenly Sean felt totally alone.

*

'Have you made your will?' Grace said, picking a strawberry from her plate and dipping it into a blob of cream on the side.

Boyd watched her eat. 'I'm not dying,' he said.

'We're all dying, Mark. Every day a little bit of us dies away. So, you need to be prepared. You saw how quickly Mam died. Not a word of warning.'

'What's brought this on?'

Grace stuffed a fat strawberry into her mouth. Chewing it slowly, she closed her eyes, enjoying the sweetness. When she'd finished it, she leaned her head to one side, appraising him.

'You're too thin. You drink too much. You smoke even though you've been told to stop. You have cancer. Do you want me to go on?'

'You're not much of a tonic.'

'What do you mean by that? How could I be a tonic? I'm a human being.'

Boyd laughed wearily. 'You should go to bed.'

'Mark. Mam is dead. You are not my mother. Do not tell me what to do.'

'Okay. I'm going to lie down and rest my head.' He sighed at the thought of his long limbs hanging over the arm of the couch for another sleepless night. There was no talking to Grace. She was on a different wavelength to everyone else.

'I'm not stupid, so don't treat me like I am.' She immersed another strawberry in the cream. 'I want to go home.'

'Grace, we have to discuss it. Not tonight, though. I'm too tired.'

'I'm not tired.'

'We'll talk about it tomorrow,' he said, moving to the couch to fix up the bedclothes. 'That's if we're all alive tomorrow after your doomsday talk.'

'I'll be alive. Not so sure about you. You look very yellow.' She stomped into the bedroom and closed the door.

Boyd plumped up the spare pillow. He had to smile. He could count on his sister to bring a dose of reality into his life. As long as he had his life, that was.

The doorbell chimed. So much for rest. He hoped Grace would go to open it, but she didn't. He sighed and went himself.

Lottie stood there, her face white, her hair in need of a wash, her clothes also in need of a turn in the washing machine, but to him she was beautiful. He wrapped his arms around her and held her. They stood like that on the doorstep for a few moments before she extricated herself and placed a soft kiss on his cheek.

'Can I come in? Or if you like, I'll sit on the step and you can bring me out a cup of tea.'

He caught her hand and brought her inside.

'I know what I'd like to do,' he said, tracing his finger along the palm of her hand.

'You're such a cliché,' she laughed. 'Is Grace asleep?'

'She's in the bedroom,' he said, lowering his voice and switching on the kettle. 'I know she's my sister, but she's doing my head in.'

He opened the cupboard for mugs and had to admire the way Grace had organised them by size. The two of them were so alike, his mam had always said. An intense sense of loss for his mother washed over him and he shuddered.

Lottie's arms eased around his waist and her head nestled between his shoulder blades.

'I'm here, Boyd. Cry if you want to.'

'I'm fine,' he said, wondering how they were so in tune with each other's emotions. 'Bad day at the office?'

'Don't move. Don't say anything. I want to stay like this for a minute, listening to the beat of your heart.'

'Now who's the cliché?'

He paused with the mugs in his hand and Lottie leaning into him like a child clinging to a departing friend trying to stop them from leaving. And he wondered what would happen to her if he didn't make it through the treatment. Maybe Grace was right. Maybe he should make a will. He put down the mugs and twisted around, putting a finger under her chin and kissing her softly on the lips. His body, which had recently been letting him down because of the chemo, reacted, and she arched into him.

'God, Lottie, I wish we were in my bedroom right this minute.' He knotted his fingers into her hair and resumed their sensual kiss.

He did not resist when she pushed him against the counter, running her fingers around his waistband. Their lips still locked, she began to loosen his belt.

'Who's there, Mark?' Grace sauntered into the living room, long nightdress flowing, buttoned to the neck as usual.

Boyd gulped for air as Lottie backed away hurriedly.

'Hiya, Grace. I just popped round for a chat and a cuppa.'

'That's nice. I'll have one too.' Grace went to sit on the couch. She folded Boyd's blanket and placed it and his pillow carefully on the floor.

Lottie swallowed a laugh and Boyd shook his head.

'We need to get our own place,' he whispered, placing tea bags into three mugs.

'That's what I came over to talk about. Leo rang. He wants to pull out of the deal.'

'What? Why?'

'He's been speaking with Tom Rickard. He told Leo that Farranstown could never be developed, which I'd neglected to tell him. In truth, I'm relieved. I didn't like the idea of deceiving him.'

'You don't owe him anything. It's not like he's been in your life for the last forty-five years.' Boyd poured the boiling water. 'What did he say?'

Lottie fetched the milk from the refrigerator. 'He knows he can't develop the land and that it's basically worthless. But he said he'll sign the house over to me.'

'That's good.' He placed the mugs on a tray, catching Lottie's eye. God, he so wanted to be in bed with her. 'Isn't it?'

'A rambling old house like that? Come on, Boyd. It'll cost me a fortune to pay the taxes, let alone figure out how to make it habitable.'

'What about Tom Rickard?'

'What about him?'

'He's a property developer. Maybe he'd buy it off you.'

'Are you joking me? Anyway, I haven't had time to digest it. Let's drink our tea and talk about it.'

As he lifted the tray to go into the living area, he noticed that Grace had fallen asleep on the couch, her legs curled under her. He winked. 'Or we could skip into the bedroom for ten minutes.'

Lottie masked her emotional need and said, 'Tea, Boyd. I need tea, and then I'm going home.'

CHAPTER FORTY-SIX

Kevin O'Keeffe had come back to the house at eleven to find Marianne wasn't at home. He'd emptied the remains of the whiskey bottle into his belly while he'd waited, and he was drunk by the time he heard the front door open. A bleary-eyed glance at his phone told him it was ten after midnight.

He heard the twang of hangers as she hung her coat in the closet under the stairs. The bottom step creaked. She was trying to sneak up to bed. Though he was inebriated, he had hit her and dragged her into the living room before she could scream or utter a word.

'Where were you?' He stared through cloudy vision, shocked at his own anger and surprised to find her at his feet on the floor. 'Answer me.'

She was lying there like a pathetic animal. He put out a toe and poked her. She moaned like a half-strangled cat. At least he hadn't killed her. Not yet, anyway. He had to get ownership of the house before he could do any real damage, and even then, he would have to be careful. His thoughts shocked him. Was it the alcohol? Or his deep-seated jealousy?

When she stirred and stretched out of the foetal position, he inhaled deeply and sat down on the nearest chair, watching her scrabbling around in the deep pile of the carpet.

'What is wrong with you?' she groaned.

'Nothing is wrong with me. It's you. Always you.'

'I did nothing.' She struggled to sit up and leaned against the door.

'Ha! You disgust me. Do you know that? You've been lying to me.'

'I could say the same about you.'

He leapt from the chair, lashing out with his bare hands, striking her on the cheek. He watched as redness spread like a watermark across her skin.

She laughed, incensing him further. He hit her again, this time in the stomach, so hard she fell and cracked the back of her head against the corner of the small table. But she kept on laughing. The hysterical cacophony bored right through his skull, striking up a brass band in his brain cells, crashing them into each other until all he could see before him was black and white spots.

'Dad! Dad! What are you at? Stop it, please … Dad!'

Ruby was on her knees, shielding her mother from another blow. Kevin looked down at his hands, surprised to see blood streaked on the knuckles.

'Dad, what's got into you?' Ruby was cradling her mother's body, her white T-shirt stained red.

Kevin tried to clear his sight, but things were melding into each other. He shook his head, frantically trying to see through the fog that had possessed him.

His daughter had witnessed it all.

He could see clearly now. Could see what Ruby could see. And it was not good enough. He'd spent so long establishing himself as the head of the house; he was not about to let that evaporate because his wife had gone out somewhere without telling him.

'I will look after your mother,' he said. 'Go back to bed.' His authoritative voice had returned.

Ruby looked at him dubiously. 'I'm not so sure, Dad. Why did you hit her?'

'It's between your mother and me. Now go back to bed. She'll be fine.'

When his daughter didn't move, Kevin stood up and brandished his fist in her face. 'Go! Now. I'll have things back to normal before you know it.'

Fear was written like graffiti across her face. Eventually she released her mother from her grip and left the room.

Marianne was breathing. Heavy and hard. Good. Kevin undressed and stuffed his clothing which was dotted with blood stains into the washing machine, then switched it on. He filled a basin with hot water, got a J-cloth, and returned to the living room where his wife lay sobbing, her laughter dissolved at last.

Naked, he began to wash the carpet clean. Marianne could wait. After all, she'd left him waiting without a word of her whereabouts. She deserved to lie in her own blood.

*

Lisa sat in the dark of her kitchen. The only light was from the moon in the sky outside.

A cry came from upstairs.

She started. Was it one of the children?

Or was it Charlie?

He'd had awful nightmares in recent weeks. He'd woken up bathed in sweat, and the look in his eyes had stopped her from asking him questions.

The kitchen door opened. A head appeared around the side of it.

'I had a nightmare.' Jack stood in his pyjama bottoms, his little chest bare and his hair stuck to his head as if he'd just stepped out of the shower. Tonight he looked so much younger than eleven. 'Dad is shouting in his sleep too. What's going on?'

'Come here and sit with me.' Lisa moved from the table to the two-seater couch that faced the patio doors. She patted the cushion. 'Come on, Jack.'

'I'm afraid, Mam.'

'Of me?'

'No. I'm afraid of whoever put the body on the railway. I'm afraid for me and Gavin. I don't think we're safe.'

'Don't worry. I can protect you. I'm like Catwoman or one of those superheroes you love.'

She had hoped to make her son laugh, but tears dropped from his eyes, running down his cheeks and onto his hands, which were clutched on his lap. She touched his chin and turned him to face her, and her heart broke into little pieces when she saw the panic in his eyes. She decided not to tell him that Tamara had rung around half past nine wondering if Gavin was with him.

'You don't even look like a Catwoman,' he said eventually.

She laughed softly, the sound easing the air around them, as though a heavy veil had been lifted.

'I suppose you're right. I look more like Buzz Lightyear since I had Maggie. Maybe I need to start walking. I could walk with you and Gavin when you get your drone back. Would you like that?'

'That's a bit gross, Mam, to be honest.' He stopped crying at last.

'Bet if Tamara wanted to walk with you, you wouldn't say no.'

Jack smiled. 'Think I'd take you over her any day.'

'Have you seen her Instagram?'

'Yeah.'

'Thought you told your dad you hadn't.'

'I didn't want him grilling me even more.'

'I'm sure he'll be in a better mood tomorrow. He's just worried about you, that's all.'

Jack twisted uneasily. 'I don't think he's worried about me. I think there's something else going on.'

Lisa felt a hard lump find its roots in the centre of her chest. 'What do you mean?'

'What you said earlier. About blood tests and stuff. That he might have cancer. Dad is dying, isn't he?'

'No, no—'

'Don't lie, Mam. I'm not stupid. He hasn't been to work in weeks. He's lost weight. He's really sick, isn't he?'

Lisa sighed. She couldn't lie to her son any longer. Not about this.

'Jack, your dad *is* sick, but we don't know how sick yet. He's seen loads of doctors, but then there was a problem with his health insurance. It's sorted now, though, and he's going to have treatment. He'll be fine.' She wasn't at all sure that Charlie would be fine. There were too many anomalies in his life at the moment.

'Why is he so angry all the time?' Jack said.

'It's just … life in general. He feels hard done by.'

'Why? He has us.'

'I know. You're too young to understand.'

'I want to understand.'

'I'm tired, Jack, and you have school tomorrow. You need to sleep.'

'Gavin isn't going to school tomorrow.'

'Why not?'

'He's on the television with his mother in the morning.'

'For fuck's sake … Sorry, Jack. You didn't hear that.'

He laughed, and his eyes crinkled. 'Like I never heard you and Dad swear before.'

'Where did you hear about the television?'

'Instagram, as usual. Gavin didn't even tell me. I'm mad at him about that, so I'm not going to speak to him ever.'

Lisa smiled. Two minutes earlier he'd been worried about Gavin, and now he was mad at him. Then she recalled Tamara's phone call. She hadn't called since, so Gavin must be tucked up in bed asleep.

'Go to bed now.' She hugged her son tightly and feathered his hair with a kiss. 'And have a shower in the morning. Your hair is stuck to your head.'

'Okay, goodnight.'

She watched him leave. 'Jack, don't be worrying. Everything will be fine.'

He stopped at the door. 'I hope so.'

She sat on the little couch for a long time. She watched the moon in the sky and the twinkling stars and listened to the wildlife outside. How much longer? she wondered. How much longer can we go on like this?

She only moved when she heard Maggie cry in her cot.

Twenty years earlier

He brought me back through the fields with him. Wordlessly.

I cried, of course I did. I was only fourteen, after all.

The house he brought me to looked nothing like ours used to look. Before the blood. Before that night …

I shivered. I felt hands take my shoulders. Cold hands. Not warm and soft like my mother's used to be. Before that night …

'The child can sleep in the box room. You can sleep on the couch.' Her voice was gruff. Not warm or motherly.

I wanted to tell her. This woman who looked nothing like my mother. I wanted to tell her the truth. Before I forgot it. Before it went all mushy like the other memories. There was something important I had to say. But I couldn't get the words from my throat to my tongue and out of my mouth.

'The child stays with me,' he said. 'Throw us down some blankets.'

'Are you going to tell me what happened?'

'No.'

'Why are you covered in blood?' Then she saw my feet. 'Good God. What happened to you, child? I'll have to get a basin of water and you can soak your feet.'

At last. A little warmth. Not that I'd been used to much warmth in my life, but it was the closest anyone had got to caring for me recently.

'Get the basin and I'll wash him.' He kept his hand on my shoulder. My bones ached under the intense pressure of his fingers.

He didn't want me out of his sight. Was he afraid of what I might tell? Of what I would say about what had gone on in our house tonight? Or was it last night? Or another night altogether? I'd lost all concept of time and place. I felt myself drifting. Floating on a bed of nails. I shook myself and flushed the images from my brain. They were too bloody. Too noisy. The screams. I remembered the screams of my sisters as they tried to escape. But there was no escape for them, from that house.

I glanced down at my bare feet and saw the blisters pulsing in the blood and the dirt. How long had I been running for? How long could I keep running from the truth?

When she left the basin of lukewarm water and a dirty tea towel, she whispered something into his ear, and he nodded and pressed his hand tighter into my shoulder.

Then she walked out the door and we were alone.

'I will do my best for you,' he said, 'but you can never, ever tell anyone what happened. We will have to stay here for a while until I figure out what we're going to do. Do you understand what I'm saying?'

I didn't.

'Answer me.'

I hadn't said the word I thought I'd said. I tried again, but I was mute. He slapped me hard across the cheek. Then again. Harder still. But his violence only added to my silence. I couldn't speak.

'You can act dumb all you like, and maybe that will help us. But if I hear you've been talking to anyone, I'll kill you. Do you understand?'

Not trusting that the words would come, I nodded. Vigorously. Somehow I knew that was the answer he wanted, and I knew that was what would keep me alive. For how long, was anyone's guess.

CHAPTER FORTY-SEVEN

Wednesday

The early-morning sunlight glinted off the shards of glass and mirrors, throwing sparkling stars against the walls of the open concrete pit.

Lottie stood at the top of the recycling pit and stared down at the little body sprawled there, limbs askew. Her eyes watered, and she had to sink to her haunches to gather her wits. Hard to tell from up here how he had died. But she knew he was dead, and she was waiting for forensics before climbing down among the detritus to carry out any further investigation.

Turning to Kirby, she said, 'This is awful. What the hell is going on?'

Kirby swallowed and shook his head slowly. 'Ah shite, that's Gavin Robinson. Is someone trying to get rid of witnesses?'

'Witnesses? There were no witnesses to any of the crimes. The frozen torso and the skull are historic murders. Try again.'

'Both of our current victims found the remains associated with the old crimes. It's the only connection I can see straight off.'

'That's what I'm thinking. But I've no idea why they needed to be killed.'

'Me neither,' Kirby said, and paced a small circle while patting his shirt pocket, stained brown from cigars, as if to ensure himself that he could soon escape for a smoke.

'Where's the man who found him? What's his name again?'

'Brandon Carthy. He's in the office getting a sugary cup of tea.'

'Is he the recycling centre manager?'

'It's his job to open up every morning except Saturdays. And it's closed on Sundays.'

'Who else was here at the time?'

'Just Carthy. The rest of the staff don't start until eight. They're all corralled in the office now.'

'How many?'

'Three.'

'Who's conducting the interviews?'

'Lynch and McKeown.'

'Right. Where the bloody hell is McGlynn?'

'Probably up to his lugs at the sites where we found the skull and the frozen body.'

'Well, this body isn't frozen. Shit, Kirby, he's decomposing in front of our eyes in this heat.' She viciously pinched the side of her leg through her jeans to remind herself to remain detached.

'Want me to buzz him again?' Kirby said.

'Do that.'

The urge to climb down into the dirt and hold Gavin's little body was overwhelming, so Lottie turned away. No point in disturbing what might help them later. She rolled up her sleeves in the morning heat. She had thought her long-sleeved T-shirt would help keep her cool today in the office. But she'd been sitting at her desk for barely five minutes when the call came in about the body. She discovered then that the night crew had been dealing with Gavin Robinson's disappearance, but no one had seen fit to contact her last night when his mother reported it.

She could barely control her anger as she walked around the top of the pit, taking in her surroundings. The wall, the fence, the railings. She set uniforms to work searching the perimeter for clues. Something that would help them identify whoever had dumped Gavin's body in the pit.

The sound of an engine and brakes screeching caused her to look around.

'Do you think I've nothing else to be doing?' Jim McGlynn stomped round his car and opened the boot. He pulled on his forensic clothing and took out his heavy equipment case.

'Thanks for getting here so quickly,' Lottie said.

'I didn't have much of a choice, did I? A child, is it? Where's the body?'

'Down there,' Lottie said, pointing into the pit of glass and mirrors.

While officers hastily erected a tent over the pit, two SOCOs went down a ladder and McGlynn climbed down gingerly after them.

'This is just what I hate,' he grumbled as his assistant held the ladder.

'What do you hate?' Lottie said. She'd suited up, and the material adhered to her arms and neck like sticky tape.

'Bodies in inaccessible locations. Agh! Shit.' He'd stepped on a shard of glass, but his rubber boots held fast. 'It'll be a nightmare preserving this scene.'

'Any sign of blood?' She was ready to descend the ladder after McGlynn.

'Will you give me a chance?' He gritted his teeth.

She wished Boyd was here to put a firm hand on her arm, to force her to keep her words secure in her mouth and prevent her from getting into a shouting match with McGlynn. To keep her from crying.

'Don't come down yet. I need to assess everything,' he said.

She stood to one side while he gave orders to his team. It was another fifteen minutes before he allowed her to join him.

'Okay, what have we got?' she said.

'Do you know the deceased?'

'He's Gavin Robinson. One of the boys who discovered the torso.'

'Right. Right. No sign of any blood, so it's safe to say he was dumped here after being killed.'

'Should there be blood?' Lottie stared at the young boy dressed in his red Manchester United football jersey and black jeans. His feet were shod in white Nike runners. No socks. By design, or had he dressed quickly? She wished the night team had called her so that she could be armed with more information and not feel like she was drowning in a pool of the unknown.

'Look at this.' McGlynn carefully moved the victim's head to one side and pulled down the neck of the jersey.

'Oh fuck,' Lottie said.

'Knife wound to his upper back.' McGlynn said. 'Deep, too. He bled a lot.' He scanned the area around the body. 'Not here, though. As I already said, he was killed at a different location.'

'Could the blood have seeped down between all the glass?'

'Could have, but it hasn't,' McGlynn said indignantly. He didn't like anyone questioning his conclusions, as Lottie had found out on more than one occasion. He added, 'Have you called the state pathologist?'

'Yes.' She tore at her hair under her hood, her gloved fingers snagging on the straggly strands and making her scalp screech in protest. She'd called the pathologist when she'd first seen the boy lying in his bed of glass, though she'd prayed it had been an accident. McGlynn's confirmation added to her growing stress levels. She wiped her forehead, and her gloved fingers almost bonded to her head like glue.

McGlynn was now in full operation mode. 'Gerry, keep that camera rolling. Don't miss anything. Bob, the video. Is it on? Jesus, lad, you know what you have to do.'

Lottie ignored his orders and carefully inserted her hands into the front pockets of the boy's trousers. Nothing. Not even loose change. She felt her way to the back pockets. Nothing in the first one. From the second, she pulled out a thin school ID card.

'Back right-hand pocket,' she said, for the video. 'Confirms it's Gavin Robinson.'

'Poor little fucker,' McGlynn said. 'You'd better check on the other boy who found the torso.'

'I'd better.' Someone offered her an evidence bag and she dropped in the card and sealed it.

'You done here?' McGlynn said. 'I need to get on with my work. Can't have you in my way.'

Lottie moved carefully back to the ladder. 'When the state pathologist has the time of death, make sure she lets me know.'

McGlynn didn't answer. He was too busy shouting orders at his team.

With one foot on the bottom rung, she turned. 'How did he get in here?'

'He didn't walk or jump, that's for sure.'

Shaking her head wryly, Lottie scaled the ladder, shrugging off McGlynn's words. He could do sarcasm too.

CHAPTER FORTY-EIGHT

Marianne opened her eyes and was surprised to see Kevin sitting on the edge of the bed tapping away on her laptop.

'That's mine,' she said. He had figured out her password. Kevin was like that, sneaky.

Her mouth felt like there was cotton wool stuffed inside, and the back of her head throbbed where she'd hit the table. She wondered if his punches had left the marks of his knuckles on her skin. Her face felt like a pin cushion, with the pins digging right into the bones. She hoped Ruby was okay. Dear God, the girl had witnessed her father's brutality. How would she ever console her?

'Shut up,' he said.

'Give it back.'

'I said shut up.' His voice rose an octave, but she was past caring. The worst he could do now was kill her, and she didn't think he'd do that. Not with Ruby in the house. Then again … he could've succeeded last night.

'There's nothing there to interest you,' she said. 'It's just my novel. It's private.'

'Nothing is private in this house.' He leaned over her, the stale stench of alcohol oozing from his breath. 'You married me. I have a right to know what you're writing, what you're doing and where you've been.' He closed the laptop, evidently not finding anything to interest him. 'I've a right to crush this to a pulp, just like I'm going to crush you one of these days.'

'You did a fair good job of it last night.' She tried to sit up, but the pillows had slipped down during the night and her back felt like a steamroller had run over her.

He slapped the bed, catching her hand. 'Where were you?'

'What do you mean?'

He twisted her fingers backwards. 'You know what I'm talking about.'

She did. And for spite, she didn't want to tell him the truth. She said, 'Out with my friend.'

'Liar. You're seeing someone else.'

She groaned in pain as he dropped her hand. 'I am not.'

'How do you explain the sheets?' he said, getting up from the bed, flicking the edge of the duvet.

'The sheets?' Had he truly slipped into madness? She had no idea what he was talking about.

'You changed the bed linen yesterday, and let me remind you, yesterday was not Saturday.' He opened the wardrobe and took out a white shirt. He checked it had been ironed before he slipped it on.

It dawned on her then. A rush of memory flushed her cheeks. Not that anything had happened, but Kevin missed nothing.

'I spilled some tea and thought it might annoy you, so I stripped the bed and put on clean sheets.'

'Liar.' He turned to her, buttoning his shirt. She recoiled at the naked hatred creasing his eyes into slits. 'Someone was here. Tell me the truth.'

'I have no reason to lie to you. You're the liar in this family.' She knew the punishment he could mete out, so why was she spitting this at him? But she couldn't stop. 'I know your secrets, Kevin, remember that.'

'You better watch your step.'

Bolder now, she said, 'Can I ask you a question?'

'I'm late for work.'

She ploughed on. 'Did you ever love me?'

He stopped and leaned his head to one side, a dangerous look in his eyes. 'Do you want the truth?'

'Yes,' she said shakily. She thought she knew the answer, but she needed to hear him say it. It would make up her mind for her.

'I don't know if I ever loved you.' He looped his tie round his neck. 'I admired your wealth. Your parents' wealth, I should say.'

'Why do you stay with me?'

'For your father's inheritance.' He laughed, then added, 'And because of Ruby. If you ever think of throwing me out, I will bring my daughter with me.'

'Our daughter! And she'd never willingly leave with you.'

'Who said anything about willingly?'

He leaned down and she dragged the duvet up to her chin, trying not to cry out with pain. He caressed her face and neck with his fingers and probed one between her lips. She felt as if he had assaulted her, more so than if he had actually slapped her. He laughed again and drew away. Took his jacket from the hanger and inserted his arms into the sleeves. At the door, he turned and smiled cruelly, then pulled it shut behind him.

CHAPTER FORTY-NINE

Lottie knew she had to speak to Tamara Robinson before the press got hold of the story. A few of the local media journalists were hovering outside the depot gate. She wanted to interview the man who had found the body, but she didn't want Tamara reading about her son's murder on Instagram or Twitter.

She left Kirby and McKeown to gather whatever evidence they could and to interview the recycling centre staff. She dragged a reluctant Lynch with her.

Climbing the steps to the Robinson apartment, Lynch said, 'Why wasn't there an FLO assigned originally?'

'Not now, Lynch.' Lottie knew there would be hell to pay for not having assigned a family liaison officer to the two boys' families, even though they'd both refused the offer. She'd have to deal with it at a later stage.

'Okay, but it's going to come up. This new super isn't like Corrigan, or McMahon for that matter. She's straight down the line.'

'What's your point?' Lottie said tersely.

'Forget it.' Lynch rang the doorbell and stuffed her hands into the pockets of her navy trousers. Lottie hoped she was sweating buckets.

The door was opened by Garda Martina Brennan, whom Lottie had dispatched to sit with Tamara. In other words, to keep the media away until the woman had been informed.

'How is she?'

'Up the walls and back down again.'

The house smelled different from the last time Lottie had been here. The fragrance of perfumes and scented candles had been replaced by the distinct scent of loss. She knew the smell. She sniffed it into her lungs every time she dealt with murder, and more so when children were involved.

Tamara sat in the small white kitchen, wearing a black sweatshirt over leggings. Her hair was tied haphazardly, knotted and sticky. She kept her head down, with her fingers around a smouldering cigarette. The room was consumed with tobacco fumes. Lottie opened the window a little before sitting beside the stricken young woman. The false eyelashes were gone and her make-up dripped like a delta along her cheeks. Lottie fought the urge to take her in her arms, carry her out of the kitchen and give her a bath. Tamara was childlike – a broken china doll that no amount of patching was ever going to fix. And this was before she'd even heard the heartbreaking news.

'Tamara? Look at me for a moment. I have—'

'Did you find him?'

'I'm sorry, but—'

'He's dead, isn't he?'

Lottie watched as the hand with the cigarette unfurled slowly and doused the butt on the table next to the saucer serving as an ashtray. Tamara hadn't been a smoker, she concluded, but she was now.

'I'm so sorry,' she said.

'Can you light me another one?' Tamara asked.

Taking the packet, Lottie tipped out a cigarette and, despite swearing off cigarettes months ago, lit one for the grieving mother.

'Tamara. I need you to talk to me.'

'Whatever happened to my Gavin, it's all my fault.' Her tears were dried like mud on her face and her eyes were wet with unshed pools.

'How can you say that?' Lottie looked around for Lynch to help her out, but the detective was in the hall chatting to Garda Brennan.

'Where is my son?' Tamara said, her voice a monotone, dead in her head. 'I want to see him.'

'Not yet. Soon, though. I can arrange it for you.'

'Where did you find him?'

There was no easy way to say it. Lottie decided to be direct. 'We found Gavin's body at the community recycling centre, on the other side of town.'

'I know where it is,' Tamara snapped. 'What was he doing there? I only sent him to the butcher's down the road to get meat for dinner.'

'When did you last see him?'

'I … I was doing my tan. That's why I sent him. I couldn't go to the shop. Gavin said I looked like an Oompa Loompa.'

Lottie smiled sadly.

Tamara inhaled deeply and coughed before placing the cigarette on the saucer. 'We were to be on the telly this morning. Me and Gavin. Someone took him. Someone didn't want him telling …' The tears came then. Big, fat ugly drops, trickling through the crevices in the muddied make-up.

'What had he to tell?' Lottie said softly.

'Nothing really. Just him and Jack finding the body. That must have been horrific for them. I didn't stop to think how it must have been for Gavin. I only thought of myself. I'm selfish. I know that now. When can I see him?'

'Soon.'

'How did he die?'

'We're not sure yet.'

Tamara wrapped her arms around her body and began banging her head off the table. Thump. Thump. Thump.

Grabbing her around the shoulders, Lottie tugged the woman against her chest. 'Stop, Tamara. Please. You'll hurt yourself.'

'Don't care. Did he suffer? If he suffered, I will make myself suffer more.'

'I don't think so. We'll know more after the post-mortem.' She held Tamara as if she was one of her own girls. 'Is there someone I can call for you?'

'I've no one. Gavin's dad died when he was little. And now Gavin is …'

'When did you become worried about him not coming home?'

Tamara shrugged. 'I thought he'd forgotten to get the meat, or couldn't be bothered because he didn't like it anyway, and had maybe walked over to Jack's house or gone somewhere with him to kick a ball. I wasn't worried. Not then. I finished applying my tan, all the time giving out about him and how I was going to kill him when he got home.' She cried out. 'Oh God, how could I say such a thing?'

'It's okay. Go on.'

'Before I knew it, it was eight o'clock and still no sign of him.'

'You didn't contact the station until eleven o'clock last night. Why the delay?'

'I honestly thought he was with Jack.'

'But did you try his phone?'

'He never answered. Jack didn't either, so I assumed the two of them were together playing football or flying that stupid drone.'

'We still have his drone at the station.'

'I wasn't thinking straight. I rang Lisa, Jack's mum. Must have been about nine or nine thirty. She said Jack was in bed and hadn't seen Gavin all day. I didn't send Gavin to school yesterday.'

'What did you do after speaking with Lisa?'

'I walked around the estate and down to the bridge. I asked the guards there if they'd seen him, and one of them thought they'd noticed him earlier but wasn't sure.'

'I'll check that with them. Go on. What did you do then?'

'Nothing. The guard I spoke to told me to report him missing, even though he said he was probably smoking a fag behind a shed somewhere. My Gavin doesn't smoke.' She stared blankly at the cigarette burning out on the saucer. 'I don't either.'

'You reported him missing at eleven o'clock. That was over an hour later.'

'I didn't know what to do. I'm all alone here. It's just been me and Gavin since his dad died. I do my best. I try. Honestly I do.'

'When did you last see Gavin?'

'Some time before six when I sent him to the shop. Might have been quarter to. I'm not sure.'

'And you had no contact with Gavin after that?'

'None.'

'Did you go to the shop to see if he had been in?'

'It would have been shut by the time I finished my tan.'

'Did you go out to any of your neighbours?'

'I don't know anyone around here.'

'Did anyone call in to you?'

Tamara hesitated, glanced at the door and back down at the table. 'No.'

'Tell me the truth, Tamara. Your son's been murdered. Even if it's something you think might be insignificant, I still need to know about it. I have to be armed with everything, if I'm to find who did this to your son.'

'Was he ... you know ... abused?'

Lottie blew out a sigh into the cloudy air. She would have no information until the post-mortem results. 'I don't know, but I doubt it. What was he wearing?'

Tamara glared at the table. 'I ... I think he had his football jersey on and his black jeans.'

'On his feet?'

'His new Nikes, even though I wanted him to keep them for the telly. He said he had to try them out.'

'Did he have socks on?' Lottie was thinking that if Tamara said yes, then the boy had been undressed and dressed again. She crossed her fingers.

'I don't know.'

'Okay. Tamara, I need to know who was here with you last night.'

'Why?'

'Because your son is dead and I need to know everything you did and everyone you spoke to.'

Tamara folded into herself again, sobbing. 'It was just a friend. She arrived in a state, very angry and upset. She'd had a row with her husband and said she had to get out of the house. She took my mind off my own worries for a time, while I tried to make her see sense and go home to her husband. She's older than me, but we met through my Instagram account, and when we realised we lived in the same town, we became good friends.'

'Who is your friend?'

'Marianne O'Keeffe.'

CHAPTER FIFTY

Lottie left Maria Lynch and Garda Brennan with Tamara. She told them that there was to be no contact with Marianne O'Keeffe until she'd had a word with her. She sent a garda to check with the butcher's shop down the road and was relieved to find it was not the shop where Jeff Cole worked. Word came back that Gavin had been there just before it closed at six. The butcher remembered, because he was just about to lock the door.

She got the number of the guard who'd been at the bridge the evening before and called him. He had a clear recollection of the boy crossing the bridge because he'd just come on duty. It was shortly after six. He had no idea where the lad had gone. She organised a team to fingertip-search the area from the bridge to Gavin's home. And another team to do door-to-door calls and pick up any dash-cam or CCTV footage that was available.

She got into her car and pulled out of the estate quickly. Stopping at the top of the road, she glanced around. In front of her, a May bush bloomed white, and to her left the narrow road led towards the main Dublin road. She shook herself and looked to her right. The roadblock on the bridge had been scaled back and traffic was being allowed through. She heard a train slinking its way out of Ragmullin station heading for Dublin, though it would probably take days to get the schedules back on track.

As she drove along the lane with grass growing up its middle, she radioed for Kirby to join her.

At the door, she gathered the edges of her cardigan closed as a wind picked up and gusted in from the canal.

The child's dismembered leg had been found in an area a good bit further up to her left. She needed the results soon on Jeff's DNA to see if the torso was that of his cousin. Polly Cole had no passport, so it was probable that she hadn't left the country. If it turned out that the torso was related to Jeff, what had gone on at number 2 Church View, his aunt's house, all those years ago? How could a mother not report her daughter missing or dead? It was inconceivable. Unless she had killed her herself. Lottie couldn't understand any of it. Maybe Jane could call in yet another favour to hurry up the DNA analysis. McKeown should be able to uncover details of the girl's whereabouts if she was still alive. But now another child was dead.

Hedges and soft-topped trees blocked her view of the canal. She shivered with the deepening chill from the breeze. While she waited for the door to be opened, she glanced at the clouds massing in the sky. She had an uneasy feeling that things were gathering pace. As if by some biblical curse, the weather usually changed when a case turned. She didn't know if this one was going nowhere, turning back on itself. Nothing made sense. She just knew that Gavin's death and that of Faye Baker were linked to both of them having found decades-old body parts. Jack Sheridan had to be protected. She had already organised a garda unit to watch the family and their house.

When she turned around, she came face to face with Lisa Sheridan, standing on the doorstep looking like a waif. Her light floral dress was pulled up on one side by the little girl sitting on her hip, exposing white legs. Her skin was paper thin and her eyes had deep dark circles of sleeplessness. She still hadn't washed her hair.

'I heard about Gavin. Come in.'

The kitchen was in disarray. The small steel bin beside the back door was overflowing, and the smell of dirty nappies permeated the air, dissolving the lemon air freshener she suspected Lisa had hurriedly sprayed before answering the door.

'Lisa, is there something you need to tell me?' She swept crumbs from the chair before sitting at the table.

'No. Nothing.' Lisa fumbled with the collar of her cotton dress, the buttons not done up properly over her chest and a faded white bra failing to support her slack breasts.

'Sit down, please.' Lottie tapped the chair beside her. Lisa remained standing, the child silent in her arms, staring at her like she was a snake about to pounce. 'I need to talk to Jack.'

'He's at school. We didn't know about Gavin earlier. Do you think I should go pick him up?'

'Can you ring the school and just confirm he's okay?'

'Sure.' Lisa made the call and confirmed that Jack was safely in school. 'This is so stressful.'

'I know, but I'm certain he's better off there. Make sure either you or Charlie goes to pick him up.'

'Okay.' Lisa clung to her daughter, looking like a little girl herself. 'I can't get my head around it. Someone cut up those bodies. That poor child. What happened to Gavin? Oh God, who is going protect my son, Inspector? Who?'

'I have a garda outside and I think you should accept our offer of a family liaison officer.'

'Okay. Yes.'

Lottie felt a wave of relief. 'I'll organise it for you. There will be a garda presence outside your home at all times too. I need to clarify a few things with you. Did Tamara phone you about Gavin?'

'Yes. She rang around half nine last night looking for him. She thought he was here with Jack. Jack was in bed and I told her we hadn't seen Gavin at all yesterday. She just hung up. Cheeky as you like. Sorry. I shouldn't say that. Not now.'

'That's okay.' Lottie glanced around the kitchen. 'Where is your husband today?'

'He's somewhere around about.' Lisa put Maggie on the floor and leaned against the sink, looking out the window. 'He might be on the canal. He likes to do a spot of riverbank fishing.'

'A large area of the canal around here is sealed off until we finish our enquiries.'

'I'm not blind. I can see the lights at night. It's disrupting our sleep.'

'It won't be for much longer. Come and sit down.'

Lisa moved away from the window and sat.

Lottie said, 'Tell me, how is Jack?'

'Disturbed, as you'd imagine. Not sleeping or eating. I wish we could return to normality.'

'Lisa, a child's dismembered body was found just metres from your home, and—'

'I know!' Lisa said. 'I know what my son found. I see what's on the news. It's horrific. A nightmare I want to wake up from. It's so unfair.'

'Things will die down eventually.'

'How can you say that? Now that Gavin is … Oh God. What's going on in this world of ours?'

A good question, Lottie thought. What could she say to this poor woman and her family? How could she help them feel safe?

Lisa twirled an open button at the neck of the dress. Lottie thought she would surely pull it from its thread.

'Lisa, there's no need to be nervous. We will get you a FLO and you can keep Jack home from school. So please try to calm down.'

Jumping up, Lisa swung around on one foot like a drunken ballerina, shaking her fist. 'Are you for real? Calm down? We've been plunged into this nightmare and you tell me to calm down! You can piss off out of here.' She turned back around so quickly she banged her knee on the open cupboard door beneath the sink. She yelped, and Maggie screeched and ran over, wrapping her small arms around her mother's knees.

'Sit down, Lisa,' Lottie said. 'I want to talk.'

Lisa picked up her daughter and kissed the top of her head. The action soothed the little girl, who stopped crying immediately. Eventually Lisa sat down opposite Lottie. She worried at a knot in the wood with a fingernail.

'I have nothing worthwhile to tell you.'

Lottie decided on small talk to try to open her up. 'I love your home. When did you buy it?'

'I don't know. Years ago. Charlie will know, he's good with things like that.'

'I saw him the other day. At Tullamore Hospital. Is he ill?'

Lisa bit her lip, trying hard not to cry. 'He's not been well for a couple of years. He's been having tests done. We're waiting for a diagnosis. He was to get the results of his biopsy yesterday, but he … he said they weren't back yet.'

'I can empathise with what you're going through,' Lottie said. 'A friend of mine is undergoing chemotherapy at the moment. Has Charlie got cancer?'

'I don't know. I'm only a nurse, not a doctor.'

'Is his consultant's name, Mr Saka?'

'I don't know. Sorry. But I can find out.'

'Okay. Where does Charlie work?'

'He was in the insurance business for years, and then two years ago, just before he became sick, he got a job with Irish Canals, mainly doing restoration work. Not a lot of money, and with three kids it's hard at times, even though I work full-time.'

'I know. I have three of my own, though two of them are adults now. And I've got a grandson.'

'Gosh, you look too young to be a granny.'

'Thank you,' Lottie said, genuinely pleased. 'Do you know Kevin O'Keeffe, then?'

Lisa dropped her head. 'Who?'

'You said Charlie used to work in insurance. I wondered if he worked with Kevin O'Keeffe. He's with A2Z Insurance in town.'

'Er, yeah. That's where Charlie worked all right.'

'And you know Kevin?' It was like talking to a traumatised child.

'I suppose. Yeah.'

'Not close friends?'

'God, no.'

'Tamara is friends with Kevin's wife, Marianne.'

Lisa lifted her head and stared, her eyes flaring like fire. 'That Tamara would sell her granny, so she's probably using them. Not that she ever told me she knew them.'

'Were they ever around here? You know, for dinner or drinks?'

'Why are you asking me about the O'Keeffes?'

'I'm trying to get a handle on all the people who have popped up in our investigation.'

'And Kevin has something to do with it?' Lisa said.

Lottie was confused. A moment ago, Lisa had claimed not to know anything about O'Keeffe; now she seemed to know a whole lot more. She knew she would have to go talk to the O'Keeffes. Based on what Karen Tierney had told her, and the fact that Tamara was friends with Marianne, she felt there might be some link. Probably nothing, but she would have to ask the question.

'Tamara is a leech,' Lisa said suddenly. 'She clings to you, sucking the life out of you until you have nothing else to give. But I wouldn't wish this on her for one minute.'

'I know. Thanks, Lisa.' Lottie felt a swell of pity for the young woman sitting across from her. 'Are things okay with you?'

'Fine. Everything is fine. Don't go hassling Charlie, Inspector. Please. I'm afraid he's going to worry himself into an early grave. How would I cope then?'

Lisa stood, shifted the two-year-old to the floor and gave her a jigsaw puzzle to play with. 'I'll see you out.'

CHAPTER FIFTY-ONE

The wind had shifted direction and blew sharply into Lottie's face. She'd hardly had her foot out the door when Lisa shut it. A squad car pulled up just as she walked towards her own car. McKeown stepped out and the car reversed and roared back down the lane.

'What's up?'

'Kirby said you needed assistance; he was doing interviews at the recycling centre, so I came instead.'

'It's okay. I left Lynch at Tamara Robinson's apartment and just wanted someone with me while I talked to the Sheridan family. But I'm done now.'

'Grand. Can I scrounge a lift? The search team want you to have a look at an old boarded-up house.'

'Which house?'

'It's just before the estate where Tamara lives.'

'Hop in. Anything I should know from the interviews?'

'No one saw anything. Usual shit.'

At the bridge, McKeown leaned towards the windscreen, the light glistening on his shaved head. 'That's it. Over there.'

She parked and turned off the engine. McKeown went to speak with the two gardaí who were standing outside the hoarding. Lottie joined them.

'Has the interior been checked?' she said.

'Waiting for you,' the garda said. 'The door looks busted.'

'You know what?' McKeown said. 'I'm not from Ragmullin, so the area isn't familiar to me, but I'm sure I've seen that house somewhere recently.'

'Really? Where?'

'Can't recall.'

'It looks like it's been boarded up for years,' Lottie said. 'But let's have a look.'

She followed McKeown to the wooden gate in the hoarding. 'The guard on the bridge said he saw Gavin on his way back home around six, but he never got there,' she said. 'Maybe something around here raised his curiosity, or he was lured inside. One thing's for certain: he wasn't killed where his body was found.'

She edged inside the gate. Dragging a board to one side, she waited for McKeown to follow her.

'It's a bit eerie-looking,' he said.

She studied the dilapidated two-storey house, once painted yellow but now faded and weather-beaten. The roof had caved in in places, and one upstairs window had been smashed. A small shrub was growing out of one of the chimneys.

They walked up the cracked pathway to the door. She could smell something sour.

'Can you smell that?'

'I can.' McKeown was staring at the ground.

She looked down and saw the small white plastic bag of meat to the left of the door. It was moving like it was alive. Flies buzzed and swarmed around it.

'Fuck,' McKeown said.

'That could be the meat Gavin bought. They never searched this house last night.' Lottie tore at her hair. 'There'll be hell to pay if he was in here and still alive when his mother reported him missing.'

'I know. But the kid was seen just after six o'clock yesterday evening and she didn't report him until eleven. Do you think she's involved?'

'Anything is possible. Call Lynch and tell her to keep a close eye on Tamara.'

'Will do.'

'And while you're at it, get someone to check our internal reports to see if this place came up in connection with the body parts found in the canal and on the railway.'

'Why?'

'All our efforts were concentrated on retrieving the body parts, but we never found where they'd been stored. McKeown, why does this place look familiar to you?'

'I'm trying to remember,' he said, and turned away to make the calls.

Lottie appraised the door, feeling sick to her stomach. The smell of the rotting meat in the bag made her queasy. Gavin had been here, she was sure of it.

She ran back to the car and pulled on forensic clothing.

Then she stepped inside the old house.

*

Kirby opened the office door at the recycling centre and was hit with a wave of stagnant air. There were too many people in the small windowless space. He glanced over his shoulder to see if there was anywhere else to relocate to. But there was just the one office.

After introducing himself, he asked everyone except for Brandon Carthy to stand outside.

Slowly the foul air filtered out with the employees. Leaving the door open, Kirby sat on a chair, making sure there was a garda at the door. The young man sitting opposite him was sweating profusely, his hair flattened to his scalp, his shirt damp to his skin. He had divested himself of his hi-vis singlet and had it bunched up in his fists. His eyes were watery as he stared at Kirby.

'I know you've been through something traumatic, Brandon, so to start off, can you tell me about your job.' Kirby needed to coax him to calm down. Get him onto safe ground, and then he would be a little clearer in his telling of how he found the body.

'My job? Here, you mean?'

'Yes. Unless you have another one.'

'Well, I do the odd stint on the door at the Last Hurdle nightclub at the weekend. But this is my real job.' He paused, a little of his colour returning to his ashen cheeks. 'What do you want to know?'

'What's the function of this facility and what's your role in it?'

'I've worked here about a year and a half. Bit of a shitty job if you want to know, but I'm not complaining.'

'What does it entail?'

'I open up. Check around. Make sure no one has dumped anything illegally over the fence during the night. That kind of thing.'

'Is that a regular occurrence?' Kirby had noticed that the depot was encircled on three sides with six-foot-high metal fencing; on the remaining side, the entrance gate was a little lower. A sliding affair.

'Not really, but it happens from time to time. Usually it's mattresses or stacks of paint cans. Sometimes people just leave them at the gate, but we have CCTV so it's a deterrent.'

Kirby's eyes shot up at this statement. Maybe they'd get lucky and find footage of whoever had dumped little Gavin's body, someone dragging him over the fence.

'Have you checked the tape for last night and early this morning?' he enquired.

'No, not yet. I haven't had time. It's so surreal, all this.'

'I want those tapes. Tell me exactly what you did this morning.'

Brandon rubbed his chin vigorously as if he'd found a spot missed by his razor. 'I arrived at seven thirty, as usual. I'm never late. I closed the gate after me because we don't open to the public until eight. I set up the computer and got the keys to the weigh bridge. Then I went to check all the skips and pits to see which needed emptying. When they're full, a truck from Athlone empties them. I can walk it with you if you want.'

'Later,' Kirby said. 'How long was it before you found the body?'

Brandon glanced at his phone on the desk, as if the inanimate object would provide him with the answer. 'I'd say it was near enough to eight. That pit is last on my circuit. It's used for glass and mirrors. The sun was quite high early on and I was sweating like a pig by the time I got up there. I glanced in and, you know, it was like being on autopilot. I'd taken maybe two steps away when I registered that it wasn't only glass and mirrors down there …'

'Would you like a drink of water?'

'I could do with a vodka and Red Bull, to be honest.' Carthy pulled at the crew neck of his T-shirt.

Kirby wouldn't mind a stiff drink himself. 'You went back to have a look, did you?'

The young man nodded. 'I'm sorry now that I did. Should have kept walking. Let someone else find him.' He looked up, his eyes sad. 'It's not like in the movies, is it?'

'No, it's not. What did you do next?'

'I couldn't believe what I was looking at. He was reflected all over the pit. Like those funny mirrors you see in carnivals. It was fucking creepy, to be honest. The sun shining off the glass was blinding me, and I doubted what I was seeing. I had to run and get one of the others to confirm it.'

Kirby glanced at McKeown's notes. 'Some of your colleagues had arrived by then, is that correct?

'Yes. I called Tommy over. Fat lot of good he was. He puked up his breakfast straight away.'

'When you'd confirmed it was a body in the pit, what did you do?'

'Me and Tommy, well we rushed down here to the office and I phoned you guys.'

'Did you notice anything unusual when you first arrived this morning?'

Brandon thought for a moment, then shook his head, droplets of sweat dripping on the desk. 'No, nothing out of the ordinary. No rubbish left at the gate or fence. No sign of a break-in or anything like that. The office was locked. Do you think maybe he fell in and cut an artery or something? On the glass?'

'We won't know cause of death until forensics complete their work and the state pathologist carries out the post-mortem.'

'This is like a nightmare. I watch all those true-crime dramas on Netflix. They always blame whoever finds the body. But I did nothing wrong. Just did my job. Swear to God.'

'No need to worry then,' Kirby said. 'Don't get alarmed, but I have to ask this. It's routine. Can you tell me where you were last night?'

'At home with my mam and dad. I had nothing to do with this.' Carthy's voice trembled and Kirby felt sorry for him being thrust into this nightmare.

'That's grand. You'll have to make a formal statement. At the station preferably. I'll accompany you there as soon as we finish up here.'

'If I have to …'

'It's procedure, Brandon.' Kirby looked around the sparse, stuffy office. 'Now, I'd like the CCTV footage for the last twenty-four hours.'

'Sure. I'll get it sorted. It will take a few minutes.'

'We need to have a garda with you. Chain of evidence and all that.'

Carthy grimaced, but Kirby knew he understood. He and his colleagues were all suspects until they figured out what they were dealing with.

Kirby had interviewed Gavin Robinson on day one. He felt a responsibility to the young boy to find out who had killed him. He suspected that Brandon Carthy was not a murderer, but Carthy's blinking eyes told him the young man was hiding something.

*

Sean loved silence. He loved being in his own head, his own space, especially at home when his sisters were arguing and his mother was shouting. His nephew was the only one he could put up with. Louis would be two in October and Sean dreaded the prospect. He'd heard his granny Rose talking to Katie about the terrible twos. But Granny Rose didn't know that Katie was planning to emigrate to New York with Louis. Come to think of it, their mother didn't know that either.

'Shit,' Sean said.

Ruby didn't answer. She was in a world of her own this morning. They were sitting on the wall outside the school eating their eleven o'clock snack. The silence was punctuated by the birds in the trees down by the canal and the thrum of traffic on the ring road.

'Do you want to hear this or not?' Sean nudged Ruby's ankle.

'Huh?'

'What my sister's planning to do.'

'Not really.'

'Mam will have a fit when she finds out. She dotes on Louis. I sometimes think he's the only one she loves in our house. Except for Boyd, but he doesn't live with us. Not yet, anyway.'

'I thought he was dying,' Ruby said, more alert now.

'No, he's not. You never listen, do you?'

'I think if you listen, sometimes you hear things you're not supposed to hear.'

'Are you having a dig at me now?'

'A dig?'

'That's what my granny calls it. Our house is small, not big and fancy like yours. The walls are paper thin, and I can't help it if I hear things I'm not supposed to hear.'

'It isn't.'

'What isn't?'

'Our house. It's not big and fancy. Okay, you don't have to roll your eyes. I know it is really, but it's no different to any other house. Shouting. Rows. Arguments. I hear it all.'

'Shit, Ruby. Your mam and dad?'

'Yeah.'

'I always thought you had the perfect family.'

'See what thought did.'

Sean watched as Ruby stuffed her uneaten sandwich into the zip pocket of her rucksack. 'Was there a big row last night?'

'You could say that.'

'Over your smoking? Your dad seemed angry about it.' Tears were now threading down Ruby's face. Sean didn't know where to look. 'It can't be that bad.'

He went to hold her hand, but she stood.

'It is.' She hoisted her bag on her back. 'Come on, we better go back in.'

Sean put his hand on Ruby's arm, gently easing her back to the wall. 'You're better off talking about it. That's what my therapist says.'

'Are you still going to her?'

Sean smiled. 'I'm supposed to be. Mam thinks I am but I'm saving the money. My running-away fund.'

'She'll kill you when she finds out.'

'Who says she's going to find out?' Sean made a face and Ruby laughed. At last.

'Won't the therapist tell her? She must give your mother a report or something.'

'It's all confidential.' But Ruby's words had planted a seed of doubt.

'He kicked her,' Ruby said.

'What?'

'My dad. He hit and kicked my mother last night.'

'That's terrible. Did you see it happen?'

'I heard them arguing. He'd been drinking. She'd been out. He doesn't like it when she does things without telling him.'

'Is he a control freak?'

'Yeah.' She was silent for a moment, her head drooping. 'Sean, it was bad. I'd never seen anything like it. Scared the hell out of me. It was worse than anything on our games. It was real. Real blood, you know.'

'What did you do?'

Sniffing, she wiped away a tear. 'I did nothing. I was a useless lump of shit. I couldn't help my mother. That frightens me more than my dad does. I went back to bed when he yelled at me. Should have stood up for her. Should have done something.'

Sean didn't know what to say.

'See, even you think I'm a freak.'

'You're not a freak. It sounds like it was a bad situation. Real bad, and maybe if you'd interfered, he'd have hurt you too.'

'Maybe.' She pulled a single crooked cigarette from her pocket and searched for a lighter.

'Is she okay? Your mother.' Sean couldn't imagine how she could be okay, but he had no idea what else to say. Maybe he should ask his mam. Then he remembered that last night she'd told him to stay away from the O'Keeffes.

Ruby said, 'I was afraid to go into her room this morning. I just made my lunch and escaped.' She lit the cigarette, and smoke streamed out of one of the creases where it had got crushed in her pocket.

'Did you see your dad this morning?'

'I never want to set eyes on him ever again.' Ruby stomped the useless cigarette under her shoe and walked away.

Sean watched her hurry up the lane to the school. He couldn't understand her comment. How could she say that about her dad? He'd love to set eyes on his dad again, even for a moment. His mind filled with the memory of his dad carrying him on his back up the stairs, telling the girls, 'Hey, pumpkins, look at this bag of potatoes I found.' Sean had been five or six at the time and he remembered it clearly. Remembered himself and his dad falling onto the floor at the top of the stairs and rolling around with laughter.

He missed his dad so much.

Suddenly the birds in the trees down by the canal sounded too loud. Way too loud.

CHAPTER FIFTY-TWO

It was cold inside the derelict house, with part of its gaping roof yawning at the sky. Birds cawed to each other across the rafters and Lottie assumed some of the upper floors must have caved in.

She found herself standing in what was once a hallway. The tiles beneath her feet might have been black and white, diamond-shaped; now they were mossy and fungal green, with wild mushrooms growing among the weeds that sprouted here and there. The wallpaper had long since been worn or torn away. There were no furnishings that she could see. No doors hanging in any of the empty frames. Holes in the walls hinted that there had once been radiators there. Funnily enough, there was no graffiti scrawled on the walls and no sign of litter, cans or other rubbish. Someone was keeping an eye on the place.

She had a look into the rooms to her right and left. Both bare, though one had a shrub spiralling out from the chimney breast. She moved to the room at the back of the house, glancing upwards every second step to ensure the remainder of the roof didn't collapse on top of her. A few cables hung precariously like icicles above her head. As she stepped through the doorway, she saw instantly what was lined up against the far wall.

Opening her mouth to shout for McKeown, she was stunned when no sound came out. Her breath hung suspended in the cool air as she stared at the three chest freezers. Gulping down her horror, she heard the sound echoing in the emptiness. She drew her eyes away from the freezers and looked around her. What she saw chilled the blood in her veins.

A solitary wooden chair stood in the centre of the floor, pieces of hemp rope hanging from the legs. The floor around and under it was wet in places and stained dry in others.

She stilled her shock with a hand to her mouth.

Blood. So much blood.

She jumped as the air behind her whooshed. 'McKeown, you scared the living daylights out of me.'

'Holy fuck,' he said.

'Yeah.'

'We need SOCOs.'

'Call them.' She was rooted to the spot. He made to move forward and she placed a hand on his arm, halting him. 'No further, McKeown. It's a crime scene.'

The big detective, with his shaved head and thick arms, was trembling. 'I bet this is where young Gavin was killed.'

'And Faye. Don't forget about Faye and her unborn baby. Holy fuck, McKeown, who is responsible for this?' It was a rhetorical question.

McKeown said nothing. He fumbled for his phone. When he had it in his hand, he stood, numb.

'SOCOs,' she reminded him.

He nodded and pointed. 'Those are freezers.'

'Yeah. Look, they all have green lights on.' She dragged her eyes along the wall. Three plugs in sockets and a makeshift mother board with fuses and trip switches. 'Even though this place looks abandoned, there's electricity coming in. To this room at least. We need to find out who's paying for it and who owns this damn place.'

'Maybe they don't know what it's being used for.'

'Oh, they know all right. Why would you leave three old freezers buzzing away in a derelict house unless you were guilty of trying to hide something?'

'Good point.'

'McKeown, can you remember why this house was familiar to you?'

He scrunched his eyes tight, thinking. 'It was something I read about when I was going through the missing persons files.' He opened his eyes. 'I'll check when I get back to the office.'

'Shake up your memory fairly promptly. I need to know.'

'Yes, boss.'

'Stay here until SOCOs arrive. And get the uniforms to wind a roll of crime-scene tape around the hoarding.'

'I will. Are you going to have a look in the freezers?'

'Yes, though I doubt there's anything in them. Everything has been dumped on the railway and in the canal. Someone wanted them empty in a hurry.'

She took another look around the room, with its stained concrete floor, single chair and three ominous-looking freezers. A wave of intense sadness and hopelessness washed over her. 'Check that Jack Sheridan is okay. Lisa called the school, but we need to double-check. I don't think I could stay in this job if I find another dead child.'

She made her way carefully over to the freezers, avoiding the pools and stains on the floor.

'Shouldn't you wait for SOCOs, boss?' McKeown said from the empty door frame.

'I have to see what's in here.'

'Thought you said they were empty.'

'I'm not God. I can't see through them.' She shrugged off the feeling that she should wait, and lifted the lid of the nearest freezer.

'Empty,' she said with a sigh of relief.

She went to the next one. Lifted the lid.

'Fuck!'

'What?'

'Stay back there, McKeown, you're not suited up.'

'What's in it?'

Lottie stared into the face of a man she'd only seen in a photograph. Pellets of frost like fresh snowdrops clung to his eyebrows and along the fringe of his hair. His mouth was frozen in the scream he had died with. He had been pushed down at an awkward angle, his face gazing up at her. She prayed he hadn't been dismembered, like the previous occupants of the freezers. A pair of spectacles, lenses cracked, was squashed in by his ear.

'Boss? Are you okay?'

'Yeah, yeah.'

'Is it a body?'

She glanced over. McKeown was standing on tiptoe, trying to see into the freezer from a distance.

'I think poor little Gavin disturbed our killer and that's why he was murdered,' she said.

'Jesus. Who is it in there?'

'I'm not sure, but I think it's Aaron Frost. I was trying to reach him yesterday. His name came up when I was talking to Jeff Cole. He's an estate agent and would've had access to Faye Baker's house.'

'He's well frosted by now.'

She did not appreciate McKeown's macabre sense of humour. She dropped the lid and looked into the third freezer. It held joints of meat. Animal meat from what she could see.

Marching back across the floor, she brushed out past the detective.

'Stay here and wait for SOCOs. Tell McGlynn, or whoever he sends, that I want evidence pointing to the killer on my desk within the hour. And keep things confidential. If this gets out before we get a proper handle on it, we are fucked, McKeown. Fucked.'

CHAPTER FIFTY-THREE

With Lynch remaining at Tamara Robinson's apartment, and McKeown waiting for SOCOs to arrive, Lottie radioed the office with instructions for someone to get her information on the derelict house.

As she headed for the station, she mulled over everything that had happened this morning, from Gavin's body being found to the discovery of Aaron Frost's in the freezer. She would need to speak to his next of kin. Why had he been murdered? Faye and Gavin were linked to the skull and torso. But Frost? What had he to do with it? Okay, he might have had access to Jeff and Faye's apartment, but had he been involved in her murder? If so, why was he now dead?

As her brain scrambled like watery eggs, she recalled Tamara's mention of Marianne O'Keeffe. Why had Tamara delayed almost five hours in reporting her son missing? As the lunchtime traffic crawled up the street, Lottie fervently hoped the woman had had nothing to do with her son's death. She phoned the station. Kirby was back, so she told him to locate Aaron's next of kin and to wait there until she returned to accompany him.

At the roundabout, she turned around and headed for the O'Keeffes'.

Lottie watched Marianne O'Keeffe sit gingerly on an armchair in her spacious living room. The recliner seemed to swallow her up, and the frightened look that had appeared in her eyes when she'd opened the door had not faded. Indeed, it had intensified.

'Your home is lovely. So tidy.' Lottie thought anywhere would seem neat to her after an hour in the derelict house, but the O'Keeffe house was exquisite. She welcomed the smell of lemons and bleach in the air, hoping it negated the stench of blood and decay that clung to her own skin and clothing.

'Thank you. Kevin is very particular,' Marianne said without further explanation.

'Is this where you write?' Lottie pointed to the large antique desk under the bay window. She'd noted Marianne's desperate attempt to disguise a bruised face with heavy make-up. She had seen all the tricks there were, and she recognised a battered woman when she saw one.

'I'll never make anything of it, but it gives me something to do.' Marianne stared at the window behind the desk as if it might be an escape route route if she needed one. 'It's good to see you, Lottie, but is there something wrong? Is it about Ruby? Has she been over at your house bothering you? She can be a bit grumpy at times. All the time, if I'm honest.' She attempted a wry laugh, but it caught in her throat and a strangled sigh escaped. 'I think she had Sean round here yesterday.'

There had been no offer of tea, or even water, and Lottie felt the thirst dry up her mouth.

'No, this is not about Ruby.' She rested her bag on her lap. 'I want to talk to you about Tamara Robinson.'

'Who?' Marianne opened her eyes wide with surprise.

She was quick, Lottie had to give her that. This was a woman who was used to lying. 'Tamara Robinson. She tells me the two of you are friends.'

'Oh, that Tamara.' Marianne lowered her head and studied her hands.

'Yes.' How many women round here had such an uncommon name? 'When did you last see her?'

Marianne looked at Lottie from under thickly powdered eyelids. 'Can I ask what this is about?'

Placing her bag on the floor, Lottie leaned forward, elbows on her knees. 'Tamara's son was found this morning—'

'Oh, that's such a relief. Tamara was so worried about him.'

Lottie sighed. *Now* Marianne knew Tamara. 'He was found dead. Someone murdered him.'

Marianne paled instantly, and her hands trembled as they flew to her mouth.

'Do you want me to fetch you some water?' Lottie said.

'No. Give me a minute. This is such a shock. Oh God. Poor Tamara.' She made to stand up, but flopped back on the chair. 'I should call over to her.'

'Were you with her last night?'

Marianne swallowed noisily and nodded, knowing she could no longer lie. 'Yes. We became friends via Instagram. I loved her make-up tutorials and she was interested in writing a book about them. I said I'd help her with it, as I love writing. Anyway, I went over to vent about Kevin because he was being a prick, but she was frantic about Gavin. Tamara can be melodramatic, but she's a good mother despite what people say. She loved her son.'

'What time did you arrive there?'

'Not sure. Maybe before seven o'clock. I just barged in with all my troubles. I think I actually frightened her.'

'How worried was she about Gavin?'

'Not overly concerned initially. It was more like ... giving out about him because she wanted the meat for dinner. She was starving. I made her a sandwich and that calmed her down.'

'Did she ring around to see if Gavin was at a friend's house?' Lottie persisted.

'She phoned the Sheridans, but they hadn't seen him at all. She'd kept him home from school yesterday and he was cooped up all day, so that's why she sent him on the errand. To get him out from under her feet.'

'While you were there, did she make any effort to find out where he was?'

'She was getting frantic as time wore on. I wasn't too worried, though. I know what kids can be like. Your Sean and my Ruby. Sean is so sweet.'

Lottie thought how Gavin was only eleven years old, not sixteen like Sean. She'd be crawling the walls if Sean disappeared like that. She shivered thinking about the terror little Gavin must have gone through. She noticed Marianne staring out of the window wistfully, clutching her elbow as if in pain.

'Is everything okay?'

'Why wouldn't it be?' Marianne visibly bristled.

'Are you hurt? You grimaced when you placed your elbow on the armrest just now.'

'I'm fine, thank you.'

Marianne wasn't going to admit to anything, so Lottie went back to the issue at hand. 'How long did you stay at Tamara's house?'

'We sat at the table chatting and she opened a bottle of wine to calm her nerves. Must have been eleven before I left.'

'Was she not worried about Gavin at all?'

'Every so often she'd look at the clock and say she was going to kill him. Figure of speech.'

'She was with you all that time?'

'Yes. Well, she did go around the estate at one stage for a quick look, but she was back in fifteen minutes or so.'

'Did she go out again after you left?'

'I've no way of knowing that. She said she was going to call the gardaí if he didn't appear in the next ten minutes. That's the last thing I remember her saying before I went home.'

'Do you have any idea why someone would kill Gavin?'

Marianne shook her head. 'He's only a little boy, for God's sake. It's too shocking to think of him being dead. How was he killed? No, I don't want to know. I'll have nightmares.'

Lottie shrugged. She wasn't going to tell her anyway. The image of the chair and the blood on the floor in the old house caused her to momentarily shake. She dug her fingers into the palms of her hands to keep calm. 'Me too.'

Marianne looked at her steadily. 'Do you think it had to do with him and Jack finding the body parts?'

'Do you?'

'I don't know.'

Lottie wondered why she was sitting here with this apparently damaged woman when there were so many people she had to interview; so many other lines to connect. Gut instinct? Ticking boxes? But it niggled away at her as to why Kevin O'Keeffe had visited Karen Tierney with knowledge about Faye's murder before it had been publicly revealed. Okay, he might have seen it online, but why the need to talk to Karen? It bugged the shit out of her.

As she stood to leave, she said, 'I spoke with Kevin yesterday.'

'Kevin?' Marianne's eyes flickered as if she'd seen a ghost appear beyond Lottie's shoulder. 'About what?'

'In relation to another case.'

'Did he do something?'

Lottie held onto the door and watched as Marianne, keeping her arm across her chest, raised herself from the chair. 'Was he at home last night?'

'I was out till after eleven. Might have been nearer midnight, because I drove around for a bit. He was here when I got in.' She winced.

Lottie didn't need a map and a compass to work out what had happened then. 'How well does Kevin know Karen Tierney?'

'They work together. That's all.'

The addition of 'that's all' made Lottie think that maybe there was more to that relationship. She'd have to quiz Kevin some more. Perhaps the only thing he was guilty of was infidelity. 'Are you sure?'

'I'm sure.'

'Okay. Do you know Faye Baker?'

'No.'

'Do you know anything about number 2 Church View?'

'I heard it mentioned on the news.'

'Faye Baker found a skull there a few days ago, and then we found her body in the boot of a car yesterday morning.'

'Jesus! Do you think Kevin had something to do with it?'

'Do you?'

Marianne bit her lip and her face closed like a fist. From between tight lips she eventually said, 'I honestly don't know.'

CHAPTER FIFTY-FOUR

Kirby filled Lottie in on his interview with Brandon Carthy at the recycling centre.

'Did you get the CCTV tape?' Lottie tried to concentrate on his words.

'Yeah. Told the lads to prioritise it.'

She told him about her conversations with Lisa, Tamara and Marianne. 'I'm waiting to see if anyone can find out who owns that derelict house. It's a horrible crime scene.'

'You're sure the body in the freezer is Aaron Frost?'

'Yes.'

'Shit.'

'And Gavin most likely met his death there too.' She needed to reassess all their evidence to see who connected to what. So far nothing seemed to be linked. Faye definitely wasn't murdered in the boot of the car where she was found, so it was possible she had been murdered in that house. Why had Kevin O'Keeffe been so quick to call to Karen Tierney to ask about the body? 'I want O'Keeffe in here for an interview. We need to know where he was last night.'

'Right so.'

'And find out who owns that old house and let me know. How did you get on with the warrant for Derry Walsh's butcher shop?'

'Got it,' Kirby said. 'The shop was searched early this morning. All clear.'

'That's good. But you still need to get one for Ferris and Frost. I want to see Aaron's diary.'

'Boss, you're giving me a lot to do,' Kirby moaned, running a pen through his bushy hair and scratching his head with it.

'Learn to delegate, Kirby. And we still have to inform Aaron Frost's mother. She'll need to identify the body.'

She was delaying that tough visit. She stood looking into her own small office with the mess of paperwork piled high. If she sat down, she felt she might never get up. Her head was muddied and tired. She sneezed and buttoned up her cardigan. She hoped she wasn't getting a cold. If she did, she'd have to stay away from Boyd. It could compromise his immune system and cause more delays to his treatment.

Boyd. She needed to hear his voice. That alone might help to release her anxiety.

She rang him.

'Hi, beautiful,' he said.

'Have you been drinking?' Just listening to him, she felt some of the tension of the morning evaporating.

'No, but I got another hospital appointment for tomorrow. They want to run my bloods again. I've had two doughnuts,' he laughed, 'trying to bring my platelets up.'

'Doesn't work that way.' How was she going to get the time off to go with him? There was only so much skiving she could get away with, and she needed to keep Superintendent Farrell off her back.

'You don't have to come with me,' he said.

She grinned. He had a habit of reading her mind. Pacing the cramped office, she said, 'I want to. No argument.'

Still holding the phone to her ear, she pushed a box file out of her way with her foot, turned the corner and stopped.

Boyd was standing there, phone to his ear, leaning against the wall outside her office. Her heart flipped in a double somersault. He was so handsome. So Boyd. She had an insane urge to rush up and kiss him. Like a teenager. God!

'Were you here all along?' she said.

He nodded. 'Just walking up the corridor when you rang. Fancy a coffee? I want to talk to you about something.'

His cheeks seemed even more hollow than last night. He looked so tired.

She was about to tell him she was too busy, but stopped herself. Yes, she had the murder investigations to juggle, including little Gavin, and to tell Mrs Frost that her son was dead, but she realised in the same instant that she had to make time for the living too.

'Come in and sit down.'

She moved a bundle of files and watched as he folded himself into the chair, one leg over his knee, trying to appear relaxed. She knew he was missing work terribly, but so far he had stayed away. Maybe he'd been in to see the super.

When she had settled herself at the desk, she said, 'Are you okay, Boyd?'

'It's Grace. She wasn't herself this morning. I'm worried about her and I don't know what to do.'

'It's been a traumatic time for you both. It will take her a good while to adjust to life without your mother.'

'Mam's death hasn't really hit me yet, but it has hit Grace quite hard. I can't let her live on her own in Galway. She wants to be self-sufficient, but you and I know that's not going to work.'

'There must be a neighbour who could keep an eye on her.'

'A neighbour? You saw how isolated our home is down there.' He looked around at the clutter. 'I'm thinking I'll have to ignore her objections and bring her to Ragmullin to live with me permanently.'

She had expected this, but hearing him say the words out loud stumped her for a moment. What about their plans to get married? His treatment? Suddenly she felt selfish, and possessive of Boyd. She folded her arms defensively; then, knowing he could read her, she unfolded them. 'What are you going to do?'

'I need your advice and wisdom.'

'I am not one bit wise. Not where you're concerned, in any case.' She smiled.

His face was etched with worry. 'We can talk about it later,' he said. 'Call round. And you don't have to drive me tomorrow. The super will be on your case over it.'

'I insist.'

'I insist too. You're busy. According to Kirby, you have two if not three cold-case victims, a young pregnant woman murdered and two new murders today. Are they all connected?'

She knew he was deflecting her. Then again, he might be able to offer some help. Against her better judgement, she found herself explaining the morning's developments.

'That's an awful lot going on,' he said when she'd finished.

'Tell me about it.'

'There has to be a connection between the frozen body parts. They were found on the same piece of track on the same day. But you say one was male and one female. Two victims. Anything else in forensics to tie them together?'

'Not so far. We're waiting for lab results.' She reminded him about the tag found on the child's torso. 'I have the team going through old missing persons reports.'

'Have you tackled the question of how they ended up on the tracks?'

'The derelict house we found earlier was overgrown and boarded off. It's like it had become part of the landscape and no one seemed to even know it was there any more. An ideal spot to hide bodies. There were three freezers plugged in. SOCOs will be inspecting them, but I'm sure they held the body parts. If so, it's possible someone put them in a wheelie bin and walked brazenly along the road and across the bridge with it.'

'Could anyone be that audacious?'

'I think the person we're dealing with is clever and cunning. They probably killed and dismembered two people, one of them a child, and hid those body parts for twenty years. Now they're killing again. They have all the traits of a serial killer.'

'But they stopped for twenty years. Doesn't make sense.'

'Who says they stopped? We just haven't found any more bodies.'

'Shit, Lottie, you know you need me on this with you.'

'I know.'

'I could go through files, knock on doors. I want to help.'

'You can't. Anyway, there aren't many houses out that way.'

'There must be farmland. Get someone to check with the farmers along the route. I seem to remember a lot of bogs between Ragmullin and Enfield. Maybe someone footing turf saw something unusual. The place could be littered with bog bodies.'

'Stop, Boyd. I've enough to contend with. I have to trace young Polly Cole. I'm convinced she's the dead child. I'm waiting for DNA results.'

'If she is the victim, then her mother must have killed her. Why else would she remain silent?'

'Patsy Cole is dead, so she isn't the one we're looking for now.'

'Someone somewhere knows something,' Boyd said.

'I'll ask Superintendent Farrell to put out another appeal. But you know how unreliable eyewitnesses are.'

'I do. Has she spoken to you yet?'

'About what?'

'Her plans for the station. Her plans for you.'

'We had a conversation. She said you wanted to return to light duties.'

'I do.'

'You know you can't do that.'

He took her hand. 'I'm going demented at home. I know I have my treatment, and I'm thankful that it's going well, but I have too much time and I'm living in my own head. I need to work, Lottie. I need a purpose. I want to be involved even if it's only sitting behind a desk trawling through missing persons reports. I can do that.'

She leaned across the desk and squeezed his hand sympathetically. 'I'll have a word with the super. See what she says.' She knew Superintendent Farrell would not allow the two of them to work together, but now wasn't the time to tell Boyd that.

He stood, walked around the desk and kissed her cheek. 'I love you, you know that, Lottie Parker.'

Smiling, she patted his thin jaw. 'I have to get back to work.'

'Okay, I'll get out of your hair.'

'About Grace. There really isn't room for the two of you in your apartment.'

'Kirby lived there with me for six months, and we didn't kill each other.'

She lowered her voice to a whisper. 'Where is he staying now?'

'Maybe with McKeown.'

'Those two?' Lottie smothered a laugh. 'They're at each other's throats all the time. I can't see them living together.' She looked over Boyd's shoulder at Kirby. He had his head down, reading something on his computer screen. 'He mentioned he spent a night at the Joyce Hotel. I'll have a word with him later.'

'Right, boss.' Boyd saluted and sauntered out the door.

He was right, though, she thought: she really could do with his help.

CHAPTER FIFTY-FIVE

The body had been removed from the freezer once Jane Dore had carried out her preliminary inspection. The information relayed to Lottie was that Aaron Frost had sustained at least two knife wounds to his upper back and had been killed within the last twenty-four hours. The wallet on his body had confirmed his identity. But all they had linking him to Faye and Jeff Baker was the fact that he had rented them the apartment. Now he was dead. And dead men couldn't speak. She hoped maybe his mother would.

While Kirby doused his cigar and placed it in his pocket, Lottie rang the doorbell of the modern semi-detached house on the old Athlone Road. A woman in her late fifties, with a hospital crutch snapped to her arm, opened the door. Her T-shirt was white with a gold-lettered logo proclaiming *I need my coffee* across her bust, and her faded denim jeans were flared.

After introducing herself, Lottie said, 'Mrs Frost, we need to talk with you. I'm afraid we have some very bad news.'

'You better come in. Is it about Aaron?'

Lottie walked behind her into a tidy sitting room. There was a couch and two armchairs, black leather. Magazines littered a small coffee table. It was an L-shaped space that led to an open-plan kitchen with double doors overlooking a garden. The kitchen, though small, appeared pleasant and warm.

Mrs Frost leaned the crutch against the arm of the chair and sat down gingerly. She bit her lip and tugged at the ends of her bobbed hair. 'My hip. Had an operation a year ago and it's worse than before. What's Aaron got himself involved in?'

Lottie had to calm her thumping heart. Informing bereaved families about the death of a loved one continued to be one of the hardest parts of her job. She could have sent someone else, but seeing the first reactions of the people closest to a murder victim could tell her a lot. She felt Kirby shuffle on the couch beside her and knew she had to speak.

'Mrs Frost—'

'It's Josie.'

Lottie smiled. A little familiarity usually helped keep things calm. She straightened her back and felt her bottom sink into the comfortable seat. She'd need Josie's crutch to get up.

'I regret to have to tell you that we found the body of a man this morning and—'

'Oh, it can't be my Aaron. He'll be at work.'

Not going to be easy, Lottie thought. 'I'm afraid there's no mistake. The body is that of your son. I'm so sorry for your loss. You will be invited to make a formal identification once the pathologist gives the go-ahead.'

Mrs Frost's fingers snared on a lock of hair at her ear. 'My Aaron? No. No. You're wrong.'

Lottie shook her head slowly, hoping Kirby might speak up. He remained mute.

Mrs Frost dropped her gaze. 'You see, Aaron is a good man. He can drink and act the Mick when he wants to, but he's good.' She glanced up, a glimmer of hope flitting across her eyes. 'Maybe it's not him?'

'I'm afraid there's no doubt. I know it's hard to take it all in at once, but I really need to ask you a few questions, if you don't mind.'

Swiping away a tear, Mrs Frost leaned forward on the chair, and Lottie gazed past her into the garden. The lawn was definitely due a trim and the bushes could do with being pruned. She returned her attention to the bereaved woman.

'Josie, we believe Aaron was murdered.'

'Oh dear God!' Josie slumped on the chair. After a moment she said, 'I suppose I knew something was wrong, with gardaí calling yesterday looking for him and now two detectives arriving at my door. I'm not stupid. But listen, Aaron has never been in trouble. Like I said, he drinks too much at times. Can't get a girl to stay long enough to call her a girlfriend. But he'll settle down in time, and then ...' She stopped speaking as the futility of her hopes for her son's future sank in. 'Sorry. Murdered, you say? How? Why?'

'We need you to tell us everything Aaron did over the last few days and nights. Do you think you can do that now?'

'Aaron does his own thing. He's an adult.' Josie stood and hobbled to the other room, leaning her head against the glass doors. Lottie watched her in silence. The woman was average build. Average height too, about five foot five, and her hair had grey roots. Maybe a little older than late fifties; it was hard to tell.

'Can I get you anything?' Lottie said, fearing Josie had slipped into a trance. 'Water? I can make a cup of tea if you'd like?'

Josie shook her head. 'It's my house and I'll make the tea if I need it.'

Still she kept her back to them. Lottie tried to rephrase her earlier question.

'Can you tell us anything about Aaron that could help us uncover the events that led to his death?' She moved to stand beside the woman at the doors.

'I've nothing else to say about Aaron.'

'We know he was out of the office yesterday. Where do you think he might have been?'

'He told me nothing about his private life. He used this house like a B&B. I even did his washing and ironing for him. I spoiled him.'

'Is his dad around?'

Josie said nothing.

'Do you want me to call your husband?'

'I haven't seen Richard in a couple of years. Went out for a packet of cigarettes and never returned.' She turned back towards Lottie. 'Left Aaron with a lot of unanswered questions, which led to a deep depression for a while. But I thought he had worked his way out of it.'

Lottie had first-hand experience and knew how hard it was to work your way out of depression. She noticed there were no longer tears in Josie's eyes. Just a dark rage burning the brown irises a deep shade of red.

'Did you report your husband's disappearance?'

'Why would I? Be a waste of time. He was fifty-nine years old. A grown man. I asked around his friends, but no one seemed to know or care. One day he was here, the next he was gone. Probably off with another woman. Wouldn't be the first time.'

Lottie wondered about that and made a note to find out all she could about Richard Frost. 'I'll try to find him. He'll need to be informed of your son's death.'

'Do what you have to do.'

'Josie, I need to know Aaron's movements. You thought he was at work today; did he have an early breakfast before he left this morning?' She knew this was impossible. Aaron had been dead for some hours.

'He never came home last night, so I've no idea if he had breakfast or not.' The woman gave a distinct shrug of her shoulders and her body contracted, her hip jutting out. She looked around and Lottie picked up the crutch and handed it to her.

'I'll send someone round to bring you to the morgue when his body is ready for identification. Is that okay?'

'It is.'

'Josie, I'd appreciate it if you could tell me anything at all about Aaron's life. Who were his friends? What did he do in his spare time? That kind of thing.'

'I knew little about him over the last few years, never mind the last few days. He was quiet, except when he'd been out on the town. Then he could roll in here at all hours, kicking up a racket. He'd wake the dead. But I let him be.'

'Would you have the names of his friends?'

'No.'

'No one you know of that he was close to?'

'I knew nothing about Aaron's friends. He never brought anyone around here.'

'But he lived with you; surely you can tell us something?'

Josie was hunched over now, hands tightly gripping her crutch. She looked to have aged by ten years.

'I can tell you nothing. I never thought my boy would meet a violent end. It was violent, I assume.'

'Yes, it was.' Recalling why she'd been looking for Aaron in the first place, Lottie said, 'Do you know a young woman called Faye Baker?'

'Wasn't she the woman found in the boot of a car? Never heard of her before it was mentioned on the news.'

'What about Jeff Cole?'

'No.'

There was no point in asking if Aaron had known them, but Lottie tried. 'Do you think Aaron might have been friends with them?'

'How would I know that?'

'We found a skull at number 2 Church View. The house had belonged to a Patsy Cole. Would Aaron have known her, or ever been in that house?' Lottie recalled the Ferris and Frost *For Sale* sign in the garden.

'Awful business. Again, I heard it on the news. You don't think my Aaron had anything to do with it, do you?'

Lottie was conscious that Josie had deflected the question with another one. She persevered. 'I need to know if there's any connection between your family and Faye Baker or Jeff Cole.'

'I can't help you there. The names mean nothing to me. Now I want to be left alone.'

'Is there someone you'd like me to call to come and sit with you?' Kirby said.

'I'm fine on my own. I'm used to it.'

'But you're not used to shocks like this,' he persisted.

'I'll be fine. Please let me know when I can see Aaron's body.'

Lottie moved towards the door. 'Would you mind if we had a quick look in Aaron's room?'

Josie sighed. 'Top of the stairs. It's the door facing you.' She nudged Kirby out of the way with her crutch and returned to her vigil at the patio doors.

Aaron's room had a double bed, unmade, a built-in wardrobe and a bedside cabinet. Clothes were strewn on a chair in the corner and socks and underwear were rolled up under the bed.

'Untidy,' Lottie said.

'Three suits and a few pair of jeans, jumpers, shirts,' Kirby said as he inspected the clothes hanging in the wardrobe.

On the shelf there was an assortment of T-shirts, all neatly folded and ironed. Two pairs of shoes and three different types of runners were lined up at the side of the bed.

Lottie opened the drawers of the bedside cabinet. 'Cables and chargers for phones.'

Kirby pulled back the duvet. 'His laptop.'

'Take it.'

'Yeah. Hopefully there'll be emails or files to tell us something.'

'The way the last few days have panned out, I doubt it,' Lottie said.

'There are no photographs.' Kirby was looking around the room.

'Do men display them?' She knew Boyd didn't.

'I used to have photos of dogs when I had my house.'

'You never had a dog, Kirby.'

'I know, but I liked looking at the photos. Cheaper and quieter than children,' he laughed.

'You're pulling my leg,' she said.

'Aye. But it is kind of sparse in here. Do you think he had somewhere else to call his own?'

As Kirby left the room with the laptop under his arm, Lottie had one last look around. She drew back the net curtain and checked the windowsill. There wasn't even a speck of dust. Obviously his mother cleaned but didn't pick up his dirty underwear. She glanced at the top of the wardrobe. Nothing. She had never known Aaron when he was alive, and now the dead man wasn't even giving her a hint of why he might have been killed. She prayed forensics found something at the old house.

*

Josie Frost watched from the window as the detectives drove off. Then, clutching her crutch, she walked back to the kitchen. She found her phone on the counter and scrolled through her contacts.

When the call was answered she said, 'Aaron's dead. What the hell have you done?'

CHAPTER FIFTY-SIX

The team were in the incident room when Lottie returned. She switched on the free-standing fan in the corner of the room and found it had little effect.

She watched McKeown add a photograph to the board of Gavin's body lying in the pit in the recycling depot, side by side with a photo of Aaron before he was extricated from the freezer. The next few photos depicted the bodies found on day one. The frozen torso and frozen hand, and the child's leg from the canal. To the left of those, a single photo of the skull discovered by Faye Baker. Then, lastly, the photo of Faye herself curled in the boot of the car.

She felt sick looking at the gruesome display. If Boyd were here, he would help alleviate some of the horror. But he wasn't. She'd better get on with it.

'SOCOs and a team of uniforms are at the derelict house where we found Aaron Frost,' McKeown said. 'The forensic guys are sure it's human blood on the floor under the chair. They're sending samples to the lab to be checked against samples from Aaron, Gavin and Faye.'

'Anything else?'

'Aaron Frost's body has been sent to the morgue. SOCOs are taking samples from the ice in all three freezers and then shipping the appliances to the forensic lab in Dublin.'

'I want Aaron's fingerprints cross-checked with the prints taken from Jeff and Faye's car.'

'On it.'

'And his movements for the last few days. Kirby, get on to Dave Murphy at the estate agent's office. Find out if Aaron had somewhere else where he stayed. And we need to see their records. Did anyone check Murphy's alibi?'

Kirby said, 'I had a word with him on the phone. He was at the Chinese and then at his girlfriend's house all night. Her parents confirmed it.'

'Okay,' Lottie said. 'Follow up on Aaron's laptop. I want to know if anything is found on it. His phone? Where is it?'

'It was in pieces beneath the body,' McKeown said. 'Tech guys have it, but I wouldn't hold out much hope of getting anything from it.'

'Right. Who is at Tamara's house?'

Lynch said, 'Garda Brennan and her colleague. Tamara keeps asking to see Gavin.'

'Only when the state pathologist says so,' Lottie said, and added, 'I'm assigning you as FLO to the Sheridans. I want you to go over there straight away. I've had confirmation that Jack is safe at school. So be there when he's picked up.'

Lynch looked like she was about to object, but remained silent.

'Let's get on with it. Has anyone contacted Kevin O'Keeffe?'

Kirby said, 'I sent uniforms to his office. Don't think that will go down well.'

Lottie said. 'He's a person of interest because it seems he knew we'd found Faye's body before it was made public. I want to know where he was last night, and for that matter, the night Faye was murdered.'

Lynch said, 'I want to know why the little boy's body was left in the recycling depot. Has it any significance?'

'Yeah, and has anyone got any idea *why* he was murdered?' Lottie asked. Blank faces stared back at her.

McKeown eventually broke the silence. 'I think Gavin noticed something when he was passing the derelict house. He then stumbled on the killer with Aaron Frost.'

'Why wasn't he stuffed in the freezer too?' Kirby said truculently.

'That's something only the killer can tell us,' Lottie said, trying to defuse the growing animosity between her detectives. 'Have we confirmed Tamara's story yet?'

'She was in her apartment with her friend all evening until about eleven,' Lynch said. 'And she reported her son missing straight afterwards.'

'How did you confirm Marianne was there?' Lottie enquired.

'One neighbour identified her car and another saw her driving off erratically. Was even going to phone her in for drunk driving but didn't. Then the squad car arrived maybe ten minutes later.'

'Okay. Do we have reports from the lab?'

'Email came in not five minutes ago.' McKeown made a big deal of tapping his iPad.

'What does it say?' Lottie said, thinking she should have scanned over her own emails before the meeting.

'DNA results on the child's torso and leg. They're a partial match for Jeff Cole.'

'It must be Jeff's cousin Polly.' Lottie looked up at the board and felt her stomach churn. 'Evidence on the skull points to blunt-force trauma inflicted with a poker-type implement. Then the little girl was cut up, possibly in the bath of her own home. If that's the case, her mother, Jeff's aunt, Patsy Cole, never reported it. Why not? Did Patsy kill her daughter? I know things have moved at a fast pace this week, but we need to discover everything we can about the family who lived at number 2 Church View.'

'I'll see what I can dig up,' McKeown said.

'Have we got the results from the bathroom?'

'The bathroom samples have DNA from two different people. One is a match for the torso and the other matches the male hand. But the two victims aren't related.'

'A real house of horrors,' Lynch said.

'Make sure the DNA is run through all the databases they can find, and also any fingerprints they managed to get from the hand.' Lottie glanced at the photos again. 'We have the partial tattoo from the hand too. See if it shows up in any missing persons reports. I'll speak to Jeff Cole again.'

'Is he a suspect now?' Kirby said.

'If this crime happened over twenty years ago, he would have been nine years old. I doubt he could have cut up a body, but stranger things have happened. We have someone watching him, haven't we?'

'Yes,' Kirby said. 'Two uniforms in a car are keeping tabs on him.'

Next Lottie ran through the details of Gavin's last-known movements. 'He was found in the same clothes he was wearing when he left his house, so hopefully we'll get DNA from those. The recycling centre CCTV, any word on it?'

McKeown said, 'I've assigned two tech guys to check it.'

'I want to know the minute anything is found. There has to be something.'

'The techies are checking to make sure it hasn't been tampered with.'

'There was hardly time for anyone to tamper with it. The body was discovered before eight this morning. First responders were on site five minutes later. Time of death has to be between six and eleven, and he was probably dumped between those hours. Once Tamara reported it, our people were all around that area looking for him.' She paused, thinking how they hadn't been looking in the right fecking place. 'There might have been too much activity in the area for a killer to move around freely with a body in his car after that. That could be the reason why Aaron's body was left at the derelict house. Who owns that house?' She felt like she was repeating herself, but until she got answers, she'd have to continue.

The loud tap of Superintendent Deborah Farrell's garda-issue shoes sounded in the corridor, and Lottie cringed. She could do without interference, especially since she didn't know the woman well enough to figure out what kind of support she might offer.

'I would have liked to have been notified about this meeting.' Farrell marched up to the top table.

'Apologies, Superintendent,' Lottie said, trying not to grovel but feeling elbowed out of the way all the same. 'We're just recapping on all we have so far.'

'You have another body, I hear.'

'Yes. Eleven-year-old Gavin Robinson. He was one of the boys who found the frozen torso on the railway. I've appointed Lynch to be FLO for his friend Jack Sheridan. She is qualified.'

'Remind me why wasn't this done initially?'

'We offered the service to both families straight after the body parts were discovered, but they declined the offer.'

'Didn't you find a body in a freezer, too?'

'Aaron Frost. A local estate agent. His only link to the current cases that we can find so far is that he would have had keys to Faye Baker's apartment, giving him an opportunity to take the car and abduct Faye. We don't know why yet.'

'Have you proof of that?'

'Not until we compare his fingerprints with those found in the car.'

'Inspector Parker, you are the senior investigating officer on the case. I expect results. And sooner rather than later. I'm the one facing a barrage from the media. I have to give them answers. And the public needs reassurances, not more bodies.'

Lottie thought of telling Farrell of her suspicions about Polly Cole being the little girl from the railway, but decided not to. She needed to hear more from Jeff first. 'I might have something later. I just need to confirm a few things before that.'

Farrell rounded on her. 'I need to be kept fully informed of all developments. Have you seen the reporters and TV crews outside? It's like a rugby scrum. I've to give a press conference in half an hour and I want everything on my desk in ten minutes.'

She turned and left, the clip of her heels resounding in the corridor outside. A collective sigh wove its way through the room.

Garda Brennan stuck her head around the door. 'We have Kevin O'Keeffe in reception.'

'Put him in an interview room. I thought you were at Tamara Robinson's.'

'Two of my colleagues took over. She was getting very upset, hysterical, so I called the doctor for her.'

'That's good. Thank you. I'll be right down.'

Lottie looked at the board filled with victims and no real suspects. 'Get a photo of Kevin O'Keeffe and slap it up there beside Aaron Frost. And notify me the second we have any DNA results or anything on that CCTV. Kirby, you come with me.'

Before she went down to the interview room, she hurried into her office and checked her emails. There was the one from the lab that McKeown had read out; the other was from Jane Dore. She had completed the preliminary post-mortem on Gavin Robinson. Death from blood loss due to a stab wound to the upper back. Time of death between 6.30 and 8.30 yesterday evening. The little boy had wandered into a killer's lair and ended up dead in a pit of glass and mirrors. Lottie felt her heart break all over again.

CHAPTER FIFTY-SEVEN

Kevin O'Keeffe looked totally pissed off. He was leaning over the table, slapping it with his hands, giving out about his privacy and rights and a whole load of stuff that Lottie tuned out of the second she saw the Band-Aid straining on his knuckles.

'When you're finished, I'd like to begin,' she said.

Kirby did the introductions for the tape.

'Can you account for your whereabouts yesterday evening from say five thirty until this morning?'

'I was at home.'

'All the time?'

'No. I got home from work at six. I went back out for a drive later and was home at ten thirty. What's this about?'

He was getting on her nerves. 'Where did you go when you went out?'

'Just drove around.'

'Can anyone verify that?'

'No. I was alone.'

'How is your wife?'

'Marianne? She's fine. Why are you asking about her?'

'Where was she during those hours?'

'How would I know? I've told you, I was out.'

'Did you know Marianne had been out too?'

Sweat appeared on his upper lip and he shifted around on the chair. 'She wasn't home when I got back. She returned around midnight.'

'Did you ask where she'd been?' Lottie felt Kirby staring at her. He had no idea what her angle was, but she was clear on the direction she was taking.

Kevin said, 'Er, she didn't tell me.'

'Do you know Tamara and Gavin Robinson?'

'Tamara is a friend of Marianne's.'

'When was the last time you saw the Robinsons?'

'Is this about the boy? Gavin? I read he'd been found dead. Awful business.'

'It is awful. When did you last see him?'

O'Keeffe shifted again, his tailored trousers squeaking. 'I … I don't know. He's a lot younger than Ruby so they're not in the same circle, not even in the same school. Ruby is friends with your lad—'

'Mr O'Keeffe, I am not talking about Ruby or my son. I'm asking when you last saw Gavin Robinson.'

'I … I can't remember.'

'A month ago? Yesterday?'

'No, not yesterday. Definitely not yesterday.'

Lottie glanced at Kirby. Had O'Keeffe denied it too strongly? 'If not yesterday, when?'

'I don't know.'

'Did you know Marianne was visiting Tamara last evening?'

'She never said.'

'Where were you?'

'I told you. I went out. We'd had a row. I drove around for hours. I arrived home before her. I didn't know she'd been with Tamara. She should have told me.'

'Oh, and if she'd told you, you wouldn't have kicked fifty shades of shite out of her, is that it?'

'What are you talking about?' He glared.

'Do you not approve of Marianne's friendship with Tamara?'

'Look, Marianne is in awe of Tamara because of her youth and beauty. But if it keeps her away from writing stuff that will never see the light of day, it doesn't bother me.'

'If you didn't know Marianne was with Tamara, who did you think she'd been with?'

'I had my suspicions.'

'You might as well spit it out.'

'She's been trying to sell the house out from under me. I know she wants to get away, but in family law it's my house too, so I won't let her do that to me.'

'What has that to do with your suspicions? Did you think she was having an affair?'

'I had no proof, but I knew someone had been in the house. I found a business card. Jesus, the fucker must be ten years younger than her.'

'Who?'

'That estate agent. Aaron Frost.'

Lottie felt Kirby nudge her elbow. 'When did you see Aaron Frost?'

'I never saw him. Never met him. Just had his card. Drove around trying to think what I was going to do about it.'

'What did you do about it?'

'Nothing.'

'I'll tell you what you did, Kevin. You beat the crap out of Marianne, then you went and found Aaron Frost.'

'I did no such thing.'

'Are you telling me you didn't beat Marianne, or that you didn't find Frost? Which is it?'

'Both.'

'I saw her, Kevin. I saw the bruises under her make-up. I saw her wince in pain.'

'You're talking pure shite.'

'Am I?'

O'Keeffe bit the inside of his cheek. Lottie could see that he was seething beneath his put-on air of nonchalance. She would do her best to shake the truth from him. 'When did you last see Gavin Robinson?'

'I don't know.'

'When did you last see Aaron Frost?'

'I never met him.'

'Did you kill Gavin Robinson?'

'What? Oh, fuck off now. You can't go around accusing me of that lad's murder. I want my solicitor.'

Lottie ignored him. 'Did you kill Aaron Frost?'

'I didn't even know he was dead.'

'He is. Do you know Faye Baker?'

'Who?'

'You know right well. I've spoken to you about her. How you went around to Karen Tierney's home after she found the body. Tell me, how did you know Faye?'

'I did not know her.'

'Why were you asking Karen about her then?'

O'Keeffe stared at the ceiling, weighing up his options, no doubt. Lottie could feel Kirby bristling beside her. They both knew what was coming next.

'I want my solicitor, and the answer to whatever else you want to ask me is no comment.'

Outside the interview room, Lottie turned to Kirby. 'We have nothing to charge him with. We'd better see if we can unravel the evidence to tie him to any of the murders.'

'It's a long piece of string, though, isn't it?' Kirby shoved a folder under his arm.

'We need to prove it one way or the other. Maybe we could get Marianne to make a complaint against him. At least then we could hold him for a few hours on that charge.'

'I wish you luck.' He patted his shirt pocket for the security of his cigar. 'I'll see how forensics are getting on.'

'I'm going home,' Lottie said. 'I feel like a cement block is sitting on my head. I need a shower, and I want to swing by the Sheridans' to see if Jack can tell me anything about Gavin. I'll call back later on.'

'Go on, boss. I'll let you know if we need you for anything.'

'Don't you have a home to go to, Kirby?'

'Actually, I don't.'

*

As Ruby slapped butter onto four slices of toast, Sean surveyed the kitchen.

'You have crumbs everywhere,' he said.

'I'll tidy up.' She put two slices in front of him, then folded hers into each other and took a large bite.

'I'm not that hungry,' Sean said. 'Here, you have mine.'

Ruby's eyes widened, staring at something behind Sean. Twisting round in the chair, he saw Mrs O'Keeffe glaring at them. He stood up quickly, knocking his rucksack from the chair beside him. His books slid out over the sparkling floor.

'Hi, Mrs O'Keeffe. I'm just leaving.' He began to scoop his belongings back into his bag.

'Sit down, Sean. I want to ask you a question.'

He sat, leaving his books half in, half out of his bag, under the table.

'You were here yesterday, and the evening before, weren't you?'

Sean glanced over at Ruby, questioning her with his eyes. What was the right answer?

Ruby said, 'Yes, he was here. We always come in after school.'

'Sometimes you see things in other people's houses, things you're not supposed to talk about.'

Sean wondered how quickly he could get his books back in the bag and escape out the door. Before he could pick up another one, Mrs O'Keeffe pulled out a chair and sat beside him. Folding her arms, she stared at him.

'Do you go home and tell your mother about us?'

'No, honestly. I hardly get time to see my mother these days. She's busy with a case.'

'What are you on about, Mum?' Ruby said. Sean could see she was close to tears. He recalled their conversation that morning about her father. Should he say something? Mrs O'Keeffe didn't look injured, but she was acting weird.

Now she put both hands on his chin and turned his face towards hers. He tried not to squirm. Her touch felt oddly inappropriate.

'You're a good boy, Sean Parker. But I think you like snooping in other people's houses and telling your mother what you see and hear.'

'What?' He tried to shake his head, but she was holding his face too tightly. 'I would never do that.'

'Don't you ever come into my home unless I'm here,' she said quietly. 'And no telling tales. Is that clear?'

'Sure.'

Sean was totally confused. He hardly spoke in his own home, never mind told tales. He glanced at Ruby, who was over by the counter, picking nervously at the crumbs. He could see that she was mortified. And for that matter, so was he. Then he realised it wasn't just mortification. Ruby was simmering with rage.

'Can I go now?' he asked.

'Remember what I said. No tittle-tattle.' With a flurry, Mrs O'Keeffe left the kitchen.

'Tittle-tattle?' Sean said.

'Don't mind her.' Ruby helped pick up Sean's books. 'She's drunk.'

But Sean knew drunk. He'd seen enough of it in his own home over the years. Ruby's mum was stone-cold sober. So, what was her problem?

CHAPTER FIFTY-EIGHT

McKeown sent Garda Brennan to fetch coffees while he viewed the CCTV from the recycling centre that his colleagues had called him in to see.

He stared at the image on the screen, timed at 20.25 the evening before. It was grainy and shadowy, but it was definitely a car backed up against the glass recycling pit. He was looking at it side on. The boot was open, masking the person bent over. He couldn't see what was being taken out or put in, but it was two minutes before the boot was closed. The head remained ducked down, so he had no way of seeing whether it was male or female. The registration number of the car was not visible. He backed up the tape to the gate. The person's hand had extended out through the car window and keyed in the code. Fuck you, Brandon Carthy, McKeown thought. He must have given out the code to someone. Or had another person working there given it out? Either way, he needed to get hold of Carthy and ask him a few awkward questions.

When Garda Brennan returned with the coffees, McKeown replayed the clip again and they both reached the same conclusion. They were looking at the shadowy image of the person who had dumped the body and who was possibly the boy's killer.

'Fancy a ride?' McKeown said.

Garda Brennan blushed.

'Oh, I'm sorry. That came out wrong.' McKeown spluttered into his coffee. He stood and his head scraped the low ceiling. 'I mean to the recycling centre.'

She threw back her head and laughed. 'I'd do anything to get out of this cubbyhole.'

'Anything?' he said.

'Don't push too far now, Detective McKeown.'

His car was filled with the floral scent Garda Brennan was wearing. It wasn't unpleasant but it did catch in the back of his throat. He was glad to step out into the fresh air.

'There's no one here, only SOCOs,' the garda at the gate informed them.

'I want to have a word with Brandon Carthy.'

'No one here, only—'

'Only SOCOs. Got that. Tell one of them to take prints from the keypad.' He pointed to the device on the wall beside the gate. They might get one that didn't belong to the staff.

As he walked back to the car, he said, 'I have Carthy's address. We might catch him at home.'

'He won't be there,' the garda said. 'He and his colleagues mentioned they were heading to Danny's Bar. Talked about getting whiskeys to dampen their shock.'

'I'll dampen their shock.' McKeown sat into the car and ducked to glance in the mirror as he reversed. 'Danny's Bar. Is that on Main Street?'

'How long have you been stationed in Ragmullin? Don't worry. I'll direct you.'

'I'm sure you will.'

Danny's Bar was buzzing with the teatime crowd. McKeown dipped his head as he entered the pub after Martina.

'Can't see him, can you?' he said.

'I've no idea what he looks like.'

'You're a fat lot of good to me then.'

'Are you saying I'm fat?' Martina thumped his elbow in jest.

'No, no,' he said.

She smiled. A nice smile, he'd give her that. And in the muted tones of the bar, he noticed how her eyes lit up. Her bulky hi-vis vest shone under the orange glow of the lights. She was equipped with radio and handcuffs if a row broke out. He smiled back at her and pushed through the young people milling around in groups, drinks in hand and bags on the floor.

'It's like Christmas Eve in here,' he said, as he was jostled roughly by a young man who only reached his shoulder.

'Summer garden party,' Martina yelled above the din.

As he pushed on, he saw a familiar figure sitting at the bar. Boyd.

'What are you doing here?' McKeown said.

'What does it look like?'

McKeown told Boyd who they were looking for.

'I don't know him,' Boyd said, 'but about an hour ago, three or four men came in, dressed in hi-vis singlets. They made their way towards the beer garden.'

'You've been here an hour, then?'

'Are you my mother, McKeown?' Boyd's eyes filled.

McKeown said, 'Sorry about your mother. Tough times for you.'

'Yeah. Tough's the word all right. How are you getting on with the new super?'

'At the beginning she was all low-key; now she's like a tornado when she sweeps into the office.'

'Care to tell me more?' Boyd said. 'I'll buy you both a drink.'

'We're still on duty,' McKeown said.

Martina Brennan looked at her watch. 'I'm not. Officially I finished five minutes ago.' She took off her cap and eased onto the stool beside Boyd. 'Captain Morgan's, seeing as you're buying.'

'Two-timing me before my very eyes,' McKeown said with mock horror. 'I better find this Brandon Carthy. I've a few questions he needs to answer.'

'Your boss won't like you interviewing suspects in a pub,' Boyd said.

'Carthy is not a suspect in anything. And I'm not interviewing him. We just need to clarify something.' He tapped Martina on the arm. 'I'll be back.'

'I'm not going anywhere, am I, Sergeant Boyd?'

McKeown shook his head as he ploughed through the bodies. Sweat and perfume mingled. A waiter carried a tray of finger food towards a group in the far corner and McKeown resisted the urge to reach out and swipe a few chicken wings.

The beer garden was even more crowded than inside. A Perspex awning acted as a temporary roof, covered in plastic vines and coloured umbrellas. A screeching band added to the noise. McKeown sensed they were out of tune, but he knew nothing about music so maybe that was the norm.

He spotted Carthy with his crew sitting on a long bench, clutching pint glasses, faces vacant, unspeaking.

'Brandon? Can I have a word?' McKeown leaned down towards the younger man.

'I've told you lot all I know; I just want a little peace and quiet.'

McKeown laughed. 'You're not in the right place if that's what you're after.' He clamped a hand on Carthy's shoulder. 'Come with me for two minutes. Then you can resume your quest to find oblivion.'

'I'm going nowhere with you.'

'If that's the way you want to play it, I can arrest you for impeding an investigation.'

Carthy stood and handed his pint to a colleague. 'I'll be back.'

Outside, McKeown blinked in the brightness of the evening sunshine. Pulling a folded A4 page from his pocket, he flattened it out in his large hand and showed it to Carthy. 'Who is that?'

'How do I know?'

'Look again. How did that person have the code to the gate?'

'I don't know.'

'Who is it, Brandon?'

'I told you, I don't know.'

Before he knew what he was doing, McKeown had the man pinned against the stone wall, his arm across his neck, and it was only when he noticed Carthy's face turning puce that he released his grip.

'That's police harassment.' Carthy coughed and spat on the ground.

'I want a straight answer.'

Carthy ducked under McKeown's arm and backed away to the edge of the footpath.

'I don't know who it is. I have a few … clients who slip me a few quid now and again in exchange for the code.'

'So how much do you make on the side?'

'Not much. Twenty here and there.'

'I want the names of everyone who bribed you.'

'It's not a bribe. For God's sake, it's only recycling.'

'Only recycling? The body of an eleven-year-old boy was dumped there, and you tell me it's only recycling.'

'My pay is just above minimum wage, not that you'd know anything about that on the money you get. It was offered, so what was I to do?'

'Tell them to fuck off and come back during opening hours maybe?'

'Well I didn't. I put my hands up. I took money. It was only two or three guys. That's all. It's not like they're going to steal anything, is it?'

McKeown paced around Carthy, stuffing his hands in his pockets to stop himself from thumping the young man. 'Look at the image again. Tell me who it is.'

'I don't know who it is. Can't you check the registration number?'

'The CCTV cameras don't appear to have captured a number plate in any of the footage we've searched.'

'It's not a high-end system. Can I go back to my drink?'

'I want the names of the people who bribed you. And I want them now. Think long and hard or you're going to be out of a job. When you've racked your brain, if you have one, I want some answers. Okay?'

'Don't get your knickers in a twist. I'll have to check. Give me your number and I'll send them on to you.'

McKeown stuffed his card into Carthy's fist and followed him back into the pub. He joined Boyd and Martina. Standing behind them, he ordered a double whiskey on the rocks.

By the time he got back to the office, McKeown's head was buzzing and his stomach gurgling with the whiskey. He slumped at his desk and glared at Kirby when he smirked.

'Shut up, Kirby. Did you find out anything from the guy at the estate agent's office?'

Kirby shrugged. 'He's adamant he wants a search warrant before releasing any information. He's lucky I didn't land him into the middle of next week.'

'You? You can't land yourself on the same bed two nights in a row.'

'What the—'

'Sorry. There was no need for that.' McKeown raised his hand in apology and began sorting the paperwork on his desk. He checked his phone, but still nothing from Carthy. Little shit. He moved a stack of twenty-year-old missing persons folders. There had been nothing in them. These were the ones that hadn't been transferred onto PULSE. As he lifted the next stack, he noticed the bundle of newspaper clippings. He put the files on the floor and skimmed through the articles again.

'Oh my God! This is where I recognised the house from.'

'The derelict house?' Kirby said, raising his head, his eyes bloodshot and angry.

'Yeah, look at this. See the photo under the headline.' McKeown jumped up and over to Kirby's desk, waving the page. 'This is the place, isn't it?'

'Let me read it.'

'I have to tell the boss. Where is she?'

'She went home for a shower. Mentioned she was going to drop in on the Sheridans to talk to Jack about Gavin. But she said to contact her if we had any developments.'

'I'll text her.'

'You better,' Kirby said, reading the article. 'Familicide?'

'Pretty horrific.' McKeown took the page back. 'It says here there's more on page three. I only have the front page.'

'Pull up the murder file. It should have all the info. No, wait. You text the boss and I'll pull the file.'

'Kirby, look at this,' McKeown said. 'Look who was the detective sergeant on the case.'

Kirby glanced at the name. 'You better call the boss.'

McKeown fumbled for his phone with one hand and opened the button on his shirt collar with the other. It was going to be a long night.

CHAPTER FIFTY-NINE

Lottie really should have gone home for a shower first, but after Lynch had made sure Jack got back safely from school, she'd asked for time to organise her own family before taking up her FLO duties at the Sheridans'. Lottie had agreed and headed there herself.

She pulled up outside the house and nodded at the garda on sentry duty. She noticed the coolness in the air and glanced over at the dark canal. SOCOs had finished their work, and the divers were doing one more day before giving up. She hoped they would find more body parts, to help identification and for completeness' sake. Not that there was anyone rushing to claim the bodies. A little girl no one cared enough about, with no one to answer her cries. Though she hadn't received any indisputable confirmation, she was convinced the torso and leg were Polly Cole's.

'Don't worry, little Polly, I will keep listening to you. Tell me what happened.' She was talking to herself again. She knew her team were doing their best to find out what had happened, but so far they'd discovered absolutely nothing.

She wandered around the side of the house, zipping up her hoodie. The weather would be cold and wet by tomorrow. A false summer, her mother had called it. Rose was always right, even when she wasn't.

The shed housed two racing bikes, and fishing rods hung neatly on hooks hammered into the wooden wall. In the centre stood a fibreglass rowboat, its oars suspended on rusted chains from the roof. It looked like it hadn't been in water for a long time. Stacks of paint cans held court in one corner beside the bins, and an old washing machine stood neglected in another. Turning away, she moved towards the back of the house.

Light poured out from the kitchen. She stood back a little and stared in at the family scene. Lisa at the stove, stirring something. Charlie reading a newspaper at the table. Maggie sitting on the floor playing contentedly with building bricks. The two boys were seated at one side of the table with books in front of them. Homework, Lottie thought. When had she last seen Sean doing his homework? She felt a glitch in her heart for all she was missing out on. She needed to sit down with her family and talk to them. Find out their fears and joys. She'd been so caught up in Boyd and his illness that she knew she'd deserted her children once again. She wiped her nose with her sleeve and brushed away her self-pitying tears.

Continuing to watch, she saw Charlie throw down the newspaper. He seemed to be shouting at the boys. He went to the refrigerator and got a bottle of beer, drinking greedily before crashing it down on the table. Lottie jumped, even though she couldn't hear anything. The boys remained with their heads buried in their homework. She wondered if Jack's little heart was breaking for his dead friend. If it was, there was no evidence before her eyes.

Lisa kept on stirring whatever was in the large saucepan. Was the strain of Jack's find and Gavin's death breaking the little family? Perhaps it was the spectre of Charlie's illness that was casting shadows over them.

As she edged back around to the front door, her phone vibrated in her pocket. She checked it before knocking. When she read McKeown's text, she let her hand fall away from the door.

*

Jack jumped when his father slammed the bottle on the table. He tried to keep the pen steady in his hand, even though he wanted to escape up to his room.

'I've finished my homework. Can I go have a shower before dinner?'

'Dinner will be ready in five minutes,' his mam said.

'You can stay where you are, Jack,' his dad added.

Tyrone sniggered but knew better than to laugh out loud.

'Please, I smell,' Jack said.

'Well then, you've got two minutes.' His dad swigged from his near-empty bottle.

'You shouldn't really be drinking,' Lisa said. 'Doctor said so.'

'Well, I'm thirsty.' He drained the bottle and went to fetch another.

Jack stuffed his books into his bag and rushed from the kitchen, closing the door softly behind him. In the hall, he thought he saw a shape through the glass in the front door. His first thought was that it was Gavin come to play a game on his laptop. And then he remembered. Gavin would never play with him again.

The shape appeared to be about to ring the bell but then moved away. He crept forward and opened the door.

The detective.

She turned and smiled. 'Hi, Jack.'

'Hi.'

'I called round to see how you were doing.'

He walked outside. 'Everything is weird.'

'I'm sure it is.' She put a hand on his shoulder. He found it strangely comforting, and the tears he'd kept at bay all day erupted in loud sobs.

'I can't believe Gavin is dead. He was my best friend.'

'I know, sweetheart. It's hard to understand.' She hugged him before holding him at arm's length and wiping his tears with her finger. It felt soft and comforting and he almost cried again.

'Thanks.' He sniffed and pulled away from her. 'Who killed him?'

'I don't know yet, but I'm going to find out, I promise.'

'When you do, will you tell me who it is?'

'I will call personally and tell you.' She leaned against her car. 'Did you and Gavin ever go to the recycling centre on the industrial estate?'

He shrugged. 'Sometimes I go there with my dad when he has a trailer-load for recycling. He says it's cheaper. But I don't think Gavin ever came with us. It's not much fun really.'

'I don't suppose it is. Did you see Gavin at all yesterday?'

'No. He wasn't at school. I didn't even text him because I was mad. You see, he was going to be on the telly and I wasn't. It was my drone, not his, that found the … the body.'

'Don't worry, it's not your fault. His mother is a bit pushy.'

Jack looked up at her. 'She is, isn't she?'

'Jack, do you know the old house over the road? The one at the bottom of Gavin's estate with the hoarding around it.'

'It's always boarded up and locked. I never went in there.'

'And Gavin? Do you think he might have sneaked in there occasionally?'

'No way. He was a big scaredy-cat. And anyway, my dad told us never to go in there because junkies always break in and use needles and stuff.'

'Ever fly your drone in to see what might be behind the boards?'

'No.' His eyes flared into wide balls of incredulity. 'Never!'

'It's okay, Jack. You better go back in before your parents come looking for you.'

He didn't move. 'Detective?'

'You can call me Lottie.'

'That's a weird name.'

'I suppose it is.'

She had a nice smile, Jack thought.

'What did you want to say?' she asked.

'When can I get my drone back?'

'I'll make arrangements for it to be sent back tomorrow. We got the SD card with the footage, so there's no reason for us to hold on to it.'

'About the SD card …'

'What about it? I can arrange for a new one for you if our guys need to keep it.'

'No, I have plenty. You see, er … that's the point.'

'What's the point?'

'Oh, nothing. Forget it. I better go back inside.'

He wanted to tell her that he sometimes flew the drone at night. That he had footage on a USB stick from the night before he found the body on the railway. But they were just blurry images. Could be foxes or badgers. So maybe it was best if he said nothing.

He stared up at the tall detective with her flyaway hair. She looked confused before a smile spread across her face. 'Is there something you want to tell me, Jack?'

'No. I just miss Gavin, that's all.'

He turned back to the door and bumped straight into his father.

'Why are you here?' Charlie said over his head to the detective.

'I called round to make sure Jack is okay in light of Gavin's death. Detective Maria Lynch, the FLO, will be here soon, but you have protection.' She pointed to the garda standing at the side of the house. 'I got an urgent call to go back to the station.' She waved her phone in the air. 'I can come back later.'

'We don't need any FLO. I can protect my family.'

Jack felt his shoulder being held tightly by his father's hand. He twisted away. 'We were only chatting about Gavin.'

'It's best you leave,' Charlie said. 'We're all disturbed by what happened to Gavin. We need time on our own as a family.'

'I'm going for now, but I have to come back and talk to you and your family. Goodnight.'

Jack ran back inside and up the stairs to his room. He heard his father shut the front door. He stood at the window. The detective stared up at him before a car arrived and a woman got out. The two of them spoke before the detective called Lottie got into her own car.

He watched as the tail-lights disappeared down the lane in an envelope of dust.

*

Marianne had found the food company on Instagram. Tamara had told her about it, and she'd jumped at the chance of not having to cook every night. Now, twice a week, wholesome ready-made dinners were delivered to her door. So far, Kevin hadn't discovered her secret.

'I'm sorry about last night, Ruby,' she said, scraping her plate into the food waste bin.

'It's okay.'

'It's not. You shouldn't have to witness something like that.'

'But it was Dad who hit you. You don't have to say sorry. He should.'

'I doubt that's going to happen.'

'Me too.' Ruby lowered her head, but Marianne caught the tail end of a sinister smile as it flitted across her daughter's face.

'Are you okay?' she said.

'You shouldn't have talked to Sean like that earlier. He's the only friend I've got and if he dumps me it will be your fault. I'll never forgive you.'

'Sean's mother was round here earlier, asking awkward questions. I thought maybe he had been telling her something he shouldn't.'

Marianne rinsed the plates under the tap before inserting them in the dishwasher in the correct slots. No point in irritating Kevin further. She glanced at the clock. He still hadn't come home from work. Hopefully he wasn't out drinking. There was no way she could put up with another night of abuse. Then she thought of Tamara. She really should call over. She'd had all day to do it but couldn't garner enough courage to go outside her own front door. She hadn't even lifted the phone. Some friend she was.

'Mum?' Ruby was lounging by the door, twisting one hand into the other.

'Yes?'

'About last night. Dad hitting you ...'

'Please, Ruby, forget it ever happened.'

'I can't. It was horrible. I felt so useless. It's not right.'

No, Marianne thought, it was far from right, and she could never let it happen again. First, though, she had things to sort, then Kevin O'Keeffe would be out of her life forever. 'Go on upstairs and finish your homework.'

'Haven't got any.'

'Well ... do something. Play a game on your PlayStation.' Anything to keep her from asking awkward questions.

She gathered up the refuse bag stuffed with the cardboard and cellophane that had come from the ready-made meal cartons and went to the outside bin. She pushed the bag right down to the bottom, where Kevin wouldn't see it. She had enough to worry about without him losing his mind over a few wrappers from food he believed was freshly cooked.

As she came back inside, she heard a key turn in the front door. Her knees weakened and she had to hold onto the edge of the table. This has to stop, she thought. I can't handle any more fear.

CHAPTER SIXTY

Lottie hadn't visited her retired superintendent in months. She found it too painful to see the once tall and rotund red-faced man diminish into a curved, grey-skinned gnome. But McKeown's text had led her here. She'd rushed by the station first to pick up the photocopy he had ready for her.

Myles Corrigan led her into the lounge, which she'd have called the sitting room. He had retained a few airs and graces even though he was quite ill.

'Don't tell me I look fecking well, Parker. You and I both know I'm on my last legs.'

'It's good to see you again.'

She sat and waited as he slowly sat into a chair plumped up with a multitude of flowery cushions. The eye he'd lost to a tumour was covered with a black patch and his hands were pulsing with sores. She'd heard the cancer was eating him alive.

'I thought you were waiting until I was in my coffin to come and see me.' He attempted a laugh, but it sounded more like an old car backfiring. 'You haven't visited me before now, have you?'

'Sorry?'

'Don't mind me too much.' He tapped the side of his head. 'My old brain gets confused. But when I'm gone, I want a good old Irish wake. Make sure everyone at the station turns up. No matter what they say about me behind my back, I'd like a good send-off.'

'There's plenty of miles in you yet.'

'Only miles left in me, young lady, is in my name.' He waited as if he wanted her to laugh before adding, 'Busy?'

'Very.'

'How are all the family?'

'Good, all good,' she said, guilt worming its way around her heart. 'Rose was asking after you.'

'Rose?'

'My mother.'

'Ah, right. Your mother is a strong woman. Listen to her,' he said. 'And Boyd? Heard he got the big C like myself.'

'Boyd is responding well to treatment. This week might see the last of the chemo.' She crossed her fingers, hoping his platelets played ball.

'If the fecking toxic poisons in it don't kill him.' Straight-talking as ever.

'Boyd's mother died suddenly last week. Set him back a bit, and he has to look after his sister. A lot of pressure.'

'Did someone tell me you're getting hitched? Will I get an invite before I kick the bucket?'

'We're nowhere near even thinking about that.'

Silence filled the space between them before he said, 'You know I was under investigation for a while there? Trying to pin old bribery charges on me. Pack of young Dublin hotshots, not knowing their fecking arse from their elbow. Kicked their arses back across the Liffey, so I did.' He looked at her as earnestly as he could with one eye. 'What brings you to my door?'

Lottie opened her bag and took out a copy of the newspaper article McKeown had found. 'This is a case you worked. You were a detective sergeant back then. It happened before PULSE was set up and it looks like the case was never transferred over.'

'That doesn't surprise me. Do you think it's one of those that was left off purposely?'

'I doubt there was any garda interference, if that's what you mean. Probably a clerical error.'

'Wouldn't be the first time.' He coughed loudly into a stained handkerchief and stuffed it down the side of the armchair.

She handed him the photocopied page from the *Ragmullin Tribune*. 'These murders were reported as familicide. Can you remember anything about the incident?' This was a long shot, because she'd heard that Corrigan, though he wasn't yet sixty, was suffering from early-onset dementia.

He glanced at the front-page photo without reading the article. 'This was well over twenty years ago. What's your interest in it now?'

She explained about the frozen body parts and the freezers in the old house. 'Today we discovered the body of a man stuffed in one of those freezers.'

'This house?' Corrigan pointed to the photograph.

'Yes. It's abandoned now. I'm trying to find out who owns it. There's still electricity being fed into it.'

'Shouldn't be hard to find out.'

'You'd think that, wouldn't you?'

'Sure, and I know how the job goes. Someone demanding a warrant, or waiting for a sharp-suited solicitor.'

'The former.' She was pissed off with Dave Murphy at Ferris and Frost. Kirby was dealing with the paperwork, and she was expecting a call to say they had a signed warrant At least he had traced the house as far as the estate agents.

'Typical.' Corrigan placed a pair of spectacles on his nose and began to read.

She sat listening to the loud and worrying rattles from his chest.

'Ah, I forget a lot of things,' he said, 'but I remember this. I was first on the scene after uniforms. Horrific sights.'

'What can you tell me about it?'

He read the article slowly, as if to refresh his mind, then said, 'It was awful. Two young girls. Stabbed. It looked to me like they'd been trying to flee, though they were on the first floor. Probably would have risked a broken neck, but they didn't get that far. One poor lassie was at the window. Blood everywhere, as you can imagine. And the smell. Afterwards we found out they'd been dead for at least thirty-six hours.' He wrinkled his nose as if the scent had leapt off the page. 'The young mother, Jesus, I couldn't even count the number of stab wounds on her body.'

'A crime of passion?'

'Hard to know. And you know what else I remember? She had a hole in the centre of her forehead. Hit with a poker. The weapon abandoned in the grate.'

'Oh, God. The small skull we found had a similar wound.'

'The father was long gone, as was the son. The boy was the eldest of the family. Thirteen or fourteen, I think. We never found a trace of either of them.'

'Fourteen, it says there.'

'Must be that, so. The general consensus was that the father abducted the boy and went on the run. Or the boy escaped, and the dad took off after him. We never found them.'

'And we haven't found any mention of them on any missing persons file. Why?'

Corrigan ran his finger around the socket of his good eye, thinking. 'That's because it was a murder investigation, not missing persons. The father was a murder suspect and the boy a victim.'

She leaned her head back. 'Did you ever discover why he might have murdered his wife and daughters?'

'Not a fecking lot.' He shook his head angrily, the eyepatch slipping slightly. 'I took the case personally. Covered all angles, but there was nothing, except maybe … Oh, it never came to anything.'

'What? Tell me.' Lottie edged closer to her former boss, inhaling the distinct odour of mothballs.

He looked at her vacantly for a few moments. 'There were rumours,' he said at last. 'But as far as I can recall, they led to nothing. But my mind isn't what it used to be.'

'Rumours of what? Come on, boss.'

'Haven't been called that in a long time.' He smiled warmly and adjusted the patch on his eye.

She said, 'I have no idea what I'm dealing with other than two, maybe three people were recently murdered in that house and it's highly likely that two bodies were kept there in freezers for at least twenty years. So far, the house is the only thing connecting them. I am grasping for proverbial straws here.'

'Two bodies kept in freezers? Could it be the father and son?'

'No, one of them was a little girl.'

'Oh. That's terrible.'

'And the girl's skull was found in a different house. I can't make sense of it all.'

'Not much hope of me making sense of it then. But you know how these cases work. All it takes is for one piece of the puzzle to unexpectedly slip into place, and the rest comes together so quickly you can't keep up.'

'I'd give up a good night's sleep this minute to find that one piece.' She stifled a yawn, feeling as if it had been days since she'd put her head on a pillow. 'Can you remember anything about those rumours you mentioned?'

He thought for a while. 'There was talk that the mother had an affair years before the murders. It's amazing how I can remember this now and I haven't a clue what I was doing before you arrived.'

'I'm like that most of the time.'

'Well, we tracked down the man it was supposed to be, but he was out of the country at the time of the murders.' He nursed his forehead.

'If there was an affair, it might have given the husband a motive for murder. Can you remember the name of the man involved?'

Corrigan shook his head slowly. 'I'm afraid there's nothing coming to me. But if I remember it, I'll let you know.'

'Please do, and thanks.'

She handed him page three from the paper, retrieved from the murder file, with a photograph of the family taking up the top half of the page.

'Ah yes. They looked so pleasant. A picture-perfect family.'

'Only they can't have been,' Lottie said. 'It's easy to paint a happy picture and at the same time hide the cracks. This seems to be similar to other cases of familicide. You and I know what people can do to the ones they love the most.'

He read out the names under the photograph, tracing each face with his finger. 'The Doyle girls were so young. Nine and eleven,' he read. 'Angela and Annie. The mother, Sinead, a beauty. Not unlike yourself, Parker.'

'Give over.'

'You can be pretty when you're not fecking scowling.' He looked up at her. 'I can say that now without a case being brought against me.'

'You've said an awful lot worse over the years,' she laughed.

'I have, so I have.'

'Does the photo jog any other memories?' she prompted.

'Poor young Karl. Hadn't many friends, but don't quote me on it. He wasn't into sports or the like, but apparently he was good academically. How do I remember that?' He shook his head, his spectacles sliding a little on his thin nose. 'Wonder where his body is.'

'If he is dead.'

'The consensus was that he escaped the slaughter and the father took off after him. Probably caught up with him, murdered him and either buried his body in a bog or weighed it down in the canal.'

'Was the canal checked at the time?'

'Half-heartedly. If he was dead, sure what could we do? We operated on the assumption that the father had killed him and fled the country.'

'Had he any money?'

'I presume he had cash because I think their bank account wasn't accessed. But check the file. He probably had a stash under a mattress.'

'That would point to a planned kill.'

'Most familicides are planned, aren't they?' He handed the page back to her.

Lottie stared at the photograph. 'The father, Harry Doyle. He was rough-looking round the edges.'

'Not one person had a bad word to say about him. Pillar of the fecking community and all that shite.'

'Not a very stable pillar then. I wonder where he fled to?'

'Most likely he changed his name and identity. Probably in the south of Spain with all the other gangsters, if he's not dead.'

'But if this article is to be believed, Harry Doyle wasn't a gangster. He was a family man until he flipped and killed them. There must have been legs to the rumour of his wife's affair.'

'Look, Parker, I think you're chasing the tail of a ghost with this angle. Find out who's paying for the electricity to the house and that will be your biggest lead.'

Lottie was silent for a few moments. In the old days, Corrigan would have roared at her to get her act together and close the case. But he was now a shadow of the man she'd worked with.

'I told you we found a child's skull the other day too.'

'That was on the news, wasn't it?'

'Yes. The house is number 2 Church View. Owned by a Patsy Cole, now deceased, inherited by her nephew Jeff Cole. Mean anything to you?'

'Not straight off. Sorry. I can't recall it having come up in the familicide case, if that's what you're asking. But as I say, if I do think of anything, I'll let you know.'

'Good.' Lottie stood and stretched before picking up her bag. She had the feeling she'd exhausted her old boss enough. 'Thanks for your time. I really appreciate it.'

'Lottie,' he said. 'You're one of the good ones. Don't let the job get to you.'

'I think it's too late for that.'

CHAPTER SIXTY-ONE

Lottie sat in the car outside her house for a full ten minutes studying the black-and-white photograph under the dim interior light. She stared into Sinead Doyle's eyes, trying to work out if there was any sadness or deceit in them, but she saw only a happy mother.

The girls, standing either side of her, wore matching dresses. She thought of how she used to dress Chloe and Katie similarly and how the girls chastised her whenever they looked at the family photos in their granny's house. A moment of nostalgia swept over her tired shoulders as she thought of all they'd lost in the house fire. Then she looked back at the photo. This was the only evidence she had so far that this family had ever existed.

She'd phoned McKeown to run a search on the Doyles, but so far he hadn't come back to her with anything. He was still waiting for Brandon Carthy to contact him with the names of people he'd let into the recycling centre after hours. She supposed he couldn't beat it out of Carthy, much as she'd like him to. She called him again and told him to visit the man at home. It was a concrete lead and she needed the names.

Her eyes travelled over to the father, Harry Doyle. His hand rested on his wife's shoulder. The gesture appeared possessive. As if his fingers were digging into her bones, claiming her as his and his alone. The photo had been taken two or three years before the massacre, going by the ages of the children when they'd been murdered. Did Doyle know back then about his wife's alleged infidelity? Could that one event have led to him taking a knife and butchering his family? Butchering. Her body convulsed in a spasm as she thought of the little girl's torso and leg. It was too awful to think about the suffering the child had gone through. She wondered if the frozen mutilated bodies were linked to the Doyle family. If so, how? The date on the tag found on the torso was a few months after the family were murdered. Could they really be connected?

Her gaze landed on the boy sitting cross-legged at his mother's feet. He appeared relaxed. A lazy smile curved his mouth, but his eyes came across as sad. What happened to you, Karl? she wondered.

Her front door opened, and she saw Sean standing there with Louis in his arms. The little boy was waving frantically, trying to escape from his young uncle. He should be in bed, Lottie thought as she put away her work and jumped out of the car. As if by magic, her weariness evaporated and she ran to take her grandson in her arms.

*

Boyd could see two of Grace when he sat on his couch. One of her was enough to deal with.

'I'm phoning Lottie,' she said.

'Go ahead, see if I care.'

'Mark, I can't believe you are my brother. What were you thinking of, going out for the afternoon and getting drunk?'

'Grace, I'm tired. I've another hospital appointment tomorrow. I need to sleep.'

'You'll be in some state.'

'It's my problem, not yours.'

'You were doing so well. What if you can't have any more treatment? What if you need a bone marrow transplant? Have you thought of that?'

'We've been through this before.'

'Yes, and you know I'm no use to you. You need to talk to Jackie.'

'What has my ex-wife got to do with any of this?'

'You never know, maybe she was pregnant when you kicked her out all those years ago. Maybe you have a son or a daughter. Someone who could be a match to you.'

'I know I've been drinking, but have you?' Boyd laughed until it hurt. 'Grace, that's the most absurd thing I've heard in a long time.'

'Mam and I talked about it before she died. I think your illness was too much for her. Too big a strain on her heart.'

The laughter died on his lips. 'So along with everything else, you're blaming me for Mam's death?'

'Yes.'

Boyd had never sobered up so quickly in all his life. 'Grace, you have deeply offended me.'

'You sound like a priest.'

'Maybe I need a priest. After all, I might be going to die too.'

'Don't be ridiculous. Make me a cup of tea, will you?'

He got up and went to the kitchen automatically. It was useless to argue with Grace. She was one of a kind. Only their mother could truly handle her. And now he was left to do it alone. It was hard enough even in full health, so how was he expected to deal with her now? Lottie would tell him off for feeling sorry for himself and she'd be right, but that didn't make him feel any better.

As he flicked the kettle on, an awful thought skittered through his brain. He turned to look at his sister.

'Grace? You haven't, have you?'

'What are you talking about?'

'Oh, no, you have. How could you do this to me?'

'Mark Boyd, I have absolutely no idea what you're referring to.' She moved his duvet to the end of the couch, sat down and folded her arms.

He had never known Grace to tell a lie, but now he was sure she was fibbing.

'You contacted Jackie. How could you?'

'Oh, that? No, I didn't, but Mam did. Anyway, Jackie didn't want to know.'

'That figures.' He turned away from her and leaned his forehead against the cool timber of the overhead cupboard. He could do without this. 'Make your own tea. I've got to go and talk to Lottie.'

'You'd better walk, because you're in no fit state to drive.'

'Would you ever shut up?'

He grabbed his jacket and keys and made sure he banged the door on the way out.

CHAPTER SIXTY-TWO

Marianne watched Kevin as he held the newspaper up to his face. She knew he was glaring at her from behind it.

'Kevin, we have to talk.'

'Now you want to talk?' he said, shaking the newspaper.

'There's no need for that tone.'

'Do you even know where I was for two hours this evening?'

'I don't know where you are any evening,' she said.

He dropped the newspaper to his lap and folded it over once, then, unable to find the original crease, balled it up and flung it across the room.

'Where were you?'

'I was in the garda station.'

'What?' She felt her heart skip a beat then thump double-time. 'I said nothing to her, I swear to God.'

'You said nothing to who?'

'Lottie Parker. Sean's mum. She was here earlier.'

'What was she doing here?'

'I don't really know. She was asking about poor Tamara and Gavin.'

'Don't feel too sorry for Tamara. She'll sell her grief all over Instagram.' Kevin gnawed at a piece of skin on his thumb and Marianne felt her stomach turn.

'Why were you in the garda station?'

'They were asking all sorts about the murders. Did you know that Aaron Frost, the estate agent, is dead?'

'What?'

'Yeah. He's been murdered.'

'Murdered? How? When?' She hoped Kevin didn't know that Aaron had been round this week. Last year he had hit the roof when she wanted to sell up and move. He'd put a stop to any valuation being made on the house. At the time, she'd thought he'd figured out she wanted the money to flee with Ruby.

'How do I know?' he said. 'I didn't do it.'

Marianne slumped back on her chair. That sweet young man who'd been here in the house only a couple of days ago. 'When was he killed?'

'I told you, I don't know.' He went to the dresser and poured himself a large drink. 'They were asking me all sorts of odd questions.'

'Kevin?'

'What?' He sat back down and kicked the newspaper to the side of the chair.

'Where were you last night?'

'Where were *you*?'

'I was at Tamara's. She didn't know where Gavin was, and I sat with her for a few hours.'

'Really?'

'Yeah, really. She's my friend. She was supposed to be on the television with Gavin this morning. I didn't know the boy was dead until Lottie Parker called round.'

'Why did she call here?'

'To ask me about Tamara.'

'Why, though?'

'How do I know? Probably because I was over there last night.' She stared at her husband as his cheeks began to redden. 'You were in a flittering rage when I got in. I'm still aching. So, where were you?'

'I was just out. Driving around. I'm under so much pressure at work. Unattainable targets. Nightmare clients. Lazy colleagues and a boss on my back. You don't know the half of it. God, Marianne, I'm so tired, but don't think you can fool me. I know all about you.'

'What do you think you know?'

'You and your toy boys.'

She laughed wryly. She wanted a drink but he hadn't even offered her one. 'You know nothing, Kevin.'

'I know you had him in the house on Monday. That's why you washed the sheets. I was a little worried about it, but not any more, because now he's dead. Suck that and see how it tastes.'

The look in his eyes was dark and demonic. Marianne pulled her feet up under her and tucked her chin down. She didn't want him to see her cry over the young man who'd run away from her.

'I don't know what you're talking about.'

'Aaron Frost. I found his card on the counter.'

'You killed him,' she said at last.

'I didn't, but if I'd known it was him, then yes, Marianne, I would have killed him.'

'You are evil.'

'I have done bad things, I will admit. I can't tell you what they are, but if you keep this up, mark my words, I will kill *you*.' He put his glass on the coffee table and picked up the newspaper. 'I'm putting this out in the bin.'

She let out a strangled cry as he exited the room. When she looked up, her daughter was standing in the doorway, her face shrouded in a mask of hatred.

*

After a late dinner, Chloe and Katie surprised Lottie by telling her to watch television in the sitting room while they cleaned up. She didn't need to be told twice.

Sean was watching a rerun of *The Chase* and shouting out the answers.

'How do you know so many of them?' she asked as she made herself comfortable in an armchair with Louis in her arms. Her grandson was dressed for bed in his colourful pyjamas.

'This is the third time I've seen this episode,' Sean said.

'Watch something else. Scroll through the menu. I'm sure there's something you haven't seen before.'

'Here, you scroll. I'm not bothered.'

Lottie took the remote control from her son. He was scrunched into the chair like an untidy pile of laundry waiting to be picked up. 'What's the matter, Sean?'

'Russia.'

'What?'

'The right answer. That dope just went for Canada.'

Pressing the off button, Lottie waited for Sean to object, but he remained where he was, staring at the blank screen.

'Peppa. Peppa,' Louis shouted.

'In a minute, pet.'

'Now, Nana.'

She switched the television back on and keyed in the code she knew by heart, the most used code on the remote. When the pink pig began to squeal, Louis nestled contentedly against her chest. She inhaled the freshness of his hair. Katie looked after him so well. She wondered if her daughter looked after herself. She needed to work or go to college, but she'd slipped into an easy way of living and Lottie was too caught up in work and Boyd's illness to discuss anything. Live and let live had become her motto. But Sean worried her.

'What's bothering you? Tell me, Sean.'

'I can't.'

'Why not?'

'I promised.'

'I'm your mother. You can tell me anything.'

'And you'll tell Boyd and he'll tell Kirby and then the whole of Ragmullin will be gossiping about the cop's son. You know how it works, Mam.'

'That's unfair. Boyd doesn't gossip.' Maybe she should ask Boyd to try find out what was bothering him.

'Forget it. I'm fine.'

Still he did not move. She knew he really did want to talk.

'Is everything okay at school?'

'Duh. Nothing's ever okay at school.'

'It's almost the summer break.'

'It's not school.'

Silence reigned between mother and son, while Louis giggled at the antics of the pink cartoon character.

'I was talking to Ruby's mother today,' Lottie said. 'She—'

'I knew it!' Sean shouted. 'I just knew it.' He jumped up, and Louis startled. Lottie held him tightly.

'Jesus, Sean, you scared Louis.'

'Jesus, Jesus,' the little boy parroted with delight, knowing he was saying something he shouldn't.

'Look, Louis, Peppa is in a muddy puddle,' Lottie said.

'Muddy puddle,' squealed the child.

'Sean. Sit down.'

He slumped back into the chair and put his feet on the coffee table, crossing his ankles. Lottie grimaced but didn't comment on the act of defiance.

'I don't want to talk about it. It's obvious you've said enough already,' Sean moaned.

'Sean Parker, I have no idea what's got into you. Have you had a falling-out with Ruby?'

'Her mother, more like. What did you say to her?'

'I called there today, but it was to do with work. She mentioned you'd been there with Ruby yesterday. That's all.'

'Well, you said something, because she practically accused me of telling you things I shouldn't, but I have no idea what she was talking about.'

Lottie smoothed Louis' hair against his scalp, trying to recall her conversation with Marianne.

'I said nothing about you, Sean. Nothing.'

'Why were you there then?'

'It was connected with a case I'm working on. It's absolutely nothing to do with you.'

'Peppa!' Louis said.

She noticed the ad break was on, so she scrolled up to the plus-one channel. Peppa lit up the screen again and Louis quietened down.

'What case?' Sean said, removing his feet from the table. Interested now.

'I can't tell you anything about it.'

'But how would Ruby's mother be able to help you? She's just a writer.'

'It was nothing to do with that.' Then it dawned on Lottie. 'What exactly did she say to you?'

'I was so shocked, I'm not sure exactly. But it was as if I'd told you something she didn't want known.'

'I would never betray your confidence. You have to believe me.' Lottie stood with her grandson in her arms. 'Time for bed, Louis.'

'More Peppa.'

'Tomorrow.'

'Mam, what's the case you're working?' Sean said.

'I have a number of cases on the go at the moment.'

'I'll put Louis to bed for you if you tell me.'

Her bones were tired from the long day and she had to be up early. She kissed Louis on the head and handed him to Sean.

'Okay. Get him off to sleep and I'll tell you some of it. Deal?'

'Deal.'

Lottie wondered just how much she could tell him, but maybe he could give her an insight into Ruby's family. She needed to find out more about them. Quickly.

Twenty years earlier

It was when he told me his version of the truth that I lashed out at him. My father. The first blow with the hammer knocked him clean off his feet. I hadn't meant to hit him so hard. I only wanted to shut him up. His words were like knives through my soul. He said he was speaking the truth. I knew it was all lies. I'd lived my life on an increasing mountain of lies until I could no longer remember the original truth.

I had to shut him up.

The others came into the room then. Horror streaked across their faces when they saw what I had done.

'You've only gone and killed him!' the woman shrieked through her drug-fuelled haze.

'I didn't mean to,' I said. 'He wouldn't shut up.'

'What are we going to do?'

Her husband was quiet. Stoned, most likely. He took the hammer from my hand and brought it down with force onto the face of the man I'd called my father for fourteen years. Bone shattered and blood spurted. He was dead now.

'He deserved it,' I said. I wasn't really sure if that was true or not, but it was the truth I would believe from now on.

'I'll never get the blood out of the curtains,' the woman complained.

'Fetch me the sharpest knife from the kitchen,' her husband told her.

'What for?'

'I need to cut him up. We can't just leave him here.'

'Jesus Christ. He was your friend,' she said. 'We have to call the guards.'

'There will be no guards coming into this house. No guards.' His voice was steelier than I'd ever heard. Violent, almost. I'd never known him to be violent, this man who was my father's friend, but I knew he'd been drinking and doing drugs. I'd seen the traces of cocaine in the bathroom when I brushed my teeth in the mornings. And here he was, with a bloody hammer in his hand, looking for a sharp knife, and my father dead at his feet.

It had to be the drugs, I thought as he took the carving knife from her and sliced it across my father's neck.

'The hammer almost decapitated him,' he said.

'What are you doing?' I asked.

'You killed him, and I have to get rid of the body.'

'I didn't kill him. You did.' But I was hoping I had killed him. He was part of my life of lies.

'Doesn't matter,' the man said, and I noticed his speech slurring. 'He's dead now. Put your arms across his chest and I'll work on the neck.'

'I'll be covered in blood,' I protested.

'You already are, you dimwit. Hold tight.'

I did as I was told. As he sliced, blood sluiced onto the floor, and I wondered how it was ever going to wash out, and where we were going to put the body pieces. So, I asked him.

'We'll cut him up small. Flush some down the toilet and the rest we'll freeze until we figure out what to do with them.'

'That's barbaric,' the woman said.

'No more damage can be done to the child. This man was a bad egg and now he has to answer to a higher court for his actions.'

For a man high on drugs and alcohol, he was thinking too clearly. I wasn't. I wasn't thinking at all, not at that time. I did what I was told, and I was relieved. After all, the one person who knew my secret was dead. I did not pause to think that there were now three of us with an even bigger secret.

It wasn't long after when I attacked again. Maybe a month after my father's death.

I never liked their daughter. She was five years younger than me, and if truth be told, she was an imbecile. Always asking why and what about absolutely everything. Never shut the fuck up. Always in the house. Never at school. Home-schooled, the woman had said through a pall of cannabis smoke.

I was minding my own business when I heard the door creak behind me as the girl tried to sneak into the room. With her croaking voice she told me she'd seen me kill him. What was I to do? I picked up the poker from the fireplace with its horrible tiger tiles and hit her. I caught her in the middle of the forehead and she fell at my feet. I wasn't sure if she was dead, so I got down on my knees and strangled the nine years of life out of her.

When the woman found us, I passed her death off as an accident.

'We were messing, and she fell,' I said. She didn't see the marks of my fingers like a necklace around her neck. She only saw her dead daughter.

'Dear God in heaven. My poor pet.' She cradled the girl's bashed skull. 'What have you done? You evil, evil child.'

That was another thing that annoyed me. Repetition. She was always repeating herself. I put it down to a lack of education, which led to her having little vocabulary. Her husband had left home shortly after freezing parts of my father's body and flushing other parts down the toilet. I couldn't stand the way he looked at me afterwards. I was glad he had left, but I admired the way he dealt with the body. That experience would help me now as I looked at the girl, dead in the junkie woman's arms.

'I'll get a knife,' I said.

'What?' she wailed. 'Call an ambulance.'

'An ambulance is of no use to her now. She's dead. We'll just cut her up and put her in the freezer. Actually, you might need to buy another freezer.'

Her eyes flared and her nostrils ran with thick white mucus. God, but I hated her. Ignoring her cries, I went to the kitchen and selected the longest and sharpest knife from the butcher's block. Then, through the window, I saw the axe sticking out of a pile of logs in the back garden. Perfect.

In the living room, she cowered, holding the dead child.

'Don't worry. I don't intend to hurt you. But listen to me carefully. If you don't keep your mouth shut and do exactly as I say, I will slice your nephew's head off. I know about Jeff, even though you haven't allowed him to visit since we arrived. You don't want his blood on your hands, do you? You can tell anyone who asks that your daughter is gone to live with your husband. End of story.'

She began to shake and shiver, and I kneeled down beside her and lifted her chin with the tip of the knife. 'Do you understand me?'

She didn't reply. She just nodded and let her child fall from her grasp to the floor. I picked up the axe and began my grim task.

CHAPTER SIXTY-THREE

Thursday

Lottie woke to a grey morning, no light streaming through the gap in the curtains. There was a mug of coffee turning cold on her bedside cabinet, and Katie was standing in the doorway.

'Morning, sweetheart,' Lottie said. 'All okay?'

'I have to talk to you.'

Patting the bed, she scooted over to the middle and waited while Katie sat down.

'This will be hard for you to swallow,' Katie said.

'I can drink any kind of coffee first thing in the morning.'

'Don't try to be funny. This is serious.'

'I've a strong constitution, so try me.' She sipped the coffee, wishing it was hotter, dreading whatever her daughter had to say.

'If it's something to do with the shit your work throws up, you're strong, but when it comes to us, your family, I think you're a pussy cat.'

Laughing, Lottie spluttered the coffee out over the white sheet. 'Oh feck.'

'I'll throw it in the wash when you're at work.'

She placed the mug back on the cabinet. This was going to be some serious shit. 'What is it, Katie?'

'I don't want to go back to college. Wait a minute before you object. I know you're hell-bent on me extending my education, but it's been too long, and I can't ever see myself back studying.'

'You will have to get a job. I'm stretched as it is.'

'That's the thing. I don't want to work here. There are only shit jobs in bars and I don't want to do that. I'm not like Chloe.'

Katie was her firstborn and Adam had spoiled her rotten. That sense of entitlement had stretched into womanhood. She was almost twenty-two and had never worked anywhere. Getting pregnant at nineteen had put paid to her studies, and once she'd had Louis, she'd not returned to college. What was she going to do with her life? Lottie tensed and her mouth dried up. She knew.

'No, Katie. I don't want you to emigrate to America. Please don't do that to me.'

'But Mam, Tom has a job lined up for me in his company, a place to stay, a nanny. It sounds perfect.'

'No,' Lottie repeated. She jumped out of bed on the far side, pulled on a hoodie and stood at the window with her back to her daughter. 'It won't work out. It's too far away. I'll never see you or Louis. Please, don't go.' She turned around. 'You don't have a green card or whatever it's called.'

'Uncle Leo said he'll help out with the visa.'

Lottie's resolve not to get angry snapped. 'He isn't your uncle. You don't know him. I don't know him. He waltzes into our lives after a … a hundred years, thinking he can fix the world. Well, he can't.'

Katie stood, picked up the mug and headed for the door. 'Mam, I have to try it out at least.'

'What about us? What about Chloe and Sean?'

'Listen, Mam, it's my life. I have to do what's best for me and Louis. Ragmullin is a hole. I'm not spending my life here. Tom has offered me an opportunity and I'm taking it.'

Lottie rushed to her, held her by her elbows, the coffee spilling onto the floor as the girl tried to steady the mug. But she didn't care. She didn't want to lose her daughter or her little grandson.

'Katie, is this about Boyd? About me and him getting married? If it is, I'll … I'll talk to him. We can put it off. Honestly. I want to keep our family together. That's what your dad would want me to do.'

Katie wrestled free. 'No, Mam. It has nothing to do with Boyd. Dad would want you to be happy. He'd want me to be happy. And right now, I'm not happy here.'

'Think of Sean and Chloe. Your granny. They all love you. I love you.'

'Mam, I want to do this. Please let me go without making me feel guilty.'

She marched out of the bedroom, her head held high, her back straight, her hair somehow gleaming in the dull morning light. She was determined and pig-headed, as headstrong as Lottie herself.

Lottie burst into tears and sank to the floor, hugging her knees to her chest like a child. Her daughter had been through so much. She deserved to make a new life for herself and her son, but at what cost?

'Stop being selfish,' she admonished herself, standing up and wiping her tears on the coffee-stained sheet. She grabbed a towel and walked to the shower. Just before she switched it on, her phone rang on the bed.

Dropping the towel on the floor, she retrieved the phone and checked the caller ID. Grace Boyd. With trembling fingers, she answered the call.

CHAPTER SIXTY-FOUR

Jack wasn't hungry. He left the bowl on the table, Weetabix congealing on the rim, and pulled back the patio doors, walking out around the back of the house. The sky had not yet awoken fully. It was grey and dull, and a few drops of rain hit his bare arms. Blackbirds huddled on the branches of the trees as if they knew something he didn't. Probably a storm on the horizon. He didn't care one way or the other. He walked round to the front and stood looking out over the canal. He saw the two gardaí keeping watch in the squad car. He wanted his drone back. Then he realised he would no longer have Gavin to fly it with, and he felt the sadness all over again.

Sitting on the damp grass, he felt around in his trouser pocket. It was there. He knew he should have told the detective about it last night. Maybe he could tell that FLO woman, but she seemed cross and moody. Or maybe he could give it to one of the guards in the car. He got up and walked towards the vehicle.

'Jack? What are you doing out there? Your breakfast is on the table. Come inside this instant and finish it. It's nearly time for school.'

His mother's voice melted his resolve. He shoved the USB stick back in his pocket and followed her into the house.

*

Breakfast was a flash point in her house, and Ruby was determined that this shite could not go on any longer. Her mother had appeared downstairs this morning without make-up; the yellow and purple bruises on her face made her look like a Picasso painting.

The two slices of toast popped up, and she jumped. Grabbing them, she set about buttering them noisily.

'I'll do you some eggs,' Marianne said. 'You like eggs. Protein for a growing girl.'

'Don't put on an act around me, Mum. I don't need it. I know what's going on in this house and sooner or later you have to kick him out.'

'Shh. Your dad is outside sorting out the bins. I hope you didn't put anything in the wrong one, or there'll be hell to pay.'

The back door opened and shut. Ruby felt the large kitchen shrink in on top of her. Kevin stood brandishing two empty plastic Coke bottles.

'How many times do I have to tell you, you have to crush the bottles and leave the lids off. This is ridiculous. Does no one in this house listen to me any more? And I told you not to buy plastic!'

Ruby chewed her toast and Marianne stood with the coffee pot in her hand, her mouth zipped shut. This morning she knew silence was the best form of defence.

'And another thing,' Kevin ranted, 'I've told you a thousand times, I'm in charge of the bins. I don't need you messing up my routine. In future, leave them to me. Because you know what? I'm the only one around here who does things right.'

'Is that what you think?'

Ruby had the words out of her mouth before she realised it. She heard the empty bottles bounce on the floor and the thump on her shoulder knocked the toast from her hand. She jumped up, sending the chair flying, and squared up to her father. She found that she was maybe half an inch taller than him, and that gave her a false sense of confidence.

'Don't you dare hit me.' She thought the voice came from someone else, but no, she'd dredged it, full of loathing, from the pit of her own stomach. 'You might be able to beat up Mum, but you won't do it to me. I've had enough of your bullying.' She was trembling all over, sweat pulsing on her skin; even her feet in her socks felt wet. 'And do not hit my mother again. Ever. Or I'll report you.'

A slow smirk widened across her father's face.

'Is that so?' he said, and moved to the back door.

Ruby thought she'd won. Her hands trembled with elation and she breathed out, but her father turned quickly and wrapped his arm around her throat, choking her.

He was going to kill her. Here in the kitchen in front of her silent mother.

'Kevin! Stop!'

Marianne's voice was strong and loud. It stilled her father and he dropped his arm, the fight appearing to desert him.

'I'm sorry. I didn't mean it,' he said, letting Ruby go.

She landed on the floor and Kevin pushed past Marianne, his footsteps echoing up the stairs.

When her mother held her in her arms, Ruby's tears fell in fat drops down her face. She knew this couldn't go on. She would have to do something. Something drastic.

CHAPTER SIXTY-FIVE

Boyd had got dressed at 6 a.m. without taking a shower, in case the noise of the water disturbed Grace. He had slipped out of the house before she opened an eye, and set off. She would be angry, but she'd get over it. And Lottie? No, he wasn't going to think about her this morning.

That was where he'd been heading last night, but he hadn't got far. Walked to the end of the road before deciding she had enough troubles of her own without him offloading his, so he'd doubled back to his apartment. He'd been relieved to find Grace in bed, the door firmly shut. Lying on the couch, he'd pulled the duvet up to his chin, determined to sort out their living arrangements the next day. After his early-morning hospital appointment. Hopefully today he would get good news; perhaps it would be the last day of his treatment. Then he could return to work. Once he got his energy back and lost the fatigue.

The nurse had taken his blood to be tested and he sat in the waiting room thinking how Lottie would go apeshit when she found out he'd come here alone. He picked up a discarded newspaper and began to flick through it without anything registering. His blood better be okay.

The door opened and in strolled the tall man who'd fled the other day. Without a glance, he moved to the farthest corner and sat on a straight-backed chair beneath a mute television streaming advertisements.

Boyd studied him. Why had he disappeared when he'd seen Lottie? Maybe it was nothing to do with her. Hadn't she said the man's son – Jack, that was his name – had found the body parts on the railway? Must have been traumatic for the boy and the family. Perhaps he had been waiting for news he might have suspected would be bad and had lost his nerve at the last minute.

The man was twisting his hands into knots; when he caught Boyd staring, he shoved them into his pockets, stretching his long legs out in front of him.

'Bit of a change in the weather,' Boyd said, folding the newspaper.

'Suppose so.'

It was clear from his body language that he didn't want to converse. Undeterred, Boyd said, 'Are you waiting for treatment?'

The man shrugged one shoulder.

Boyd said, 'I'm hoping today sees my last chemo. That's if my platelets behave. Damn things were so far down the scale the other day they had to send out a search party.' He'd thought the quip might make the man grin, but his face remained like a concrete block.

He added, 'But I'm hopeful.'

'Aye.'

'And yourself? Is it chemo or radium?'

'Don't want to talk about it.'

'It's good to talk.' Not wanting to bore the man with the specifics of his disease, Boyd decided to generalise. 'I've got leukaemia. Not the worst form as far as I can determine, but it's still cancer.'

The man nodded silently.

'And yourself?' he persisted.

'Waiting for results.'

'The waiting is the worst. I thought I might need a bone marrow transplant or stem cells, whatever they call it, but I hope it won't come to that. I've no one that I can ask to donate, and the donor lists are a minefield.'

'What do you mean?'

'Oh, not enough people registered. Or something like that.' In truth Boyd wasn't sure how the donor lists worked and hoped he would never have to find out.

The man said, 'I checked it out. Just in case.'

'And do you have a relative that can donate if you need it?'

The man stared up at the flickering fluorescent light. A buzzing fly was caught in the surrounding casing. 'It's complicated. My son …' His voice faltered. 'It's complicated.'

Boyd could see flashes of anger in his eyes. Obviously the man didn't want to put his son through the procedure. 'Hard on a young fellow. What age is he?'

'Who?'

'Your son.'

'Er … nine.'

'Very young. Hopefully it won't come to that then.'

A nurse opened the door, 'Charlie Sheridan? Mr Saka will see you now.'

'Nice to meet you,' Charlie said as he passed.

Left to his thoughts, Boyd wondered why the man was so on edge. He'd have a word with Lottie when he got back, if she was still speaking to him once she found out he'd driven to the hospital alone.

CHAPTER SIXTY-SIX

The coffee was tepid. Lottie grimaced as she reread the various forensic reports that had just arrived. The words flickered in and out of focus. Her mind was full of the conversation with Katie, which was quickly followed by Grace's angry phone call about Boyd driving himself to the hospital. Boyd was a stubborn fool. She shook away her frustration and tried to concentrate on the reports, noting down the salient points.

Fingerprints found on the inside of the boot of Faye Baker's car were a match for Aaron Frost. Shit, she thought. Frost was dead, so she couldn't question him. Obviously. They'd also found plenty of other DNA in the boot, which had been rushed through the Dublin forensics lab. Plenty of unexplained DNA. But they'd identified Jeff's, Faye's and Aaron's, and one other that made Lottie raise her eyebrows as she read. DNA had been recovered from a hair attached to Faye's body. It was not a match for anything in their database, but there were enough markers to point to it being a relative of Aaron. Interesting. She'd have to interrogate Mrs Frost again.

The next report informed her that fibres from the carpet at 2 Church View matched those found on the frozen torso. And here was the kicker. The fingerprints from the hand matched unidentified fingerprints taken at the Doyle crime scene over twenty years previously. Was this the father, Harry Doyle? Or someone else who had massacred the Doyle family? She shook her head, trying to clear it. There had been no DNA filed at the time of the Doyle case, only fingerprints. It was too far back, an era before DNA databases were compiled in Ireland. Harry Doyle had absconded and disappeared, so at the time there was no way to confirm if the fingerprints were his or not.

'This gets weirder,' Lottie said, as McKeown loped into her office.

'I can add to it,' he said. 'Brandon Carthy sent me the list of people he'd given the gate code to.'

'Many on it?' Lottie despaired of ever getting a lead if it was a long one.

'Four names.'

'And?'

'One of them is Kevin O'Keeffe.'

'What the f—'

'Exactly. I checked the CCTV images again, and the car is similar to the saloon O'Keeffe drives, though we can't determine the registration number on the image.'

'Get O'Keeffe in here, and his car too. What about the other names on the list?'

'None of the others have a car similar to the one on the CCTV, and their alibis all check out for the relevant time.'

'Right, we need to talk to O'Keeffe, so,' Lottie said.

Kirby peered around McKeown's large frame. 'I've news too. Marianne O'Keeffe has just been on the phone. She was looking for you, but you'd said you weren't to be disturbed, so I spoke with her.'

'What did she say?'

'She wants to make a complaint about her husband. Says he beat her up the night before last. The same night that Aaron Frost was murdered. She said she had a thing with Aaron – a non-thing really because he didn't accept her advances. However, she believes Kevin somehow found out and followed Aaron and killed him.'

'Under normal circumstances I'd say that's some leap in deduction, but O'Keeffe couldn't give us an alibi for that night. If it is his car dumping Gavin's body, I'm inclined to give Marianne's hypothesis some credence. Is he our killer? If he is, what reason has he for killing a defenceless eleven-year-old boy?'

McKeown said, 'I still think Gavin stumbled on Aaron's murder and was killed for it. O'Keeffe is a bastard. I'll bring him in.'

'Hold on a minute.' Lottie stood up but sat down quickly again. The office was tiny, and with three of them in there, the air had thinned considerably. 'We can be sure O'Keeffe will reply no comment to our questions, so we need to be certain of everything. I want all the evidence studied in light of this new information. Find out where O'Keeffe is and stick someone on him so that he doesn't make a run for it. See if his car has turned up on any other CCTV over the last few days. We need to see where he went and what he did.'

'Right, boss,' McKeown said.

'Find me the evidence and then we can arrest him. We've slipped up in the past making arrests before we've had an airtight case, and people have walked. Look at the evidence with a critical eye. In the meantime, prepare a warrant and get it signed so that we can search his car. Kirby, is Marianne coming in to make a statement?'

'She was adamant she wanted to speak with you, so I kind of promised you'd call to her house this morning. Hope that's okay.'

'It's not. I haven't got time. Did she say where her husband is?'

'She said he took their daughter to school and then he's heading to work.'

'Make sure he's being watched.' Lottie looked over at McKeown. 'We need to get our heads around all this. Find someone to replace Lynch at the Sheridans'.'

'Okay.'

'I know we're doubling up here, but I asked you for everything you could find on the Doyle familicide case. Did you track down the file?'

'Yeah. Eventually found it listed on PULSE. It had been entered incorrectly, but that's another day's work.'

'I need to go through it. The forensic report is back and the fingerprints from the dismembered hand are a near match for prints taken from the original crime scene twenty years ago. There was a lot of deterioration, but they found enough markers to be confident. It's possible the hand is that of Harry Doyle, who allegedly murdered his family and absconded with his son.'

'Jesus. I'll get the file,' McKeown said.

Once she was alone, Lottie scrutinised the forensic report again. No matter which way she looked at it, she could not figure out how the current murders were linked, but they were. She knew it in her gut.

CHAPTER SIXTY-SEVEN

Kirby was munching his way through a Happy Meal, his food of choice when he was broke. Lottie stood beside him.

'I thought I told you to find O'Keeffe and have him watched,' she said.

'I've sent a squad to sit outside his office. I got the file on the derelict house at Canal Lane from Ferris and Frost.'

'Oh good.' Lottie stole his coffee, removed the lid and gulped down a good mouthful, even though it was cold. 'And bring Jeff Cole in for interview. I want to talk to him again now that we know his DNA is a partial match to the torso.'

Kirby stuffed a chicken nugget in his mouth. He chewed then swallowed. 'Sorry, I bought this on the way in and hadn't time to eat it.'

'What else did you get from the estate agent's?'

'First off, Dave Murphy says Aaron didn't have an apartment anywhere else.' He handed her the file. 'But Ferris and Frost have a caretaker agreement on the abandoned house. Aaron Frost was the registered occupier for electricity bills. The agreement came into force two years ago. Nothing to say who owned it before. I'm going to check that out as soon as I can.'

'Yes, do that. We'll need to speak with Aaron's mother again. Did the tech guys find anything on his laptop?'

'Still working on it, but so far, not even a porn site. They're talking about shipping it off to Dublin to see if the experts there can find anything.'

'Why would Aaron end up dead in a freezer in a derelict house that was the scene of horrific murders years ago?'

'Questions beget questions.'

'Don't think that's the correct quote, Kirby.' She sat on the edge of his desk and tried to think straight. 'Aaron's fingerprints were in Faye's car and he had access to the keys, so we could deduce therefore that he disposed of Faye Baker and her unborn child. Did he kill her too? Did he kill Gavin? But if he did, who killed *him*? Which brings me to Kevin O'Keeffe. How does he fit into the picture? A few minutes ago, I had him down for all the murders, but none of it makes sense.'

Kirby munched a handful of fries. 'What's O'Keeffe got to do with Faye Baker?'

'I believe he knew Faye was dead before the fact was released to the media, though we know that means fuck all nowadays. But here's the thing. We've yet to prove it, but it's likely O'Keeffe's car was used to dump young Gavin's body.'

'We have to bring him in!'

'Wait. We must be sure of all the evidence first. McKeown is working on a warrant for the car. It needs to be forensically searched.'

Kirby crushed the empty Happy Meal box and stuffed it in his already overflowing waste bin. 'You said to look at all the evidence. I've been thinking about the blue paint flecks found on the torso. The lab said they were from a recycling bin. We should get McKeown to extend the warrant for O'Keeffe's bins while he's at it.'

'Not sure we have enough to ask for a full house search. It's possible we might be able to place his car at the recycling depot, but not the man himself. Ask the tech guys if the CCTV footage can be digitally enhanced. We need to be certain of everything before I fuck it up.'

'Holy Mother of God, boss, you couldn't fuck it up if you tried.' He ran his greasy hands through his unruly bush of hair, leaving it standing on end.

'Too early in the morning for sarcasm, Kirby.'

'I was serious.'

Lottie heard her phone ringing. If it was Boyd, now was definitely not a good time. But it was her old boss, Corrigan.

'I saw the news last night and it came back to me,' he said without preamble.

'What came back to you?'

'What we were discussing yesterday. About the Doyle murder case all those years ago.'

'Yes, of course.'

'You have to bear with me. This brain of mine is fecked. But I remembered the name of the man Sinead Doyle was rumoured to have had an affair with. It was Frost.'

When Lottie hung up to the sound of her old boss chortling down the phone, delighted he could still be of some use to an active case despite dementia chewing up his brain, she had two texts on her mobile. Both from Boyd. Things were gathering pace in the investigation. What if he had bad news? Could she handle it? Oh God, she thought, not now, Boyd.

Ignoring the texts, she grabbed her jacket from the back of the chair and her bag from the floor, and with Lynch not yet back from the Sheridans' and everyone else busy, headed out on her own.

Could she be on the verge of finding the connection between Aaron Frost and the dismembered bodies?

*

McKeown secured the warrant for O'Keeffe's car without delay. When Lynch was relieved of her FLO duties by Garda Martina Brennan, he headed into town with her. They walked around the small car park at the back of the office where Kevin O'Keeffe worked.

'I can't see his car here,' he said.

'That's because it's not here.' Lynch moved around the side of the building and opened the door. 'You know I should be home in bed?'

'Not now, Lynch.'

'Just saying.'

He followed her up a flight of stairs and into the open-plan office.

'Hi,' a young woman said, lifting her head from the computer screen in front of her. 'Can I help you?'

McKeown and Lynch introduced themselves and showed their ID.

'What's your name, miss?' McKeown said, wondering how her eyelids could hold the weight of her lashes.

'Karen Tierney.'

'Well, Karen, we'd like a word with Mr O'Keeffe.'

'Kevin isn't in yet. Some days he's a bit late, but Shane, our manager, has let it go so far.'

'Is that so?' McKeown flashed his widest smile and Karen actually blushed.

'Between you and me, he has a lot to contend with at home. It's all *her* fault.'

'Whose fault?'

'The wife. Marianne. She drinks, according to Kevin. He spends the morning cleaning up after her. So he says.'

'So he says,' McKeown repeated, and threw Lynch a knowing glance. 'Here's my number. When Kevin arrives, please don't say we were here. Just ring me.'

'Has he done something wrong?' Karen looked around frantically at her colleagues. 'Have we reason to be worried?'

Lynch butted in. 'Just ring us when he comes in.'

'You have me terrified now. You see, I found that poor girl's body in the car at the station, and Kevin went a bit loopy with me after that.'

'Loopy?' McKeown moved to the edge of her desk. 'What do you mean?'

'He came to my flat asking all sorts of questions. I told the other detective. I think she's an inspector.'

'That'd be Detective Inspector Lottie Parker,' he said.

'Did you not know about it?' Karen asked.

'It's very busy at the station with all the murders. Just mind yourself. And phone us if Kevin arrives.'

McKeown followed Lynch out of the office without a backward glance at the terrified young woman he'd left behind. It was better to have her warned, especially if she was working with a murderer.

*

Ruby O'Keeffe could not remember the last time her father had driven her to school. But he'd been contrite after their morning spat, and apologised, saying his job was getting to him. She had agreed to his offer of a lift, despite an urge to tell him to stuff it up his hole.

She had sat into the car, earbuds firmly in to block out his conversation, and left her mother peering out the window with a worried expression creased into her brow.

But her father did not drive her to school. Instead he headed out of town, along the lake road, and now they were sitting in the car on the shores of Lough Cullion. A narrow road along by the railway tracks had brought them here, and she wondered what it was her father wanted to tell her. So far, the only sound was Ryan Tubridy talking nineteen to the dozen on the radio.

'Dad, why are we here?' she said, freeing her ears of the buds.

'We have to talk.'

'Why are we in Mum's car?'

'Because mine was out of diesel.'

'I should be in school. This is the last week before the holidays, and I know I usually hate school, but I don't want to miss the last couple of days. Me and Sean, well, we have our project to complete.'

In truth, the prospect of school was not as awful as sitting here with her dad.

'Fuck Sean,' he said.

'Dad?'

'And fuck you. Fuck your mother. Fuck everyone.'

Ruby said nothing. Was she about to pay for her earlier outburst? She wanted to kill her father, to smash his face in, but suddenly she felt powerless to do anything other than sit beside this man she felt she hated.

She huddled against the side window, her legs stretched out in the footwell, her bag on the seat between them, and said nothing. The water lapped hungrily up over the stones on the shore. A family of swans glided gracefully across the grey surface. At peace. Ruby wished she could experience some peace without her father around. She wished she was at home in her room, living in her virtual world of computer gaming.

Silence filled the car.

Then her father spoke.

'I haven't been a great dad to you. Haven't been a great husband to your mother. There are things going on in my life that I can't talk about. I've messed up badly. Very badly. I did things because I was greedy. I was offered a way to make some money, and I lost sight of what was important. I think your mother will report me for beating her. I've been under pressure at work and … other things. I was out of control and I'm a person who likes to be able to control everything and everyone. The guards have interviewed me. They will do so again, and a lot of things will be revealed in the coming days and weeks. But I want you to believe this. I never did anything to intentionally hurt you.'

'You hurt Mum.'

'That woman brings it on herself. I know you see me as the villain. I know all that. But it's her own fucking fault.'

'Dad, there is no justification for hitting another human being. None.' She surprised herself with the conviction in her tone. 'You're just a big bully. Like the kids in my school who don't get their own way. You use your fists to show your superiority and—'

'Shut the fuck up.'

The slap caught her unawares. A clanging noise reverberated deep in the chambers of her ear. She'd thought they were having a father–daughter talk. She was wrong. The only way her father could talk, could get his point across, was with his fists.

She knew she had to get out of the car. To get away from this man who no longer acted like a true dad should. But the door was locked. She was trapped with a madman.

'Unlock the door, Dad. You're scaring me.'

'You will sit there and keep your mouth shut and listen to what I have to tell you.'

Without any other option, Ruby nodded. She would have to bide her time. There was no way her father was getting away with this. No way on earth.

And then he started to talk, and she realised just how terrifying her situation was.

While Kevin spoke, Ruby worked her fingers on the phone in her pocket. She had to let someone know where she was.

CHAPTER SIXTY-EIGHT

Lottie knew that Corrigan's information might have nothing to do with anything. Because of his illness, he could be totally wrong, but she had to talk to Aaron Frost's mother. She also needed to find out how Aaron came to be connected to the derelict house.

Josie Frost opened the front door, her face sunken. She looked like Boyd did after treatment. Lottie supposed her pallor was from grief. Her black shirt was on inside out, with the collar turned up, and she wore creased black trousers. The crutch had been abandoned and she hobbled down the narrow hallway, her hands brushing the walls to support herself.

'They won't let me bring my son's body home. Can't you do anything about it?'

'I have to wait until the pathologist has finished all her tests. It takes time. I'm sorry.'

'Sit down. Why are you here?' Josie's grief was quickly turning to impatience.

Lottie decided to tackle what Corrigan had told her first. 'I want to ask you about your husband.'

'Richard? What about him?'

'You said he left a few years ago. Is that correct?'

'It is. Why are you asking about him?'

'There's an old abandoned house out by the canal, near the new apartments on Canal Lane. Two years ago, Aaron's name became associated with it.'

'What are you talking about? Aaron lives here. He never told me about any house.'

'Really?'

'Was it making money for him? If it was, he should have handed over more.'

'It's derelict, Josie, uninhabitable, but there was electricity being fed into it. Aaron is on the network lease as occupier.'

'He was paying the bills? Why in God's name would he do that?'

'I thought you might be able to answer that.'

'I didn't even know about it.' The woman crossed her arms indignantly.

'That same house was the site of brutal murders over twenty years ago.'

'Oh sweet Jesus. That's macabre. What would Aaron want with a place like that?'

Lottie pressed on, ignoring the question. 'A mother and her two daughters were killed there. The mother was Sinead Doyle. Ring any bells?'

Josie's eyes blinked rapidly, her lips moving and her teeth rattling as if she was chewing an imaginary piece of food. 'I do recall the murders, now that you mention it. It was all over the papers at the time. Did you work the case?'

'No, I wasn't long out of training and I think I was based in Athlone then. Sinead Doyle,' Lottie repeated. 'Does that name mean anything to you?'

Josie shook her head, but Lottie had enough experience reading suspects and witnesses to recognise that she knew exactly who Sinead Doyle was.

'It's important, Josie. Aaron is dead. You have to tell me what you know.'

After a dramatic sigh, Josie said, 'There were plenty of rumours. Rumours that broke my heart at the time. My husband, Richard, did not kill that family. He was in London all that week, visiting his mother. A rude detective hounded him when he arrived home, but Richard could prove he was nowhere near Ragmullin when they were killed.'

'What were the rumours?'

'You're going to persist until I tell you, aren't you?'

'I need to know.'

Josie clamped her lips shut. They were so dry, Lottie thought she heard them crack.

'Come on, Josie. I'm investigating current murders including that of your own son, a young pregnant woman and an eleven-year-old boy.' She grabbed the other woman's parchment-like fingers. 'Please. You have to help me.'

After a moment, Josie gave Lottie's hand a squeeze and sat back slowly. Her eyes filled with tears.

'I thought it was over and done with. He admitted it. The affair. Said it was years before that awful event. Years before the family were killed. He told me that Harry, Sinead's husband, knew all about it and was eaten crossways with jealousy. Richard thought that maybe a row had broken out that night and Harry lost it. Stabbed them all and fled the country with the boy.'

Closing her eyes, imagining the scene, Lottie couldn't understand how Harry Doyle would murder his family that particular night if he'd known about the affair years previously. 'There had to have been something else.'

'There was.' Josie found a tissue and tore it to strips between her fingers as she spoke. 'Sinead got pregnant from the affair. She had a child with Richard.'

'Oh!'

'Oh is right. Harry stood by her, and as far as the town knew, they were happily married. No one could figure out why he did what he did. Killing them all. Shocking.'

'And this child of Sinead's,' Lottie knew she had to tread carefully, 'was it Aaron?'

'Good God, no! Aaron is mine and Richard's.'

There went that theory, Lottie thought. 'Do you know which of the Doyle children was Richard's?'

'The eldest. The boy. After the murders, the rumours started to fly around town, and it got so bad that Richard confessed to me. I believe it broke his heart to think that Harry had absconded with the boy, and most likely killed him, because no one ever found his body.'

There was so much to digest, Lottie was sorry she hadn't brought Kirby with her to take notes. She looked over at Josie, wondering if she had anything to do with the current murders, and how in the name of God they were all connected. Because she was one hundred per cent sure they had to be.

Josie filled the awkward silence. 'If Harry didn't kill the boy at the time, the general consensus was that he probably fled to Spain and changed their names.'

'When did your husband leave home?'

'Two years ago.'

Lottie regained perspective. 'So two years ago, your husband left home and Aaron became owner of the Doyles' old house.'

'So?'

'What happened here two years ago?'

'Nothing. Nothing at all.' The tissue was in shreds, covering Josie's trouser legs like snowflakes.

'Maybe the missing Doyle boy has come back,' Lottie said.

'Maybe Harry came back,' Josie said.

'No, he did not.' She couldn't tell Josie how she knew that. She believed that the fingerprints found on the hand from the railway tracks would prove it was Harry Doyle's. Even though they did not have the rest of his body, she was sure he'd been dead a long time. She tried to recall the name of the Doyle boy. It had been mentioned in the article.

'Josie, do you know anyone called Karl Doyle?'

'No. But if he's still alive, he could have changed his name.'

Thinking out loud, Lottie said, 'But if he is alive, and had done nothing wrong, why wouldn't he reveal himself?'

'That I can't answer for you, Inspector.'

'Are you sure you don't know where Richard is? I really need to speak with him.'

'I have no idea. He upped sticks and left me and Aaron for no good reason. I thought that Doyle business was all water under the bridge. Now I'm not so sure.'

'Me neither,' Lottie said. 'Thanks for your help. I'll contact the pathologist to see when she'll release Aaron's body to you.'

'Thank you. I just want my son home.'

CHAPTER SIXTY-NINE

As she returned to the office, Lottie's mind was churning around all she'd learned from Josie Frost.

Kirby was at his desk going through a page of illegible notes. 'I did an online search, and then I phoned the land registry.'

'And?'

'The former registered owner of the property was Harry Doyle. No one else registered until it was transferred to Aaron Frost.'

'We know Harry Doyle is dead, so who transferred it?'

'It was done through a solicitor. The woman on the phone said the documents appeared in order.'

'Get on to the electricity company. See who was paying for the power before Aaron took over. Doyle's house is key.'

'Will do. By the way, while you were out, Jeff Cole arrived. He's been keeping his nose clean, according to the team who were monitoring him. You said you wanted to talk to him. He's in Interview Room 1.'

'Good. You come with me.'

Lottie dropped her bag and jacket and tried to line up her thoughts. She had to find out how Jeff's aunt's house was connected to Doyle's house. The only obvious connection was that the child's body had possibly been hidden there, in the freezers. But why?

*

Sitting next to Kirby in the interview room, Lottie thought she would faint with the smell of French fries wafting to her nose every time he moved his hands. She'd have to talk to him about his personal hygiene.

Jeff Cole was hunched on a steel chair opposite them, his padded jacket wrapped around him even though it was sweltering in the airless interview room. He appeared gaunt, and Lottie wondered when he'd last eaten.

'I miss Faye so much,' he blurted. 'It's funny how much I depended on her. My boss, Derry, is about to give me the boot. So much for compassionate leave. I'll probably have to sell my aunt's house too. Have you found who killed my Faye?' The young man's thoughts were coming out of his mouth in a ramble of incoherent words.

'We're making progress,' Lottie said, without commitment in her tone. 'That's why I asked you to come in.'

'You probably think I killed her.'

'No, I don't. I want to go over the conversation we had previously, about your aunt and cousin. We think Polly is the young girl whose body we found.' She didn't add that it was also her skull that Faye had found in his aunt's house.

'You proved it, then?'

'Your DNA is a familial match. Not a direct match, but enough to prove you were at least cousins.'

'Oh God. The poor child. Why? Who?'

'Jeff, you said you used to visit your aunt's house regularly and then suddenly it all stopped. Do you have any recollection of why that might have been?'

He shook his head slowly, as if he was denying it but thinking it over at the same time.

'I was only nine. Me and Polly were friends. I just know I was upset that I couldn't go over there any more. My mother told me that Aunt Patsy was going through a tough time and had broken off all ties with the family. On her deathbed, she admitted that Patsy and Noel had been deep into drugs. When Patsy eventually contacted me after my mother's death, she refused to talk about my cousin. The story was that Polly had gone to England with her father. Patsy seemed to be deeply hurt, and she always had a terrified look in her eyes. Maybe I should have pressed her more. But she was addicted to prescription drugs by then, and she was very fragile.'

'I want you to try to remember back to when you were nine. Can you recall anything significant happening that resulted in you being prevented from seeing your aunt and cousin?'

'It was a long time ago.'

Lottie was not about to let it go that easily. 'At around that time, a woman called Sinead Doyle, and her two daughters, Annie and Angela, were murdered in Ragmullin. Her husband Harry and son Karl disappeared. Do those names mean anything to you?'

She watched Jeff as he churned over this information. 'Harry Doyle? That name rings a bell.'

Opening the file she'd brought in with her, she slid the Doyle family photo across the table. 'Do you recognise anyone in this photo?'

He stared at it and shook his head. 'No. Am I supposed to know who they are?'

'Look at the man standing at the back.'

'Sorry. I don't recognise anyone.'

'Why do you think you remember the name Harry Doyle?'

'I'm not really sure, to be honest. I think my uncle Noel, Patsy's husband, used to work with a Doyle man. I was just a kid. Wait a minute. Yes. Patsy was always giving out when he was late in from work, and he'd tell her he was only in the pub throwing darts with Harry Doyle. I remember now because I couldn't understand how she'd get so annoyed about them playing darts. I had my own dart board hanging in my bedroom and I thought it was great fun. But now ... I suppose it was really the drinking after work that annoyed her. Does that help?'

'Yes, it does. Thank you.'

She turned to Kirby and he nodded. They now had a link between the murdered Doyle family and Patsy Cole's house at Church View where the skull was found. But how did it all link to the murders this week?

'Where is your uncle Noel now?'

'Aunt Patsy said he died years ago from a stroke. In hindsight, it was probably from drugs. If my mother was still alive, she'd be able to tell you. Aunt Patsy too, for that matter, but they're all dead. All dead, including my Faye.' He whimpered into his sleeve, childlike.

Lottie thought that even if Jeff's aunt was still alive, she was hardly going to enlighten them as to what had occurred in her house twenty years ago. 'One final question, and then you can leave,' she said. 'Do you know Kevin O'Keeffe?'

'The insurance guy? Yeah. He gave us a quote for Aunt Patsy's house. Traipsed all over it telling us how expensive it was going to be to insure it because of its state of disrepair.'

Shit, Lottie thought. Even if she proved a link to him, Kevin O'Keeffe had an excuse for his DNA being at 2 Church View. One step forward, ten steps backwards. Welcome to my world, she thought as she shook hands with Jeff and watched Kirby lead him out.

Lottie tasked Garda Brennan to trace Aaron's father, Richard Frost. They had already tried to find out what they could about Jeff's relatives, the Cole family, and come up blank. If Polly had been murdered in that house, why had no one reported it? It was looking likely that either the mother or the father had killed the child in some drug-fuelled scenario. After Faye's murder, the neighbours in Church View had been canvassed, but no one could throw any light on why a skull had been hidden there.

She had another email. Jane Dore, with the time of death for Aaron Frost.

McKeown arrived. 'Boss, I've good news and bad news. Which do you want to hear first?'

'Just tell me.'

'We can't locate Kevin O'Keeffe. His wife said he took their daughter to school in her car and was then to go to work. He's not at his office. We checked. But his car was sitting outside the family home and SOCOs examined it. Guess what?'

'McKeown! Now isn't the time for riddles.'

'They opened the boot and the smell of bleach hit them like a tsunami. It was cleaned out recently. I think that gives us grounds to arrest him.'

'No, it doesn't. Marianne said he's very particular. Her word. Their house is shining. The presence of bleach doesn't mean a thing.'

'But with the CCTV and Carthy's statement, we can make a case that he at least dumped Gavin's body.'

'Tentative at best; it's just his car.'

'Maybe it was Marianne,' McKeown offered eagerly.

'No, she was with Tamara. But even though we don't have proof it was Kevin at the recycling centre, I think we have enough to bring him in for questioning as a person of interest. Find him.'

'I'll put out an alert.'

McKeown headed out and Lottie went to the incident room and stood in front of the photo board. She studied Harry Doyle in the family photo. His hand pressing hard on his wife's shoulder, the white cuff of his shirt visible below the sleeve of his jacket. She glanced over at the photos of the body parts. The hand. The end of a tattoo on the wrist. Tearing the photo from the board, she held it up to the family picture.

There. She could just about make it out. The ink of a tattoo on Harry Doyle's hand. If they could match the tattoo, it would prove beyond doubt that Harry Doyle had been dead almost as long as his wife and daughters. But who had killed him? And why pick now to dispose of his frozen, dismembered body? And where was the rest of it?

Questions beget questions, as Kirby had said.

Aaron's DNA was in the car where Faye's body had been found, so it was possible he had killed her. But there was no way he'd murdered Gavin Robinson. According to Jane Dore, Aaron was already dead before Gavin was killed.

Who else was involved? She stared at the photos. They'd kept tabs on Jeff since Faye's murder, so she knew it wasn't him. It had to be Kevin O'Keeffe. His wife, Marianne, had thought Kevin had killed Aaron because he suspected she was having an affair with him. But why kill the others? What the hell was she missing?

CHAPTER SEVENTY

Her father had been rambling on and on, and Ruby tuned out. She was desperate to get out of the car.

'You see, Ruby, I haven't always been faithful to your mother. It's got me in trouble more times than I can count.'

She heard that bit. 'You've been with more women than you can count?'

'That's not what I mean. But Marianne takes every opportunity to regurgitate my affairs when it suits her.'

'I don't blame her.' Ruby wondered why her mother had never kicked Kevin out.

'She's always chasing someone younger than herself. I suspect she's bisexual. Do you know what that means?'

'I'm not stupid.'

'No, I don't suppose you are. I was sure she was having it off with that Tamara one.'

'*That Tamara one*, as you call her, has just had her son murdered. You are pathetic.'

'Maybe I am.' Kevin's gaze never left the fogged-up windscreen.

'Where is all this leading?' Ruby thought her father was imagining things. Her mother was just good friends with Tamara. He was jealous. She'd never seen him with a friend. Pathetic old man.

'Let me tell this my own way,' he said, 'then I won't get mad and do something stupid.'

'Go on.'

'Your mother holds it over my head all the time that the money for our house came from her family. I know the law says I'd be entitled to half if we ever divorced, but it gets to me. No property. No savings. I needed my own money to have some sway over her. Then, two years ago, I was presented with an opportunity. It was traumatic but I thought I'd make money.' He paused, and Ruby rolled her eyes. He'd already told her this shite. But she felt the hairs on the back of her neck prickle when he added, 'That was what I was promised. But you see, Ruby, there wasn't any money. Now people have been killed and I am involved.'

'What?' Ruby said.

'I got dragged into something dark. Very dark.' He lapsed into silence.

She squashed herself against the locked door. Her father was terrifying her. She had her hand on her phone in her pocket. Blindly she drafted a text. She couldn't see what she was typing, but she was proficient enough to know it might make some sense to Sean.

*

Sean's phone vibrated against his leg and he took it from his pocket. A text from Ruby. The teacher was rambling on about questions for exams and how they were to read over old papers. Right.

Ruby's message consisted of four words.

Da mad help lake

He squinted at the screen again. She hadn't turned up for school, and her father had been acting weird the last few times Sean had been in their house. Holding his phone under the desk, he reread the text for the third time. Ruby was in trouble.

'Sean Parker, if that's your phone you're holding in your hand, you'd better put it away or it will be in the principal's office, along with you, in five seconds flat.'

Sean groaned and stopped himself saying that it took three minutes, not five seconds, to walk there.

'Sorry, miss, I'm not holding my phone. I just need to use the toilet.'

The young teacher curled up her nose and pointed to the door. 'Don't be all day.'

Sean slid out of his chair and escaped.

In the bathroom, he stared at the screen again. Should he text back? That could make things worse for Ruby. And what lake was she on about?

Maybe he should tell his mother. But she was stressed over the investigations she was running. She wouldn't have time for nonsensical texts. Maybe Ruby had skipped school and wanted Sean to join her. No, she'd have been more specific. He texted back.

Where are you?

Waited.

No reply.

What was he to do? Then he remembered the conversation he'd had with his mother last night. There was no way around it. He'd have to tell her about Ruby's text.

The guard on the front desk was young and uninterested.

'Look, I've had to tell a pack of lies to get out of school and I need to see my mother.'

The guard laughed. 'What lies?'

'I told the principal that my mam was dying.'

'You did not.'

'Did so. And I need to speak with her. It's urgent.'

'Detective Inspector Parker is busy. Leave a message and I'll get it to her.'

'You don't understand.'

'Try me.'

'Piss off,' Sean muttered under his breath.

'Your mother wouldn't like to hear you've been abusing me with bad language.'

'When she hears what I've to tell her, I don't think she will give a flying fu— flute what you say.'

The door with the code opened and two guards walked out. Sean took his chance and scooted in behind them, catching it before it shut.

'Hey, you can't go in there.'

He scampered up the stairs and skidded along the corridor, trying to remember which was his mother's office.

A woman marched towards him. 'Young man, are you lost?'

'I want to speak to my mother.'

'Who would that be?'

'Lottie Parker.'

The woman's face crunched into itself. 'Have you been kicked out of school?'

'No.'

'Well you shouldn't be up here. Come with me. You can wait in reception. Someone will tell your mother.'

'Fuck this,' Sean said, and darted out of the way. He careened through the door of the nearest office and stopped short in front of the board of photographs. Graphic, twisted images of death. On the other board, undead people. Slap bang in the middle of those photos was Ruby's dad, Kevin O'Keeffe.

*

Ruby didn't want to hear any more, but her father kept talking.

'The boy. He was so young. So fragile. So light to lift and carry. It was awful. I'm terrified now.'

'What are you talking about?'

'The boy that died. Tamara's son. Gavin.'

'You ... I don't believe it. You killed a little boy?'

'No, Ruby, don't go accusing me, I'm just trying to tell you what happened. You see, someone threatened to kill my own child. I had to do what they asked.'

'Are you for real? Who asked you?'

'That doesn't matter now.'

'You killed a child!' Ruby trembled and felt the tears trickling down her face, but her fear quickly turned to rage. 'You're a murderer! I don't want to hear any more. I want to go home. Let me out.' She pulled at the handle, but the door wouldn't budge.

'I'm sorry,' Kevin said.

'Fuck you and your excuses. You're evil. I want to go home!'

'Where is home? Where is anything of value? I abandoned all that I love when I got caught up in the darkness.'

Ruby had heard enough. She shoved her rucksack hard into his side, grabbed the key fob from the dash, pressed the door-unlock button and leapt out of the car.

As she ran, like she'd never run before, she felt her belly fat flap and her feet thump against the pebbles on the ground.

She didn't dare look behind her to see if her father was following. She just ran and ran.

And she cried and cried, her face a mask of horror.

*

Lottie looked up to find Superintendent Farrell standing in the doorway with Sean skulking behind her.

'Superintendent? Sean? What's going on?'

'This young man is as impertinent as you. I would advise you to put some manners on him, and then I want to talk to you in my office.'

'Of course.'

Farrell stomped out with irritated steps. Sean wrinkled his nose and instinctively Lottie wanted to shake him.

'What are you doing here? Did something happen to you at school?'

'Nothing happened.'

'Tell me then.' She knew it had to be important. Sean was conscientious and law-abiding. Most of the time.

He handed her his phone. 'After seeing all those photos, I think this is serious.'

'What photos?'

'On the boards. In the other office.'

'You shouldn't have been in there.'

'Look, Mam, that text is from Ruby. I think she's in trouble.'

The words on the screen made no sense, but with all that had gone on, they actually did.

'Did you text back?' She scrolled down.

'Yes, but there's been no reply. I didn't try again, because if she's in danger I thought I might make it worse. What should I do?'

What indeed? Lottie stared at the words.

Da mad help lake

'Which lake do you think she means?'

'I've no idea. Can't you trace it?'

'It'd take time. I'll contact Marianne. Leave your phone with me in case Ruby sends another message. Go back to school. I'll sort it.'

'Ruby's my friend.'

'I know, Sean. I'll find her. I promise.'

CHAPTER SEVENTY-ONE

A scowl flashed across Marianne's face when she opened the door.

'I didn't expect my house to be turned into a crime scene, Lottie. I shouldn't have made that complaint. I was only—'

'Shut up, Marianne.' Lottie bundled the woman back into the house and grabbed her elbows, whirling her around to look at her. 'Do you know which is Kevin's favourite lake?'

'Lake? What are you on about?'

'Kevin has Ruby. I think your daughter is in danger. They're at a lake. I've no idea which one. Think, Marianne.'

'Ruby. Oh God. Jesus.' Marianne swayed against the wall. 'I … I don't know.'

Behind her, Lottie could see SOCOs working their way through the kitchen.

'This is urgent. Phone me if you think of anything.' She moved back outside.

'I'll get my coat,' Marianne said. 'I'm coming with you.'

'Where?'

'Lough Cullion. It's where we used to go for picnics when Ruby was younger.'

'You're staying here.'

'No. If anyone can talk sense into Kevin, I can.'

Lottie wasn't so sure, but time was against her. She relented and headed to the car.

Marianne slid in beside her. 'What has Kevin done?'

'I don't think you really want to know the answer to that question.'

She stuck the blue flashing strobe light on, and as the car screamed out of the driveway, she radioed for backup to meet them at Lough Cullion.

*

Kirby stood looking over Gary's shoulder. The technical guru still had Aaron's laptop on his desk.

'I thought you were sending it to the Dublin experts.'

'I don't like things getting the better of me.'

'What have you found?'

'Tell me I'm a genius first.' Gary squinted over his spectacles.

'You're a genius,' Kirby said. 'Now what the fuck have you found?'

'The site most visited was TraceMyGenes.'

'What's that when it's at home?'

'An ancestry DNA site. You take your DNA and post it in, and then they match it up with other people who've submitted theirs.'

'And who did Aaron find?'

'It's more like who found Aaron.'

'Come on, Gary. I'm knee-deep in corpses. Tell me.'

'The site itself won't tell us anything, but I've successfully restored his deleted emails and printed them out for you. It seems Aaron first registered on the site trying to find a Richard Frost. But then someone else made contact with him. The name is there.'

Kirby scanned the page. 'Holy shit. Thanks, Gary. You truly are a genius.'

He raced down the stairs and flew into Lottie's office. Empty. A phone was sliding around on the desk with an incoming call. Boyd's name. He answered it.

'Hi, bud,' Kirby said. 'Could do with your help here.'

'Where's Lottie?'

'I haven't the foggiest.'

'Get her to call me. I need to talk to her. It's urgent.'

'Will do.'

Kirby hung up, scratching his head. His belly rumbled, and he didn't know which way to turn.

*

The level-crossing barrier was down. A train was due.

Marianne said, 'Drive through it!'

'Calm down.' Lottie glanced in her rear-view mirror. The backup crews were sitting helplessly in their cars behind her. She had an awful sense of déjà vu. Of sitting here helplessly on a chase with Boyd, frantic that their suspect was getting away. She shook off the memory and thought of the unread texts from Boyd earlier. She felt for the phone in her back pocket and eased it out.

'Damn.'

'What?'

'I took Sean's phone in case Ruby contacted him again, but I never brought mine.'

As she slid the phone onto the dashboard, she noticed a figure streaking up the lane on the far side of the tracks. A teenager, slightly overweight, with short hair, her face white, mouth stretched with the exertion of her run.

She jumped out of the car and ran to the barrier.

'Ruby!' Marianne screeched as she followed.

The rumble of the train echoed up the tracks and Lottie shot out a hand, holding back the frantic mother. The train screamed past them like a fast-forwarded movie, silver-grey images merging and stretching. Lottie's imagination conjured up horrific images of Ruby being caught by her pursuer and thrust under the speeding train, her body ending up like the torso Jack and Gavin had found.

Then the train was gone. A void of stillness in its wake. She was deaf in the silence and she still couldn't see the girl. Without waiting for the barrier to rise, she ducked under it and ran across the tracks sunken in the road.

'Ruby? Ruby!' Marianne shouted.

Lottie saw the teenager then, lying on her side in the long grass, holding her chest, trying to catch her breath. She looked so young in her school uniform, and Lottie was grateful Sean hadn't tried to find her on his own.

'She's going to be okay,' she said.

Marianne cradled her daughter in her arms, crying relentlessly.

Lottie hunkered down beside them as uniforms swarmed around like flies. 'Ruby, are you hurt?'

The girl shook her head.

'Where's your dad? Where's Kevin?'

'Lake. Car.' Ruby was breathless but did not appear to be harmed. 'Said ... horrible things. I think he murdered Gavin Robinson. Oh, God!'

Lottie instructed two uniforms to bring the girl to the hospital to have her checked over, then told the crew of the other squad car to follow her.

Kevin was still sitting in the car, facing the water. His head leaning on the steering wheel. Lottie unholstered her weapon and approached the vehicle, giving orders for the others to stay well back.

'Kevin O'Keeffe, come out and put your hands on your head.'

If a gun battle ensued, she'd get a right bollocking from Farrell for not calling in the armed response unit. Then again, she'd most likely be dead, so she wouldn't have to worry about it.

Her hand wavered. She wasn't all that brave. Without moving closer, she stood behind the vehicle.

'Kevin? Get out of the car.'

She held her breath as the door opened slowly.

One foot appeared. Shiny black shoe. Then the other. Pin-stripe trousers with a neat press down the seam. And then he stood out of the car, his face ashen, his hands in the air.

'Put your hands on your head and face the car.'

He did as she ordered.

Slowly she approached, alert for any sudden movement. But Kevin O'Keeffe was spent.

She cuffed him. Read him his right to remain silent and arrested him for kidnapping his daughter. Then, even without any evidence other than Ruby's garbled words, she tagged on the murder of Gavin Robinson for good measure.

O'Keeffe did not utter a word in reply.

The sudden elation of capturing her prey had dissipated as soon as O'Keeffe was taken away. The car would need to be impounded, even though it was Marianne's. Lottie left a crew with it until that happened.

She drove to the station, her head thumping, her body feeling strangely empty. There would be a hundred forms to fill, a thousand reports to file, and the scale of winding up the investigation was so overpowering that she yearned to go home to bed.

Kirby was pacing.

'Well done on the arrest, boss. It came in over the radio. I was looking for you, actually.'

'Not now, Kirby. I need to put my head on the desk for five minutes. Then we'll talk.'

'Boyd wants you to ring him. Says it's urgent. And I have new information.'

Lottie felt the blood stop flowing in her veins, and her head lightened. 'Oh God, Kirby. I bet he got bad news this morning. I don't think I can handle it. I really don't.'

'He did sound a bit off.'

She stared at the detective, with his flushed fat face and wild hair, his shirt straining over a stomach that had consumed way too many Happy Meals. Her knees wobbled. He put out a hand to steady her but she shooed him away.

'Don't fuss. I'm fine. I'll ring him.'

'You sure? I'll get you a coffee. A hot one. You like that.'

'Not now, Kirby.'

'Sorry.'

She sat on the nearest chair. It was Boyd's old desk, and a sense of loss swamped her. She shoved the keyboard to one side and laid her head on the cool surface.

'I'm getting you that coffee,' Kirby said.

Then she recalled what he'd said a few moments ago. With a laborious sigh, she raised her head. 'What's this new information?'

'I'm not sure, but it might help tie up loose ends.'

'What loose ends? We have Kevin O'Keeffe for the murders. I can't wait to interview him. I really need to find out his relationship to Polly Cole and Harry Doyle.'

'That's the thing …'

'What is it, Kirby?'

'I think there's someone else involved.'

'Well, we know Aaron Frost is. His prints were found in Faye's car.'

'Gary, the tech guy, he unlocked Aaron's laptop.'

A shiver convulsed her spine.

'I'm not going to like this, am I?'

CHAPTER SEVENTY-TWO

Jack was surprised to see his dad outside the door of the principal's office. He'd been dragged out of class without a reason. Just told to bring his books and school bag.

'Hi, Dad! Am I getting a day off?'

'Come on. We have to go.'

Jack followed the long, loping figure down the narrow corridor and his young brain filled up quickly with terrible thoughts.

'Dad? Is something wrong? Is Maggie okay? Mam?'

'They're fine.'

'Is it because of Gavin? You know I miss him and don't know how to act about it in school, and—'

'Jack, be quiet and just follow me.'

He drove them through town and out along the main road, past the road where they lived.

'Are we not going home?'

'Not yet. The house is like a fortress with the guards on duty there. I need head space. I want to show you a restoration project I've been working on.'

'I thought you were off work sick.'

'Irish Canals is a good employer. I can work any day I feel up to it. And today, I feel up to it.'

Jack knew all about the lock gates that Charlie had been working on. He and Tyrone sometimes helped him to paint the walls and cut the grass.

When they got out of the car, Jack looked at the gates. All painted and newly oiled.

'They're working now,' Charlie said. 'I'll show you.'

'I know how they work,' Jack said. 'I read about it online.'

'Nothing like seeing the real thing, is there?'

'Suppose not.'

Jack was bored already. He wished he had his drone. It would be cool to fly it along this section of the canal. Way cooler than lock gates that must be two hundred years old.

As he stood on the small gantry, the rush of water gushed through Jack's ears. He heard the train make its way along the tracks that ran parallel to the canal, though he couldn't see it because of the bushes and trees. He glanced down at the water. A rat scampered along the concrete edge of the lock then disappeared into the long grass, making its appearance again with a splash as it cut through the green slime that hugged the reeds. The slime separated in its wake, rousing the smell of deadness and decay from the water.

'How deep is it?' Jack asked.

'Must be twenty feet.'

'Good place to hide a body,' he said softly.

'Why do you say that?'

'You know, just with finding the body parts the other day and all that's happened. Dad, why would someone want to leave them out in the open and not in a place like here, where they'd never be found?'

'Oh, they'd be found. Bodies are always found. Even bog bodies are found thousands of years later. Nothing is hidden forever.'

'Still,' Jack said.

Charlie said, 'I used to come here a lot as a boy. My father … he used to bring me. That was before I discovered the darkest thing in my life. Now I have to tell you the darkest thing in yours.'

Jack leaned on the heavy balance beam to get a better look at his dad, who was turning the windlass. He knew the equipment. Charlie was filling the lock chamber with water.

*

'Jack is at school,' Lisa said. She was dressed in her white nurse's tunic and navy slacks and seemed to be ready to walk out the door. Her colour was a little better. Her hair was washed and scooped at the back of her neck. Garda Brennan was chatting to the other garda at the squad car.

Lottie said, 'I've called the school. They told me Jack's dad picked him up. Where would they go?'

'Charlie?'

'Yes.' Lottie was frantic. She'd seen the emails on Aaron's laptop. She knew they were running out of time.

Lisa pulled the door shut and locked it. 'I've to drop Maggie to the crèche. Charlie had an early hospital appointment. God, I hope he didn't get bad news.'

This made Lottie think of Boyd's texts again. Not now, she warned herself. The boy could be in danger. 'Where would Charlie take Jack?'

'I don't understand. He'd come home. He'd no reason to take him out of school. What are you talking about?' Lisa brushed past her and stood at the car door, watching Maggie sitting quietly in the back.

'Did you know that Charlie and Aaron Frost were related?'

Lisa whirled around, stones crunching underfoot. 'What on earth are you on about?'

'There are emails. Charlie thought he might need a bone marrow transplant. He signed up to an online site to trace near relatives. Why would he do that when he has sons?'

'What do you mean? Charlie doesn't need a transplant. He must have been searching for some other reason.'

'I've seen his correspondence with Aaron,' Lottie said. Her phone rang. 'Give me one minute.'

She walked a little way down the lane, bracing herself for what she might hear.

'Boyd. I'm up to my ears. I hope you're okay, otherwise I'm going to kill you.'

'I met that guy Charlie Sheridan at the hospital this morning.'

'Is everything all right?' Instinctively, Lottie pulled her jacket tight to her chest.

'I don't know, but I was trying to draw him out about his illness. We talked about bone marrow and I asked if he had anyone to donate for him if he ever needed it. He said he had a nine-year-old son but he was too young. Then I remembered about Jack finding the torso. He's eleven, isn't he?'

'Yes.'

'So why did Charlie only mention the nine-year-old?'

'I'll find out. Thanks, Boyd. You okay?'

'I'm fine. I know you're busy. I just wanted to pass that on. I'll call round later.'

Lottie walked back to Lisa Sheridan. 'Lisa, you need to tell me everything.'

'I've to go to work. I've missed so much lately.'

'The sooner you talk, the sooner you can go. Where is Charlie?'

'I don't know.'

'Why would he take Jack from school?'

'I don't know. You have to believe me.' Lisa's forehead bubbled with perspiration.

'Jack could be in danger.'

'Jesus, no. Do you think he's going to harm him?'

'I don't know,' Lottie said honestly.

Lisa gulped and shook her head. Tears were streaming down her face. 'Jack doesn't know.'

'Doesn't know what?'

'That Charlie isn't his dad.'

'Oh.' Lottie had half expected to hear this declaration after Boyd's call. 'How did Charlie find out?'

'That's not important. We have to find him.'

'We will, but I have to know what I'm dealing with first.'

Lisa shrugged her shoulders wearily. 'It's a long story, but back when Charlie first started to feel sick, he had all these symptoms and I foolishly told him he might have leukaemia. He had blood tests done and the doctors initially suspected he might have a mild form of the disease. It turned him into a hypochondriac. He insisted that we all be tested in case he ever needed bone marrow. He became irrational about it, obsessive. I couldn't talk sense into him. I refused to put my children through unnecessary testing and so … and so I had to tell him.'

'What was his reaction?'

Lisa cried softly. 'He was like a madman. Talking about history repeating itself. Hammered the daylights out of me. I was pregnant with Maggie at the time. This was two years ago. I've lived with his anger and paranoia every day since.'

'How was he with Jack?'

'Offhand. Rude. Angry. Never hit him, though. He wouldn't hurt him. I know he wouldn't.'

'Did you tell Charlie the name of the father?'

Lisa nodded. 'It was the only way to stop the beatings.'

'Who is it?'

Lottie was sure the answer would be Aaron Frost.

She was wrong.

*

Jack stood and watched his father operate the lock gates.

'Why are you showing me this, Dad? I know how it works.'

'I have to do something or I'm going to kill someone.'

'You're scaring me.'

'Good.'

Jack thought of running then. Running as fast and as hard as he could. But Charlie stopped twisting the windlass and walked over to him. He sat on the beam and took Jack's hand in his. Stared at it before dropping it.

'Jack, listen to me. I found out about my dad the hard way. It darkened my soul for a long time. I raged at everyone. I was delirious, demented.' He paused. Jack wondered about the monotone flatness of his voice.

Charlie continued. 'It got so bad that one night I killed them all. I wasn't sorry. They were laughing behind my back. The bastard son, that's what I heard them saying. My mother hadn't even the decency to tell me the truth. I had to overhear it in an argument between her and that fucking excuse for a father. Not my real dad. Never met him. He's still out there somewhere, but I will find him. Mark my words. And he will suffer too.'

'Dad, what are you saying? You're really scaring me now.'

'That's the thing, Jack. I'm not your dad. Your mother slept with someone else and then passed you off as mine. I was so excited when she was pregnant. At last I was going to have my own kid, after years living in exile. At last I had something of my own. But like everything in my life, it was a lie. Everything was lies.'

'I ... I don't understand, Dad.'

'Don't call me that. I am not your father. You are not my son.'

'Of course I am.'

Jack was knocked from the beam as Charlie hit him. He landed on the concrete, a sharp pain shooting through his coccyx bone. He screamed in agony, biting his tongue as Charlie slapped him to shut him up. Blood filled his mouth.

'I know you saw me that night. With your drone. I know you downloaded the images. What did you save them on? Don't tell me they're on your laptop, because I checked and they're not.'

Jack scrambled backwards, crying in pain. 'It's just shadows.'

'Where is it?'

He didn't know whether to lie or tell the truth. What would help him? 'I gave the USB to the detective, Lottie something.'

'If you'd done that, she'd have arrested me by now. Don't lie to me. Where is it?'

'You can't see anything on it anyway. You have to believe me.'

Jack had no idea where he was finding his bravery. As he crawled, scuffing the palms of his hands, he felt the USB stick in his pocket, and he wished, oh how he wished, he had dumped it.

Charlie turned around. His face, usually pale and wan, was now purple with anger. In his hand he held a large knife. The steel was dull beneath the cloudy sky, but it was bright enough to scare the shit out of Jack.

Instead of doubling over with the pain again, he blocked out the agony, shot upright and began to run. He ran like he was in the Olympics. He ran like the devil himself was on his heels. Because he knew that if he did not outrun Charlie, he would lie with the bones of the dead that were surely in the bottom of the canal lock chamber.

CHAPTER SEVENTY-THREE

Lottie flung open the station doors, scanned her ID card and raced down the stairs to the cells.

'Open it. Now, for fuck's sake,' she yelled at the guard.

Inside, she hauled Kevin O'Keeffe up off the bench and thrust him against the wall.

'You have one chance to tell me the truth. One fucking chance.'

'Okay.'

She let go of his shoulder and pushed away from him, breathing heavily as she tried to get her thoughts in order.

'Charlie Sheridan,' she said.

'What about him?'

'Where would he take your son?'

'My son? I don't—'

'Your son Jack. Jack Sheridan.'

'You know?'

'I do. Talk. Jack is in danger. Charlie has taken him.'

Kevin fell back onto the bench and buried his head in his hands. 'He's deranged. I've seen what he can do.'

'You'd better start telling me what you know, if you want to save Jack's life.'

'Oh God almighty,' Kevin said. 'Charlie contacted me. About two years ago. Said he knew about me and Lisa. I wasn't sure what he was talking about. There was nothing to know really. Charlie used to work at A2Z Insurance, that's how I knew them. It was just a drunken one-night stand. Lisa wasn't long married at the time and I don't know why it happened, but it did. Next I knew, she was pregnant and then she had Jack. I assumed he was Charlie's. She never told me. I never knew. Not until Charlie came hammering on my door in a flittering rage one night. He threatened to kill Ruby in front of me. To tear her limb from limb and then do the same to Marianne.'

'Jesus.'

'I'd have done anything to stop him.' Kevin lifted his head and stared up at the grated fluorescent light. 'In the end, I did.'

'Who did you kill?' She wanted to shake the words out of him, but she couldn't move. Her feet were rooted to the spot.

He shook his head quickly. 'Oh no, don't get me wrong. Charlie killed them all. Faye, Aaron and that poor innocent boy Gavin Robinson.' He was crying now, the smart businessman a bubbling wreck of snot and tears. He looked at Lottie. 'I admit I helped him empty the freezers. His original plan was to leave the body parts on the rail track, in the hope that the trains would smash them to pieces. But it would have been tough getting the bins onto the tracks, so in the end he must have dumped them in the canal.'

'Why did he want to get rid of them?'

'Something to do with having to sell the derelict house because he thought he was going to die. I don't know.'

'Good God, Kevin, do you even know what you've done?'

'I killed no one, I swear to God.'

'You keep telling me that. Go on.'

'I moved Gavin's body for Charlie. He wouldn't leave me alone. I was sure he was going to kill Ruby before my eyes. I was terrified. I drank. I took it out on Marianne.'

'How did he frighten you so much? Surely words alone wouldn't make you do what you've done.'

Kevin was silent.

'I asked you a fucking question.' She slammed her fist against the wall. He shuddered.

'He told me stuff he'd done. Horrific crimes. Crimes no one could link to him. He showed me those bodies in the freezer. A little girl and a man. He said he had killed them years and years ago and kept the bodies to remind himself who he really was. He was only fourteen years old at the time and he'd murdered people and terrified others into silence. Don't ask me how or why he did it.'

'I can't understand it. You're telling me Charlie Sheridan killed a nine-year-old girl twenty years ago? When he was just fourteen.'

'Yes. He told me he killed his mother and sisters too. And then he killed the man who claimed to be his father.'

'But ...' Lottie moved then, in small, sharp circles. 'The family was called Doyle. Sinead, Annie and Angela. The father was Harry Doyle. Harry killed his family and absconded with his son, Karl.'

'That's not what Charlie told me. He says he killed them. He really put the wind up me. He described it. Knives and stabbing.'

'Are you telling me that Charlie Sheridan is Karl?'

'Yeah. He rebranded himself as Charlie Sheridan. Made a new life for himself until he thought he was dying of cancer. Then he dragged that halfwit Aaron Frost into his mad schemes too.'

'Shit.' Lottie stopped pacing and tore at the roots of her hair. 'Did he ever talk about anything that might tell us where he is now?'

'The old family home. The Doyle house. He killed Gavin and Aaron there, and probably Faye Baker too. He made that poor sod Aaron pick her up and drive her to her death and then dump her body.'

'But why Faye?'

'When she found the skull, he thought she had discovered his secret. That she knew what he had done. That's how deranged he is.'

'Fuck.' Lottie stared at Kevin, a broken man, destined for years in prison. In that instant, she realised she shouldn't be questioning him alone in the cell. But she had a little boy to find and Kevin might unlock the mystery of his whereabouts. 'The Doyle house is cordoned off. We have SOCOs working their way through it. He can't be there. Where else is there?'

'I honestly don't know. Please find Jack.'

'You'll need to make a full statement. Thanks for being so candid.' She turned towards the door.

Kevin said, 'There was something he mentioned that might help you.'

'Go on.'

'He told me his love of the canal had come from Harry Doyle, the man who wasn't even his real father. He said Harry and some fellow called Noel worked for the Canal Board. It's called Irish Canals now. And he said wasn't it funny how he ended up working on the canals too.'

'Canals. Okay.'

She raced up the stairs into the incident room. Kirby, McKeown and Lynch stared at her. Waiting for instructions.

'Find out what part of the canal Charlie Sheridan was working on. Ring Irish Canals. Someone. Call out air support. Move. We have to find him or he's going to kill Jack.'

Lottie scoured every piece of information they'd accumulated since Jack and Gavin had found the torso. She reread the emails from Aaron's laptop. Charlie and Aaron were half-brothers. Aaron's father, Richard Frost, had fathered Charlie, aka Karl, with Sinead Doyle. Two years ago, Richard had left Ragmullin, and at the same time Charlie had discovered he was related to the Frosts by registering with an ancestry DNA site.

'Did anyone have any luck finding out where Richard Frost went to when he left home?'

'I put in a request to trace his passport,' McKeown said. 'Nothing back yet.'

A thought struck her, and she raced up to the tech room.

'Gary. Do you still have Aaron Frost's laptop?'

'I do.'

'We have a printout of emails between Aaron and Charlie Sheridan. Are there other emails?'

'Loads. But I only printed the ones in relation to the DNA site.' He was opening the laptop as he spoke. Tapping and prodding.

'Search for a Richard Frost.'

'Here we are. There are a few. In what order do you want them?' She peered over his shoulder. 'The most recent.'

'This one hasn't been opened. It has a phone number under the name. Looks like a UK number.' Gary moved to one side and let her read.

Lottie tapped the number into her phone and waited.

'Is that Richard Frost?'

'It is.'

She introduced herself and said, 'Richard, I know you don't want to be found, but Aaron tracked you down. And you may or may not know that Aaron has been murdered.'

'Josie rang me. Blamed me, as usual. I'm totally devastated.'

'I'm sorry. She knew where you were all the time?'

'Yes.'

Lottie could not think of Josie Frost's lies right now. 'Richard, I have a small boy in mortal danger. Do you remember Sinead Doyle?'

'That was a long time ago.'

'You had a son together. Charlie Sheridan. He used to be called Karl Doyle. I need to find him. Is there anything in the Doyles' history that might help me discover where he's taken the boy?'

'Let me think.' After a long pause he said, 'Sinead's husband Harry worked on the canals. He'd been working on the lock gates beside an old lock house at the time his family were murdered.'

'Do you think that's where Charlie could be now? This lock house?'

'I don't know, but you asked and that's all I can think of.'

'Would you know where it is?'

And he told her.

CHAPTER SEVENTY-FOUR

Jack felt his collarbone snap under Charlie's hand. The pain shot up his neck and down his spine and into every crevice of his body.

'You little fucker,' Charlie snarled, dragging him through the reeds and grasses, rats and moorhens and ducks scattering in all directions.

'Let me go,' Jack screamed. 'I did nothing.'

'You were born, weren't you? And you saw me dump the frozen body parts with your drone.'

'I didn't see you. I told you, it was just shadows. I won't tell anyone, I promise.'

Jack yelped as his trousers tore and ripped, and his legs bumped over stones and gravel. Blood poured from the cuts, and the smell of the canal clogged his throat along with mucus and snot. He thought he might die before Charlie had a chance to kill him.

He swallowed, then screamed as loudly as he could. He heard the birds taking flight from the trees, and the sky darkened with heavy clouds. The summer appeared to have deserted the earth like everyone had deserted him.

Charlie threw him down on the concrete and the lock chamber opened up before him, full of water.

'Dad ... I have it. The USB. In my pocket.'

Charlie laughed then. Loud and harsh. Maniacal. Like something Jack and Gavin would be afraid of if they heard it in one of their games. Jack missed Gavin. And he understood in that moment what his father had done.

'Did you kill Gavin because he was my friend?'

'No, but he was a nosy little fucker. He stumbled on me by accident while I was getting rid of … Well, he heard a man scream and shout and wandered in where he shouldn't have been.'

Jack sobbed long and hard, and then he noticed the silence all around him. He lifted his head, trying not to shout with the torture of his injured shoulder. A car. A siren in the distance. Charlie heard it too. He was standing as still as a statue.

The sky lit up blue. Bright blue, then white, then red.

A helicopter hovered overhead and cars parked up somewhere close by. Doors opened and slammed.

Shouts rang out and commands and orders filled the air. Jack rolled into a ball in the shelter of the big iron windlass and covered his head.

He heard the voice of the woman detective.

'Charlie Sheridan. Or should I say Karl Doyle? Put the knife down. You are surrounded by armed gardaí. Walk towards me slowly with your hands on your head.'

Jack felt Charlie pull him from the ground and grab him to his chest, the knife at his throat. He elbowed Charlie in the stomach before everything went fuzzy.

As he closed his eyes, he thought he saw Gavin up above giving him a high-five.

*

Lottie saw Jack drop at Charlie's feet as the knife fell into the water. She couldn't be sure if he had another weapon or not.

'Charlie,' she yelled, 'move away from Jack. Come slowly towards me.'

'Like fuck.' Charlie swung around.

The boy was unmoving. She had to get him out of there. She noticed the armed response unit circling around behind Charlie. She had to distract him; get him talking.

'Why, Charlie?'

'Why what?'

'Your mother. Your sisters.'

'Ha! I was the bastard son of Richard Frost. I knew my family talked about me behind my back. I had to get rid of them to clear my brain of their cackles. I eventually got the old man too.'

'How did you manage that?' The ARU were now just metres away.

'Harry arrived home to the carnage that night, and before I could knife him, he chased me. But he wasn't a killer. When he caught me, he didn't know what to do with me. The police were after him, not me. He thought he would be found guilty of the murders. No one would have believed a fourteen-year-old could slaughter his mother and sisters. So he brought me to his workmate's house.' Charlie's lips curled in a wicked sneer.

'What workmate?'

'Noel Cole. They worked together on that fucking lock house right over there. Harry couldn't turn me in because I told him I'd tell the guards he'd done it, so I was foisted on another family who didn't want me while he tried to figure it all out. And in the process, I was landed with another girl who didn't want me around and laughed at me with her sick fucking head on her. I soon stopped that, once I'd taken Harry out of the equation.'

'But the Coles never reported any of this. Why?'

'They were junkies, the pair of them. Spaced out and easy to threaten. You see, if you leave the threat of death hanging over a family member, you can scare people shitless. I told the Patsy one I'd gut her nephew if she opened her mouth, and then she'd have his blood on her hands too. She lived for years with the dismembered remains of her daughter in a freezer in her kitchen.' Charlie started to laugh, and the sound curdled Lottie's blood.

'I understand, Charlie,' Lottie said, wanting to wring his neck there and then. She had to keep him talking. 'But that little girl, Polly. Why?'

'Why not? She reminded me of my sisters. Always had a stupid grin on her face. Then one evening she went too far. Said she'd seen me kill Harry. That was that. I hit her with a poker and then squeezed the life out of her. Useless piece of shit she was.'

'And then you dismembered her. Why leave her head separate from the rest of her body, though?'

'I did it to remind Patsy that she was implicated. Tore down the plaster beside the fireplace where there used to be a range. Put the head in and then plastered it up again. Neat job.'

Lottie shook her head in confusion. 'But the freezers, they were found in the Doyle house, your family home.'

'I moved them years later. I think that's what did old Patsy in. When I arrived with a truck at her door. The look on her face when she saw me!' He let out another demonic laugh that shook the birds from the trees.

The ARU were close to Charlie now, sneaking silently behind him. Lottie edged forward, ready to catch Jack if Charlie kicked him into the deep lock chamber.

'Why did you remove the bodies from the freezers? Surely if you'd left them, no one would have known anything.'

'I wanted Aaron to sell the house for me. I had to move the bodies. I thought if I left them on the railway the trains would make them unrecognisable. But it was too difficult and I ended up throwing some of the remains into the canal. I didn't bank on that Baker woman finding the skull the same week, or my own son and his dumb friend spotting the torso on the tracks. Fate is funny. I don't trust those doctors telling me it's just low platelets I've got. I'm a sick man and I'm dying.'

Lottie inched closer as one of the ARU grabbed Charlie, sticking the muzzle of a gun to the side of his head.

'You're sick all right, and you're fucking paranoid,' she said, and dived for Jack, grabbing him before Charlie's foot could connect with him. She wrapped the unconscious boy in her arms as the murderer was led away.

CHAPTER SEVENTY-FIVE

Lottie stood in the centre of Superintendent Farrell's office. The air was stuffy and stale, like something had died in it and was still decaying in a corner. Farrell sat like a squat sergeant major and did not offer Lottie a seat, so she remained on her tired feet.

She knew it was not going to be a congratulatory meeting. There would be no commendation for saving a young boy and capturing a killer who'd evaded the law for over twenty years. A killer who'd killed three innocent people in the last week and would have killed more if Lottie and her team had not been so good at their job. Or plain lucky. She knew most cases hinged on luck and timing. Circumstance and opportunity. She did not feel very lucky at this particular moment. She was just knackered.

'Detective Inspector Parker, earlier today I ordered you to come to my office and you did not.'

Lottie tried to remember. Did she mean when Sean was there? Must be that. 'At that time Ruby O'Keeffe was missing, in danger, and I had to save—'

'Did you save her?'

'Yes. Well, she saved herself actually.'

'Then there was no need to disobey an order.'

'With all due respect—'

'Don't make excuses.'

'But we successfully found Kevin O'Keeffe, and then—'

'Was he even missing?'

'We couldn't locate him at first and his wife said he was a danger. We suspected him of murdering Aaron Frost.'

'Did he murder Aaron Frost?'

'No, but he was complicit in—'

'Did you interview O'Keeffe with another officer present? Did you read him his rights?'

'I read him his rights at the lake.'

'Was there an officer present in the cell? Did you record the interview?'

'No, but I had to find Jack Sheridan and—'

'Detective Inspector Parker, you couldn't obey an order if your life depended on it. I want to play fair and I want you to play fair, but you make it so difficult for me. If you can't play by my rules, there have to be consequences.'

Lottie swayed on her feet. She wanted to sit, so badly.

'I'm sorry, Superintendent. It won't happen again.' She gulped down her pride and her anger.

'Too bloody right it won't. I have a list of complaints here about you. I'm going to read them out and you have a right of reply when I've finished.'

'Do I have the right to a garda representative, or do I need my solicitor?'

'Have you got a rep?' Farrell folded her arms.

'I can find one.'

'Okay. If you want to formalise this, on your head be it.'

'No, no, read them out. Then I'll see what I need to do.'

Lottie's exhaustion was replaced by anger as Farrell began.

'First up, you interviewed Jeff Cole in the cell with no one else present.'

'Best way to get information at the time.'

'But it's not following protocol. Why did you do it?'

'I just did.' She knew she sounded like one of her kids. When they were five years old, maybe.

'You interviewed him alone, without recording it. On your own!' Farrell raised her voice.

'Not unusual for me. I've been doing it for—' Lottie shut her mouth when Farrell stared. No point in digging a deeper grave. She needed to dump the shovel.

'You did not assign FLOs to the families of the two boys who found the body parts. Why?'

'They initially refused them. I can only offer, I can't coerce.'

'Could have fooled me,' Farrell said drily. 'You visited the Sheridan family alone without other officers present. You interviewed Josie Frost and Marianne O'Keeffe alone.'

'So?'

Farrell ignored her. 'On garda time you attended hospital visits with Detective Sergeant Boyd. While you were in the middle of an investigation, I might add.'

Lottie clenched her hands into fists as her anger threatened to spill over. She said nothing.

Farrell continued to read, and Lottie knew Maria Lynch had hung her out to dry. Well, Detective Lynch, she thought, what goes around fucking comes around.

CHAPTER SEVENTY-SIX

One week later

Ruby O'Keeffe stuffed her earbuds into her jeans pocket and stepped into Tamara's kitchen. She shuddered. The room pulsed with a sense of loss. She hugged Tamara and went to sit beside Marianne.

'I'm so sorry, Tamara,' she said. 'We're sure my dad didn't kill Gavin, but I'll never forgive him for what he did afterwards.'

'I don't care about Kevin.' Tamara sucked on a cigarette, her eyes glazed with grief. 'Nothing can bring my little boy back.'

Ruby waited for her mother to say something, though Marianne was consumed with hatred, and anything that came from her lips might be better left unsaid.

'I've been offered a lot of money to write about my husband's role in all this,' Marianne said eventually. 'He spent our married life trying to get his hands on my money, threatening to reveal to all and sundry that I'd coerced my father into leaving everything to me, and I've lived the last two years threatening to tell everyone about his illegitimate child. Now I know that a life built on threats can only lead to disaster.'

'It's not your fault,' Tamara said.

'My dream has always been for my words to be published in a book, but let me tell you, I will not write one word about this tragedy.'

'Write it,' Tamara said. 'Make loads of money. He can rot in jail while you spend it.'

'I hope he does rot, but I'm not going to benefit from what he's done. What are you going to do?'

Tamara doused her cigarette and lit another one. She looked up sadly, her cheeks stained black from all her tears. 'I am going to cry forever for my angel.'

A soft knock came on the front door. Ruby went to answer it.

Lisa Sheridan stood there with Maggie in her arms and Tyrone clutching her hand.

'I need to speak with Tamara,' she said. The wind caught her hair and blew it across her harried face.

'I … I'm not sure that's a good—' Ruby began.

'Tell her to come in,' Tamara said. 'We have a lot to talk about.'

Ruby stood back and watched the sad little family move past her. 'Where's Jack?'

Lisa nodded towards the street.

Ruby went down the concrete steps and stood beside the young boy. 'Jack?'

He was staring down the road at the boarded-up house that had seen the slaughter of the Doyle family twenty years previously.

'It was there all the time,' he whispered. 'We walked by it every single day, me and Gavin. We knew there was a house there, behind the hoarding, but we never sneaked in or went near it. Do you think there was a supernatural force keeping us away?'

Ruby put her arm around him and hugged him. 'Whatever it was, it's gone now.'

'They're all gone. Gavin and that woman Faye and my dad's … Charlie's half-brother Aaron. All murdered. Why?'

'I don't know, Jack. But that house wasn't evil. Charlie was.'

'He wasn't always, you know. He used to be caring and loving. But when he thought he was going to die, he changed.' Ruby thought those were wise words from an eleven-year-old. He added, 'It's like the past was resurrected and he continued where he had left off at fourteen years old.' He looked up into her face, pleading. 'I'm afraid the same will happen to me.'

'No, Jack, it won't, because Charlie wasn't your real dad. And hey, listen. This is the best bit ever. I'm your big sister. How cool is that?'

'Gross,' Jack said, but beneath the sorrow swimming in his eyes, Ruby saw the faintest glimmer of a smile.

*

Jeff Cole stood on the pavement outside number 2 Church View. He could hear the forensic people working inside. Pulling up floorboards, tearing plaster from the walls. A white-suited technician appeared at the door, struggling beneath the weight of a toilet bowl. Jeff wanted to go in, to bear witness to the continuing search of his aunt's house. He wanted to tear every last tile off the walls, to twist out the nails from each piece of timber and hinge. He wanted to dismantle the house one cement block at a time, to fling the tiles from the roof and shout at the top of his voice. He wanted to destroy it; only then could he forget what it had been.

Instead he stood in silence at the crime-scene tape while the light breeze whipped around him, and mourned Faye and their unborn child. He didn't mourn his cousin Polly. He couldn't remember much about her, if he was totally honest. But the more he thought back to the time when he was a boy and tried to see it through the eyes of a man, the more he recalled the drunken, drug-fuelled existence of his aunt and uncle. Had Patsy really stayed silent about the death of her daughter because of a threat to his own life? Or – and he assumed now that this was the more credible scenario – had she not wanted to bring the gardaí to her door, where they would discover evidence of her collusion in covering up two crimes and confirmation of her drug habit?

He would never know.

He took a last look at the window with its yellowing curtains, and for a second he thought he saw Faye standing there, her hair soft and light, her smile wide and infectious, her hand cupping the little bump that would grow no bigger. He thought he heard her laughing and calling him. Thinking was driving him crazy.

He walked slowly away, his six-foot frame now slouched and sorrowful. He had a funeral to organise.

EPILOGUE

Two weeks later

Lottie sat with Boyd in the sitting room. He had a glass of wine in his hand. Grace was in the kitchen talking with Chloe and Katie. Sean was upstairs on his computer and Louis was fast asleep. Rose had dropped off a cooked dinner, but Lottie had no appetite.

'Do you think your friend Father Joe could marry us?' Boyd said.

'You're divorced. We can't have a church wedding.'

'Oh, does that mean he can't officiate at my funeral either?'

'Stop talking like that.'

'Only asking.'

'Anyway, he can't.'

'Why not?'

'Because he's on a sabbatical.'

'Another one? That man is out of the priesthood more than he's in it.'

'He's trying for full access to his daughter. It's awkward for him.'

'I should say it is.' Boyd sipped his wine.

Lottie looked longingly at the glass in his hand and took a slug of her Diet Coke. 'He's been denied his daughter for so long, like his mother was denied all knowledge of him, so I understand it. Though he could take my daughters for a while if he wants them.'

Boyd laughed heartily.

It was good to hear that sound. When she looked at him, she felt her love grow another root, though the roots were constantly being tangled with the winding ivy of guilt. She could not undo her love for Adam. She couldn't unlove him. She couldn't unlove Boyd, either. She had to learn to live with the ghost of one love while experiencing the newness of another.

'Everything I do, Boyd, I do for my kids, but they don't get it.'

'That's because they're kids.'

'Katie and Chloe are so-called adults. Why aren't they satisfied?'

'Like I said, they're still only kids.'

'Katie wants to move to New York with Louis,' she said, tears nipping at her eyes.

'When?'

'Soon. That's not a safe place to raise a child.'

'Can't be much worse than Ragmullin. Listen, Lottie, I've told you before and I'll tell you again, you have to let them go.'

'I can't. I love all of them equally, but I love little Louis differently. I can't bear not to have him around me. I missed so much of my kids' childhoods. I was working every hour that God gave. I don't want to miss my grandson growing up.'

'You're overcompensating because Adam is no longer here, but you have me now.'

'I know that, Boyd, but it's a different kind of love. Children find a home in your heart, and when one of them leaves, a big fat hole remains that nothing can fill. Adam left me like that, and I try to cram it with work, but it's just fleeting. I need a constant.'

'I'll be your constant,' he said, and trailed his arm around her shoulder. 'And if Farrell suspends you, you'll have plenty of time to do all the things you can't do because of work.'

'Like what? Join a knitting group with my mother.'

He laughed again and she smiled. He sat up straight and put his glass on the coffee table. 'I've got an idea.'

'Go on. Dazzle me.'

'You know how Leo is talking about giving you Farranstown House?'

'What about it?'

'Well, why not go over to the States with Katie. Help her settle in and at the same time meet up with Leo face to face and see what he's up to.'

'That's the best idea you've had in ages, Boyd.' And she knew in her heart that was what she'd been leading up to all along. 'On one condition,' she added.

'Anything.'

'You have to finish your treatment, and when you get the all-clear, we can go together.'

'A honeymoon? I'll drink to that, but first I have to do this.'

He leaned over and drew her face to his, and Lottie let herself be kissed by the man she realised she loved more than he would ever know.

From upstairs came a loud cry.

Louis was awake.

A LETTER FROM PATRICIA

Hello, dear reader,

Sincere thanks to you for reading my eighth novel, *Buried Angels*.

I'm so grateful to you for sharing your time with Lottie Parker, her family and her team in this the latest book in the series. I hope you enjoyed *Buried Angels*, and I'd love it if you could follow Lottie throughout the series of novels.

You can connect with me on my Facebook author page and Twitter. I also have a website (which I try to keep up to date).

To those of you who have already read the other seven Lottie Parker books, *The Missing Ones, The Stolen Girls, The Lost Child, No Safe Place, Tell Nobody, Final Betrayal* and *Broken Souls,* I thank you for your support and reviews. And if *Buried Angels* is your first encounter with Lottie, I hope you are in for a treat with the previous books in the series.

I'm embarrassed to ask, but I'm always humbled when readers leave reviews, so it would be fantastic if you could post a review on Amazon, or indeed on the site where you purchased the eBook, paperback or audio book. It would mean so much to me. And thank you so much for the reviews received so far.

Thanks again for reading *Buried Angels*.

I hope you will join me for book nine in the series.

Love,

Patricia

www.patriciagibney.com

trisha460

@trisha460

patricia_gibney_author

ACKNOWLEDGEMENTS

I want to start by thanking you for reading *Buried Angels*, and to everyone who continues to follow Lottie's journey, thank you for reading my other books too.

I want to sincerely thank my agent Ger Nichol of the Book Bureau, who works tirelessly on my behalf and has become a true confidante. Also thanks to Marianne Gunn O'Connor. Thanks to Hannah at the Rights People for sourcing foreign translation publishers for my books.

Lydia Vassar-Smith is the most patient and professional editor I could wish for. I am lucky to have her working with me. Thank you for helping me bring *Buried Angels* to life.

Thank you to Kim Nash, head of publicity at Bookouture, for all the PR work and your encouragement and support. Thanks also to Noelle Holten and those who work directly on my books at Bookouture: Alexandra Holmes (production), Leodora Darlington, Alex Crow and Jules Macadam (marketing). I'm also forever grateful to Jane Selley for her excellent copyediting skills.

I want to wish Olly Rhodes best of good luck as he leaves Book-outure. Thanks, Olly, for all your support and for taking me on as a debut author three years ago. Look where we are now! Best wishes in your new ventures and adventures. Congratulations to Jenny Geras on taking the role of steering the ship.

Thank you to Sphere, Hachette Ireland and Grand Central Publishing, who publish my books in paperback, and to all my foreign translation publishers for bringing my books to readers in their native languages.

Michele Moran is the incredible voice on the audio format of all my books, bringing Lottie to life in the ears of those who listen on audio. Thanks, Michele, and your team at the Audiobook Producers.

Book bloggers and reviewers, book shops and libraries, thank you. You help readers to find my books, and I am grateful to every reader who has posted a review, because you all make a difference. The writing community is very supportive of me and my work. Thank you to all who have listened to me, chatted and advised me, especially my fellow Bookouture authors.

Special thanks to John Quinn for his speedy responses to my pleas for clarification and advice. I write crime fiction and seek advice where necessary, but inaccuracies are all my own. I tend to fictionalise police procedures to move the story along. It is fiction after all!

Shane Barkey, thank you for demonstrating how a drone works. I really had no idea until you showed me.

My friends keep me going when I am knee-deep in writing and edits. I am blessed to have good people around me. Antoinette Hegarty, Jo Kelly, Jackie Walsh, Niamh Brennan and Grainne Daly, thank you for your words of encouragement, trips away and of course the retail therapy and crystals.

This year my mother and father celebrate sixty years of marriage, so I want to congratulate them. My parents have been the constant throughout my life. Thank you, Kathleen and William Ward.

Thanks to my mother-in-law, Lily Gibney, and her family, who have been in my life since the day I met Aidan. I dedicate this book to Lily.

My sisters and brother support me in all that I do. Thank you, Cathy Thornton, Gerry Ward and Marie Brennan. Special thanks to Marie for helping me with edits and proofreading *Buried Angels*.

I want to say a special thanks to my children, Aisling, Orla and Cathal. As young teenagers, they lost their dad, Aidan, to cancer. They had to work their way through the dark days and rough times, and have come out the other side three beautiful, caring and considerate adults. If Aidan was alive today, he would have a big smile on his face telling them how proud he is of them. I want to say now how proud *I* am, and thankful to have you in my life. And thank you for bringing me pure joy with my four grandchildren, Daisy and Caitlyn, Shay and Lola. I love you all.

All the characters in my books are fictional, as is Lottie's town of Ragmullin. Mullingar, situated in the heart of Ireland, is the town of my birth, my home town, and I'm forever grateful for the support that I've received from everyone there.

I won't delay you any longer. I have to write book nine in the series!

Keep reading from an extract from the next book in Patricia Gibney's Lottie Parker series, *Silent Voices*.

Nine years earlier

The boy tried not to cry. He'd thought he knew the way home, but now he wasn't so sure. It was dark in the fields, far away from the lights of the house he'd just left. He'd been told to go home. They didn't want him there. Had even laughed at him. Big boys were not supposed to cry, but he was crying now. He hoped his mum and dad would be at home, like he'd just been told, even though they were supposed to be away for the night.

He walked across the field, up the lane, and gingerly stepped over the stile. He let his feet sink in the sandy ground. The dew was heavy underfoot and the distance ahead of him appeared shortened by the stubborn fog lying far too low. The trail should be familiar, bred deep in his mind from his treks with his daddy to check on the work at the quarry. Some days he never saw his dad. Long days and never-ending nights, the air punctured by the thud of drills and the hum of machinery. He loved that noise. His daddy had told him it was only a small operation but that one day the boy might make it great. He didn't like the way the green of the hedges had become grey with dust and stone after the summer and the nests had begun to empty. But his family didn't seem to worry about nature.

The silence wrapped itself around his shoulders and the fog dampened his hair as he trudged on. He wished he'd worn his wellington boots, because his runners were wet and sluiced up and down as he walked. Maybe he could have a look at the quarry before he crested the hill. There'd be no one there at this time of night, but he knew a way in. Anyway, that was the shortest way home. He eased through the gap in the wire fence and kept going.

He only realised he was close to the lip of the quarry when he heard the stones he'd kicked up as he walked hitting the water. The cavernous space opened up as all around him the fog rose mystically into the sky and the stone and grass split the earth before him. The boy felt he was alone with nature. Just then, he thought he heard a noise behind him. No, only silly people would come up here in the dark. Did that make him silly? There it was again. A rustle. Leaves shifting on the branches. The wind? No, the night was still with the fog hovering around him. Why did it have to be so dark? As he went to move away from the edge, the rustling came closer and stones crunched underfoot. He made to turn around, and felt a hand pressing between his shoulder blades.

'No!'

He thought he'd said the word out loud, but maybe he hadn't. Instead the air was filled with a hysterical laugh. Not his laugh. Then a choked scream left his body as the hand on his back pushed, and he was flying through the air.

The water was thick and viscous. It rushed into his screaming mouth and travelled into his lungs as quickly as his head dipped below the water.

He was strangely calm.

PROLOGUE

Saturday 25 November

It might only have been built in the last ten years but the little chapel house looked like it dated back to the time when the monks set up the first Christian churches in Ireland. At a push it held a hundred people, but today it was laid out for less than thirty.

Sprays of baby's breath interspersed with fragrant freesias were tied in little bunches with white satin ribbons on the backs of the chairs that lined the short aisle. When the first guests began to arrive and the door was opened, a miasma of scent wafted towards them in a wave of freshness. Light filtered through the small arched windows, casting rainbows on the stone walls and bathing the interior in a mystical aura.

A coolness permeated the inside of the chapel, even though outdoors the midday air was warm. Three pillar candles stood on the flower-draped altar, one each for the bride and groom, while the third candle had the names of dead family members inscribed in gold filigree.

Chatter preceded the guests as they took their seats. Family in the first two rows with friends behind them, followed by colleagues. The friends' section was mainly colleagues, but that didn't matter.

In the bedroom of the stone cottage adjacent to the chapel, Lottie stared at herself in the long mirror. She had to admit she didn't recognise the reflected image. Below a tight satin bodice, the chiffon cream dress floated out from her waist, and with the light streaming in through the window, she thought it looked magical. She hardly ever – never – wore dresses, and she would have got married in her jeans and T-shirt if she'd thought she could get away with it. But her daughters had been adamant, so she'd given in. A small victory for the girls, but she was surprisingly happy with her reflection. Her hair had been coloured a little lighter than normal – a box job last night; Chloe had insisted – though she wasn't sure if it was strawberry blonde or out-and-out blonde. She never fussed about such things. A few stray flowers placed strategically around her head hid the clips that held her hair in place. Katie had worked her magic with make-up and eyeshadow and a whole load of other shite Lottie had never used before, but she was pleased with the effect. At least it hid the bruises.

'It's smashing,' she said, hugging her elder daughter.

'You look ten years younger,' Katie said, a wide smile lighting up her eyes.

'Go away! I'm only forty-five,' Lottie said playfully. She'd turned forty-six in June. 'Is Louis ready?' Louis was Katie's two-year-old son, Lottie's grandson.

'He's ready, but I can't guarantee he'll do what he's supposed to do.'

'It doesn't matter. As long as Boyd is there, along with you, Chloe and Sean and little Louis, I'll be happy.'

'I know you haven't met Chloe's boyfriend yet, Mam, but he's not what you'd expect—'

'Not today, Katie.'

'Just giving you a little warning.'

'Thanks,' Lottie said. 'And I love your dress.' Katie was dressed in a fuchsia-pink floaty number from Macy's, while Chloe was wearing a similar style in blue (end-of-line sale). Lottie's own dress was from a charity shop, but they all looked quite expensive. No point in wasting money I don't have, she thought. 'Is Sean ready?'

'Sean is never ready,' Katie groaned. 'I'll go check on him.'

'Thanks. And Katie?'

'Yes?'

'Please don't let Granny Rose near me before the ceremony. She'll say something to upset me, and I can't be dealing with that today of all days.'

'Sure thing.'

Alone, Lottie felt her heart balloon with happiness. It was a feeling she'd thought she'd never again experience after her husband, Adam, had died five years ago. A period of hell had enveloped her then, and she'd floundered in the depths of addiction and sorrow, but eventually, with the help of her colleague, friend and soon-to-be husband Mark Boyd, she had arrived at this day, after a week of storms and torrential rain, with the sun shining brighter than she ever remembered at the end of November.

Sitting at the small dressing table, she stared at the gift her mother had given her. A gold locket. 'It was my mother's,' Rose had told her. 'It's an irreplaceable heirloom. Don't lose it. I put a photo in it, just for you.' There had been no expression of love or good wishes. Just that statement. *Don't lose it.* Lottie wanted to say, why give it as a gift if you're attaching orders? But she'd only murmured a thank you and let Rose off.

Opening the locket now, she stared at the small, crudely cut-out photograph of Adam's face. Her heart lurched in her chest before dipping dramatically somewhere into her belly, and her breath caught in the back of her throat. Tears threatened to override her sense of happiness. Was Rose just being her usual tactless self, or did she really think she was doing the right thing? Lottie snapped the locket shut and dropped it into Katie's make-up bag. Out of sight and all that. Not that she had forgotten Adam. She missed him and loved him still. But she loved Boyd in a different way. A new way. He was part of her present, not her past. He was here for her. She trusted him. Believed in him. Loved him. Didn't she? When she wasn't taking unnecessary risks and almost getting him killed!

Wiping away her tears before they ruined her make-up, she opened the lid of the blue velvet box that Boyd had given her. A thin silver chain with two interlinked hearts. Hand-crafted. Simple. Profound. Thoughtful. It was truly beautiful. Clipping it around her neck, she admired it in the mirror. A smile reached her green eyes which glinted like emeralds in sunshine. Enough! she admonished herself.

She slipped her feet into the cream silk shoes that Chloe had insisted she buy. Despite the price for something she'd never wear again, she'd given in and purchased them. Anything to keep her girls happy. Ready at last, she opened the door and stepped into the small living room, where her family awaited her.

'Oh my God! You look amazing,' Chloe enthused, grabbing Lottie's hands and twirling her round the room. A mesh of cream and blue chiffon swished in the air and Louis squealed with delight.

'What do you think, Sean?' Lottie said, regaining her balance as Chloe let her go.

Her son gripped his bottom lip with his teeth and his eyes glimmered with tears. His fair hair was cut tightly around his head, but his fringe still hung low towards his blue eyes. Adam's eyes. She felt her hand fly to her chest and gulped.

'You look stunning, Mam,' he said eventually. 'Beautiful.'

'Am I not always beautiful?' she joked, trying to release some of the tension which was in danger of simmering out of control.

Sean hugged her tightly, then stepped back. 'Are we Parkers ready to get this show on the road?'

An expectant silence descended on them, and Lottie inhaled the floral scent of her daughters' perfume.

'Who's got my bouquet?'

Katie took the bunch of wild flowers from the kitchenette sink and wiped the stems with a tea towel before handing them to her.

'I'm ready if you are,' Lottie said, and for the first time in five years, she felt truly happy. 'Let's get the next phase of our lives started.'

The nervy butterflies swarmed in the pit of her stomach as she stepped outside the door, walking behind her daughters and grandson. Sean grasped her elbow a little too tightly, then eased his fingers and let them rest softly on her arm.

'You okay, Mam?'

'I'm a little nervous. What if Boyd doesn't turn up?'

'Of course he'll turn up.'

As they walked across the cobbled stones of the courtyard, she glanced to the cottage where she hoped Boyd had arrived this morning to change into his new suit. It looked deserted.

'Stop fretting,' Sean said.

They rounded the corner and approached the chapel, and she felt the first wave of anxiety. Why was there a huddle of people outside? They should be inside. Chloe and Boyd had planned this down to the last detail, the last second. Boyd was like that. OCD. He'd drummed the schedule into her brain. 'Twelve noon. Not a second later.' How many times had he said it? Too many to count. She started to smile, but stopped as her mother approached with Grace, Boyd's sister.

'What's wrong?' Lottie said. 'The celebrant not shown up?'

'No, *she's* here,' Rose said, disdain greasing her words. She was old-fashioned and wasn't about to change.

Lottie caught Grace's arm. 'Where are you going, Grace? Boyd … Mark will be annoyed if we're a second late.'

'He's the one who's late,' Grace said.

Turning, Lottie saw Kirby exiting the cottage Boyd had been allocated. 'What's up?'

'We might need to hold off on the ceremony for a while,' Kirby said, lighting up a cigar. He looked unusually neat and tidy, though the buttons on his white shirt strained across his belly, and he'd put gel or something in his hair to calm down his unruly curls.

Her chest split in a schism of panic. 'Where's Boyd?'

'I don't know.'

'Weren't you with him this morning? To help him pin on his flower or something?'

'You know Boyd better than anyone, and you know that only he can do it right.' Kirby took a long drag on his cigar, topped it and palmed it. 'We agreed to meet at the chapel door at ten to twelve. It's now midday, and I just went to see why he was late and—'

'Oh for God's sake, Kirby, stop rambling.' Lottie shoved her bouquet into his hand and headed for the cottage. It was a studio-type design, neat and tidy. Typical Boyd.

His wedding suit hung on the back of a door, still in its plastic wrapping. Twirling around, she looked for a sign, for anything at all to tell her what was going on. She found it on the small kitchen table.

A note. Folded in two. Cream vellum paper. The name *Mark Boyd* on the outside of the fold.

She opened it up, and as she read, she could feel her blood turning to ice and her knees to jelly. Shivers ran up and down her spine.

The words blurred as she reread it. No signature. Hand-written in small, neat letters.

Before you make the biggest mistake of your life, meet me. If you don't, her blood will be on your hands. She is with me. You know where to find us.

Lottie sank to the floor in a whoosh of chiffon.